The Grey Wig by Israel Zangwill

A Collection of Stories and Novelettes

Israel Zangwill was born in London on 21st January 1864, to a family of Jewish immigrants from the Russian Empire.

Zangwill was initially educated in Plymouth and Bristol. At age 9 he was enrolled in the Jews' Free School in Spitalfields in east London. Zangwill excelled here. He began to teach part-time at the school and eventually full time. Whilst teaching he also studied with the University of London and by 1884 had earned his BA with triple honours in philosophy, history, and the sciences.

His writing earned him the sobriquet "the Dickens of the Ghetto" primarily based on his much lauded novel 'Children of the Ghetto: A Study of a Peculiar People' in 1892 and its glimpse of the poverty-stricken life in London's Jewish quarter.

As a writer he was keen to reflect on his political and social outlooks. His simulation of Yiddish sentence structure in English aroused great interest. His mystery work, 'The Big Bow Mystery' (1892) was the first locked room mystery novel.

Zangwill was also involved with narrowly focused Jewish issues as an assimilationist, an early Zionist, and later a territorialist. In the early 1890s he had joined the Lovers of Zion movement in England. In 1897 he joined Theodor Herzl (considered the father of modern political Zionism) in founding the World Zionist Organization.

Zangwill quit the established philosophy of Zionism when his plan for a homeland in Uganda was rejected and founded his own organisation; the Jewish Territorialist Organization. Its stated goal was to create a Jewish homeland in whatever territory in the world could be found for them.

Amongst the challenges in his life he found time to write poetry. He had translated a medieval Jewish poet in 1903 and his volume 'Blind Children' in 1908 shows his promise in this new endeavour.

'The Melting Pot' in 1909 made Zangwill's name as an admired playwright. When the play opened in Washington D.C., former President Theodore Roosevelt leaned over the edge of his box and shouted, "That's a great play, Mr. Zangwill, that's a great play."

Israel Zangwill died on 1st August 1926 in Midhurst, West Sussex.

Index of Contents

THE BIG BOW MYSTERY
MERELY MARY ANN
THE SERIO-COMIC GOVERNESS
ISRAEL ZANGHILL - A SHORT BIOGRAPHY
ISRAEL ZANGHILL – A CONCISE BIBLIOGRAPHY

THE GREY WIG

I

They both styled themselves "Madame," but only the younger of the old ladies had been married. Madame Valière was still a demoiselle, but as she drew towards sixty it had seemed more convenable to possess a mature label. Certainly Madame Dépine had no visible matrimonial advantages over her fellow-lodger at the Hôtel des Tourterelles, though in the symmetrical cemetery of Montparnasse (Section 22) wreaths of glass beads testified to a copious domesticity in the far past, and a newspaper picture of a chasseur d'Afrique pinned over her bed recalled—though only the uniform was the dead soldier's—the son she had contributed to France's colonial empire. Practically it was two old maids—or two lone widows—whose boots turned pointed toes towards each other in the dark cranny of the rambling, fusty corridor of the sky-floor. Madame Dépine was round, and grew dumpier with age; "Madame" Valière was long, and grew slimmer. Otherwise their lives ran parallel. For the true madame of the establishment you had to turn to Madame la Propriétaire, with her buxom bookkeeper of a daughter and her tame baggage-bearing husband. This full-blooded, jovial creature, with her swart moustache, represented the only Parisian success of three provincial lives, and, in her good-nature, had permitted her decayed townswomen—at as low a rent as was compatible with prudence—to shelter themselves under her roof and as near it as possible. Her house being a profitable warren of American art-students, tempered by native journalists and decadent poets, she could, moreover, afford to let the old ladies off coffee and candles. They were at liberty to prepare their own déjeuner in winter or to buy it outside in summer; they could burn their own candles or sit in the dark, as the heart in them pleased; and thus they were as cheaply niched as any one in the gay city. Rentières after their meticulous fashion, they drew a ridiculous but regular amount from the mysterious coffers of the Crédit Lyonnais.

But though they met continuously in the musty corridor, and even dined—when they did dine—at the same crémerie, they never spoke to each other. Madame la Propriétaire was the channel through which they sucked each other's history, for though they had both known her in their girlish days at Tonnerre, in the department of Yonne, they had not known each other. Madame Valière (Madame Dépine learnt, and it seemed to explain the frigidity of her neighbour's manner) still trailed clouds of glory from the service of a Princess a quarter of a century before. Her refusal to wink at the Princess's goings-on, her austere, if provincial, regard for the convenances, had cost her the place, and from these purpureal heights she had fallen lower and lower, till she struck the attic of the Hôtel des Tourterelles.

But even a haloed past does not give one a licence to annoy one's neighbours. Madame Dépine felt resentfully, and she hated Madame Valière as a haughty minion of royalty, who kept a cough, which barked loudest in the silence of the night.

"Why doesn't she go to the hospital, your Princess?" she complained to Madame la Propriétaire.

"Since she is able to nurse herself at home," the opulent-bosomed hostess replied with a shrug.

"At the expense of other people," Madame Dépine retorted bitterly. "I shall die of her cough, I am sure of it."

Madame showed her white teeth sweetly. "Then it is you who should go to the hospital."

II

Time wrote wrinkles enough on the brows of the two old ladies, but his frosty finger never touched their glossy brown hair, for both wore wigs of nearly the same shade. These wigs were almost symbolic of the evenness of their existence, which had got beyond the reach of happenings. The Church calendar, so richly dyed with figures of saints and martyrs, filled life with colour enough, and fast-days were almost as welcome as feast-days, for if the latter warmed the general air, the former cloaked economy with dignity. As for Mardi Gras, that shook you up for weeks, even though you did not venture out of your apartment; the gay serpentine streamers remained round one's soul as round the trees.

At intervals, indeed, secular excitements broke the even tenor. A country cousin would call upon the important Parisian relative, and be received, not in the little bedroom, but in state in the mustily magnificent salon of the hotel—all gold mirrors and mouldiness—which the poor country mouse vaguely accepted as part of the glories of Paris and success. Madame Dépine would don her ponderous gold brooch, sole salvage of her bourgeois prosperity; while, if the visitor were for Madame Valière, that grande dame would hang from her yellow, shrivelled neck the long gold chain and the old-fashioned watch, whose hands still seemed to point to regal hours.

Another break in the monotony was the day on which the lottery was drawn—the day of the pagan god of Luck. What delicious hopes of wealth flamed in these withered breasts, only to turn grey and cold when the blank was theirs again, but not the less to soar up again, with each fresh investment, towards the heaven of the hundred thousand francs! But if ever Madame Dépine stumbled on Madame Valière buying a section of a billet at the lottery agent's, she insisted on having her own slice cut from another number. Fortune itself would be robbed of its sweet if the "Princess" should share it. Even their common failure to win a sou did not draw them from their freezing depths of silence, from which every passing year made it more difficult to emerge. Some greater conjuncture was needed for that.

It came when Madame la Propriétaire made her début one fine morning in a grey wig.

III

Hitherto that portly lady's hair had been black. But now, as suddenly as darkness vanishes in a tropic dawn, it was become light. No gradual approach of the grey, for the black had been equally artificial. The wig is the region without twilight. Only in the swart moustache had the grey crept on, so that perhaps the growing incongruity had necessitated the sudden surrender to age.

To both Madame Dépine and Madame Valière the grey wig came like a blow on the heart.

It was a grisly embodiment of their secret griefs, a tantalising vision of the unattainable. To glide reputably into a grey wig had been for years their dearest desire. As each saw herself getting older and older, saw her complexion fade and the crow's-feet gather, and her eyes grow hollow, and her teeth fall out and her cheeks fall in, so did the impropriety of her brown wig strike more and more humiliatingly to her soul. But how should a poor old woman ever accumulate enough for a new wig? One might as well cry for the moon—or a set of false teeth. Unless, indeed, the lottery—?

And so, when Madame Dépine received a sister-in-law from Tonnerre, or Madame Valière's nephew came up by the excursion train from that same quiet and incongruously christened townlet, the Parisian personage would receive the visitor in the darkest corner of the salon, with her back to the light, and a big bonnet on her head—an imposing figure repeated duskily in the gold mirrors. These visits, instead of a relief, became a terror. Even a provincial knows it is not convenable for an old woman to wear a brown wig. And Tonnerre kept strict record of birthdays.

Tears of shame and misery had wetted the old ladies' hired pillows, as under the threat of a provincial visitation they had tossed sleepless in similar solicitude, and their wigs, had they not been wigs, would have turned grey of themselves. Their only consolation had been that neither outdid the other, and so long as each saw the other's brown wig, they had refrained from facing the dread possibility of having to sell off their jewellery in a desperate effort of emulation. Gradually Madame Dépine had grown to wear her wig with vindictive endurance, and Madame Valière to wear hers with gentle resignation. And now, here was Madame la Propriétaire, a woman five years younger and ten years better preserved, putting them both to the public blush, drawing the hotel's attention to what the hotel might have overlooked, in its long habituation to their surmounting brownness.

More morbidly conscious than ever of a young head on old shoulders, the old ladies no longer paused at the bureau to exchange the news with Madame or even with her black-haired bookkeeping daughter. No more lounging against the newel under the carved torch-bearer, while the journalist of the fourth floor spat at the Dreyfusites, and the poet of the entresol threw versified vitriol at perfidious Albion. For the first time, too—losing their channel of communication—they grew out of touch with each other's microscopic affairs, and their mutual detestation increased with their resentful ignorance. And so, shrinking and silent, and protected as far as possible by their big bonnets, the squat Madame Dépine and the skinny Madame Valière toiled up and down the dark, fusty stairs of the Hôtel des Tourterelles, often brushing against each other, yet sundered by icy infinities. And the endurance on Madame Dépine's round face became more vindictive, and gentler grew the resignation on the angular visage of Madame Valière.

IV

"Tiens! Madame Dépine, one never sees you now." Madame la Propriétaire was blocking the threshold, preventing her exit. "I was almost thinking you had veritably died of Madame Valière's cough."

"One has received my rent, the Monday," the little old lady replied frigidly.

"Oh! là! là!" Madame waved her plump hands. "And La Valière, too, makes herself invisible. What has then happened to both of you? Is it that you are doing a penance together?"

"Hist!" said Madame Dépine, flushing.

For at this moment Madame Valière appeared on the pavement outside bearing a long French roll and a bag of figs, which made an excellent lunch at low water. Madame la Propriétaire, dominatingly bestriding her doorstep, was sandwiched between the two old ladies, her wig aggressively grey between the two browns. Madame Valière halted awkwardly, a bronze blush mounting to match her wig. To be seen by Madame Dépine carrying in her meagre provisions was humiliation enough; to be juxtaposited with a grey wig was unbearable.

"Maman, maman, the English monsieur will not pay two francs for his dinner!" And the distressed bookkeeper, bill in hand, shattered the trio.

"And why will he not pay?" Fire leapt into the black eyes.

"He says you told him the night he came that by arrangement he could have his dinners for one franc fifty."

Madame la Propriétaire made two strides towards the refractory English monsieur. "I told you one franc fifty? For déjeuner, yes, as many luncheons as you can eat. But for dinner? You eat with us as one of the family, and vin compris and café likewise, and it should be all for one franc fifty! Mon Dieu! it is to ruin oneself. Come here." And she seized the surprised Anglo-Saxon by the wrist and dragged him towards a painted tablet of prices that hung in a dark niche of the hall. "I have kept this hotel for twenty years, I have grown grey in the service of artists and students, and this is the first time one has demanded dinner for one franc fifty!"

"She has grown grey!" contemptuously muttered Madame Valière.

"Grey? She!" repeated Madame Dépine, with no less bitterness. "It is only to give herself the air of a grande dame!"

Then both started, and coloured to the roots of their wigs. Simultaneously they realised that they had spoken to each other.

V

As they went up the stairs together—for Madame Dépine had quite forgotten she was going out—an immense relief enlarged their souls. Merely to mention the grey wig had been a vent for all this morbid brooding; to abuse Madame la Propriétaire into the bargain was to pass from the long isolation into a subtle sympathy.

"I wonder if she did say one franc fifty," observed Madame Valière, reflectively.

"Without doubt," Madame Dépine replied viciously. "And fifty centimes a day soon mount up to a grey wig."

"Not so soon," sighed Madame Valière.

"But then it is not only one client that she cheats."

"Ah! at that rate wigs fall from the skies," admitted Madame Valière.

"Especially if one has not to give dowries to one's nieces," said Madame Dépine, boldly.

"And if one is mean on New Year's Day," returned Madame Valière, with a shade less of mendacity.

They inhaled the immemorial airlessness of the staircase as if they were breathing the free air of the forests depicted on its dirty-brown wall-paper. It was the new atmosphere of self-respect that they were really absorbing. Each had at last explained herself and her brown wig to the other. An immaculate honesty (that would scorn to overcharge fifty centimes even to un Anglais), complicated with unwedded nieces in one case, with a royal shower of New Year's gifts in the other, had kept them from selfish, if seemly, hoary-headedness.

"Ah! here is my floor," panted Madame Valière at length, with an air of indicating it to a thorough stranger. "Will you not come into my room and eat a fig? They are very healthy between meals."

Madame Dépine accepted the invitation, and entering her own corner of the corridor with a responsive air of foreign exploration, passed behind the door through whose keyhole she had so often peered. Ah! no wonder she had detected nothing abnormal. The room was a facsimile of her own—the same bed with the same quilt over it and the same crucifix above it, the same little table with the same books of devotion, the same washstand with the same tiny jug and basin, the same rusted, fireless grate. The wardrobe, like her own, was merely a pair of moth-eaten tartan curtains, concealing both pegs and garments from her curiosity. The only sense of difference came subtly from the folding windows, below whose railed balcony showed another view of the quarter, with steam-trams—diminished to toy trains—puffing past to the suburbs. But as Madame Dépine's eyes roved from these to the mantel-piece, she caught sight of an oval miniature of an elegant young woman, who was jewelled in many places, and corresponded exactly with her idea of a Princess!

To disguise her access of respect, she said abruptly, "It must be very noisy here from the steam-trams."

"It is what I love, the bustle of life," replied Madame Valière, simply.

"Ah!" said Madame Dépine, impressed beyond masking-point, "I suppose when one has had the habit of Courts—"

Madame Valière shuddered unexpectedly. "Let us not speak of it. Take a fig."

But Madame Dépine persisted—though she took the fig. "Ah! those were brave days when we had still an Emperor and an Empress to drive to the Bois with their equipages and outriders. Ah, how pretty it was!"

"But the President has also"—a fit of coughing interrupted Madame Valière—"has also outriders."

"But he is so bourgeois—a mere man of the people," said Madame Dépine.

"They are the most decent sort of folk. But do you not feel cold? I will light a fire." She bent towards the wood-box.

"No, no; do not trouble. I shall be going in a moment. I have a large fire blazing in my room."

"Then suppose we go and sit there," said poor Madame Valière.

Poor Madame Dépine was seized with a cough, more protracted than any of which she had complained.

"Provided it has not gone out in my absence," she stammered at last. "I will go first and see if it is in good trim."

"No, no; it is not worth the trouble of moving." And Madame Valière drew her street-cloak closer round her slim form. "But I have lived so long in Russia, I forget people call this cold."

"Ah! the Princess travelled far?" said Madame Dépine, eagerly.

"Too far," replied Madame Valière, with a flash of Gallic wit. "But who has told you of the Princess?"

"Madame la Propriétaire, naturally."

"She talks too much—she and her wig!"

"If only she didn't imagine herself a powdered marquise in it! To see her standing before the mirror in the salon!"

"The beautiful spectacle!" assented Madame Valière.

"Ah! but I don't forget—if she does—that her mother wheeled a fruit-barrow through the streets of Tonnerre!"

"Ah! yes, I knew you were from Tonnerre—dear Tonnerre!"

"How did you know?"

"Naturally, Madame la Propriétaire."

"The old gossip!" cried Madame Dépine—"though not so old as she feigns. But did she tell you of her mother, too, and the fruit-barrow?"

"I knew her mother—une brave femme."

"I do not say not," said Madame Dépine, a whit disconcerted. "Nevertheless, when one's mother is a merchant of the four seasons—"

"Provided she sold fruit as good as this! Take another fig, I beg of you."

"Thank you. These are indeed excellent," said Madame Dépine. "She owed all her good fortune to a coup in the lottery."

"Ah! the lottery!" Madame Valière sighed. Before the eyes of both rose the vision of a lucky number and a grey wig.

The acquaintanceship ripened. It was not only their common grievances against fate and Madame la Propriétaire: they were linked by the sheer physical fact that each was the only person to whom the other could talk without the morbid consciousness of an eye scrutinising the unseemly brown wig. It became quite natural, therefore, for Madame Dépine to stroll into her "Princess's" room, and they soon slid into dividing the cost of the fire. That was more than an economy, for neither could afford a fire alone. It was an easy transition to the discovery that coffee could be made more cheaply for two, and that the same candle would light two persons, provided they sat in the same room. And if they did not fall out of the habit of companionship even at the crémerie, though "two portions for one" were not served, their union at least kept the sexagenarians in countenance. Two brown wigs give each other a moral support, are on the way to a fashion.

But there was more than wigs and cheese-parings in their camaraderie. Madame Dépine found a fathomless mine of edification in Madame Valière's reminiscences, which she skilfully extracted from her, finding the average ore rich with noble streaks, though the old tirewoman had an obstinate way of harking back to her girlhood, which made some delvings result in mere earth.

On the Day of the Dead Madame Dépine emerged into importance, taking her friend with her to the Cemetery Montparnasse to see the glass flowers blooming immortally over the graves of her husband and children. Madame Dépine paid the omnibus for both (inside places), and felt, for once, superior to the poor "Princess," who had never known the realities of love and death.

Two months passed. Another of Madame Valière's teeth fell out. Madame Dépine's cheeks grew more pendulous. But their brown wigs remained as fadeless as the cemetery flowers.

One day they passed the hairdresser's shop together. It was indeed next to the tobacconist's, so not easy to avoid, whenever one wanted a stamp or a postcard. In the window, amid pendent plaits of divers hues, bloomed two wax busts of females—the one young and coquettish and golden-haired, the other aristocratic in a distinguished grey wig. Both wore diamond rosettes in their hair and ropes of pearls round their necks. The old ladies' eyes met, then turned away.

"If one demanded the price!" said Madame Dépine (who had already done so twice).

"It is an idea!" agreed Madame Valière.

"The day will come when one's nieces will be married."

"But scarcely when New Year's Day shall cease to be," the "Princess" sighed.

"Still, one might win in the lottery!"

"Ah! true. Let us enter, then."

"One will be enough. You go." Madame Dépine rather dreaded the coiffeur, whom intercourse with jocose students had made severe.

But Madame Valière shrank back shyly. "No, let us both go." She added, with a smile to cover her timidity, "Two heads are better than one."

"You are right. He will name a lower price in the hope of two orders." And, pushing the "Princess" before her like a turret of defence, Madame Dépine wheeled her into the ladies' department.

The coiffeur, who was washing the head of an American girl, looked up ungraciously. As he perceived the outer circumference of Madame Dépine projecting on either side of her turret, he emitted a glacial "Bon jour, mesdames."

"Those grey wigs—" faltered Madame Valière

"I have already told your friend." He rubbed the American head viciously.

Madame Dépine coloured. "But—but we are two. Is there no reduction on taking a quantity?"

"And why then? A wig is a wig. Twice a hundred francs are two hundred francs."

"One hundred francs for a wig!" said Madame Valière, paling. "I did not pay that for the one I wear."

"I well believe it, madame. A grey wig is not a brown wig."

"But you just said a wig is a wig."

The coiffeur gave angry rubs at the head, in time with his explosive phrases. "You want real hair, I presume—and to your measure—and to look natural—and convenable!" (Both old ladies shuddered at the word.) "Of course, if you want it merely for private theatricals—"

"Private theatricals!" repeated Madame Dépine, aghast.

"A comédienne's wig I can sell you for a bagatelle. That passes at a distance."

Madame Valière ignored the suggestion. "But why should a grey wig cost more than any other?"

The coiffeur shrugged his shoulders. "Since there are less grey hairs in the world—"

"Comment!" repeated Madame Valière, in amazement.

"It stands to reason," said the coiffeur. "Since most persons do not live to be old—or only live to be bald." He grew animated, professorial almost, seeing the weight his words carried to unthinking bosoms. "And since one must provide a fine hair-net for a groundwork, to imitate the flesh-tint of the scalp, and since each hair of the parting must be treated separately, and since the natural wave of the hair must be reproduced, and since you will also need a block for it to stand on at nights to guard its shape—"

"But since one has already blocks," interposed Madame Dépine.

"But since a conscientious artist cannot trust another's block! Represent to yourself also that the shape of the head does not remain as fixed as the dome of the Invalides, and that—"

"Eh bien, we will think," interrupted Madame Valière, with dignity.

VIII

They walked slowly towards the Hôtel des Tourterelles.

"If one could share a wig!" Madame Dépine exclaimed suddenly.

"It is an idea," replied Madame Valière. And then each stared involuntarily at the other's head. They had shared so many things that this new possibility sounded like a discovery. Pleasing pictures flitted before their eyes—the country cousin received (on a Box and Cox basis) by a Parisian old gentlewoman sans peur and sans reproche; a day of seclusion for each alternating with a day of ostentatious publicity.

But the light died out of their eyes, as Madame Dépine recognised that the "Princess's" skull was hopelessly long, and Madame Valière recognised that Madame Dépine's cranium was hopelessly round. Decidedly either head would be a bad block for the other's wig to repose on.

"It would be more sensible to acquire a wig together, and draw lots for it," said Madame Dépine.

The "Princess's" eyes rekindled. "Yes, and then save up again to buy the loser a wig."

"Parfaitement" said Madame Dépine. They had slid out of pretending that they had large sums immediately available. Certain sums still existed in vague stockings for dowries or presents, but these, of course, could not be touched. For practical purposes it was understood that neither had the advantage of the other, and that the few francs a month by which Madame Dépine's income exceeded Madame Valière's were neutralised by the superior rent she paid for her comparative immunity from steam-trams. The accumulation of fifty francs apiece was thus a limitless perspective.

They discussed their budget. It was really almost impossible to cut down anything. By incredible economies they saw their way to saving a franc a week each. But fifty weeks! A whole year, allowing for sickness and other breakdowns! Who can do penance for a whole year? They thought of moving to an even cheaper hotel; but then in the course of years Madame Valière had fallen three weeks behind with the rent, and Madame Dépine a fortnight, and these arrears would have to be paid up. The first council ended in despair. But in the silence of the night Madame Dépine had another inspiration. If one suppressed the lottery for a season!

On the average each speculated a full franc a week, with scarcely a gleam of encouragement. Two francs a week each—already the year becomes six months! For six months one can hold out. Hardships shared are halved, too. It will seem scarce three months. Ah, how good are the blessed saints!

But over the morning coffee Madame Valière objected that they might win the whole hundred francs in a week!

It was true; it was heartbreaking.

Madame Dépine made a reckless reference to her brooch, but the Princess had a gesture of horror. "And wear your heart on your shawl when your friends come?" she exclaimed poetically. "Sooner my watch shall go, since that at least is hidden in my bosom!"

"Heaven forbid!" ejaculated Madame Dépine. "But if you sold the other things hidden in your bosom!"

"How do you mean?"

"The Royal Secrets."

The "Princess" blushed. "What are you thinking of?"

"The journalist below us tells me that gossip about the great sells like Easter buns."

"He is truly below us," said Madame Valière, witheringly. "What! sell one's memories! No, no; it would not be convenable. There are even people living—"

"But nobody would know," urged Madame Dépine.

"One must carry the head high, even if it is not grey."

It was almost a quarrel. Far below the steam-tram was puffing past. At the window across the street a woman was beating her carpet with swift, spasmodic thwacks, as one who knew the legal time was nearly up. In the tragic silence which followed Madame Valière's rebuke, these sounds acquired a curious intensity.

"I prefer to sacrifice the lottery rather than honour," she added, in more conciliatory accents.

IX

The long quasi-Lenten weeks went by, and unflinchingly the two old ladies pursued their pious quest of the grey wig. Butter had vanished from their bread, and beans from their coffee. Their morning brew was confected of charred crusts, and as they sipped it solemnly they exchanged the reflection that it was quite equal to the coffee at the crémerie. Positively one was safer drinking one's own messes. Figs, no longer posing as a pastime of the palate, were accepted seriously as pièces de résistance. The Spring was still cold, yet fires could be left to die after breakfast. The chill had been taken off, and by mid-day the sun was in its full power. Each sustained the other by a desperate cheerfulness. When they took their morning walk in the Luxembourg Gardens—what time the blue-aproned Jacques was polishing their waxed floors with his legs for broom-handles—they went into ecstasies over everything, drawing each other's attention to the sky, the trees, the water. And, indeed, of a sunshiny morning it was heartening to sit by the pond and watch the wavering sheet of beaten gold water, reflecting all shades of green in a restless shimmer against the shadowed grass around. Madame Valière always had a bit of dry bread to feed the pigeons withal—it gave a cheerful sense of superfluity, and her manner of sprinkling the crumbs revived Madame Dépine's faded images of a Princess scattering New Year largess.

But beneath all these pretences of content lay a hollow sense of desolation. It was not the want of butter nor the diminished meat; it was the total removal from life of that intangible splendour of hope produced by the lottery ticket. Ah! every day was drawn blank now. This gloom, this gnawing emptiness at the heart, was worse than either had foreseen or now confessed. Malicious Fate, too, they felt, would even crown with the grand prix the number they would have chosen. But for the prospective draw for the Wig—which reintroduced the aleatory—life would scarcely have been bearable.

Madame Dépine's sister-in-law's visit by the June excursion train was a not unexpected catastrophe. It only lasted a day, but it put back the Grey Wig by a week, for Madame Choucrou had to be fed at Duval's, and Madame Valière magnanimously insisted on being of the party: whether to run parallel with her friend, or to carry off the brown wig, she alone knew. Fortunately, Madame Choucrou was both short-sighted and colour-blind. On the other hand, she liked a petit verre with her coffee, and both at a separate restaurant. But never had Madame Valière appeared to Madame Dépine's eyes more like the "Princess," more gay and polished and debonair, than at this little round table on the sunlit Boulevard. Little trills of laughter came from the half-toothless gums; long gloved fingers toyed with the liqueur glass or drew out the old-fashioned watch to see that Madame Choucrou did not miss her train; she spent her sou royally on a hawked journal. When they had seen Madame Choucrou off, she proposed to dock meat entirely for a fortnight so as to regain the week. Madame Dépine accepted in the same heroic spirit, and even suggested the elimination of the figs: one could lunch quite well on bread and milk, now the sunshine was here. But Madame Valière only agreed to a week's trial of this, for she had a sweet tooth among the few in her gums.

The very next morning, as they walked in the Luxembourg Gardens, Madame Dépine's foot kicked against something. She stooped and saw a shining glory—a five-franc piece!

"What is it?" said Madame Valière.

"Nothing," said Madame Dépine, covering the coin with her foot. "My bootlace." And she bent down—to pick up the coin, to fumble at her bootlace, and to cover her furious blush. It was not that she wished to keep the godsend to herself,—one saw on the instant that le bon Dieu was paying for Madame Choucrou,—it was an instantaneous dread of the "Princess's" quixotic code of honour. La Valière was capable of flying in the face of Providence, of taking the windfall to a bureau de police. As if the inspector wouldn't stick to it himself! A purse—yes. But a five-franc piece, one of a flock of sheep!

The treasure-trove was added to the heap of which her stocking was guardian, and thus honestly divided. The trouble, however, was that, as she dared not inform the "Princess," she could not decently back out of the meatless fortnight. Providence, as it turned out, was making them gain a week. As to the figs, however, she confessed on the third day that she hungered sore for them, and Madame Valière readily agreed to make this concession to her weakness.

This little episode coloured for Madame Dépine the whole dreary period that remained. Life was never again so depressingly definite; though curiously enough the "Princess" mistook for gloom her steady earthward glance, as they sauntered about the sweltering city. With anxious solicitude Madame Valière would direct her attention to sunsets, to clouds, to the rising moon; but heaven had ceased to have attraction, except as a place from which five-francs fell, and as soon as the "Princess's" eye was off her, her own sought the ground again. But this imaginary need of cheering up Madame Dépine kept Madame Valière herself from collapsing. At last, when the first red leaves began to litter the Gardens and cover up possible coins, the francs in the stocking approached their century.

What a happy time was that! The privations were become second nature; the weather was still fine. The morning Gardens were a glow of pink and purple and dripping diamonds, and on some of the trees was the delicate green of a second blossoming, like hope in the heart of age. They could scarcely refrain from betraying their exultation to the Hôtel des Tourterelles, from which they had concealed their sufferings. But the polyglot population seething round its malodorous stairs and tortuous corridors remained ignorant that anything was passing in the life of these faded old creatures, and even on the day of drawing lots for the Wig the exuberant hotel retained its imperturbable activity.

Not that they really drew lots. That was a figure of speech, difficult to translate into facts. They preferred to spin a coin. Madame Dépine was to toss, the "Princess" to cry pile ou face. From the stocking Madame Dépine drew, naturally enough, the solitary five-franc piece. It whirled in the air; the "Princess" cried face. The puff-puff of the steam-tram sounded like the panting of anxious Fate. The great coin fell, rolled, balanced itself between two destinies, then subsided, pile upwards. The poor "Princess's" face grew even longer; but for the life of her Madame Dépine could not make her own face other than a round red glow, like the sun in a fog. In fact, she looked so young at this supreme moment that the brown wig quite became her.

"I congratulate you," said Madame Valière, after the steam-tram had become a far-away rumble.

"Before next summer we shall have yours too," the winner reminded her consolingly.

XI

They had not waited till the hundred francs were actually in the stocking. The last few would accumulate while the wig was making. As they sat at their joyous breakfast the next morning, ere starting for the hairdresser's, the casement open to the October sunshine, Jacques brought up a letter for Madame Valière—an infrequent incident. Both old women paled with instinctive distrust of life. And as the "Princess" read her letter, all the sympathetic happiness died out of her face.

"What is the matter, then?" breathed Madame Dépine.

The "Princess" recovered herself. "Nothing, nothing. Only my nephew who is marrying."

"Soon?"

"The middle of next month."

"Then you will need to give presents!"

"One gives a watch, a bagatelle, and then—there is time. It is nothing. How good the coffee is this morning!"

They had not changed the name of the brew: it is not only in religious evolutions that old names are a comfort.

They walked to the hairdresser's in silence. The triumphal procession had become almost a dead march. Only once was the silence broken.

"I suppose they have invited you down for the wedding?" said Madame Dépine.

"Yes," said Madame Valière.

They walked on.

The coiffeur was at his door, sunning his aproned stomach, and twisting his moustache as if it were a customer's. Emotion overcame Madame Dépine at the sight of him. She pushed Madame Valière into the tobacconist's instead.

"I have need of a stamp," she explained, and demanded one for five centimes. She leaned over the counter babbling aimlessly to the proprietor, postponing the great moment. Madame Valière lost the clue to her movements, felt her suddenly as a stranger. But finally Madame Dépine drew herself together and led the way into the coiffeurs. The proprietor, who had reëntered his parlour, reëmerged gloomily.

Madame Valière took the word. "We are thinking of ordering a wig."

"Cash in advance, of course," said the coiffeur.

"Comment!" cried Madame Valière, indignantly. "You do not trust my friend!"

"Madame Valière has moved in the best society," added Madame Dépine.

"But you cannot expect me to do two hundred francs of work and then be left planted with the wigs!"

"But who said two hundred francs?" cried Madame Dépine. "It is only one wig that we demand—to-day at least."

He shrugged his shoulders. "A hundred francs, then."

"And why should we trust you with one hundred francs?" asked Madame Dépine. "You might botch the work."

"Or fly to Italy," added the "Princess."

In the end it was agreed he should have fifty down and fifty on delivery.

"Measure us, while we are here," said Madame Dépine. "I will bring you the fifty francs immediately."

"Very well," he murmured. "Which of you?"

But Madame Valière was already affectionately untying Madame Dépine's bonnet-strings. "It is for my friend," she cried. "And let it be as chic and convenable as possible!"

He bowed. "An artist remains always an artist."

Madame Dépine removed her wig and exposed her poor old scalp, with its thin, forlorn wisps and patches of grey hair, grotesque, almost indecent, in its nudity. But the coiffeur measured it in sublime seriousness, putting his tape this way and that way, while Madame Valière's eyes danced in sympathetic excitement.

"You may as well measure my friend too," remarked Madame Dépine, as she reassumed her glossy brown wig (which seemed propriety itself compared with the bald cranium).

"What an idea!" ejaculated Madame Valière. "To what end?"

"Since you are here," returned Madame Dépine, indifferently. "You may as well leave your measurements. Then when you decide yourself—Is it not so, monsieur?"

The coiffeur, like a good man of business, eagerly endorsed the suggestion. "Perfectly, madame."

"But if one's head should change!" said Madame Valière, trembling with excitement at the vivid imminence of the visioned wig.

"Souvent femme varie, madame," said the coiffeur. "But it is the inside, not the outside of the head."

"But you said one is not the dome of the Invalides," Madame Valière reminded him.

"He spoke of our old blocks," Madame Dépine intervened hastily. "At our age one changes no more."

Thus persuaded, the "Princess" in her turn denuded herself of her wealth of wig, and Madame Dépine watched with unsmiling satisfaction the stretchings of tape across the ungainly cranium.

"C'est bien," she said. "I return with your fifty francs on the instant."

And having seen her "Princess" safely ensconced in the attic, she rifled the stocking, and returned to the coiffeur.

When she emerged from the shop, the vindictive endurance had vanished from her face, and in its place reigned an angelic exaltation.

Eleven days later Madame Valière and Madame Dépine set out on the great expedition to the hairdresser's to try on the Wig. The "Princess's" excitement was no less tense than the fortunate winner's. Neither had slept a wink the night before, but the November morning was keen and bright, and supplied an excellent tonic. They conversed with animation on the English in Egypt, and Madame Dépine recalled the gallant death of her son, the chasseur.

The coiffeur saluted them amiably. Yes, mesdames, it was a beautiful morning. The wig was quite ready. Behold it there—on its block.

Madame Valière's eyes turned thither, then grew clouded, and returned to Madame Dépine's head and thence back to the Grey Wig.

"It is not this one?" she said dubiously.

"Mais, oui." Madame Dépine was nodding, a great smile transfiguring the emaciated orb of her face. The artist's eyes twinkled.

"But this will not fit you," Madame Valière gasped.

"It is a little error, I know," replied Madame Dépine.

"But it is a great error," cried Madame Valière, aghast. And her angry gaze transfixed the coiffeur.

"It is not his fault—I ought not to have let him measure you."

"Ha! Did I not tell you so?" Triumph softened her anger. "He has mixed up the two measurements!"

"Yes. I suspected as much when I went in to inquire the other day; but I was afraid to tell you, lest it shouldn't even fit you."

"Fit me!" breathed Madame Valière.

"But whom else?" replied Madame Dépine, impatiently, as she whipped off the "Princess's" wig. "If only it fits you, one can pardon him. Let us see. Stand still, ma chère," and with shaking hands she seized the grey wig.

"But—but—" The "Princess" was gasping, coughing, her ridiculous scalp bare.

"But stand still, then! What is the matter? Are you a little infant? Ah! that is better. Look at yourself, then, in the mirror. But it is perfect!" "A true Princess," she muttered beatifically to herself. "Ah, how she will show up the fruit-vendor's daughter!"

As the "Princess" gazed at the majestic figure in the mirror, crowned with the dignity of age, two great tears trickled down her pendulous cheeks.

"I shall be able to go to the wedding," she murmured chokingly.

"The wedding!" Madame Dépine opened her eyes. "What wedding?"

"My nephew's, of course!"

"Your nephew is marrying? I congratulate you. But why did you not tell me?"

"I did mention it. That day I had a letter!"

"Ah! I seem to remember. I had not thought of it." Then briskly: "Well, that makes all for the best again. Ah! I was right not to scold monsieur le coiffeur too much, was I not?"

"You are very good to be so patient," said Madame Valière, with a sob in her voice.

Madame Dépine shot her a dignified glance. "We will discuss our affairs at home. Here it only remains to say whether you are satisfied with the fit."

Madame Valière patted the wig, as much in approbation as in adjustment. "But it fits me to a miracle!"

"Then we will pay our friend, and wish him le bon jour." She produced the fifty francs—two gold pieces, well sounding, for which she had exchanged her silver and copper, and two five-franc pieces. "And voilà," she added, putting down a franc for pourboire, "we are very content with the artist."

The "Princess" stared at her, with a new admiration.

"Merci bien," said the coiffeur, fervently, as he counted the cash. "Would that all customers' heads lent themselves so easily to artistic treatment!"

"And when will my friend's wig be ready?" said the "Princess."

"Madame Valière! What are you saying there? Monsieur will set to work when I bring him the fifty francs."

"Mais non, madame. I commence immediately. In a week it shall be ready, and you shall only pay on delivery."

"You are very good. But I shall not need it yet—not till the winter—when the snows come," said Madame Dépine, vaguely. "Bon jour, monsieur;" and, thrusting the old wig on the new block, and both under her shawl, she dragged the "Princess" out of the shop. Then, looking back through the door, "Do not lose the measurement, monsieur," she cried. "One of these days!"

XIII

The grey wig soon showed its dark side. Its possession, indeed, enabled Madame Valière to loiter on the more lighted stairs, or dawdle in the hall with Madame la Propriétaire; but Madame Dépine was not only debarred from these dignified domestic attitudes, but found a new awkwardness in bearing Madame Valière company in their walks abroad. Instead of keeping each other in countenance—duoe contra mundum—they might now have served as an advertisement for the coiffeur and the convenable. Before the grey wig—after the grey wig.

Wherefore Madame Dépine was not so very sorry when, after a few weeks of this discomforting contrast, the hour drew near of the "Princess's" departure for the family wedding; especially as she was only losing her for two days. She had insisted, of course, that the savings for the second wig were not to commence till the return, so that Madame Valière might carry with her a present worthy of her position and her port. They had anxious consultations over this present. Madame Dépine was for a cheap but showy article from the Bon Marché; but Madame Valière reminded her that the price-lists of this enterprising firm knocked at the doors of Tonnerre. Something distinguished (in silver) was her own idea. Madame Dépine frequently wept during these discussions, reminded of her own wedding. Oh, the roundabouts at Robinson, and that delicious wedding-lunch up the tree! One was gay then, my dear.

At last they purchased a tiny metal Louis Quinze timepiece for eleven francs seventy-five centimes, congratulating themselves on the surplus of twenty-five centimes from their three weeks' savings. Madame Valière packed it with her impedimenta into the carpet-bag lent her by Madame la Propriétaire. She was going by a night train from the Gare de Lyon, and sternly refused to let Madame Dépine see her off.

"And how would you go back—an old woman, alone in these dark November nights, with the papers all full of crimes of violence? It is not convenable, either."

Madame Dépine yielded to the latter consideration; but as Madame Valière, carrying the bulging carpet-bag, was crying "La porte, s'il vous plaît" to the concierge, she heard Madame Dépine come tearing and puffing after her like the steam-tram, and, looking back, saw her breathlessly brandishing her gold brooch. "Tiens!" she panted, fastening the "Princess's" cloak with it. "That will give thee an air."

"But—it is too valuable. Thou must not." They had never "thou'd" each other before, and this enhanced the tremulousness of the moment.

"I do not give it thee," Madame Dépine laughed through her tears. "Au revoir, mon amie."

"Adieu, ma chérie! I will tell my dear ones of my Paris comrade." And for the first time their lips met, and the brown wig brushed the grey.

XIV

Madame Dépine had two drearier days than she had foreseen. She kept to her own room, creeping out only at night, when, like all cats, all wigs are grey. After an eternity of loneliness the third day dawned, and she went by pre-arrangement to meet the morning train. Ah, how gaily gleamed the kiosks on the boulevards through the grey mist! What jolly red faces glowed under the cabmen's white hats! How blithely the birds sang in the bird-shops!

The train was late. Her spirits fell as she stood impatiently at the barrier, shivering in her thin clothes, and morbidly conscious of all those eyes on her wig. At length the train glided in unconcernedly, and shot out a medley of passengers. Her poor old eyes strained towards them. They surged through the gate in animated masses, but Madame Valière's form did not disentangle itself from them, though every instant she expected it to jump at her eyes. Her heart contracted painfully—there was no "Princess." She rushed round to another exit, then outside, to the gates at the end of the drive; she peered into every cab even, as it rumbled past. What had happened? She trudged home as hastily as her legs could bear her. No, Madame Valière had not arrived.

"They have persuaded her to stay another day," said Madame la Propriétaire. "She will come by the evening train, or she will write."

Madame Dépine passed the evening at the Gare de Lyon, and came home heavy of heart and weary of foot. The "Princess" might still arrive at midnight, though, and Madame Dépine lay down dressed in her bed, waiting for the familiar step in the corridor. About three o'clock she fell into a heavy doze, and woke in broad day. She jumped to her feet, her overwrought brain still heavy with the vapours of sleep, and threw open her door.

"Ah! she has already taken in her boots," she thought confusedly. "I shall be late for coffee." She gave her perfunctory knock, and turned the door-handle. But the door would not budge.

"Jacques! Jacques!" she cried, with a clammy fear at her heart. The garçon, who was pottering about with pails, opened the door with his key. An emptiness struck cold from the neat bed, the bare walls, the parted wardrobe-curtains that revealed nothing. She fled down the stairs, into the bureau.

"Madame Valière is not returned?" she cried.

Madame la Propriétaire shook her head.

"And she has not written?"

"No letter in her writing has come—for anybody."

"O mon Dieu! She has been murdered. She would go alone by night."

"She owes me three weeks' rent," grimly returned Madame la Propriétaire.

"What do you insinuate?" Madame Dépine's eyes flared.

Madame la Propriétaire shrugged her shoulders. "I am not at my first communion. I have grown grey in the service of lodgers. And this is how they reward me." She called Jacques, who had followed uneasily in Madame Dépine's wake. "Is there anything in the room?"

"Empty as an egg-shell, madame."

"Not even the miniature of her sister?"

"Not even the miniature of her sister."

"Of her sister?" repeated Madame Dépine.

"Yes; did I never tell you of her? A handsome creature, but she threw her bonnet over the mills."

"But I thought that was the Princess."

"The Princess, too. Her bonnet will also be found lying there."

"No, no; I mean I thought the portrait was the Princess's."

Madame la Propriétaire laughed. "She told you so?"

"No, no; but—but I imagined so."

"Without doubt, she gave you the idea. Quelle farceuse! I don't believe there ever was a Princess. The family was always inflated."

All Madame Dépine's world seemed toppling. Somehow her own mistake added to her sense of having been exploited.

"Still," said Madame la Propriétaire with a shrug, "it is only three weeks' rent."

"If you lose it, I will pay!" Madame Dépine had an heroic burst of faith.

"As you please. But I ought to have been on my guard. Where did she take the funds for a grey wig?"

"Ah, the brown wig!" cried Madame Dépine, joyfully. "She must have left that behind, and any coiffeur will give you three weeks' rent for that alone."

"We shall see," replied Madame la Propriétaire, ambiguously.

The trio mounted the stairs, and hunted high and low, disturbing the peaceful spider-webs. They peered under the very bed. Not even the old block was to be seen. As far as Madame Valière's own chattels were concerned, the room was indeed "empty as an egg-shell."

"She has carried it away with the three weeks' rent," sneered Madame la Propriétaire. "In my own carpet-bag," she added with a terrible recollection.

"She wished to wear it at night against the hard back of the carriage, and guard the other all glossy for the wedding." Madame Dépine quavered pleadingly, but she could not quite believe herself.

"The wedding had no more existence than the Princess," returned Madame la Propriétaire, believing herself more and more.

"Then she will have cheated me out of the grey wig from the first," cried Madame Dépine, involuntarily. "And I who sacrificed myself to her!"

"Comment! It was your wig?"

"No, no." She flushed and stammered. "But enfin—and then, oh, heaven! my brooch!"

"She has stolen your brooch?"

Great tears rolled down the wrinkled, ashen cheeks. So this was her reward for secretly instructing the coiffeur to make the "Princess's" wig first. The Princess, indeed! Ah, the adventuress! She felt choking; she shook her fist in the air. Not even the brooch to show when her family came up from Tonnerre, to say nothing of the wig. Was there a God in the world at all? Oh, holy Mother! No wonder the trickstress would not be escorted to the station—she never went to the station. No wonder she would not sell the royal secrets to the journalist—there were none to sell. Oh! it was all of a piece.

"If I were you I should go to the bureau of police!" said Madame la Propriétaire.

Yes, she would go; the wretch should be captured, should be haled to gaol. Even her half of the Louis Quinze timepiece recurred to poor Madame Dépine's brain.

"Add that she has stolen my carpet-bag."

The local bureau telegraphed first to Tonnerre.

There had been the wedding, but no Madame Valière. She had accepted the invitation, had given notice of her arrival; one had awaited the midnight train. The family was still wondering why the rich aunt had turned sulky at the last hour. But she was always an eccentric; a capricious and haughty personage.

Poor Madame Dépine's recurrent "My wig! my brooch!" reduced the official mind to the same muddle as her own.

"No doubt a sudden impulse of senescent kleptomania," said the superintendent, sagely, when he had noted down for transference to headquarters Madame Dépine's verbose and vociferous description of the traits and garments of the runagate. "But we will do our best to recover your brooch and your wig." Then, with a spasm of supreme sagacity, "Without doubt they are in the carpet-bag."

XV

Madame Dépine left the bureau and wandered about in a daze. That monster of ingratitude! That arch-adventuress, more vicious even than her bejewelled sister! All the long months of more than Lenten rigour recurred to her self-pitiful mood, that futile half-year of semi-starvation. How Madame Valière must have gorged on the sly, the rich eccentric! She crossed a bridge to the Ile de la Cité, and came to the gargoyled portals of Notre Dame, and let herself be drawn through the open door, and all the gloom and glory of the building fell around her like a soothing caress. She dropped before an altar and poured out her grief to the Mother of Sorrows. At last she arose, and tottered up the aisle, and the great rose-window glowed like the window of heaven. She imagined her husband and the dead children looking through it. Probably they wondered, as they gazed down, why her head remained so young.

Ah! but she was old, so very old. Surely God would take her soon. How should she endure the long years of loneliness and social ignominy?

As she stumbled out of the Cathedral, the cold, hard day smote her full in the face. People stared at her, and she knew it was at the brown wig. But could they expect her to starve herself for a whole year?

"Mon Dieu! Starve yourselves, my good friends. At my age, one needs fuel."

She escaped from them, and ran, muttering, across the road, and almost into the low grey shed.

Ah! the Morgue! Blessed idea! That should be the end of her. A moment's struggle, and then—the rose-window of heaven! Hell? No, no; the Madonna would plead for her; she who always looked so beautiful, so convenable.

She would peep in. Let her see how she would look when they found her. Would they clap a grey wig upon her, or expose her humiliation even in death?

"A-a-a-h!" A long scream tore her lips apart. There, behind the glass, in terrible waxen peace, a gash on her forehead, lay the "Princess," so uncanny-looking without any wig at all, that she would not have recognised her but for that moment of measurement at the hairdresser's. She fell sobbing before the cold glass wall of the death-chamber. Ah, God! Her first fear had been right; her brooch had but added to the murderer's temptation. And she had just traduced this martyred saint to the police.

"Forgive me, ma chérie, forgive me," she moaned, not even conscious that the attendant was lifting her to her feet with professional interest.

For in that instant everything passed from her but the great yearning for love and reconciliation, and for the first time a grey wig seemed a petty and futile aspiration.

CHASSÉ-CROISÉ

I

SET TO PARTNERS

"Oh, look, dear, there's that poor Walter Bassett."

Amber Roan looked down from the roof of the drag at the crossing restless shuttles, weaving with feminine woof and masculine warp the multi-coloured web of Society in London's cricket Coliseum.

"Where?" she murmured, her eye wandering over the little tract of sunlit green between the coaches with their rival Eton and Harrow favours. Before Lady Chelmer had time to bend her pink parasol a little more definitely, a thunder of applause turned Amber Roan's face back towards the wickets, with a piqued expression.

"It's real mean," she said. "What have I missed now?"

"Only a good catch," said the Hon. Tolshunt Darcy, whose eyes had never faltered from her face.

"My, that's just the one thing I've been dying for," she pouted self-mockingly.

"Poor Walter Bassett," Lady Chelmer repeated. "I knew his mother."

"Where?" Amber asked again.

"In Huntingdonshire, before the property went to Algy—"

"No, no, Lady Chelmer; I mean, where is poor Walter Whatsaname now?"

"Why, right here," said Lady Chelmer, involuntarily borrowing from the vocabulary of her young American protégée.

"Walter Bassett!" said the Hon. Tolshunt, languidly. "Isn't that the chap that's always getting chucked out of Parliament?"

"But his name doesn't sound Irish?" queried Amber.

"What are you talking about, Amber!" cried Lady Chelmer. "Why, he comes of a good old Huntingdon family. If he had been his own elder brother, he'd have got in long ago."

"Oh, you mean he never gets into Parliament," said Amber.

"Serve him right. I believe he's one of those independent nuisances," said the old Marquis of Woodham. "How is one ever to govern the country, if every man is a party unto himself?" He said "one," but only out of modesty; for having once accepted a minor post in a Ministry that the Premier in posse had not succeeded in forming, he had retained a Cabinet air ever since.

"Well, the beggar will scarcely come up at Highmead for a third licking," observed the Hon. Tolshunt.

"No, poor Walter," said Lady Chelmer. "He thought he'd be sure to get in this time, but he's quite crushed now. Wasn't it actually two thousand votes less than last time?"

"Two thousand and thirty-three," replied Lord Woodham, with punctilious inaccuracy.

Involuntarily Amber's eyes turned in search of the crushed candidate whom she almost saw flattened beneath the 2033 votes, and whom it would scarcely have been a surprise to find asquat under a carriage, humbly assisting the footmen to pack the dirty plates. But before she had time to decide which of the unlively men, loitering round the carriages or helping stout old dowagers up slim iron ladders, was sufficiently lugubrious to be identified as the martyr of the ballot-box, she was absorbed by a tall, masterful figure, whose face had the radiance of easeful success, and whose hands were clapping at some nuance of style which had escaped the palms of the great circular mob.

"I can't see any Walter Bassett," she murmured absently.

"Why, you are staring straight at him," said Lady Chelmer.

Miss Roan did not reply, but her face was eloquent of her astonishment, and when her face spoke, it was with that vivacity which is the American accent of beauty. What wonder if the Hon. Tolshunt Darcy paid heed to it, although he liked what it said less than the form of expression! As he used to put it in after days, "She gave one look, and threw herself away from the top of that drag." The more literal truth was that she drew Walter Bassett up to the top of that drag.

Lady Chelmer protested in vain that she could not halloo to the man.

"You knew his mother," Amber replied. "And he's got no seat."

"Quite symbolical! He, he, he!" and the old Marquis chuckled and cackled in solitary amusement. "Let's offer him one," he went on, half to enjoy the joke a little longer, half to utilise the opportunity of bringing his Ministerial wisdom to bear upon this erratic young man.

"I don't see where there's room," said the Hon. Tolshunt Darcy, sulkily.

"There's room on the front bench," cackled the Marquis, shaking his sides.

"Oh, I don't want you to roll off for him," said Miss Roan, who treated Ministerial Marquises with a contempt that bred in them a delightful sense of familiarity. "Tolshunt can sit opposite me—he's stared at the cricket long enough."

Tolshunt blushed with apparent irrelevance. But even the prospect of staring at Amber more comfortably did not reconcile him to displacement. "It's so awkward meeting a fellow who's had a tumble," he grumbled. "It's like having to condole with a man fresh from a funeral."

"There doesn't seem much black about Walter Bassett," Amber laughed. And at this moment—the dull end of a "maiden over"—the radiant personage in question turned his head, and perceiving Lady Chelmer's massive smile, acknowledged her recognition with respectful superiority, whereupon her Ladyship beckoned him with her best parasol manner.

"I want to introduce you to my friend, Miss Roan," she said, as he climbed to her side.

"I've been reading so much about you," said that young lady, with a sweet smile. "But you shouldn't be so independent, you know, you really shouldn't."

He smiled back. "I'm only independent till they come to my way of thinking."

Lady Chelmer gasped. "Then you still have hopes of Highmead!"

"I won a moral victory there each time, Lady Chelmer."

"How so, sir?" put in the Marquis. "Your opponent increased the Government majority—"

"And my reputation. A tiresome twaddler. Unfortunately," and he smiled again, "two moral victories are as bad as a defeat. On the other hand, a defeat at a bye-election equals a victory at a general. You play a solo—and on your own trumpet." A burst of cheering rounded off these remarks. This time Amber did not even inquire what it indicated—she was almost content to take it as an endorsement of Walter Bassett's epigrams. But Lord Woodham eagerly improved the situation. "A fine stroke that," he said, "but a batsman outside a team doesn't play the game."

"It will be a good time for the country, Lord Woodham," Mr. Bassett returned quietly, "when people cease to regard the Parliamentary session as a cricket match, one side trying to bowl over or catch out the other. But then England always has been a sporting nation."

"Ah, you allow some good in the old country," said Lady Chelmer, pleased. "Look at the trouble we all take to come here to encourage the dear boys;" and the words ended with a tired sigh.

"Yes, of course, that is the side on which they need encouragement," he rejoined drily. "Majuba was lost on the playing-field of Lord's."

There was a moment of shocked surprise. Lady Chelmer, herself a martyr to the religion of sport thus blasphemed—of which she understood as little as of any other religion—hastily tried to pour tea on the troubled waters. But they had been troubled too deeply. For full eight minutes the top of the drag became a political platform for Marquis-Ministerial denunciations of Mr. Gladstone, to a hail of repartee from the profane young man.

At the end of those eight minutes—when Lady Chelmer was at last able to reinsinuate tea into the discussion—Miss Amber Roan realised with a sudden shock that she had not "chipped in" once, and that "poor Walter Bassett" had commanded her ear for all that time without pouring into it a single compliment, or, indeed, addressing to it any observation whatever. For the first time since her début in the Milwaukee parlour at the age of five, this spoiled daughter of the dollar had lost sight of herself. As they walked towards the tea-tent, through the throng of clergymen and parasols and tanned men with field-glasses, and young bloods and pretty girls, she noted uneasily that his eyes wandered from her to these types of English beauty, these flower-faces under witching hats. Indeed, he had led her out of the way to plough past a row of open carriages. "The shortest cut," he said, "is past the prettiest woman."

But he had to face her at the tea-table, where she blocked his view of the tables beyond and plied him with strawberries and smiles under the sullen glances of the Hon. Tolshunt Darcy and the timid cough of her chaperon.

"I wonder you waste your time on the silly elections," she said. "We don't take much stock in Senators in America."

"It's just because M.P.'s are at such a discount that I want to get in. In the realm of the blind the one-eyed is a king."

"They must be blind not to let you in," she answered with equal frankness.

"No, they see too well, if you mean the voters. They've got their eye on the price of their vote."

"What!" she cried. "You can't buy votes in England!"

"Oh, can't you—"

"But I'm sure I read about it in the English histories—it was all abolished."

"A good many things were abolished by the Decalogue even earlier," he replied grimly. "Half an hour before the poll closed I could have bought a thousand votes at a shilling each."

"Well, that seems reasonable enough," said Lady Chelmer.

"It was beyond my pocket."

"What! Fifty pounds?" cried Amber, incredulously.

The blush that followed was hers, not his. "But what became of the thousand votes?" she asked hurriedly.

He laughed. "Half an hour before the poll closed they had gone down to sixpence apiece—like fish that wouldn't keep."

"My! And were they all wasted?"

"No. My rival bought them up. Vide the newspapers—'the polling was unusually heavy towards the close.'"

"Really!" intervened Lady Chelmer. "Then at that rate you can unseat him for bribery."

"At that rate—or higher," he replied drily. "To unseat another is even more expensive than to seat oneself."

"Why, it seems all a question of money," said Miss Amber Roan, naively.

II

CHASSÉ

Lady Chelmer was glad when the season came to an end and the dancing mice had no longer to spin dizzyingly in their gilded cage. "The Prisoner of Pleasure" was Walter Bassett's phrase for her. Even now she was a convict on circuit. Some of the dungeons were in ancient castles, from which Bassett was barred, but all of which opened to Amber's golden keys, though only because Lady Chelmer knew how to turn them. He, however, penetrated the ducal doors through the letter-box.

The Hon. Tolshunt and Lord Woodham, in their apprehension of the common foe, began to find each other endurable. If it was politics that attracted her, Tolshunt felt he too could stoop to a career. As for the Marquis, he began to meditate resuming office. Both had freely hinted to her Ladyship that to give a millionaire bride to a man who hadn't a penny savoured of Socialism.

Galled by such terrible insinuations, Lady Chelmer had dared to sound the girl.

"I love his letters," gushed Amber, bafflingly. "He writes such cute things."

"He doesn't dress very well," said Lady Chelmer, feebly fighting.

"Oh, of course, he doesn't bother as much as Tolly, who looks as if he had been poured into his clothes—"

"Yes, the mould of fashion," quoted Lady Chelmer, vaguely.

An eruption of Walter Bassett in the Press did not tend to allay her Ladyship's alarm, especially as Amber began to dally with the morning paper and the evening.

Opening a new People's Library at Highmead—in the absence abroad of the successful candidate—he had contrived to set the newspapers sneering. He had told the People that although they might temporarily accept such gifts as "Capital's conscience-money," yet it was as much the duty of the parish to supply light as to supply street-lamps; which was considered both ungracious and unsound. The donor he described as "a millionaire of means," which was considered wilfully paradoxical by those who did not know how great capitals are locked up in industries. But what worked up the Press most was his denunciation of modern journalism, in malodorous comparison with the literature this Library would bring the People. "The journalist," he said tersely, "is Satan's secretary." No shorter cut to notoriety could have been devised, for it was the "Silly Season," and Satan found plenty of mischief for his idle hands to do.

"Oh, you poor man!" Amber wrote Walter. "Why don't you say you were thinking of America—yellow journalism, and all that? The yellow is, of course, Satan's sulphur. You would hardly believe what his secretaries have written even of poor little me! And you should see the pictures of 'The Milwaukee Millionairess' in the Sunday numbers!"

Walter Bassett did not reply regularly and punctually to Amber's letters, and it was a novel sensation to the jaded beauty who had often thrown aside masculine missives after a glance at the envelope, to find herself eagerly shuffling her morning correspondence in the hope of turning up a trump-card. A card, indeed, it often proved, though never a postcard, and Amber meekly repaid it fourfold. She found it delicious to pour herself out to him; it had the pleasure of abandonment without its humiliation. Verbally, this was the least flirtatious correspondence she had ever maintained with the opposite sex.

So when at last, towards the end of the holiday season, the pair met in the flesh at a country house (Lady Chelmer still protests it was a coincidence), Walter Bassett had no apprehension of danger, and his expression of pleasure at the coincidence was unfeigned, for he felt his correspondence would be lightened. In nothing did he feel the want of pence more keenly than in his inability to keep a secretary for his public work. "Money is time," he used to complain; "the millionaire is your only Methuselah."

The house had an old-world garden, and it was here they had their first duologue. Amber had quickly discovered that Walter was interested in the apiaries that lay at the foot of its slope, and so he found her standing in poetic grace among the tall sweet-peas, with their whites and pinks and faint purples, a basket of roses in one hand and a pair of scissors in the other.

As he came to her under the quaint trellised arch, "I always feel like a croquet ball going through the hoop," he said.

"But the ball is always driven," she said.

"Oh, I dare say it has the illusion of freewill. Doubtless the pieces in that chess game, which Eastern monarchs are said to play with human figures, come to think they move of themselves. The knight chuckles as he makes his tortuous jump at the queen, and the bishop swoops down on the castle with holy joy."

She came imperceptibly closer to him. "Then you don't think any of us move of ourselves?"

"One or two of us in each generation. They make the puppets dance."

"You admire Bismarck, I see."

"Yes. A pity he didn't emigrate to your country, like so many Germans."

"Do you think we need him? But he couldn't have been President. You must be born in America."

"True. Then I shall remain on here."

"You're terrible ambitious, Mr. Bassett."

"Yes, terrible," he repeated mockingly.

"Then come and help me pick blackberries," she said, and caught him by his own love of the unexpected. They left the formal garden, and came out into the rabbit-warren, and toiled up and down hillocks in search of ripe bushes, paying, as Walter said, "many pricks to the pint." And when Amber urged him to scramble to the back of tangled bushes, through coils of bristling briars, "You were right," he laughed; "this is terrible ambitious." The best of the blackberries plucked, Amber began a new campaign against mushrooms, and had frequent opportunities to rebuke his clumsiness in crumbling the prizes he uprooted. She knelt at his side to teach him, and once laid her deft fingers instructively upon his.

And just at that moment he irritatingly discovered a dead mole, and fell to philosophising upon it and its soft, velvet, dainty skin—as if a girl's fingers were not softer and daintier! "Look at its poor little pale-red mouth," he went on, "gaspingly open, as in surprise at the strange great forces that had made and killed it."

"I dare say it had a good time," said Amber, pettishly.

After the harvest had been carried indoors they scarcely exchanged a word till she found him watching the bees the next morning.

"Are you interested in bees?" she inquired in tones of surprise.

"Yes," he said. "They are the most striking example of Nature's Bismarckism—her habit of using her creatures to work her will through their own. Sic vos non vobis."

"I learnt enough Latin at College to understand that," she said; "but I don't see how one finds out anything by just watching them hover over their hives. I've never even been able to find the queen bee. Won't you come and see what beautiful woods there are behind the house? Lady Chelmer is walking there, and I ought to be joining her."

"You ought to be taking her an umbrella," he said coldly. Amber looked up at the sky. Had it been blue, she would have felt it grey. As it was grey, she felt it black.

"Oh, if you're afraid of a drop of rain—" And Amber walked on witheringly. It was a clever move.

Walter followed in silence. Amber did not become aware of him till she was in the middle of an embryonic footpath through tall bracken that made way, courtseying, for the rare pedestrian.

"Oh!" She gave a little scream. "I thought you were studying the bees—or the moles."

"I have only been studying your graceful back."

"How mean! Behind my back!" She laughed, pleased. "I hope you haven't discovered anything Bismarckian about my back."

"Only in the sense that I followed it, and must follow—till the path widens."

"Ah, how you must hate following—you, so terrible ambitious."

"The path will widen," he said composedly.

She planted her feet firm on Mother Earth—as though it were literally her own mother—and turned a mocking head over a tantalising shoulder. "I shall stay still right here."

He smiled maliciously. "And I, too; I follow you no farther."

"Oh, you are just too cute," she said with a laugh of vexation and pleasure. "You make me go on just to make you follow; but it is really you that make me lead. That's what you mean by Bismarckism, isn't it?"

"You put it beautifully."

She swung round to face him. "Is there nothing you admire but Force?"

"Not Force—Power!"

"What's the difference?"

"Force is blind."

"So is love," she said. "Do you scorn that?" And her smile was daring and dazzling.

Ere he could reply Nature outdid her in dazzlement, and superadded a crash of thunder.

"Yes," he said, as though there had been no interruption. "I scorn all that is blind—even this storm that may strike you and me. Ah! the rain," as the great drops began to fall. "Poor Lady Chelmer—without an umbrella."

"We can shelter by these shrubs." In an instant she was crouching amid the ferns on a carpet of autumn leaves, making space for him beside her.

"Thank you—I will stand," he said coldly. "But I don't know if you're aware these are oak-shrubs."

"What of it?"

"I was only thinking of the Swiss proverb about lightning, 'Vor den Eichen sollst du weichen.' We ought to make for the beeches."

"I'm not going to leave my umbrella. I am sorry you won't accept a bit of it." And she bent the tall ferns invitingly towards him.

"I don't like cowering even before the rain," he laughed. "How it brings out the beautiful earthy smell."

"One enjoys the beautiful earthy smell the better for being nearer to the earth."

He did not reply.

"Oh, you dear fool," she thought. Hadn't she had heaps of Power from childhood—over her stern old father, over her weakling mother, over her governesses, and later over the whole tribe of "the boys," and now in Europe over Marquises and Honourables—and could it all compare in intensity to this delicious, poignant sense of being caught up into a masterful personality! No, not Power but Powerlessness was life's central reality; not to turn with iron hand the great wheels of Fate, but to faint at a dear touch, to be sucked up as a moth in the flame. And for him, too, it were surely as sweet to leave this strenuous quest for dominance, or to be content with dominating her alone. Oh, she would bring him to clear vision, to live for nothing but her, even as she asked for nothing but him.

The harsh scream of a bluejay struck a discord through her reverie. She remembered that he had yet to be won.

"But didn't you tell me people can't get power without money?" she said, forgetting the hiatus in the conversation.

"Nor with it generally," he replied, without surprise. "Money is but a lever. You cannot move the earth unless you have force and fulcrum, too."

"But I guess a man like you must get real mad to see so many levers lying about idle."

"Oh, I shall get on without a lever, like primitive man. I have muscles."

"But it seems too bad not to be able to afford machinery."

"I shall be hand-made."

"Yes, and by your own hand. But won't it be slow?"

"It will be sure."

Every one of his speeches rang like the stroke of a hammer. Yes, indeed he had muscles.

"But how much surer with money! You ought to turn your career into a company. Surely it would pay a dividend to its promoters."

"The directors would interfere."

"You could be chairman—with a veto."

He shook his head. "The rain is dripping through your umbrella. Don't you think we might run to the house?"

"It's only an old hat." It was fresh from Paris, broad-brimmed, beautiful, and bewitching. "Why don't you find"—she smiled nervously—"a millionaire of means?"

"And what would be his reward?"

"Just Virtue's. Won't you be a light to England? And isn't it the duty of parishes and millionaires to supply light?" She was plucking a fern-leaf to pieces.

"Millionaires' minds don't run that way."

"Not male millionaires, perhaps," she said, turning her face from him so jerkily that she shook the oak-shrub and it became a shower-bath.

He looked at her, slightly startled. It was the first emotion she had ever provoked in him, and her heart beat faster.

"I really do think it is giving over now," he said, gazing at her sopping hat.

'Twas as if he had shaken the shrub again and drenched her with cold water. He was mocking her, her and her dollars and her love.

"It is quite over," she said savagely, springing up, and growing even angrier when she found the rain had really stopped, so that her indignation sounded only like acquiescence. She strode ahead of him, silent, through the wet bracken, her frock growing a limp rag as it brushed aside the glistening ferns.

As she struck the broader path to the house, the cackling laugh of a goat chained to a roadside log followed her cynically. Where had she heard this bleat before? Ah, yes, from the Marquis of Woodham.

III

BALANCEZ

Walter Bassett had spoken truly. He did not admire love—that blind force. Women seemed to him delightfully aesthetic objects—to be kept at a distance, however closely one embraced them. They were unreasoning beings at the best, even when unbiassed by that supreme prejudice—love.

It was not his conception of the strong man that he must needs become as water at some woman's touch and go dancing and babbling like a sylvan brook. Women were the light of life—he was willing enough to admit it, but one must be able to switch the light on and off at will. All these were reasons for not falling in love—they were not reasons for not marrying. And so, Amber being determined to marry him, there was really less difficulty than if it had been necessary for him to fall in love with her.

It took, however, many letters and interviews, full of the subtlest comedy, infinite advancing and retiring, and recrossing and bowing, and courtesying and facing and half-turning, before this leap-year dance could end in the solemn Wedding March.

"You know," she said once, "how I should love the fun of seeing you plough your way through all the mediocrities."

"That is the means, not the end," he reminded her, rebukingly. "One only wants the world to swallow one's pills for the world's sake."

"I don't believe you," she said frankly. "Else you'd move mountains to get the money for the pills, not turn up your nose at the mountain when it comes to you."

He laughed heartily. "What a delightful confusion of metaphors! I'm sure you've got Irish blood somewhere."

"Of course I have. Did I never tell you I am descended from the kings of Ireland?"

He took off his hat mockingly. "I salute Miss Brian Boru."

"You're an awfully good fellow," he told her on a later occasion. "I almost believe I'd take your money if you were not a woman." "If I were not a woman I should not offer it to you—I should want a career of my own."

"And my career would content you?" he asked, touched.

"Absolutely," she lied. "The interest I should take in it—wouldn't that be sufficient interest on the loan?"

"There is one thing you have taught me," he said slowly—"how conventional I am! But every prejudice in me shrinks from your proposition, much as I admire your manliness."

"Perhaps it could be put on more conventional lines—superficially," she suggested in a letter that harked back to this conversation. "One might go through conventional forms. That adorable Disraeli—I have just been reading his letters. How right he was not to marry for love!"

The penultimate stage of the pre-nuptial comedy was reached in the lobby of the Opera, while Society was squeezing to its carriage. It was after the Rheingold, and poor Lady Chelmer could hardly keep her eyes open, and actually dozed off as she leaned against a wall, in patient martyrdom. Walter Bassett had been specially irritating, for he had not come up to the box once, and everybody knows (as the Hon. Tolshunt had said, with unwonted brilliance) the Rheingold is in heavy bars.

"I didn't know you admired Wagner so much," Amber said scathingly, as Walter pushed through the grooms. "Such a rapt devotee!"

"Wagner is the greatest man of the century. He alone has been able to change London's dinner-hour."

Amber could not help smiling. "Poor Lady Chelmer!" she said, nodding towards the drowsing dowager. "Since half-past six!"

"Is that our carriage?" said the "Prisoner of Pleasure," opening her eyes.

"No, dear—I guess we are some fifty behind. Tolly and the Marquis are watching from the pavement."

The poor lady sighed and went to sleep again.

"Behold the compensations of poverty," observed Walter Bassett. "The gallery-folk have to wait and squeeze before the opera; the carriage-folk after the opera."

"You forget the places they occupy during the opera. Poor Wagner! What a fight! I wish I could have helped his career." And Amber set a wistful smile in the becoming frame of her white hood.

"The form of the career appears to be indifferent to you," he said, with a little laugh.

"As indifferent as the man," she replied, meeting his eyes calmly.

The faint scent of her hair mingled with his pleasurable sense of her frank originality. For the first time the bargain really appealed to him. He could not but see that she was easily the fairest of that crush of fair women, and to have her prostrated at the foot of his career was more subtly delicious than to have her surrender to his person. The ball was at his foot in surely the most tempting form that a ball could take. And the fact that he must leave her hurriedly to write the musical criticism that was the price of his stall, was not calculated to diminish his appreciation of all the kingdoms of the world which his temptress was showing him from her high mountain.

"Alas! I must go and write a notice," he sighed.

"Satan's Secretary?" she queried mischievously.

He started. Had he not been just thinking of her as a Satan in skirts?

"En attendant that I become Satan's master," he replied ambiguously, as he raised his hat.

"Oh, to drive off with him into the peace and solitude of Love—away from the grinding paths of ambition," thought Amber, when the horses pranced up.

"Women, not measures," said the reigning wit anent the administration which Amber's Salon held together, and in which her husband occupied a position quite disproportionate to his nominal office, and still more so to the almost unparalleled brevity of his career as a private member.

Few, indeed, were the recalcitrants who could resist Amber's smiles, or her still more seductive sulkiness. Walter Bassett's many enemies declared that the young Cabinet Minister owed his career entirely to his wife. His admirers indignantly pointed out that he had represented Highmead for two sessions before he met Miss Roan. The germ of truth in this was that he had stipulated to himself that he would not accept the contract unless Amber, too, must admit "Value received," and in contributing a career already self-launched, and a good old Huntingdon name, his pride was satisfied. This, however, had wasted a year or so, while the Government was getting itself turned out, and it never entered his brain that his crushing victory at the General Election could owe anything to a corner in votes—at five dollars a head—secretly made by a fair American financier.

It was in the thick of the season, and Amber had just said good-bye to the Bishop, the last of her dinner-guests. "I always say grace when the church goes," she laughed, as she turned to her budget of unread correspondence and shuffled the letters, as in the old days, when she hoped to draw a letter of Walter's. But her method had become more scientific. Recognising the writers by their crests or mottoes, she would arrange the letters in order of precedence, alleging it was to keep her hand in, otherwise she would always be making the most horrible mistakes in "your Mediæval British etiquette."

"Who goes first to-night?" said her husband, watching her movements from a voluptuous arm-chair.

"Only Lady Chelmer," Amber yawned, as she broke the seal.

"Didn't I see the scrawl of the Honourable Tolly?"

"Yes, poor dear. I do so want to know if he is happy in British Honduras. But he must take his turn."

"If he had taken his turn," Walter laughed, "he never would have got the appointment there."

"No, poor dear; it was very good of you."

"Of me?" Walter's tone was even more amused. His eyes roved round the vast drawing-room, as if with the thought that he had as little to do with its dignified grandeur. Then his gaze rested once more on his wife; she seemed a delicious harmony of silks and flowers and creamy flesh-tones.

"Mrs. Bassett," he said softly, lingering on the proprietorial term.

"Yes, Walter," she said, not looking up from her letter.

"Do you realise this is the first time we have been alone together this month?"

"No? Really?" She glanced up absently.

"Never mind that muddle-headed old Chelmer. I dare say she only wants another hundred or two." He came over, took the letter and her hand with it. "I have a great secret to tell you."

Now he had captured her attention as well as her hand. Her eyes sparkled. "A Cabinet Secret?" she said.

"Yes. At this moment every newspaper office is in a fever—to-morrow all England will be ringing with the news. It is a thunderbolt."

She started up, snatching her hand away, every nerve a-quiver with excitement. "And you kept this from me all through dinner?"

"I hadn't a chance, darling—I came straight from the scrimmage."

"You won't gloss it over by calling me novel names. I hate stale thunderbolts. You might have breathed a word in my ear."

"I shall make amends by beginning with the part that is only for your ear. Do you know what next Monday is?"

"The day you address your constituents, of course. Oh, I see, this thunderbolt is going to change your speech."

"Is going to change my speech altogether. Next Monday is the seventh anniversary of our wedding."

"Is it? But what has that to do with your speech at Highmead?"

"Everything." He smiled mysteriously, then went on softly, "Amber, do you remember our honeymoon?"

She smiled faintly. "Oh, I haven't quite forgotten."

"If you had quite forgotten the misery of it, I should be glad."

"I have quite forgotten."

"You are kinder than I deserve. But I was so startled to find my career was less to you than a kiss that I was more churlish than I need have been. I even wished that you might have a child, so that you might be taken up with it instead of with me."

She blushed. "Yes, I dare say I showed my hand clumsily as soon as it held all the aces."

"Ah, Amber, you were an angel and I was a beast. How gallantly you swallowed your disappointment in your bargain, how loyally you worked heart and soul that I might gain my one ideal—Power!"

"It was a labour of love," she said deprecatingly.

"My noble Amber. But did you think, selfishly engrossed though I have been with the Fight for Power, that this love-labour of yours was lost on me? No, 'terrible ambitious' as I was, I could still see I got the blackberries and you little more than the scratches, and the less you began to press your claim upon my heart, the more my heart was opening out with an answering passion. I began to watch the play of your eyes, the shimmer of light across your cheek, the roguish pout of your lips, the lock that strayed across your temple—as it is straying now."

She pushed it back impatiently. "But what has all this to do with the Cabinet Secret?"

"Patience, darling! How much nicer to listen to you than to the Opposition."

"I shall be in the Opposition unless you get along faster."

"That is what I want—your face opposite me always, instead of bald-headed babblers. Ah, if you knew how often, of late, it has floated before me in the House, reducing historic wrangles to the rocking of children's boats in stormy ponds, accentuating the ponderous futility." He took her hand again, and a great joy filled him as he felt its gentle responsive pressure.

"Ponderous, perhaps," she said, smiling faintly; "but not futile, Walter."

"Futile, so far as I am concerned, dearest. Ah, you are right. Love is the only reality—everything else a game played with counters. What are our winnings? A few cheers drowned in the roar that greets the winning jockey, a few leading articles, stale as yesterday's newspaper."

"But the good to the masses—" she reminded him.

"Don't mock me with my own phrases, darling. The masses have done me more good than I can ever do them. Next Monday, dear Amber Roan, we'll try our honeymoon over again." And his lips sought hers.

She drew back. "Yes, yes, after the Speech. But now—the Secret!"

"There will be no speech—that is the secret."

She drew away from him altogether. "No speech!" she gasped.

"None save to your adorable ear—and the moonlit waters. Woodham has lent us his yacht—"

"In the middle of a Cabinet Crisis?"

"Which concerns me less than anybody." And he beamed happily.

"Less than anybody?" she repeated.

"Yes—since it is my resignation that makes the crisis."

She fell back into a chair, white and trembling. "You have resigned!"

"For ever. And now, hey for the great round, wonderful world! Don't you hear our keel cutting the shimmering waters?"

"No," she said savagely. "I hear only Woodham's mocking laughter!... And it sounds like a goat bleating."

"Darling!" he cried in amaze.

"I told you not to 'darling' me. How dared you change our lives without a word of consultation?"

"Amber!" His voice was pained now. "I prepared a surprise for the anniversary of our wedding. One can't consult about surprises."

"Keep your quibbles for the House! But perhaps there is no House, either."

"Naturally. I have done with it all. I have written for the Chiltern Hundreds."

"You are mad, Walter. You must take it all back."

"I can't, Amber. I have quarrelled hopelessly with the Party. The Prime Minister will never forgive what I said at the Council to-day. The luxury of speaking one's mind is expensive. I ought never to have joined any Party. I am only fit to be Independent."

"Independence leads nowhere." She rose angrily. "And this is to be the end of your Career! The Career you married me for!"

"I did wrong, Amber. But before one finds the true God, one worships idols."

"And what is the true God, pray?"

"The one whose angel and minister you have always been, Amber"—he lowered his voice reverently—"Love."

"Love!" Her voice was bitter. "Any bench in the Park, any alley in Highmead, swarms with Love." 'Twas as if Cæsar had skipped from his imperial chariot to a sociable.

All her childish passion for directing the life of the household, all her girlish relish in keeping lovers in leading strings, all that unconscious love of Power which—inversely—had attracted her to Walter Bassett, and which had found so delightful a scope in her political activities, leapt—now that her Salon was threatened with extinction—into agonised consciousness of itself.

Through this brilliant husband of hers, she had touched the destinies of England, pulled the strings of Empire. Oh, the intoxication of the fight—the fight for which she had seconded and sponged him! Oh, the rapture of intriguing against his enemies—himself included—the feminine triumph of managing Goodman Waverer or Badman Badgerer!

And now—oh, she could no longer control her sobs!

He tried to soothe her, to caress her, but she repulsed him.

"Go to your yacht—to your miserable shimmering waters. I shall spend my honeymoon here alone.... You discovered I was Irish."

THE WOMAN BEATER

She came "to meet John Lefolle," but John Lefolle did not know he was to meet Winifred Glamorys. He did not even know he was himself the meeting-point of all the brilliant and beautiful persons, assembled in the publisher's Saturday Salon, for although a youthful minor poet, he was modest and lovable. Perhaps his Oxford tutorship was sobering. At any rate his head remained unturned by his precocious fame, and to meet these other young men and women—his reverend seniors on the slopes of Parnassus—gave him more pleasure than the receipt of "royalties." Not that his publisher afforded him much opportunity of contrasting the two pleasures. The profits of the Muse went to provide this room of old furniture and roses, this beautiful garden a-twinkle with Japanese lanterns, like gorgeous fire-flowers blossoming under the white crescent-moon of early June.

Winifred Glamorys was not literary herself. She was better than a poetess, she was a poem. The publisher always threw in a few realities, and some beautiful brainless creature would generally be found the nucleus of a crowd, while Clio in spectacles languished in a corner. Winifred Glamorys, however, was reputed to have a tongue that matched her eye; paralleling with whimsies and epigrams its freakish fires and witcheries, and, assuredly, flitting in her white gown through the dark balmy garden, she seemed the very spirit of moonlight, the subtle incarnation of night and roses.

When John Lefolle met her, Cecilia was with her, and the first conversation was triangular. Cecilia fired most of the shots; she was a bouncing, rattling beauty, chockful of confidence and high spirits, except when asked to do the one thing she could do—sing! Then she became—quite genuinely—a nervous, hesitant, pale little thing. However, the suppliant hostess bore her off, and presently her rich contralto notes passed through the garden, adding to its passion and mystery, and through the open French windows, John could see her standing against the wall near the piano, her head thrown back, her eyes half-closed, her creamy throat swelling in the very abandonment of artistic ecstasy.

"What a charming creature!" he exclaimed involuntarily.

"That is what everybody thinks, except her husband," Winifred laughed.

"Is he blind then?" asked John with his cloistral naïveté.

"Blind? No, love is blind. Marriage is never blind."

The bitterness in her tone pierced John. He felt vaguely the passing of some icy current from unknown seas of experience. Cecilia's voice soared out enchantingly.

"Then, marriage must be deaf," he said, "or such music as that would charm it."

She smiled sadly. Her smile was the tricksy play of moonlight among clouds of faëry.

"You have never been married," she said simply.

"Do you mean that you, too, are neglected?" something impelled him to exclaim.

"Worse," she murmured.

"It is incredible!" he cried. "You!"

"Hush! My husband will hear you."

Her warning whisper brought him into a delicious conspiracy with her. "Which is your husband?" he whispered back.

"There! Near the casement, standing gazing open-mouthed at Cecilia. He always opens his mouth when she sings. It is like two toys moved by the same wire."

He looked at the tall, stalwart, ruddy-haired Anglo-Saxon. "Do you mean to say he—?"

"I mean to say nothing."

"But you said—"

"I said 'worse.'"

"Why, what can be worse?"

She put her hand over her face. "I am ashamed to tell you." How adorable was that half-divined blush!

"But you must tell me everything." He scarcely knew how he had leapt into this rôle of confessor. He only felt they were "moved by the same wire."

Her head drooped on her breast. "He—beats—me."

"What!" John forgot to whisper. It was the greatest shock his recluse life had known, compact as it was of horror at the revelation, shamed confusion at her candour, and delicious pleasure in her confidence.

This fragile, exquisite creature under the rod of a brutal bully!

Once he had gone to a wedding reception, and among the serious presents some grinning Philistine drew his attention to an uncouth club—"a wife-beater" he called it. The flippancy had jarred upon John terribly: this intrusive reminder of the customs of the slums. It grated like Billingsgate in a boudoir. Now that savage weapon recurred to him—for a lurid instant he saw Winifred's husband wielding it. Oh, abomination of his sex! And did he stand there, in his immaculate evening dress, posing as an English gentleman? Even so might some gentleman burglar bear through a salon his imperturbable swallow-tail.

Beat a woman! Beat that essence of charm and purity, God's best gift to man, redeeming him from his own grossness! Could such things be? John Lefolle would as soon have credited the French legend that English wives are sold in Smithfield. No! it could not be real that this flower-like figure was thrashed.

"Do you mean to say—?" he cried. The rapidity of her confidence alone made him feel it all of a dreamlike unreality.

"Hush! Cecilia's singing!" she admonished him with an unexpected smile, as her fingers fell from her face.

"Oh, you have been making fun of me." He was vastly relieved. "He beats you—at chess—or at lawn-tennis?"

"Does one wear a high-necked dress to conceal the traces of chess, or lawn-tennis?"

He had not noticed her dress before, save for its spiritual whiteness. Susceptible though he was to beautiful shoulders, Winifred's enchanting face had been sufficiently distracting. Now the thought of physical bruises gave him a second spasm of righteous horror. That delicate rose-leaf flesh abraded and lacerated!

"The ruffian! Does he use a stick or a fist?"

"Both! But as a rule he just takes me by the arms and shakes me like a terrier. I'm all black and blue now."

"Poor butterfly!" he murmured poetically.

"Why did I tell you?" she murmured back with subtler poetry.

The poet thrilled in every vein. "Love at first sight," of which he had often read and often written, was then a reality! It could be as mutual, too, as Romeo's and Juliet's. But how awkward that Juliet should be married and her husband a Bill Sykes in broadcloth!

II

Mrs. Glamorys herself gave "At Homes," every Sunday afternoon, and so, on the morrow, after a sleepless night mitigated by perpended sonnets, the love-sick young tutor presented himself by invitation at the beautiful old house in Hampstead. He was enchanted to find his heart's mistress set in an eighteenth-century frame of small-paned windows and of high oak-panelling, and at once began to image her dancing minuets and playing on virginals. Her husband was absent, but a broad band of velvet round Winifred's neck was a painful reminder of his possibilities. Winifred, however, said it was only a touch of sore throat caught in the garden. Her eyes added that there was nothing in the pathological dictionary which she would not willingly have caught for the sake of those divine, if draughty moments; but that, alas! it was more than a mere bodily ailment she had caught there.

There were a great many visitors in the two delightfully quaint rooms, among whom he wandered disconsolate and admired, jealous of her scattered smiles, but presently he found himself seated by her side on a "cosy corner" near the open folding-doors, with all the other guests huddled round a violinist in the inner room. How Winifred had managed it he did not know, but she sat plausibly in the outer room, awaiting new-comers, and this particular niche was invisible, save to a determined eye. He took her unresisting hand—that dear, warm hand, with its begemmed artistic fingers, and held it in uneasy beatitude. How wonderful! She—the beautiful and adored hostess, of whose sweetness and charm he heard even her own guests murmur to one another—it was her actual flesh-and-blood hand that lay in his—thrillingly tangible. Oh, adventure beyond all merit, beyond all hoping!

But every now and then, the outer door facing them would open on some new-comer, and John had hastily to release her soft magnetic fingers and sit demure, and jealously overhear her effusive welcome to those innocent intruders, nor did his brow clear till she had shepherded them within the inner fold. Fortunately, the refreshments were in this section, so that once therein, few of the sheep strayed back, and the jiggling wail of the violin was succeeded by a shrill babble of tongues and the clatter of cups and spoons. "Get me an ice, please—strawberry," she ordered John during one of these forced intervals in manual flirtation; and when he had steered laboriously to and fro, he found a young actor beside her their hands dispart. He stood over them with a sickly smile, while Winifred ate her ice. When he returned from depositing the empty saucer, the player-fellow was gone, and in remorse for his mad suspicion he stooped and reverently lifted her fragrant finger-tips to his lips. The door behind his back opened abruptly.

"Good-by," she said, rising in a flash. The words had the calm conventional cadence, and instantly extorted from him—amid all his dazedness—the corresponding "Good-by." When he turned and saw it was Mr. Glamorys who had come in, his heart leapt wildly at the nearness of his escape. As he passed this masked ruffian, he nodded perfunctorily and received a cordial smile. Yes, he was handsome and fascinating enough externally, this blonde savage.

"A man may smile and smile and be a villain," John thought. "I wonder how he'd feel, if he knew I knew he beats women."

Already John had generalised the charge. "I hope Cecilia will keep him at arm's length," he had said to Winifred, "if only that she may not smart for it some day."

He lingered purposely in the hall to get an impression of the brute, who had begun talking loudly to a friend with irritating bursts of laughter, speciously frank-ringing. Golf, fishing, comic operas—ah, the Boeotian! These were the men who monopolised the ethereal divinities.

But this brusque separation from his particular divinity was disconcerting. How to see her again? He must go up to Oxford in the morning, he wrote her that night, but if she could possibly let him call during the week he would manage to run down again.

"Oh, my dear, dreaming poet," she wrote to Oxford, "how could you possibly send me a letter to be laid on the breakfast-table beside The Times! With a poem in it, too. Fortunately my husband was in a hurry to get down to the City, and he neglected to read my correspondence. ('The unchivalrous blackguard,' John commented. 'But what can be expected of a woman beater?') Never, never write to me again at the house. A letter, care of Mrs. Best, 8A Foley Street, W.C., will always find me. She is my maid's mother. And you must not come here either, my dear handsome head-in-the-clouds, except to my 'At Homes,' and then only at judicious intervals. I shall be walking round the pond in Kensington Gardens at four next Wednesday, unless Mrs. Best brings me a letter to the contrary. And now thank you for your delicious poem; I do not recognise my humble self in the dainty lines, but I shall always be proud to think I inspired them. Will it be in the new volume? I have never been in print before; it will be a novel sensation. I cannot pay you song for song, only feeling for feeling. Oh, John Lefolle, why did we not meet when I had still my girlish dreams? Now, I have grown to distrust all men—to fear the brute beneath the cavalier...."

Mrs. Best did bring her a letter, but it was not to cancel the appointment, only to say he was not surprised at her horror of the male sex, but that she must beware of false generalisations. Life was still a wonderful and beautiful thing—vide poem enclosed. He was counting the minutes till Wednesday afternoon. It was surely a popular mistake that only sixty went to the hour.

This chronometrical reflection recurred to him even more poignantly in the hour that he circumambulated the pond in Kensington Gardens. Had she forgotten—had her husband locked her up? What could have happened? It seemed six hundred minutes, ere, at ten past five she came tripping daintily towards him. His brain had been reduced to insanely devising problems for his pupils—if a man walks two strides of one and a half feet a second round a lake fifty acres in area, in how many turns will he overtake a lady who walks half as fast and isn't there?—but the moment her pink parasol loomed on the horizon, all his long misery vanished in an ineffable peace and uplifting. He hurried, bare-headed, to clasp her little gloved hand. He had forgotten her unpunctuality, nor did she remind him of it.

"How sweet of you to come all that way," was all she said, and it was a sufficient reward for the hours in the train and the six hundred minutes among the nursemaids and perambulators. The elms were in their glory, the birds were singing briskly, the water sparkled, the sunlit sward stretched fresh and green—it was the loveliest, coolest moment of the afternoon. John instinctively turned down a leafy avenue. Nature and Love! What more could poet ask?

"No, we can't have tea by the Kiosk," Mrs. Glamorys protested. "Of course I love anything that savours of Paris, but it's become so fashionable. There will be heaps of people who know me. I suppose you've forgotten it's the height of the season. I know a quiet little place in the High Street." She led him, unresisting but bemused, towards the gate, and into a confectioner's. Conversation languished on the way.

"Tea," he was about to instruct the pretty attendant.

"Strawberry ices," Mrs. Glamorys remarked gently. "And some of those nice French cakes."

The ice restored his spirits, it was really delicious, and he had got so hot and tired, pacing round the pond. Decidedly Winifred was a practical person and he was a dreamer. The pastry he dared not touch—being a genius—but he was charmed at the gaiety with which Winifred crammed cake after cake into her rosebud of a mouth. What an enchanting creature! How bravely she covered up her life's tragedy!

The thought made him glance at her velvet band—it was broader than ever.

"He has beaten you again!" he murmured furiously. Her joyous eyes saddened, she hung her head, and her fingers crumbled the cake. "What is his pretext?" he asked, his blood burning.

"Jealousy," she whispered.

His blood lost its glow, ran cold. He felt the bully's blows on his own skin, his romance turning suddenly sordid. But he recovered his courage. He, too, had muscles. "But I thought he just missed seeing me kiss your hand."

She opened her eyes wide. "It wasn't you, you darling old dreamer."

He was relieved and disturbed in one.

"Somebody else?" he murmured. Somehow the vision of the player-fellow came up.

She nodded. "Isn't it lucky he has himself drawn a red-herring across the track? I didn't mind his blows— you were safe!" Then, with one of her adorable transitions, "I am dreaming of another ice," she cried with roguish wistfulness.

"I was afraid to confess my own greediness," he said, laughing. He beckoned the waitress. "Two more."

"We haven't got any more strawberries," was her unexpected reply. "There's been such a run on them to-day."

Winifred's face grew overcast. "Oh, nonsense!" she pouted. To John the moment seemed tragic.

"Won't you have another kind?" he queried. He himself liked any kind, but he could scarcely eat a second ice without her.

Winifred meditated. "Coffee?" she queried.

The waitress went away and returned with a face as gloomy as Winifred's. "It's been such a hot day," she said deprecatingly. "There is only one ice in the place and that's Neapolitan."

"Well, bring two Neapolitans," John ventured.

"I mean there is only one Neapolitan ice left."

"Well, bring that. I don't really want one."

He watched Mrs. Glamorys daintily devouring the solitary ice, and felt a certain pathos about the parti-coloured oblong, a something of the haunting sadness of "The Last Rose of Summer." It would make a graceful, serio-comic triolet, he was thinking. But at the last spoonful, his beautiful companion dislocated his rhymes by her sudden upspringing.

"Goodness gracious," she cried, "how late it is!"

"Oh, you're not leaving me yet!" he said. A world of things sprang to his brain, things that he was going to say—to arrange. They had said nothing—not a word of their love even; nothing but cakes and ices.

"Poet!" she laughed. "Have you forgotten I live at Hampstead?" She picked up her parasol. "Put me into a hansom, or my husband will be raving at his lonely dinner-table."

He was so dazed as to be surprised when the waitress blocked his departure with a bill. When Winifred was spirited away, he remembered she might, without much risk, have given him a lift to Paddington.

He hailed another hansom and caught the next train to Oxford. But he was too late for his own dinner in Hall.

III

He was kept very busy for the next few days, and could only exchange a passionate letter or two with her. For some time the examination fever had been raging, and in every college poor patients sat with wet towels round their heads. Some, who had neglected their tutor all the term, now strove to absorb his omniscience in a sitting.

On the Monday, John Lefolle was good-naturedly giving a special audience to a muscular dunce, trying to explain to him the political effects of the Crusades, when there was a knock at the sitting-room door, and the scout ushered in Mrs. Glamorys. She was bewitchingly dressed in white, and stood in the open doorway, smiling—an embodiment of the summer he was neglecting. He rose, but his tongue was paralysed. The dunce became suddenly important—a symbol of the decorum he had been outraging. His soul, torn so abruptly from history to romance, could not get up the right emotion. Why this imprudence of Winifred's? She had been so careful heretofore.

"What a lot of boots there are on your staircase!" she said gaily.

He laughed. The spell was broken. "Yes, the heap to be cleaned is rather obtrusive," he said, "but I suppose it is a sort of tradition."

"I think I've got hold of the thing pretty well now, sir." The dunce rose and smiled, and his tutor realised how little the dunce had to learn in some things. He felt quite grateful to him.

"Oh, well, you'll come and see me again after lunch, won't you, if one or two points occur to you for elucidation," he said, feeling vaguely a liar, and generally guilty. But when, on the departure of the dunce, Winifred held out her arms, everything fell from him but the sense of the exquisite moment. Their lips met for the first time, but only for an instant. He had scarcely time to realise that this wonderful thing had happened before the mobile creature had darted to his book-shelves and was examining a Thucydides upside down.

"How clever to know Greek!" she exclaimed. "And do you really talk it with the other dons?"

"No, we never talk shop," he laughed. "But, Winifred, what made you come here?"

"I had never seen Oxford. Isn't it beautiful?"

"There's nothing beautiful here," he said, looking round his sober study.

"No," she admitted; "there's nothing I care for here," and had left another celestial kiss on his lips before he knew it. "And now you must take me to lunch and on the river."

He stammered, "I have—work."

She pouted. "But I can't stay beyond to-morrow morning, and I want so much to see all your celebrated oarsmen practising."

"You are not staying over the night?" he gasped.

"Yes, I am," and she threw him a dazzling glance.

His heart went pit-a-pat. "Where?" he murmured.

"Oh, some poky little hotel near the station. The swell hotels are full."

He was glad to hear she was not conspicuously quartered.

"So many people have come down already for Commem," he said. "I suppose they are anxious to see the Generals get their degrees. But hadn't we better go somewhere and lunch?"

They went down the stone staircase, past the battalion of boots, and across the quad. He felt that all the windows were alive with eyes, but she insisted on standing still and admiring their ivied picturesqueness. After lunch he shamefacedly borrowed the dunce's punt. The necessities of punting, which kept him far from her, and demanded much adroit labour, gradually restored his self-respect, and he was able to look the uncelebrated oarsmen they met in the eyes, except when they were accompanied by their parents and sisters, which subtly made him feel uncomfortable again. But Winifred, piquant under her pink parasol, was singularly at ease, enraptured with the changing beauty of the river, applauding with childish glee the wild flowers on the banks, or the rippling reflections in the water.

"Look, look!" she cried once, pointing skyward. He stared upwards, expecting a balloon at least. But it was only "Keats' little rosy cloud," she explained. It was not her fault if he did not find the excursion unreservedly idyllic.

"How stupid," she reflected, "to keep all those nice boys cooped up reading dead languages in a spot made for life and love."

"I'm afraid they don't disturb the dead languages so much as you think," he reassured her, smiling. "And there will be plenty of love-making during Commem."

"I am so glad. I suppose there are lots of engagements that week."

"Oh, yes—but not one per cent come to anything."

"Really? Oh, how fickle men are!"

That seemed rather question-begging, but he was so thrilled by the implicit revelation that she could not even imagine feminine inconstancy, that he forebore to draw her attention to her inadequate logic.

So childish and thoughtless indeed was she that day that nothing would content her but attending a "Viva," which he had incautiously informed her was public.

"Nobody will notice us," she urged with strange unconsciousness of her loveliness. "Besides, they don't know I'm not your sister."

"The Oxford intellect is sceptical," he said, laughing. "It cultivates philosophical doubt."

But, putting a bold face on the matter, and assuming a fraternal air, he took her to the torture-chamber, in which candidates sat dolefully on a row of chairs against the wall, waiting their turn to come before the three grand inquisitors at the table. Fortunately, Winifred and he were the only spectators; but unfortunately they blundered in at the very moment when the poor owner of the punt was on the rack. The central inquisitor was trying to extract from him information about à Becket, almost prompting him with the very words, but without penetrating through the duncical denseness. John Lefolle breathed more freely when the Crusades were broached; but, alas, it very soon became evident that the dunce had by no means "got hold of the thing." As the dunce passed out sadly, obviously ploughed, John Lefolle suffered more than he. So conscience-stricken was he that, when he had accompanied Winifred as far as her hotel, he refused her invitation to come in, pleading the compulsoriness of duty and dinner in Hall. But he could not get away without promising to call in during the evening.

The prospect of this visit was with him all through dinner, at once tempting and terrifying. Assuredly there was a skeleton at his feast, as he sat at the high table, facing the Master. The venerable portraits round the Hall seemed to rebuke his romantic waywardness. In the common-room, he sipped his port uneasily, listening as in a daze to the discussion on Free Will, which an eminent stranger had stirred up. How academic it seemed, compared with the passionate realities of life. But somehow he found himself lingering on at the academic discussion, postponing the realities of life. Every now and again, he was impelled to glance at his watch; but suddenly murmuring, "It is very late," he pulled himself together, and took leave of his learned brethren. But in the street the sight of a telegraph office drew his steps to it, and almost mechanically he wrote out the message: "Regret detained. Will call early in morning."

When he did call in the morning, he was told she had gone back to London the night before on receipt of a telegram. He turned away with a bitter pang of disappointment and regret.

IV

Their subsequent correspondence was only the more amorous. The reason she had fled from the hotel, she explained, was that she could not endure the night in those stuffy quarters. He consoled himself with the hope of seeing much of her during the Long Vacation. He did see her once at her own reception, but this time her husband wandered about the two rooms. The cosy corner was impossible, and they could only manage to gasp out a few mutual endearments amid the buzz and movement, and to arrange a rendezvous for the end of July. When the day came, he received a heart-broken letter, stating that her husband had borne her away to Goodwood. In a postscript she informed him that "Quicksilver was a sure thing." Much correspondence passed without another meeting being effected, and he lent her five pounds to pay a debt of honour incurred through her husband's "absurd confidence in Quicksilver." A week later this horsey husband of hers brought her on to Brighton for the races there, and hither John Lefolle flew. But her husband shadowed her, and he could only lift his hat to her as they passed each other on the Lawns. Sometimes he saw her sitting pensively on a chair while her lord and thrasher perused a pink sporting-paper. Such tantalising proximity raised their correspondence through the Hove Post Office to fever heat. Life apart, they felt, was impossible, and, removed from the sobering influences of his cap and gown, John Lefolle dreamed of throwing everything to the winds. His literary reputation had opened out a new career. The Winifred lyrics alone had brought in a tidy sum, and though he had expended that and more on despatches of flowers and trifles to her, yet he felt this extravagance would become extinguished under daily companionship, and the poems provoked by her charms would go far towards their daily maintenance. Yes, he could throw up the University. He would rescue her from this bully, this gentleman bruiser. They would live openly and nobly in the world's eye. A poet was not even expected to be conventional.

She, on her side, was no less ardent for the great step. She raged against the world's law, the injustice by which a husband's cruelty was not sufficient ground for divorce. "But we finer souls must take the law into our own hands," she wrote. "We must teach society that the ethics of a barbarous age are unfitted for our century of enlightenment." But somehow the actual time and place of the elopement could never get itself fixed. In September her husband dragged her to Scotland, in October after the pheasants. When the dramatic day was actually fixed, Winifred wrote by the next post deferring it for a week. Even the few actual preliminary meetings they planned for Kensington Gardens or Hampstead Heath rarely came off. He lived in a whirling atmosphere of express letters of excuse, and telegrams that transformed the situation from hour to hour. Not that her passion in any way abated, or her romantic resolution really altered: it was only that her conception of time and place and ways and means was dizzily mutable.

But after nigh six months of palpitating negotiations with the adorable Mrs. Glamorys, the poet, in a moment of dejection, penned the prose apophthegm, "It is of no use trying to change a changeable person."

V

But at last she astonished him by a sketch plan of the elopement, so detailed, even to band-boxes and the Paris night route viâ Dieppe, that no further room for doubt was left in his intoxicated soul, and he was actually further astonished when, just as he was putting his handbag into the hansom, a telegram was handed to him saying: "Gone to Homburg. Letter follows."

He stood still for a moment on the pavement in utter distraction. What did it mean? Had she failed him again? Or was it simply that she had changed the city of refuge from Paris to Homburg? He was about to name the new station to the cabman, but then, "letter follows." Surely that meant that he was to wait for it. Perplexed and miserable, he stood with the telegram crumpled up in his fist. What a ridiculous situation! He had wrought himself up to the point of breaking with the world and his past, and now—it only remained to satisfy the cabman!

He tossed feverishly all night, seeking to soothe himself, but really exciting himself the more by a hundred plausible explanations. He was now strung up to such a pitch of uncertainty that he was astonished for the third time when the "letter" did duly "follow."

"Dearest," it ran, "as I explained in my telegram, my husband became suddenly ill"—("if she had only put that in the telegram," he groaned)—"and was ordered to Homburg. Of course it was impossible to leave him in this crisis, both for practical and sentimental reasons. You yourself, darling, would not like me to have aggravated his illness by my flight just at this moment, and thus possibly have his death on my conscience." ("Darling, you are always right," he said, kissing the letter.) "Let us possess our souls in patience a little longer. I need not tell you how vexatious it will be to find myself nursing him in

Homburg—out of the season even—instead of the prospect to which I had looked forward with my whole heart and soul. But what can one do? How true is the French proverb, 'Nothing happens but the unexpected'! Write to me immediately Poste Restante, that I may at least console myself with your dear words."

The unexpected did indeed happen. Despite draughts of Elizabethbrunnen and promenades on the Kurhaus terrace, the stalwart woman beater succumbed to his malady. The curt telegram from Winifred gave no indication of her emotions. He sent a reply-telegram of sympathy with her trouble. Although he could not pretend to grieve at this sudden providential solution of their life-problem, still he did sincerely sympathise with the distress inevitable in connection with a death, especially on foreign soil.

He was not able to see her till her husband's body had been brought across the North Sea and committed to the green repose of the old Hampstead churchyard. He found her pathetically altered— her face wan and spiritualised, and all in subtle harmony with the exquisite black gown. In the first interview, he did not dare speak of their love at all. They discussed the immortality of the soul, and she quoted George Herbert. But with the weeks the question of their future began to force its way back to his lips.

"We could not decently marry before six months," she said, when definitely confronted with the problem.

"Six months!" he gasped.

"Well, surely you don't want to outrage everybody," she said, pouting.

At first he was outraged himself. What! She who had been ready to flutter the world with a fantastic dance was now measuring her footsteps. But on reflection he saw that Mrs. Glamorys was right once more. Since Providence had been good enough to rescue them, why should they fly in its face? A little patience, and a blameless happiness lay before them. Let him not blind himself to the immense relief he really felt at being spared social obloquy. After all, a poet could be unconventional in his work—he had no need of the practical outlet demanded for the less gifted.

VI

They scarcely met at all during the next six months—it had, naturally, in this grateful reaction against their recklessness, become a sacred period, even more charged with tremulous emotion than the engagement periods of those who have not so nearly scorched themselves. Even in her presence he found a certain pleasure in combining distant adoration with the confident expectation of proximity, and thus she was restored to the sanctity which she had risked by her former easiness. And so all was for the best in the best of all possible worlds.

When the six months had gone by, he came to claim her hand. She was quite astonished. "You promised to marry me at the end of six months," he reminded her.

"Surely it isn't six months already," she said.

He referred her to the calendar, recalled the date of her husband's death.

"You are strangely literal for a poet," she said. "Of course I said six months, but six months doesn't mean twenty-six weeks by the clock. All I meant was that a decent period must intervene. But even to myself it seems only yesterday that poor Harold was walking beside me in the Kurhaus Park." She burst into tears, and in the face of them he could not pursue the argument.

Gradually, after several interviews and letters, it was agreed that they should wait another six months.

"She is right," he reflected again. "We have waited so long, we may as well wait a little longer and leave malice no handle."

The second six months seemed to him much longer than the first. The charm of respectful adoration had lost its novelty, and once again his breast was racked by fitful fevers which could scarcely calm themselves even by conversion into sonnets. The one point of repose was that shining fixed star of marriage. Still smarting under Winifred's reproach of his unpoetic literality, he did not intend to force her to marry him exactly at the end of the twelve-month. But he was determined that she should have no later than this exact date for at least "naming the day." Not the most punctilious stickler for convention, he felt, could deny that Mrs. Grundy's claim had been paid to the last minute.

The publication of his new volume—containing the Winifred lyrics—had served to colour these months of intolerable delay. Even the reaction of the critics against his poetry, that conventional revolt against every second volume, that parrot cry of over-praise from the very throats that had praised him, though it pained and perplexed him, was perhaps really helpful. At any rate, the long waiting was over at last. He felt like Jacob after his years of service for Rachel.

The fateful morning dawned bright and blue, and, as the towers of Oxford were left behind him he recalled that distant Saturday when he had first gone down to meet the literary lights of London in his publisher's salon. How much older he was now than then—and yet how much younger! The nebulous melancholy of youth, the clouds of philosophy, had vanished before this beautiful creature of sunshine whose radiance cut out a clear line for his future through the confusion of life.

At a florist's in the High Street of Hampstead he bought a costly bouquet of white flowers, and walked airily to the house and rang the bell jubilantly. He could scarcely believe his ears when the maid told him her mistress was not at home. How dared the girl stare at him so impassively? Did she not know by what appointment—on what errand—he had come? Had he not written to her mistress a week ago that he would present himself that afternoon?

"Not at home!" he gasped. "But when will she be home?"

"I fancy she won't be long. She went out an hour ago, and she has an appointment with her dressmaker at five."

"Do you know in what direction she'd have gone?"

"Oh, she generally walks on the Heath before tea."

The world suddenly grew rosy again. "I will come back again," he said. Yes, a walk in this glorious air—heathward—would do him good.

As the door shut he remembered he might have left the flowers, but he would not ring again, and besides, it was, perhaps, better he should present them with his own hand, than let her find them on the hall table. Still, it seemed rather awkward to walk about the streets with a bouquet, and he was glad, accidentally to strike the old Hampstead Church, and to seek a momentary seclusion in passing through its avenue of quiet gravestones on his heathward way.

Mounting the few steps, he paused idly a moment on the verge of this green "God's-acre" to read a perpendicular slab on a wall, and his face broadened into a smile as he followed the absurdly elaborate biography of a rich, self-made merchant who had taught himself to read. "Reader, go thou and do likewise," was the delicious bull at the end. As he turned away, the smile still lingering about his lips, he saw a dainty figure tripping down the stony graveyard path, and though he was somehow startled to find her still in black, there was no mistaking Mrs. Glamorys. She ran to meet him with a glad cry, which filled his eyes with happy tears.

"How good of you to remember!" she said, as she took the bouquet from his unresisting hand, and turned again on her footsteps. He followed her wonderingly across the uneven road towards a narrow aisle of graves on the left. In another instant she had stooped before a shining white stone, and laid his bouquet reverently upon it. As he reached her side, he saw that his flowers were almost lost in the vast mass of floral offerings with which the grave of the woman beater was bestrewn.

"How good of you to remember the anniversary," she murmured again.

"How could I forget it?" he stammered, astonished. "Is not this the end of the terrible twelve-month?"

The soft gratitude died out of her face. "Oh, is that what you were thinking of?"

"What else?" he murmured, pale with conflicting emotions.

"What else! I think decency demanded that this day, at least, should be sacred to his memory. Oh, what brutes men are!" And she burst into tears.

His patient breast revolted at last. "You said he was the brute!" he retorted, outraged.

"Is that your chivalry to the dead? Oh, my poor Harold, my poor Harold!"

For once her tears could not extinguish the flame of his anger. "But you told me he beat you," he cried.

"And if he did, I dare say I deserved it. Oh, my darling, my darling!" She laid her face on the stone and sobbed.

John Lefolle stood by in silent torture. As he helplessly watched her white throat swell and fall with the sobs, he was suddenly struck by the absence of the black velvet band—the truer mourning she had worn in the lifetime of the so lamented. A faint scar, only perceptible to his conscious eye, added to his painful bewilderment.

At last she rose and walked unsteadily forward. He followed her in mute misery. In a moment or two they found themselves on the outskirts of the deserted heath. How beautiful stretched the gorsy rolling country! The sun was setting in great burning furrows of gold and green—a panorama to take one's breath away. The beauty and peace of Nature passed into the poet's soul.

"Forgive me, dearest," he begged, taking her hand.

She drew it away sharply. "I cannot forgive you. You have shown yourself in your true colours."

Her unreasonableness angered him again. "What do you mean? I only came in accordance with our long-standing arrangement. You have put me off long enough."

"It is fortunate I did put you off long enough to discover what you are."

He gasped. He thought of all the weary months of waiting, all the long comedy of telegrams and express letters, the far-off flirtations of the cosy corner, the baffled elopement to Paris. "Then you won't marry me?"

"I cannot marry a man I neither love nor respect."

"You don't love me!" Her spontaneous kiss in his sober Oxford study seemed to burn on his angry lips.

"No, I never loved you."

He took her by the arms and turned her round roughly. "Look me in the face and dare to say you have never loved me."

His memory was buzzing with passionate phrases from her endless letters. They stung like a swarm of bees. The sunset was like blood-red mist before his eyes.

"I have never loved you," she said obstinately.

"You—!" His grasp on her arms tightened. He shook her.

"You are bruising me," she cried.

His grasp fell from her arms as though they were red-hot. He had become a woman beater.

THE ETERNAL FEMININE

He wore a curious costume, representing the devil carrying off his corpse; but I recognised him at once as the lesser lion of a London evening party last season. Then he had just returned from a Polar expedition, and wore the glacier of civilisation on his breast. To-night he was among the maddest of the mad, dancing savagely with the Bacchantes of the Latin Quarter at the art students' ball, and some of his fellow-Americans told me that he was the best marine painter in the atelier which he had joined. More they did not pause to tell me, for they were anxious to celebrate this night of nights, when, in that fine spirit of equality born of belonging to two Republics, the artist lowers himself to the level of his model.

The young Arctic explorer, so entirely at home in this more tropical clime, had relapsed into respectability when I spoke to him. He was sitting at a supper-table smoking a cigarette, and gazing somewhat sadly—it seemed to me—at the pandemoniac phantasmagoria of screaming dancers, the glittering cosmopolitan chaos that multiplied itself riotously in the mirrored walls of the great flaring ball-room, where under-dressed women, waving many-coloured paper lanterns, rode on the shoulders of grotesquely clad men prancing to joyous music. For some time he had been trying hard to get some one to take the money for his supper; but the frenzied waiters suspected he was clamouring for something to eat, and would not be cajoled into attention.

Moved by an impulse of mischief, I went up to him and clapped him on his corpse, which he wore behind.

There was a death-mask of papier-maché on the back of his head with appropriate funereal drapings down the body.

"I'll take your money," I said.

He started, and turned his devil upon me. The face was made Mephistophelian, and the front half of him wore scarlet.

"Thanks," he said, laughing roguishly, when he recognised me. "It's darned queer that Paris should be the place where they refuse to take the devil's money."

I suggested smilingly that it was the corpse they fought shy of.

"I guess not," he retorted. "It's dead men's money that keeps this place lively. I wish I'd had the chance of some anyhow; but a rolling stone gathers no moss, they say—not even from graveyards, I suppose."

He spoke disconsolately, in a tone more befitting the back than the front of him, and quite out of accord with the reckless revelry around him.

"Oh! you'll make lots of money with your pictures," I said heartily.

He shook his head. "That's the chap who's going to scoop in the dollars," he said, indicating a brawny Frenchman attired in a blanket that girdled his loins, and black feathers that decorated his hair. "That fellow's got the touch of Velasquez. You should see the portrait he's doing for the Salon."

"Well, I don't see much art in his costume, anyhow," I retorted. "Yours is an inspiration of genius."

"Yes; so prophetic, don't you know," he replied modestly. "But you are not the only one who has complimented me. To it I owe the proudest moment of my life—when I shook hands with a European prince." And he laughed with returning merriment.

"Indeed!" I exclaimed. "With which?"

"Ah! I see your admiration for my rig is mounting. No; it wasn't with the Prince of Wales—confess your admiration is going down already. Come, you shall guess. Je vous le donne en trois."

After teasing me a little he told me it was the Kronprinds of Denmark. "At the Kunstner Karneval in Copenhagen," he explained briefly. His front face had grown sad again.

"Did you study art in Copenhagen?" I inquired.

"Yes, before I joined that expedition," he said. "It was from there I started."

"Yes, of course," I replied. "I remember now. It was a Danish expedition. But what made you chuck up your studies so suddenly?"

"Oh! I don't know. I guess I was just about sick of most things. My stars! Look at that little gypsy-girl dancing the can-can; isn't she fresh? Isn't she wonderful? How awful to think she'll be used up in a year or two!"

"I suppose there was a woman—the eternal feminine," I said, sticking him to the point, for I was more interested in him than in the seething saturnalia, our common sobriety amid which seemed somehow to raise our casual acquaintanceship to the plane of confidential friendship.

"Yes, I suppose there was a woman," he echoed in low tones. "The eternal feminine!" And a strange unfathomable light leapt into his eyes, which he raised slightly towards the gilded ceiling, where countless lustres glittered.

"Deceived you, eh?" I said lightly.

His expression changed. "Deceived me, as you say," he murmured, with a faint, sad smile, that made me conjure up a vision of a passionate lovely face with cruel eyes.

"Won't you tell me about it?" I asked, as I tendered him a fresh cigarette, for while we spoke his half-smoked one had been snatched from his mouth by a beautiful Mænad, who whirled off puffing it.

"I reckon you'll be making copy out of it," he said, his smile growing whimsical.

"If it's good enough," I replied candidly. "That's why I am here."

"What a lovely excuse! But there's nothing in my affair to make a story of."

I smiled majestically.

"You stick to your art—leave me to manage mine." And I put a light to his cigarette.

"Ah, but you'll be disappointed this time, I warrant," he said laughingly, as the smoke circled round his diabolically handsome face. Then, becoming serious again, he went on: "It's so terribly plebeian, yet it all befell through that very Kunstner Karneval. I was telling you of when I first wore this composite costume which gained me the smile of royalty. It was a very swell affair, of course, not a bit like this, but it was given in hell."

"In hell!" I cried, startled.

"Yes. Underverden they call it in their lingo. The ball-room of the palace (the Palaeet, an old disused mansion) was got up to represent the infernal regions—you tumble?—and everybody had to dress appropriately. That was what gave me the idea of this costume. The staircase up which you entered was made the mouth of a great dragon, and as you trod on the first step his eye gleamed blazes and brimstone. There were great monsters all about, and dark grottoes radiating around; and when you took your dame into one of them, your tread flooded them with light. If, however, the cavalier modestly conducted his mistress into one of the lighted caves, virtue was rewarded by instantaneous darkness."

"That was really artistic," I said, laughing.

"You bet! The artists spent any amount of money over the affair. The whole of Hades bristled with ingenious devices in every corner. I had got a couple of tickets, and had designed the dress of my best girl, as well as my own, and the morning before (there being little work done in the studios that day, as you may well imagine) I called upon her to see her try it on. To my chagrin I found she was down with influenza, or something of that sort appropriate to the bitter winter we were having. And it did freeze that year, by Jove!—so hard that Denmark and Sweden were united—to their mutual disgust, I fancy— by a broad causeway of ice. I remember, as I walked back from the girl's house towards the town along the Langelinie, my mortification was somewhat allayed by the picturesque appearance of the Sound, in whose white expanse boats of every species and colour were embedded, looking like trapped creatures unable to stir oar or sail. But as I left the Promenade and came into the narrow old streets of the town, with their cobblestones and their quaint, many-windowed houses, my ill-humour returned. I had had some trouble in getting the second ticket, and now it looked as if I should get left. I went over in my mind the girls I could ask, and what with not caring more for one than for another, and not knowing which were booked already, and what with the imminence of the ball, I felt the little brains I had getting addled in my head. At last, in sheer despair, I had what is called a happy thought. I resolved to ask the first girl of my acquaintance I met in my walk. Instantly my spirits rose like a thermometer in a Turkish bath. The clouds of irresolution rolled away, and the touch of adventure made my walk joyous again. I peered eagerly into every female face I met, but it was not till I approached the market-place that I knew my fate. Then, turning a corner, I came suddenly and violently face to face with Fröken Jensen."

He paused and relit his cigarette, and the maddening music of brass instruments and brazen creatures, which his story had shut out, crashed again upon my ears. "I reckon if you were telling this, you'd stop here," he said, "and put down 'to be continued in our next.'" There seemed a trace of huskiness in his flippant tones, as if he were trying to keep under some genuine emotion.

"Never you mind," I returned, smiling. "You're not a writer, anyhow, so just keep straight on."

"Well, Fröken Jensen was absolutely the ugliest girl I have seen in all my globe-trottings.... On second thoughts, that is the place to stop, isn't it?"

"Not at all; it's only in long novels one stops for refreshment. So go ahead, and—I say—do cut your interruptions à la Fielding and Thackeray. C'est vieux jeu."

"All right, don't get mad. Fröken Jensen had the most irregular and ungainly features that ever crippled a woman's career; her nose was—But no! I won't describe her, poor girl. She was about twenty-six years old, but one of those girls whose years no one counts, who are old maids at seventeen. Well, you can fancy what a fix I was in. It was no good pretending to myself that I hadn't seen her, for we nearly bowled each other over—she was coming along quick trot with a basket on her arm—and it seemed kind of shuffling to back out of my promise to her, though she didn't know anything about it. It was like betting with yourself and wanting to cheat yourself when you lost. I felt I should never trust myself again, if I turned welsher—that's the word, isn't it?"

"It's like Jephtha," I said. "He swore, you know, he would sacrifice the first creature that he saw on his triumphant return from the wars, and his daughter came out and had to be sacrificed."

"Thank you for the compliment," he said, with a grimace. "But I'm not up in the classics, so the comparison didn't strike me. But what did strike me, after the first moment of annoyance, was the humour of the situation. I turned and walked beside her—under cover of an elaborate apology for my dashing behaviour. She seemed quite concerned at my regret, and insisted that it was she that had dashed—it was her marketing-day, and she was late. You must know she kept a boarding-house for art and university students, and it was there that I had made her acquaintance, when I went to dine once or twice with a studio chum who was quartered there. I had never exchanged two sentences with her before, as you can well imagine. She was not inviting to the artistic eye; indeed, I rather wondered how my friend could tolerate her at the head of the table, till he jestingly told me it was reckoned off the bill. The place was indeed suited to the student's pocket. But this morning I was surprised at the sprightliness of her share in the dialogue of mutual apologies. Her mind seemed as alert as her step, her voice was pleasing and gentle, and there was a refreshing gaiety in her attitude towards the situation.

"'But I am quite sure it was my fault,' I wound up rather lamely at last, 'and, if you will allow me to make you amends, I shall be pleased to send you a ticket for the ball to-morrow night.'

"She stood still. 'For the Kunstner Karneval!' she cried eagerly, while her poor absurd face lit up.

"'Yes, Fröken; and I shall be happy to escort you there if you will give me the pleasure.'

"She looked at me with sudden suspicion—the idea that I was chaffing her must have crossed her mind. I felt myself flushing furiously, feeling somehow half-guilty by my secret thoughts of her a few moments ago. We had arrived at the Amagertorv—the market-place—and I recollect getting a sudden impression of the quaint stalls and the picturesque Amager-women—one with a preternaturally hideous face—and the frozen canal in the middle, with the ice-bound fruit-boats from the islands, and the red sails of the Norwegian boats, and the Egyptian architecture of Thorwaldsen's Museum in the background, making up my mind to paint it all, in the brief instant before I added in my most convincing tones, 'The Kronprinds will be there.'

"Her incredulous expression became tempered by wistfulness, and with an inspiration I drew out the ticket and thrust it into her hand. I saw her eyes fill with tears as she turned her head away and examined some vegetables.

"'You will excuse me,' she said presently, holding the ticket limply in her hand, 'but I fear it is impossible for me to accept your kind invitation. You see I have so much to do, and my children will be so uncomfortable without me.'

"'Your children will be at the ball to a man,' I retorted.

"'But I haven't any fancy costume,' she pleaded, and tendered me the ticket back. It struck me—almost with a pang—that her hand was bare of glove, and the work-a-day costume she was wearing was ill adapted to the rigour of the weather.

"'Oh! Come anyhow,' I said. 'Ordinary evening dress. Of course, you will need a mask.'

"I saw her lip twitch at this unfortunate way of putting it, and hastened to affect unconsciousness of my blunder.

"'She wouldn't,' I added with feigned jocularity, nodding towards the preternaturally hideous Amager-woman.

"'Poor old thing,' she said gently. 'I shall be sorry when she dies.'

"'Why?' I murmured.

"'Because then I shall be the ugliest woman in Copenhagen,' she answered gaily.

"Something in that remark sent a thrill down my backbone—there seemed an infinite pathos and lovableness in her courageous recognition of facts. It dispensed me from the painful necessity of pretending to be unaware of her ugliness—nay, gave it almost a cachet—made it as possible a topic of light conversation as beauty itself. I pressed her more fervently to come, and at last she consented, stipulating only that I should call for her rather late, after she had quite finished her household duties and the other boarders had gone off to the ball.

"Well, I took her to the ball (it was as brilliant and gay as this without being riotous), and—will you believe it?—she made quite a little sensation. With a black domino covering her impossible face, and a simple evening dress, she looked as distinguée as my best girl would have done. Her skin was good, and her figure, freed from the distracting companionship of her face, was rather elegant, while the lively humour of her conversation had now fair play. She danced well, too, with a natural grace. I believe she enjoyed her incog. almost as much as the ball, and I began to feel quite like a fairy godmother who was giving poor little Cinderella an outing, and to regret that I had not the power to make her beautiful for ever, or at least to make life one eternal fancy ball, at which silk masks might veil the horrors of reality. I dare say, too, she got a certain kudos through dancing so much with me, for, as I have told you ad nauseam, this lovely costume of mine was the hit of the evening, and the Kronprinds asked for the honour of an introduction to me. It was rather funny—the circuitous etiquette. I had to be first introduced to his aide-de-camp. This was done through an actress of the Kongelige Theatre, with whom I had been polking (he knew all the soubrettes, that aide-de-camp!). Then he introduced me to the Kronprinds, and I held out my hand and shook his royal paw heartily. He was very gracious to me, learning I was an American, and complimented me on my dress and my dancing, and I answered him affably; and the natives, gathered round at a respectful distance, eyed me with reverent curiosity. But at last, when the music struck up again, I said, 'Excuse me, I am engaged for this waltz!' and hurried off to dance with my Cinderella, much to the amazement of the Danes, who wondered audibly what mighty foreign potentate His Royal Highness had been making himself agreeable to."

"It was plain enough," I broke in. "His Satanic Majesty, of course."

"I am glad you interrupted me," he said, "for you give me an opening to state that the Kronprinds has nothing to do with the story. You, of course, would have left him out; but I am only an amateur, and I get my threads mixed."

"Shut up!" I cried. "I mean—go on."

"Oh, well, perhaps, he has got a little to do with the story, after all; for after that, Fröken Jensen became more important—sharing in my reflected glory—or, perhaps, now I come to think of it, it was only then that she became important. Anyway, important she was; and, among others, Axel Larson—who was got up as an ancient Gallic warrior, to show off his fine figure—came up and asked me to introduce him. I don't think I should have done so ordinarily, for he was the filthiest-mouthed fellow in the atelier—a great swaggering Don Juan Baron Munchausen sort of chap, handsome enough in his raffish way—a tall, stalwart Swede, blue-eyed and yellow-haired. But the fun of the position was that Axel Larson was one of my Cinderella's 'children,' so I could not resist introducing him formally to 'Fröken Jensen.' His happy air of expectation was replaced by a scowl of surprise and disgust.

"'What, thou, Ingeborg!' he cried.

"I could have knocked the man down. The familiar tutoiement, the Christian name—these, perhaps, he had a right to use; but nothing could justify the contempt of his tone. It reminded me disagreeably of the ugliness I had nigh forgotten. I felt Ingeborg's arm tremble in mine.

"'Yes, it is I, Herr Larson,' she said, with her wonted gentleness, and almost apologetically. 'This gentleman was good enough to bring me.' She spoke as if her presence needed explanation—with the timidity of one shut out from the pleasures of life. I could feel her poor little heart fluttering wildly, and knew that her face was alternating from red to white beneath the mask.

"Axel Larson shot a swift glance of surprise at me, which was followed by a more malicious bolt. 'I congratulate you, Ingeborg,' he said, 'on the property you seem to have come into.' It was a clever double entente—the man was witty after his coarse fashion—but the sarcasm scarcely stung either of us. I, of course, had none of the motives the cad imagined; and as for Ingeborg, I fancy she thought he alluded merely to the conquest of myself, and was only pained by the fear I might resent so ludicrous a suggestion. Having thrown the shadow of his cynicism over our innocent relation, Axel turned away highly pleased with himself, rudely neglecting to ask Ingeborg for a dance. I felt like giving him 'Hail Columbia,' but I restrained myself.

"Some days after this—in response to Ingeborg's grateful anxiety to return my hospitality—I went to dine with her 'children.' I found Axel occupying the seat of honour, and grumbling at the soup and the sauces like a sort of autocrat of the dinner-table, and generally making things unpleasant. I had to cling to my knife and fork so as not to throw the water-bottle at his head. Ingeborg presided meekly over the dishes, her ugliness more rampant than ever after the illusion of the mask. I remembered now he had been disagreeable when I had dined there before, though, not being interested in Ingeborg then, I had not resented his ill-humour, contenting myself with remarking to my friend that I understood now why the Danes disliked the Swedes so much—a generalisation that was probably as unjust as most of one's judgments of other peoples. After dinner I asked her why she tolerated the fellow. She flushed painfully and murmured that times were hard. I protested that she could easily get another boarder to replace him, but she said Axel Larson had been there so long—nearly two years—and was comfortable, and knew the ways of the house, and it would be very discourteous to ask him to go. I insisted that rather than see her suffer I would move into Larson's room myself, but she urged tremulously that she didn't suffer at all from his rudeness, it was only his surface-manner; it deceived strangers, but there was a good heart underneath, as who could know better than she? Besides, he was a genius with the brush, and everybody knew well that geniuses were bears. And, finally, she could not afford to lose boarders—there were already two vacancies.

"It ended—as I dare say you have guessed—by my filling up one of those two vacancies, partly to help her pecuniarily, partly to act as a buffer between her and the swaggering Swede. He was quite flabbergasted by my installation in the house, and took me aside in the atelier and asked me if Ingeborg had really come into any money. I was boiling over, but I kept the lid on by main force, and answered curtly that Ingeborg had a heart of gold. He laughed boisterously, and said one could not raise anything on that; adding, with an air of authority, that he believed I spoke the truth, for it was not likely the hag would have kept anything from her oldest boarder. 'I dare say the real truth is,' he wound up, 'that you are hard up, like me, and want to do the thing cheap.'

"'I wasn't aware you were hard up,' I said, for I had seen him often enough flaunting it in the theatres and restaurants.

"'Not for luxuries,' he retorted with a guffaw, 'but for necessities—yes. And there comes in the value of our domestic eyesore. Why, I haven't paid her a skilling for six months!'

"I thought of poor Ingeborg's thin winter attire, and would have liked to reply with my fist, only the reply didn't seem quite logical. It was not my business, after all; but I thought I understood now why Ingeborg was so reluctant to part with him—it is the immemorial fallacy of economical souls to throw good money after bad; though when I saw the patience with which she bore his querulous complaints and the solicitude with which she attended to his wants, I sometimes imagined he had some secret hold over her. Often I saw her cower and flush piteously, as with terror, before his insolent gaze. But I decided finally his was merely the ascendency of the strong over the weak—of the bully over his victims, who serve him more loyally because he kicks them. The bad-tempered have the best of it in this vile world. I cannot tell you how I grew to pity that poor girl. Living in her daily presence, I marked the thousand and one trials of which her life was made up, all borne with the same sweetness and good-humour. I discovered that she had a bed-ridden mother, whom she kept in the attic, and whom she stole up to attend to fifty times a day, sitting with her when her work was done and the moonlight on the Sound tempted one to be out enjoying one's youth. Alone she managed and financed the entire establishment, aided only by a little maid-of-all-work, just squeezing out a scanty living for herself and her mother. If ever there was an angel on earth it was Ingeborg Jensen. I tell you, when I see the angels of the Italian masters I feel they are all wrong: I don't want flaxen-haired cherubs to give me an idea of heaven in this hell of a world. I just want to see good honest faces, full of suffering and sacrifice, and if ever I paint an angel its phiz shall have the unflinching ugliness of Ingeborg Jensen, God bless her! To be near her was to live in an atmosphere of purity and pity and tenderness, and everything that is sweet and sacred."

As he spoke I became suddenly aware that the gas-lights were paling, and glancing towards the window on my left I saw the splendour of the sunrise breaking fresh and clear over the city of diabolical night, where in the sombre eastern sky—

"God made himself an awful rose of dawn."

A breath of coolness and purity seemed to waft into the feverish ball-room; a ray of fresh morning sunlight. I looked curiously at the young artist. He seemed transfigured. I could scarcely realise that an hour ago he had been among the rowdiest of the Comus crew, whose shrieks and laughter still rang all around us. Even his duplex costume seemed to have grown subtly symbolical, the diabolical part typical of all that is bestial and selfish in man, the death-mask speaking silently of renunciation and the peace of the tomb. He went on, after a moment of emotion: "They say that pity is akin to love, but I am not sure that I ever loved her, for I suppose that love involves passion, and I never arrived at that. I only came to feel that I wanted to be with her always, to guard her, to protect her, to work for her, to suffer for her if need be, to give her life something of the joy and sweetness that God owed her. I felt I wasn't much use in the world, and that would be something to do. And so one day—though not without much mental tossing, for we are curiously, complexly built, and I dreaded ridicule and the long years of comment from unsympathetic strangers—I asked her to be my wife. Her surprise, her agitation, was painful to witness. But she was not incredulous, as before; she had learned to know that I respected her.

"Nevertheless, her immediate impulse was one of refusal.

"'It cannot be,' she said, and her bosom heaved spasmodically.

"I protested that it could and would be, but she shook her head.

"'You are very kind to me! God bless you!' she said. 'You have always been kind to me. But you do not love me.'

"I assured her I did, and in that moment I dare say I spoke the truth. For in that moment of her reluctance and diffidence to snatch at proffered joy, when the suggestion of rejection made her appear doubly precious, she seemed to me the most adorable creature in the world.

"But still she shook her head. 'No one can love me,' she said sadly.

"I took her hand in mute protestation, but she withdrew it gently.

"'I cannot be your wife,' she persisted.

"'Why not, Ingeborg?' I asked passionately.

"She hesitated, panting and colouring painfully, then—the words are echoing in my brain—she answered softly, 'Jeg kan ikke elske Dem' (I cannot love you).

"It was like a shaft of lightning piercing me, rending and illuminating. In my blind conceit the obverse side of the question had never presented itself to me. I had taken it for granted I had only to ask to be jumped at. But now, in one great flash of insight, I seemed to see everything plain.

"'You love Axel Larson!' I cried chokingly, as I thought of all the insults he had heaped upon her in her presence, all the sneers and vile jocosities of which she had been the butt behind her back, in return for the care she had lavished upon his comfort, for her pinching to make both ends meet without the money he should have contributed.

"She did not reply. The tears came into her eyes, she let her head droop on her heaving breast. As in those visions that are said to come to the dying, I saw Axel Larson feeding day by day at her board, brutally conscious of her passion, yet not deigning even to sacrifice her to it; I saw him ultimately leave the schools and the town to carry his clever brush to the welcome of a wider world, without a word or a thought of thanks for the creature who had worshipped and waited upon him hand and foot; and then I saw her life from day to day unroll its long monotonous folds, all in the same pattern, all drab duty and joyless sacrifice, and hopeless undying love.

"I took her hand again in a passion of pity. She understood my sympathy, and the hot tears started from her eyes and rolled down her poor wan cheeks. And in that holy moment I saw into the inner heaven of woman's love, which purifies and atones for the world. The eternal feminine!"

The sentimental young artist ceased, and buried his devil's face in his hands. I looked around and started. We were alone in the abandoned supper-room. The gorgeously grotesque company was seated in a gigantic circle upon the ball-room floor furiously applauding the efforts of two sweetly pretty girls who were performing the celebrated danse du ventre.

"The eternal feminine!" I echoed pensively.

THE SILENT SISTERS

They had quarrelled in girlhood, and mutually declared their intention never to speak to each other again, wetting and drying their forefingers to the accompaniment of an ancient childish incantation, and while they lived on the paternal farm they kept their foolish oath with the stubbornness of a slow country stock, despite the alternate coaxing and chastisement of their parents, notwithstanding the perpetual everyday contact of their lives, through every vicissitude of season and weather, of sowing and reaping, of sun and shade, of joy and sorrow.

Death and misfortune did not reconcile them, and when their father died and the old farm was sold up, they travelled to London in the same silence, by the same train, in search of similar situations. Service separated them for years, though there was only a stone's throw between them. They often stared at each other in the streets.

Honor, the elder, married a local artisan, and two and a half years later, Mercy, the younger, married a fellow-workman of Honor's husband. The two husbands were friends, and often visited each other's houses, which were on opposite sides of the same sordid street, and the wives made them welcome. Neither Honor nor Mercy suffered an allusion to their breach; it was understood that their silence must be received in silence. Each of the children had a quiverful of children who played and quarrelled together in the streets and in one another's houses, but not even the street affrays and mutual grievances of the children could provoke the mothers to words. They stood at their doors in impotent fury, almost bursting with the torture of keeping their mouths shut against the effervescence of angry speech. When either lost a child the other watched the funeral from her window, dumb as the mutes.

The years rolled on, and still the river of silence flowed between their lives. Their good looks faded, the burden of life and child-bearing was heavy upon them. Grey hairs streaked their brown tresses, then brown hairs streaked their grey tresses. The puckers of age replaced the dimples of youth. The years rolled on, and Death grew busy among the families. Honor's husband died, and Mercy lost a son, who died a week after his wife. Cholera took several of the younger children. But the sisters themselves lived on, bent and shrivelled by toil and sorrow, even more than by the slow frost of the years.

Then one day Mercy took to her death-bed. An internal disease, too long neglected, would carry her off within a week. So the doctor told Jim, Mercy's husband.

Through him, the news travelled to Honor's eldest son, who still lived with her. By the evening it reached Honor.

She went upstairs abruptly when her son told her, leaving him wondering at her stony aspect. When she came down she was bonneted and shawled. He was filled with joyous amaze to see her hobble across the street and for the first time in her life pass over her sister Mercy's threshold.

As Honor entered the sick-room, with pursed lips, a light leapt into the wasted, wrinkled countenance of the dying creature. She raised herself slightly in bed, her lips parted, then shut tightly, and her face darkened.

Honor turned angrily to Mercy's husband, who hung about impotently. "Why did you let her run down so low?" she said.

"I didn't know," the old man stammered, taken aback by her presence even more than by her question. "She was always a woman to say nothin'."

Honor put him impatiently aside and examined the medicine bottle on the bedside table.

"Isn't it time she took her dose?"

"I dessay."

Honor snorted wrathfully. "What's the use of a man?" she inquired, as she carefully measured out the fluid and put it to her sister's lips, which opened to receive it, and then closed tightly again.

"How is your wife feeling now?" Honor asked after a pause.

"How are you, now, Mercy?" asked the old man awkwardly.

The old woman shook her head. "I'm a-goin' fast, Jim," she grumbled weakly, and a tear of self-pity trickled down her parchment cheek.

"What rubbidge she do talk!" cried Honor, sharply. "Why d'ye stand there like a tailor's dummy? Why don't you tell her to cheer up?"

"Cheer up, Mercy," quavered the old man, hoarsely.

But Mercy groaned instead, and turned fretfully on her other side, with her face to the wall.

"I'm too old, I'm too old," she moaned, "this is the end o' me."

"Did you ever hear the like?" Honor asked Jim, angrily, as she smoothed his wife's pillow. "She was always conceited about her age, settin' herself up as the equals of her elders, and here am I, her elder sister, as carried her in my arms when I was five and she was two, still hale and strong, and with no mind for underground for many a day. Nigh three times her age I was once, mind you, and now she has the imperence to talk of dyin' before me."

She took off her bonnet and shawl. "Send one o' the kids to tell my boy I'm stayin' here," she said, "and then just you get 'em all to bed—there's too much noise about the house."

The children, who were orphaned grandchildren of the dying woman, were sent to bed, and then Jim himself was packed off to refresh himself for the next day's labours, for the poor old fellow still doddered about the workshop.

The silence of the sick-room spread over the whole house. About ten o'clock the doctor came again and instructed Honor how to alleviate the patient's last hours. All night long she sat watching her dying sister, hand and eye alert to anticipate every wish. No word broke the awful stillness.

The first thing in the morning, Mercy's married daughter, the only child of hers living in London, arrived to nurse her mother. But Honor indignantly refused to be dispossessed.

"A nice daughter you are," she said, "to leave your mother lay a day and a night without a sight o' your ugly face."

"I had to look after the good man, and the little 'uns," the daughter pleaded.

"Then what do you mean by desertin' them now?" the irate old woman retorted. "First you deserts your mother, and then your husband and children. You must go back to them as needs your care. I carried your mother in my arms before you was born, and if she wants anybody else now to look after her, let her just tell me so, and I'll be off in a brace o' shakes."

She looked defiantly at the yellow, dried-up creature in the bed. Mercy's withered lips twitched, but no sound came from them. Jim, strung up by the situation, took the word. "You can't do no good up here, the doctor says. You might look after the kids downstairs a bit, when you can spare an hour, and I've got to go to the shop. I'll send you a telegraph if there's a change," he whispered to the daughter, and she, not wholly discontented to return to her living interests, kissed her mother, lingered a little, and then stole quietly away.

All that day the old women remained together in solemn silence, broken only by the doctor's visit. He reported that Mercy might last a couple of days more. In the evening Jim replaced his sister-in-law, who slept perforce. At midnight she reappeared and sent him to bed. The sufferer tossed about restlessly. At half-past two she awoke, and Honor fed her with some broth, as she would have fed a baby. Mercy, indeed, looked scarcely bigger than an infant, and Honor only had the advantage of her by being puffed out with clothes. A church clock in the distance struck three. Then the silence fell deeper. The watcher drowsed, the lamp flickered, tossing her shadow about the walls as if she, too, were turning feverishly from side to side. A strange ticking made itself heard in the wainscoting. Mercy sat up with a scream of terror. "Jim!" she shrieked, "Jim!"

Honor started up, opened her mouth to cry "Hush!" then checked herself, suddenly frozen.

"Jim," cried the dying woman, "listen! Is that the death spider?"

Honor listened, her blood curdling. Then she went towards the door and opened it. "Jim," she said, in low tones, speaking towards the landing, "tell her it's nothing, it's only a mouse. She was always a nervous little thing." And she closed the door softly, and pressing her trembling sister tenderly back on the pillow, tucked her up snugly in the blanket.

Next morning, when Jim was really present, the patient begged pathetically to have a grandchild with her in the room, day and night. "Don't leave me alone again," she quavered, "don't leave me alone with not a soul to talk to." Honor winced, but said nothing.

The youngest child, who did not have to go to school, was brought—a pretty little boy with brown curls, which the sun, streaming through the panes, turned to gold. The morning passed slowly. About noon Mercy took the child's hand, and smoothed his curls.

"My sister Honor had golden curls like that," she whispered.

"They were in the family, Bobby," Honor answered. "Your granny had them, too, when she was a girl."

There was a long pause. Mercy's eyes were half-glazed. But her vision was inward now.

"The mignonette will be growin' in the gardens, Bobby," she murmured.

"Yes, Bobby, and the heart's-ease," said Honor, softly. "We lived in the country, you know, Bobby."

"There is flowers in the country," Bobby declared gravely.

"Yes, and trees," said Honor. "I wonder if your granny remembers when we were larruped for stealin' apples."

"Ay, that I do, Bobby, he, he," croaked the dying creature, with a burst of enthusiasm. "We was a pair o' tomboys. The farmer he ran after us cryin' 'Ye! ye!' but we wouldn't take no gar. He, he, he!"

Honor wept at the laughter. The native idiom, unheard for half a century, made her face shine under the tears. "Don't let your granny excite herself, Bobby. Let me give her her drink." She moved the boy aside, and Mercy's lips automatically opened to the draught.

"Tom was wi' us, Bobby," she gurgled, still vibrating with amusement, "and he tumbled over on the heather. He, he!"

"Tom is dead this forty year, Bobby," whispered Honor.

Mercy's head fell back, and an expression of supreme exhaustion came over the face. Half an hour passed. Bobby was called down to dinner. The doctor had been sent for. The silent sisters were alone. Suddenly Mercy sat up with a jerk.

"It be growin' dark, Tom," she said hoarsely, "'haint it time to call the cattle home from the ma'shes?"

"She's talkin' rubbidge again," said Honor, chokingly. "Tell her she's in London, Bobby."

A wave of intelligence traversed the sallow face. Still sitting up, Mercy bent towards the side of the bed. "Ah, is Honor still there? Kiss me—Bobby." Her hands groped blindly. Honor bent down and the old women's withered lips met.

And in that kiss Mercy passed away into the greater Silence.

THE BIG BOW MYSTERY

I

On a memorable morning of early December, London opened its eyes on a frigid grey mist. There are mornings when King Fog masses his molecules of carbon in serried squadrons in the city, while he scatters them tenuously in the suburbs; so that your morning train may bear you from twilight to darkness. But to-day the enemy's manoeuvring was more monotonous. From Bow even unto Hammersmith there draggled a dull, wretched vapour, like the wraith of an impecunious suicide come into a fortune immediately after the fatal deed. The barometers and thermometers had sympathetically shared its depression, and their spirits (when they had any) were low. The cold cut like a many-bladed knife.

Mrs. Drabdump, of 11 Glover Street, Bow, was one of the few persons in London whom fog did not depress. She went about her work quite as cheerlessly as usual. She had been among the earliest to be aware of the enemy's advent, picking out the strands of fog from the coils of darkness the moment she rolled up her bedroom blind and unveiled the sombre picture of the winter morning. She knew that the fog had come to stay for the day at least, and that the gas-bill for the quarter was going to beat the record in high-jumping. She also knew that this was because she had allowed her new gentleman lodger, Mr. Arthur Constant, to pay a fixed sum of a shilling a week for gas, instead of charging him a proportion of the actual account for the whole house. The meteorologists might have saved the credit of their science if they had reckoned with Mrs. Drabdump's next gas-bill when they predicted the weather and made "Snow" the favourite, and said that "Fog" would be nowhere. Fog was everywhere, yet Mrs. Drabdump took no credit to herself for her prescience. Mrs. Drabdump indeed took no credit for anything, paying her way along doggedly, and struggling through life like a wearied swimmer trying to touch the horizon. That things always went as badly as she had foreseen did not exhilarate her in the least.

Mrs. Drabdump was a widow. Widows are not born but made, else you might have fancied Mrs. Drabdump had always been a widow. Nature had given her that tall, spare form, and that pale, thin-lipped, elongated, hard-eyed visage, and that painfully precise hair, which are always associated with widowhood in low life. It is only in higher circles that women can lose their husbands and yet remain bewitching. The late Mr. Drabdump had scratched the base of his thumb with a rusty nail, and Mrs. Drabdump's foreboding that he would die of lockjaw had not prevented her wrestling day and night with the shadow of Death, as she had wrestled with it vainly twice before, when Katie died of diphtheria and little Johnny of scarlet fever. Perhaps it is from overwork among the poor that Death has been reduced to a shadow.

Mrs. Drabdump was lighting the kitchen fire. She did it very scientifically, as knowing the contrariety of coal and the anxiety of flaming sticks to end in smoke unless rigidly kept up to the mark. Science was a success as usual; and Mrs. Drabdump rose from her knees content, like a Parsee priestess who had duly paid her morning devotions to her deity. Then she started violently, and nearly lost her balance. Her eye had caught the hands of the clock on the mantel. They pointed to fifteen minutes to seven. Mrs. Drabdump's devotion to the kitchen fire invariably terminated at fifteen minutes past six. What was the matter with the clock?

Mrs. Drabdump had an immediate vision of Snoppet, the neighbouring horologist, keeping the clock in hand for weeks and then returning it only superficially repaired and secretly injured more vitally "for the good of the trade." The evil vision vanished as quickly as it came, exorcised by the deep boom of St. Dunstan's bells chiming the three-quarters. In its place a great horror surged. Instinct had failed; Mrs. Drabdump had risen at half-past six instead of six. Now she understood why she had been feeling so dazed and strange and sleepy. She had overslept herself.

Chagrined and puzzled, she hastily set the kettle over the crackling coal, discovering a second later that she had overslept herself because Mr. Constant wished to be woke three-quarters of an hour earlier than usual, and to have his breakfast at seven, having to speak at an early meeting of discontented tram-men. She ran at once, candle in hand, to his bedroom. It was upstairs. All "upstairs" was Arthur Constant's domain, for it consisted of but two mutually independent rooms. Mrs. Drabdump knocked viciously at the door of the one he used for a bedroom, crying, "Seven o'clock, sir. You'll be late, sir. You must get up at once." The usual slumbrous "All right" was not forthcoming; but, as she herself had varied her morning salute, her ear was less expectant of the echo. She went downstairs, with no foreboding save that the kettle would come off second best in the race between its boiling and her lodger's dressing.

For she knew there was no fear of Arthur Constant's lying deaf to the call of Duty—temporarily represented by Mrs. Drabdump. He was a light sleeper, and the tram-conductors' bells were probably ringing in his ears, summoning him to the meeting. Why Arthur Constant, B.A.—white-handed and while-shirted, and gentleman to the very purse of him—should concern himself with tram-men, when fortune had confined his necessary relations with drivers to cabmen at the least, Mrs. Drabdump could not quite make out. He probably aspired to represent Bow in Parliament; but then it would surely have been wiser to lodge with a landlady who possessed a vote by having a husband alive. Nor was there much practical wisdom in his wish to black his own boots (an occupation in which he shone but little), and to live in every way like a Bow working man. Bow working men were not so lavish in their patronage of water, whether existing in drinking-glasses, morning tubs, or laundress's establishments. Nor did they eat the delicacies with which Mrs. Drabdump supplied him, with the assurance that they were the artisan's appanage. She could not bear to see him eat things unbefitting his station. Arthur Constant opened his mouth and ate what his landlady gave him, not first deliberately shutting his eyes according to the formula, the rather pluming himself on keeping them very wide open. But it is difficult for saints to see through their own halos; and in practice an aureola about the head is often indistinguishable from a mist.

The tea to be scalded in Mr. Constant's pot, when that cantankerous kettle should boil, was not the coarse mixture of black and green sacred to herself and Mr. Mortlake, of whom the thoughts of breakfast now reminded her. Poor Mr. Mortlake, gone off without any to Devonport, somewhere about four in the fog-thickened darkness of a winter night! Well, she hoped his journey would be duly rewarded, that his perks would be heavy, and that he would make as good a thing out of the "travelling expenses" as rival labour leaders roundly accused him of to other people's faces. She did not grudge him his gains, nor was it her business if, as they alleged, in introducing Mr. Constant to her vacant rooms, his idea was not merely to benefit his landlady. He had done her an uncommon good turn, queer as was the lodger thus introduced. His own apostleship to the sons of toil gave Mrs. Drabdump no twinges of perplexity. Tom Mortlake had been a compositor; and apostleship was obviously a profession better paid and of a higher social status. Tom Mortlake—the hero of a hundred strikes—set up in print on a poster, was unmistakably superior to Tom Mortlake setting up other men's names at a case. Still, the work was not all beer and skittles, and Mrs. Drabdump felt that Tom's latest job was not enviable.

She shook his door as she passed it on her way back to the kitchen, but there was no response. The street door was only a few feet off down the passage, and a glance at it dispelled the last hope that Tom had abandoned the journey. The door was unbolted and unchained, and the only security was the latch-key lock. Mrs. Drabdump felt a whit uneasy, though, to give her her due, she never suffered as much as most good housewives do from criminals who never come. Not quite opposite, but still only a few doors off, on the other side of the street, lived the celebrated ex-detective Grodman, and, illogically enough, his presence in the street gave Mrs. Drabdump a curious sense of security, as of a believer living under the shadow of the fane. That any human being of ill odour should consciously come within a mile of the scent of so famous a sleuth-hound seemed to her highly improbable. Grodman had retired (with a competence) and was only a sleeping dog now; still, even criminals would have sense enough to let him lie.

So Mrs. Drabdump did not really feel that there had been any danger, especially as a second glance at the street door showed that Mortlake had been thoughtful enough to slip the loop that held back the bolt of the big lock. She allowed herself another throb of sympathy for the labour leader whirling on his dreary way towards Devonport Dockyard. Not that he had told her anything of his journey, beyond the town; but she knew Devonport had a Dockyard because Jessie Dymond—Tom's sweetheart—once mentioned that her aunt lived near there, and it lay on the surface that Tom had gone to help the dockers, who were imitating their London brethren. Mrs. Drabdump did not need to be told things to be aware of them. She went back to prepare Mr. Constant's superfine tea, vaguely wondering why people were so discontented nowadays. But when she brought up the tea and the toast and the eggs to Mr. Constant's sitting-room (which adjoined his bedroom, though without communicating with it), Mr. Constant was not sitting in it. She lit the gas, and laid the cloth; then she returned to the landing and beat at the bedroom door with an imperative palm. Silence alone answered her. She called him by name and told him the hour, but hers was the only voice she heard, and it sounded strangely to her in the shadows of the staircase. Then, muttering, "Poor gentleman, he had the toothache last night; and p'r'aps he's only just got a wink o' sleep. Pity to disturb him for the sake of them grizzling conductors. I'll let him sleep his usual time," she bore the tea-pot downstairs with a mournful, almost poetic, consciousness that soft-boiled eggs (like love) must grow cold.

Half-past seven came—and she knocked again. But Constant slept on.

His letters, always a strange assortment, arrived at eight, and a telegram came soon after. Mrs. Drabdump rattled his door, shouted, and at last put the wire under it. Her heart was beating fast enough now, though there seemed to be a cold, clammy snake curling round it. She went downstairs again and turned the handle of Mortlake's room, and went in without knowing why. The coverlet of the bed showed that the occupant had only lain down in his clothes, as if fearing to miss the early train. She had not for a moment expected to find him in the room; yet somehow the consciousness that she was alone in the house with the sleeping Constant seemed to flash for the first time upon her, and the clammy snake tightened its folds round her heart.

She opened the street door, and her eye wandered nervously up and down. It was half-past eight. The little street stretched cold and still in the grey mist, blinking bleary eyes at either end, where the street lamps smouldered on. No one was visible for the moment, though smoke was rising from many of the chimneys to greet its sister mist. At the house of the detective across the way the blinds were still down and the shutters up. Yet the familiar, prosaic aspect of the street calmed her. The bleak air set her coughing; she slammed the door to, and returned to the kitchen to make fresh tea for Constant, who could only be in a deep sleep. But the canister trembled in her grasp. She did not know whether she dropped it or threw it down, but there was nothing in the hand that battered again a moment later at the bedroom door. No sound within answered the clamour without. She rained blow upon blow in a sort of spasm of frenzy, scarce remembering that her object was merely to wake her lodger, and almost staving in the lower panels with her kicks. Then she turned the handle and tried to open the door, but it was locked. The resistance recalled her to herself—she had a moment of shocked decency at the thought that she had been about to enter Constant's bedroom. Then the terror came over her afresh. She felt that she was alone in the house with a corpse. She sank to the floor, cowering; with difficulty stifling a desire to scream. Then she rose with a jerk and raced down the stairs without looking behind her, and threw open the door and ran out into the street, only pulling up with her hand violently agitating Grodman's door-knocker. In a moment the first-floor window was raised—the little house was of the same pattern as her own—and Grodman's full fleshy face loomed through the fog in sleepy irritation from under a nightcap. Despite its scowl the ex-detective's face dawned upon her like the sun upon an occupant of the haunted chamber.

"What in the devil's the matter?" he growled. Grodman was not an early bird, now that he had no worms to catch. He could afford to despise proverbs now, for the house in which he lived was his, and he lived in it because several other houses in the street were also his, and it is well for the landlord to be about his own estate in Bow, where poachers often shoot the moon. Perhaps the desire to enjoy his greatness among his early cronies counted for something, too, for he had been born and bred at Bow, receiving when a youth his first engagement from the local police quarters, whence he had drawn a few shillings a week as an amateur detective in his leisure hours.

Grodman was still a bachelor. In the celestial matrimonial bureau a partner might have been selected for him, but he had never been able to discover her. It was his one failure as a detective. He was a self-sufficing person, who preferred a gas stove to a domestic; but in deference to Glover Street opinion he admitted a female factotum between ten A.M. and ten P.M., and, equally in deference to Glover Street opinion, excluded her between ten P.M. and ten A.M.

"I want you to come across at once," Mrs. Drabdump gasped. "Something has happened to Mr. Constant."

"What! Not bludgeoned by the police at the meeting this morning, I hope?"

"No, no! He didn't go. He is dead."

"Dead?" Grodman's face grew very serious now.

"Yes. Murdered!"

"What?" almost shouted the ex-detective. "How? When? Where? Who?"

"I don't know. I can't get to him. I have beaten at his door. He does not answer."

Grodman's face lit up with relief.

"You silly woman! Is that all? I shall have a cold in my head. Bitter weather. He's dog-tired after yesterday—processions, three speeches, kindergarten, lecture on 'the moon,' article on cooperation. That's his style." It was also Grodman's style. He never wasted words.

"No," Mrs. Drabdump breathed up at him solemnly, "he's dead."

"All right; go back. Don't alarm the neighbourhood unnecessarily. Wait for me. Down in five minutes." Grodman did not take this Cassandra of the kitchen too seriously. Probably he knew his woman. His small, bead-like eyes glittered with an almost amused smile as he withdrew them from Mrs. Drabdump's ken, and shut down the sash with a bang. The poor woman ran back across the road and through her door, which she would not close behind her. It seemed to shut her in with the dead. She waited in the passage. After an age—seven minutes by any honest clock—Grodman made his appearance, looking as dressed as usual, but with unkempt hair and with disconsolate side-whisker. He was not quite used to that side-whisker yet, for it had only recently come within the margin of cultivation. In active service Grodman had been clean-shaven, like all members of the profession—for surely your detective is the most versatile of actors. Mrs. Drabdump closed the street door quietly, and pointed to the stairs, fear operating like a polite desire to give him precedence. Grodman ascended, amusement still glimmering in his eyes. Arrived on the landing he knocked peremptorily at the door, crying, "Nine o'clock, Mr. Constant; nine o'clock!" When he ceased there was no other sound or movement. His face grew more serious. He waited, then knocked, and cried louder. He turned the handle but the door was fast. He tried to peer through the keyhole, but it was blocked. He shook the upper panels, but the door seemed bolted as well as locked. He stood still, his face set and rigid, for he liked and esteemed the man.

"Ay, knock your loudest," whispered the pale-faced woman. "You'll not wake him now."

The grey mist had followed them through the street door, and hovered about the staircase, charging the air with a moist sepulchral odour.

"Locked and bolted," muttered Grodman, shaking the door afresh.

"Burst it open," breathed the woman, trembling violently all over, and holding her hands before her as if to ward off the dreadful vision. Without another word, Grodman applied his shoulder to the door, and made a violent muscular effort. He had been an athlete in his time, and the sap was yet in him. The door creaked, little by little it began to give, the woodwork enclosing the bolt of the lock splintered, the panels bent inwards, the large upper bolt tore off its iron staple; the door flew back with a crash. Grodman rushed in.

"My God!" he cried. The woman shrieked. The sight was too terrible.

Within a few hours the jubilant newsboys were shrieking "Horrible Suicide in Bow," and The Moon poster added, for the satisfaction of those too poor to purchase, "A Philanthropist Cuts His Throat."

II

But the newspapers were premature. Scotland Yard refused to prejudice the case despite the penny-a-liners. Several arrests were made, so that the later editions were compelled to soften "Suicide" into "Mystery." The people arrested were a nondescript collection of tramps. Most of them had committed other offences for which the police had not arrested them. One bewildered-looking gentleman gave himself up (as if he were a riddle), but the police would have none of him, and restored him forthwith to his friends and keepers. The number of candidates for each new opening in Newgate is astonishing.

The full significance of this tragedy of a noble young life cut short had hardly time to filter into the public mind, when a fresh sensation absorbed it. Tom Mortlake had been arrested the same day at Liverpool on suspicion of being concerned in the death of his fellow-lodger. The news fell like a bombshell upon a land in which Tom Mortlake's name was a household word. That the gifted artisan orator, who had never shrunk upon occasion from launching red rhetoric at society, should actually have shed blood seemed too startling, especially as the blood shed was not blue, but the property of a lovable young middle-class idealist, who had now literally given his life to the Cause. But this supplementary sensation did not grow to a head, and everybody (save a few labour leaders) was relieved to hear that Tom had been released almost immediately, being merely subpoenaed to appear at the inquest. In an interview which he accorded to the representative of a Liverpool paper the same afternoon, he stated that he put his arrest down entirely to the enmity and rancour entertained towards him by the police throughout the country. He had come to Liverpool to trace the movements of a friend about whom he was very uneasy, and he was making anxious inquiries at the docks to discover at what times steamers left for America, when the detectives stationed there had, in accordance with instructions from headquarters, arrested him as a suspicious-looking character. "Though," said Tom, "they must very well have known my phiz, as I have been sketched and caricatured all over the shop. When I told them who I was they had the decency to let me go. They thought they'd scored off me enough, I reckon. Yes, it certainly is a strange coincidence that I might actually have had something to do with the poor fellow's death, which has cut me up as much as anybody; though if they had known I had just come from the 'scene of the crime,' and actually lived in the house, they would probably have—let me alone." He laughed sarcastically. "They are a queer lot of muddle-heads, are the police. Their motto is, 'First catch your man, then cook the evidence.' If you're on the spot you're guilty because you're there, and if you're elsewhere you're guilty because you have gone away. Oh, I know them! If they could have seen their way to clap me in quod, they'd ha' done it. Luckily I know the number of the cabman who took me to Euston before five this morning."

"If they clapped you in quod," the interviewer reported himself as facetiously observing, "the prisoners would be on strike in a week."

"Yes, but there would be so many blacklegs ready to take their places," Mortlake flashed back, "that I'm afraid it 'ould be no go. But do excuse me. I am so upset about my friend. I'm afraid he has left England, and I have to make inquiries; and now there's poor Constant gone—horrible! horrible! and I'm due in London at the inquest. I must really run away. Good-by. Tell your readers it's all a police grudge."

"One last word, Mr. Mortlake, if you please. Is it true that you were billed to preside at a great meeting of clerks at St. James's Hall between one and two to-day to protest against the German invasion?"

"Whew! so I was. But the beggars arrested me just before one, when I was going to wire, and then the news of poor Constant's end drove it out of my head. What a nuisance! Lord, how troubles do come together! Well, good-by, send me a copy of the paper."

Tom Mortlake's evidence at the inquest added little beyond this to the public knowledge of his movements on the morning of the Mystery. The cabman who drove him to Euston had written indignantly to the papers to say that he picked up his celebrated fare at Bow Railway Station at about half-past four A.M., and the arrest was a deliberate insult to democracy, and he offered to make an affidavit to that effect, leaving it dubious to which effect. But Scotland Yard betrayed no itch for the affidavit in question, and No. 2138 subsided again into the obscurity of his rank. Mortlake—whose face was very pale below the black mane brushed back from his fine forehead—gave his evidence in low, sympathetic tones. He had known the deceased for over a year, coming constantly across him in their common political and social work, and had found the furnished rooms for him in Glover Street at his own request, they just being to let when Constant resolved to leave his rooms at Oxford House in Bethnal Green, and to share the actual life of the people. The locality suited the deceased, as being near the People's Palace. He respected and admired the deceased, whose genuine goodness had won all hearts. The deceased was an untiring worker; never grumbled, was always in fair spirits, regarded his life and wealth as a sacred trust to be used for the benefit of humanity. He had last seen him at a quarter past nine P.M. on the day preceding his death. He (witness) had received a letter by the last post which made him uneasy about a friend. He went up to consult deceased about it. Deceased was evidently suffering from toothache, and was fixing a piece of cotton-wool in a hollow tooth, but he did not complain. Deceased seemed rather upset by the news he brought, and they both discussed it rather excitedly.

By a JURYMAN: Did the news concern him?

MORTLAKE: Only impersonally. He knew my friend, and was keenly sympathetic when one was in trouble.

CORONER: Could you show the jury the letter you received?

MORTLAKE: I have mislaid it, and cannot make out where it has got to. If you, sir, think it relevant or essential, I will state what the trouble was.

CORONER: Was the toothache very violent?

MORTLAKE: I cannot tell. I think not, though he told me it had disturbed his rest the night before.

CORONER: What time did you leave him?

MORTLAKE: About twenty to ten.

CORONER: And what did you do then?

MORTLAKE: I went out for an hour or so to make some inquiries. Then I returned, and told my landlady I should be leaving by an early train for—for the country.

CORONER: And that was the last you saw of the deceased?

MORTLAKE (with emotion): The last.

CORONER: How was he when you left him?

MORTLAKE: Mainly concerned about my trouble.

CORONER: Otherwise you saw nothing unusual about him?

MORTLAKE: Nothing.

CORONER: What time did you leave the house on Tuesday morning?

MORTLAKE: At about five-and-twenty minutes past four.

CORONER: Are you sure that you shut the street door?

MORTLAKE: Quite sure. Knowing my landlady was rather a timid person, I even slipped the bolt of the big lock, which was usually tied back. It was impossible for any one to get in, even with a latch-key.

Mrs. Drabdump's evidence (which, of course, preceded his) was more important, and occupied a considerable time, unduly eked out by Drabdumpian padding. Thus she not only deposed that Mr. Constant had the toothache, but that it was going to last about a week; in tragi-comic indifference to the radical cure that had been effected. Her account of the last hours of the deceased tallied with Mortlake's, only that she feared Mortlake was quarrelling with him over something in the letter that came by the nine o'clock post. Deceased had left the house a little after Mortlake, but had returned before him, and had gone straight to his bedroom. She had not actually seen him come in, having been in the kitchen, but she heard his latch-key, followed by his light step up the stairs.

A JURYMAN: How do you know it was not somebody else? (Sensation, of which the juryman tries to look unconscious.)

WITNESS: He called down to me over the banisters, and says in his sweetish voice, "Be hextra sure to wake me at a quarter to seven, Mrs. Drabdump, or else I shan't get to my tram meeting." (Juryman collapses.)

CORONER: And did you wake him?

MRS. DRABDUMP (breaking down): Oh, my lud, how can you ask?

CORONER: There, there, compose yourself. I mean did you try to wake him?

MRS. DRABDUMP: I have taken in and done for lodgers this seventeen years, my lud, and have always gave satisfaction; and Mr. Mortlake, he wouldn't ha' recommended me otherwise, though I wish to Heaven the poor gentleman had never—

CORONER: Yes, yes, of course. You tried to rouse him?

But it was some time before Mrs. Drabdump was sufficiently calm to explain that, though she had overslept herself, and though it would have been all the same anyhow, she had come up to time. Bit by bit the tragic story was forced from her lips—a tragedy that even her telling could not make tawdry. She told with superfluous detail how—when Mr. Grodman broke in the door—she saw her unhappy gentleman-lodger lying on his back in bed, stone dead, with a gaping red wound in his throat; how her stronger-minded companion calmed her a little by spreading a handkerchief over the distorted face; how they then looked vainly about and under the bed for any instrument by which the deed could have been done, the veteran detective carefully making a rapid inventory of the contents of the room, and taking notes of the precise position and condition of the body before anything was disturbed by the arrival of gapers or bunglers; how she had pointed out to him that both the windows were firmly bolted to keep out the cold night air; how, having noted this down with a puzzled, pitying shake of the head, he had opened the window to summon the police, and espied in the fog one Denzil Cantercot, whom he called, and told to run to the nearest police-station and ask them to send on an inspector and a surgeon; how they both remained in the room till the police arrived, Grodman pondering deeply the while and making notes every now and again, as fresh points occurred to him, and asking her questions about the poor, weak-headed young man. Pressed as to what she meant by calling the deceased "weak-headed," she replied that some of her neighbours wrote him begging letters, though, Heaven knew, they were better off than herself, who had to scrape her fingers to the bone for every penny she earned. Under further pressure from Mr. Talbot, who was watching the inquiry on behalf of Arthur Constant's family, Mrs. Drabdump admitted that the deceased had behaved like a human being, nor was there anything externally eccentric or queer in his conduct. He was always cheerful and pleasant spoken, though certainly soft—God rest his soul. No; he never shaved, but wore all the hair that Heaven had given him.

By a JURYMAN: She thought deceased was in the habit of locking his door when he went to bed. Of course, she couldn't say for certain. (Laughter.) There was no need to bolt the door as well. The bolt slid upwards, and was at the top of the door. When she first let lodgings, her reasons for which she seemed anxious to publish, there had only been a bolt, but a suspicious lodger, she would not call him a gentleman, had complained that he could not fasten his door behind him, and so she had been put to the expense of having a lock made. The complaining lodger went off soon after without paying his rent. (Laughter.) She had always known he would.

The CORONER: Was deceased at all nervous?

WITNESS: No, he was a very nice gentleman. (A laugh.)

CORONER: I mean did he seem afraid of being robbed?

WITNESS: No, he was always goin' to demonstrations. (Laughter.) I told him to be careful. I told him I lost a purse with 3s. 2d. myself on Jubilee Day.

Mrs. Drabdump resumed her seat, weeping vaguely.

The CORONER: Gentlemen, we shall have an opportunity of viewing the room shortly.

The story of the discovery of the body was retold, though more scientifically, by Mr. George Grodman, whose unexpected resurgence into the realm of his early exploits excited as keen a curiosity as the reappearance "for this occasion only" of a retired prima donna. His book, Criminals I have Caught, passed from the twenty-third to the twenty-fourth edition merely on the strength of it. Mr. Grodman stated that the body was still warm when he found it. He thought that death was quite recent. The door he had had to burst was bolted as well as locked. He confirmed Mrs. Drabdump's statement about the windows; the chimney was very narrow. The cut looked as if done by a razor. There was no instrument lying about the room. He had known the deceased about a month. He seemed a very earnest, simple-minded young fellow, who spoke a great deal about the brotherhood of man. (The hardened old man-hunter's voice was not free from a tremor as he spoke jerkily of the dead man's enthusiasms.) He should have thought the deceased the last man in the world to commit suicide.

Mr. DENZIL CANTERCOT was next called: He was a poet. (Laughter.) He was on his way to Mr. Grodman's house to tell him he had been unable to do some writing for him because he was suffering from writer's cramp, when Mr. Grodman called to him from the window of No. 11 and asked him to run for the police. No, he did not run; he was a philosopher. (Laughter.) He returned with them to the door, but did not go up. He had no stomach for crude sensations. (Laughter.) The grey fog was sufficiently unbeautiful for him for one morning. (Laughter.)

Inspector HOWLETT said: About 9.45 on the morning of Tuesday, 4th December, from information received, he went with Sergeant Runnymede and Dr. Robinson to 11 Glover Street, Bow, and there found the dead body of a young man, lying on his back with his throat cut. The door of the room had been smashed in, and the lock and the bolt evidently forced. The room was tidy. There were no marks of blood on the floor. A purse full of gold was on the dressing-table beside a big book. A hip-bath, with cold water, stood beside the bed, over which was a hanging bookcase. There was a large wardrobe against the wall next to the door. The chimney was very narrow. There were two windows, one bolted. It was about eighteen feet to the pavement. There was no way of climbing up. No one could possibly have got out of the room, and then bolted the doors and windows behind him; and he had searched all parts of the room in which any one might have been concealed. He had been unable to find any instrument in the room in spite of exhaustive search, there being not even a penknife in the pockets of the clothes of the deceased, which lay on a chair. The house and the back yard, and the adjacent pavement, had also been fruitlessly searched.

Sergeant RUNNYMEDE made an identical statement, saving only that he had gone with Dr. Robinson and Inspector Howlett.

Dr. ROBINSON, divisional surgeon, said: "The deceased was lying on his back, with his throat cut. The body was not yet cold, the abdominal region being quite warm. Rigor mortis had set in in the lower jaw, neck, and upper extremities. The muscles contracted when beaten. I inferred that life had been extinct some two or three hours, probably not longer, it might have been less. The bed-clothes would keep the lower part warm for some time. The wound, which was a deep one, was five and a half inches from right to left across the throat to a point under the left ear. The upper portion of the windpipe was severed, and likewise the jugular vein. The muscular coating of the carotid artery was divided. There was a slight cut, as if in continuation of the wound, on the thumb of the left hand. The hands were clasped underneath the head. There was no blood on the right hand. The wound could not have been self-inflicted. A sharp instrument had been used, such as a razor. The cut might have been made by a left-handed person. No doubt death was practically instantaneous. I saw no signs of a struggle about the body or the room. I noticed a purse on the dressing-table, lying next to Madame Blavatsky's big book on Theosophy. Sergeant Runnymede drew my attention to the fact that the door had evidently been locked and bolted from within."

By a JURYMAN: I do not say the cuts could not have been made by a right-handed person. I can offer no suggestion as to how the inflictor of the wound got in or out. Extremely improbable that the cut was self-inflicted. There was little trace of the outside fog in the room.

Police constable Williams said he was on duty in the early hours of the morning of the 4th inst. Glover Street lay within his beat. He saw or heard nothing suspicious. The fog was never very dense, though nasty to the throat. He had passed through Glover Street about half-past four. He had not seen Mr. Mortlake or anybody else leave the house.

The Court here adjourned, the coroner and the jury repairing in a body to 11 Glover Street, to view the house and the bedroom of the deceased. And the evening posters announced "The Bow Mystery Thickens."

III

Before the inquiry was resumed, all the poor wretches in custody had been released on suspicion that they were innocent; there was not a single case even for a magistrate. Clues, which at such seasons are gathered by the police like blackberries off the hedges, were scanty and unripe. Inferior specimens were offered them by bushels, but there was not a good one among the lot. The police could not even manufacture a clue.

Arthur Constant's death was already the theme of every hearth, railway-carriage, and public-house. The dead idealist had points of contact with so many spheres. The East-end and the West-end alike were moved and excited, the Democratic Leagues and the Churches, the Doss-houses and the Universities. The pity of it! And then the impenetrable mystery of it!

The evidence given in the concluding portion of the investigation was necessarily less sensational. There were no more witnesses to bring the scent of blood over the coroner's table; those who had yet to be heard were merely relatives and friends of the deceased, who spoke of him as he had been in life. His parents were dead, perhaps happily for them; his relatives had seen little of him, and had scarce heard as much about him as the outside world. No man is a prophet in his own country, and, even if he migrates, it is advisable for him to leave his family at home. His friends were a motley crew; friends of the same friend are not necessarily friends of one another. But their diversity only made the congruity of the tale they had to tell more striking. It was the tale of a man who had never made an enemy even by benefiting him, nor lost a friend even by refusing his favours; the tale of a man whose heart overflowed with peace and goodwill to all men all the year round; of a man to whom Christmas came not once, but three hundred and sixty-five times a year; it was the tale of a brilliant intellect, who gave up to mankind what was meant for himself, and worked as a labourer in the vineyard of humanity, never crying that the grapes were sour; of a man uniformly cheerful and of good courage, living in that forgetfulness of self which is the truest antidote to despair. And yet there was not quite wanting the note of pain to jar the harmony and make it human. Richard Elton, his chum from boyhood, and vicar of Somerton, in Midlandshire, handed to the coroner a letter received from the deceased about ten days before his death, containing some passages which the coroner read aloud:—"Do you know anything of Schopenhauer? I mean anything beyond the current misconceptions? I have been making his acquaintance lately. He is an agreeable rattle of a pessimist; his essay on 'The Misery of Mankind' is quite lively reading. At first his assimilation of Christianity and Pessimism (it occurs in his essay on 'Suicide') dazzled me as an audacious paradox. But there is truth in it. Verily the whole creation groaneth and travaileth, and man is a degraded monster, and sin is over all. Ah, my friend, I have shed many of my illusions since I came to this seething hive of misery and wrongdoing. What shall one man's life—a million men's lives—avail against the corruption, the vulgarity, and the squalor of civilisation? Sometimes I feel like a farthing rushlight in the Hall of Eblis. Selfishness is so long and life so short. And the worst of it is that everybody is so beastly contented. The poor no more desire comfort than the rich culture. The woman, to whom a penny school fee for her child represents an appreciable slice of her income, is satisfied that the rich we shall always have with us.

"The real old Tories are the paupers in the Workhouse. The radical working men are jealous of their own leaders, and the leaders are jealous of one another. Schopenhauer must have organised a Labour Party in his salad days. And yet one can't help feeling that he committed suicide as a philosopher by not committing it as a man. He claims kinship with Buddha, too; though Esoteric Buddhism at least seems spheres removed from the philosophy of 'the Will and the Idea.' What a wonderful woman Madame Blavatsky must be! I can't say I follow her, for she is up in the clouds nearly all the time, and I haven't as yet developed an astral body. Shall I send you on her book? It is fascinating.... I am becoming quite a fluent orator. One soon gets into the way of it. The horrible thing is that you catch yourself saying things to lead up to 'Cheers' instead of sticking to the plain realities of the business. Lucy is still doing the galleries in Italy. It used to pain me sometimes to think of my darling's happiness when I came across a flat-chested factory-girl. Now I feel her happiness is as important as a factory-girl's."

Lucy, the witness explained, was Lucy Brent, the betrothed of the deceased. The poor girl had been telegraphed for, and had started for England. The witness stated that the outburst of despondency in this letter was almost a solitary one, most of the letters in his possession being bright, buoyant, and hopeful. Even this letter ended with a humorous statement of the writer's manifold plans and projects for the New Year. The deceased was a good Churchman.

CORONER: Was there any private trouble in his own life to account for the temporary despondency?

WITNESS: Not so far as I am aware. His financial position was exceptionally favourable.

CORONER: There had been no quarrel with Miss Brent?

WITNESS: I have the best authority for saying that no shadow of difference had ever come between them.

CORONER: Was the deceased left-handed?

WITNESS: Certainly not. He was not even ambidexter.

A JURYMAN: Isn't Shoppinhour one of the infidel writers, published by the Freethought Publication Society?

WITNESS: I do not know who publishes his books.

The JURYMAN (a small grocer and big raw-boned Scotchman, rejoicing in the name of Sandy Sanderson and the dignities of deaconry and membership of the committee of the Bow Conservative Association): No equeevocation, sir. Is he not a secularist, who has lectured at the Hall of Science?

WITNESS: No, he is a foreign writer—(Mr. Sanderson was heard to thank heaven for this small mercy)— who believes that life is not worth living.

The JURYMAN: Were you not shocked to find the friend of a meenister reading such impure leeterature?

WITNESS: The deceased read everything. Schopenhauer is the author of a system of philosophy, and not what you seem to imagine. Perhaps you would like to inspect the book? (Laughter.)

The JURYMAN: I would na' touch it with a pitchfork. Such books should be burnt. And this Madame Blavatsky's book—what is that? Is that also pheelosophy?

WITNESS: No. It is Theosophy. (Laughter.)

Mr. Allan Smith, secretary of the Tram-men's Union, stated that he had had an interview with the deceased on the day before his death, when he (the deceased) spoke hopefully of the prospects of the movement, and wrote him out a check for ten guineas for his Union. Deceased promised to speak at a meeting called for a quarter past seven A.M. the next day.

Mr. Edward Wimp, of the Scotland Yard Detective Department, said that the letters and papers of the deceased threw no light upon the manner of his death, and they would be handed back to the family. His Department had not formed any theory on the subject.

The coroner proceeded to sum up the evidence. "We have to deal, gentlemen," he said, "with a most incomprehensible and mysterious case, the details of which are yet astonishingly simple. On the morning of Tuesday, the 4th inst., Mrs. Drabdump, a worthy hard-working widow, who lets lodgings at 11 Glover Street, Bow, was unable to arouse the deceased, who occupied the entire upper floor of the house. Becoming alarmed, she went across to fetch Mr. George Grodman, a gentleman known to us all by reputation, and to whose clear and scientific evidence we are much indebted, and got him to batter in the door. They found the deceased lying back in bed with a deep wound in his throat. Life had only recently become extinct. There was no trace of any instrument by which the cut could have been effected: there was no trace of any person who could have effected the cut. No person could apparently have got in or out. The medical evidence goes to show that the deceased could not have inflicted the wound himself. And yet, gentlemen, there are, in the nature of things, two—and only two—alternative explanations of his death. Either the wound was inflicted by his own hand, or it was inflicted by another's. I shall take each of these possibilities separately. First, did the deceased commit suicide? The medical evidence says deceased was lying with his hands clasped behind his head. Now the wound was made from right to left, and terminated by a cut on the left thumb. If the deceased had made it he would have had to do it with his right hand, while his left hand remained under his head—a most peculiar and unnatural position to assume. Moreover, in making a cut with the right hand, one would naturally move the hand from left to right. It is unlikely that the deceased would move his right hand so awkwardly and unnaturally, unless, of course, his object was to baffle suspicion. Another point is that on this hypothesis, the deceased would have had to replace his right hand beneath his head. But Dr. Robinson believes that death was instantaneous. If so, deceased could have had no time to pose so neatly. It is just possible the cut was made with the left hand, but then the deceased was right-handed. The absence of any signs of a possible weapon undoubtedly goes to corroborate the medical evidence. The police have made an exhaustive search in all places where the razor or other weapon or instrument might by any possibility have been concealed, including the bed-clothes, the mattress, the pillow, and the street into which it might have been dropped. But all theories involving the wilful concealment of the fatal instrument have to reckon with the fact or probability that death was instantaneous, also with the fact that there was no blood about the floor. Finally, the instrument used was in all likelihood a razor, and the deceased did not shave, and was never known to be in possession of any such instrument. If, then, we were to confine ourselves to the medical and police evidence, there would, I think, be little hesitation in dismissing the idea of suicide. Nevertheless, it is well to forget the physical aspect of the case for a moment and to apply our minds to an unprejudiced inquiry into the mental aspect of it. Was there any reason why the deceased should wish to take his own life? He was young, wealthy, and popular, loving and loved; life stretched fair before him. He had no vices. Plain living, high thinking, and noble doing were the three guiding stars of his life. If he had had ambition, an illustrious public career was within his reach. He was an orator of no mean power, a brilliant and industrious man. His outlook was always on the future—he was always sketching out ways in which he could be useful to his fellow-men. His purse and his time were ever at the command of whosoever could show fair claim upon them. If such a man were likely to end his own life, the science of human nature would be at an end. Still, some of the shadows of the picture have been presented to us. The man had his moments of despondency—as which of us has not? But they seem to have been few and passing. Anyhow, he was cheerful enough on the day before his death. He was suffering, too, from toothache. But it does not seem to have been violent, nor did he complain. Possibly, of course, the pain became very acute in the night. Nor must we forget that he may have overworked himself, and got his nerves into a morbid state. He worked very hard, never rising later than half-past seven, and doing far more than the professional 'labour leader.' He taught, and wrote, as well as spoke and organised. But on the other hand all witnesses agreed that he was looking forward eagerly to the meeting of tram-men on the morning of the 4th inst. His whole heart was in the movement. Is it likely that this was the night he would choose for quitting the scene of his usefulness? Is it likely that if he had chosen it, he would not have left letters and a statement behind, or made a last will and testament? Mr. Wimp has found no possible clue to such conduct in his papers. Or is it likely he would have concealed the instrument? The only positive sign of intention is the bolting of his door in addition to the usual locking of it, but one cannot lay much stress on that. Regarding the mental aspects alone, the balance is largely against suicide; looking at the physical aspects, suicide is well-nigh impossible. Putting the two together, the case against suicide is all but mathematically complete. The answer, then, to our first question, Did the deceased commit suicide? is, that he did not."

The coroner paused, and everybody drew a long breath. The lucid exposition had been followed with admiration. If the coroner had stopped now, the jury would have unhesitatingly returned a verdict of "murder." But the coroner swallowed a mouthful of water and went on:—

"We now come to the second alternative—was the deceased the victim of homicide? In order to answer that question in the affirmative it is essential that we should be able to form some conception of the modus operandi. It is all very well for Dr. Robinson to say the cut was made by another hand; but in the absence of any theory as to how the cut could possibly have been made by that other hand, we should be driven back to the theory of self-infliction, however improbable it may seem to medical gentlemen. Now, what are the facts? When Mrs. Drabdump and Mr. Grodman found the body it was yet warm, and Mr. Grodman, a witness fortunately qualified by special experience, states that death had been quite recent. This tallies closely enough with the view of Dr. Robinson, who, examining the body about an hour later, put the time of death at two or three hours before, say seven o'clock. Mrs. Drabdump had attempted to wake the deceased at a quarter to seven, which would put back the act to a little earlier. As I understand from Dr. Robinson, that it is impossible to fix the time very precisely, death may have very well taken place several hours before Mrs. Drabdump's first attempt to wake deceased. Of course, it may have taken place between the first and second calls, as he may merely have been sound asleep at first; it may also not impossibly have taken place considerably earlier than the first call, for all the physical data seem to prove. Nevertheless, on the whole, I think we shall be least likely to err if we assume the time of death to be half-past six. Gentlemen, let us picture to ourselves No. 11 Glover Street, at half-past six. We have seen the house; we know exactly how it is constructed. On the ground floor a front room tenanted by Mr. Mortlake, with two windows giving on the street, both securely bolted; a back room occupied by the landlady; and a kitchen. Mrs. Drabdump did not leave her bedroom till half-past six, so that we may be sure all the various doors and windows have not yet been unfastened; while the season of the year is a guarantee that nothing had been left open. The front door, through which Mr. Mortlake has gone out before half-past four, is guarded by the latch-key lock and the big lock. On the upper floor are two rooms—a front room used by deceased for a bedroom, and a back room which he used as a sitting-room. The back room has been left open, with the key inside, but the window is fastened. The door of the front room is not only locked but bolted. We have seen the splintered mortice and the staple of the upper bolt violently forced from the woodwork and resting on the pin. The windows are bolted, the fasteners being firmly fixed in the catches. The chimney is too narrow to admit of the passage of even a child. This room, in fact, is as firmly barred in as if besieged. It has no communication with any other part of the house. It is as absolutely self-centred and isolated as if it were a fort in the sea or a log-hut in the forest. Even if any strange person is in the house, nay, in the very sitting-room of the deceased, he cannot get into the bedroom, for the house is one built for the poor, with no communication between the different rooms, so that separate families, if need be, may inhabit each. Now, however, let us grant that some person has achieved the miracle of getting into the front room, first floor, 18 feet from the ground. At half-past six, or thereabouts, he cuts the throat of the sleeping occupant. How is he then to get out without attracting the attention of the now roused landlady? But let us concede him that miracle, too. How is he to go away and yet leave the doors and windows locked and bolted from within? This is a degree of miracle at which my credulity must draw the line. No, the room had been closed all night—there is scarce a trace of fog in it. No one could get in or out. Finally, murders do not take place without motive. Robbery and revenge are the only conceivable motives. The deceased had not an enemy in the world; his money and valuables were left untouched. Everything was in order. There were no signs of a struggle. The answer, then, to our second inquiry, Was the deceased killed by another person? is, that he was not.

"Gentlemen, I am aware that this sounds impossible and contradictory. But it is the facts that contradict themselves. It seems clear that the deceased did not commit suicide. It seems equally clear that the deceased was not murdered. There is nothing for it, therefore, gentlemen, but to return a verdict tantamount to an acknowledgment of our incompetence to come to any adequately grounded conviction whatever as to the means or the manner by which the deceased met his death. It is the most inexplicable mystery in all my experience." (Sensation.)

The FOREMAN (after a colloquy with Mr. Sandy Sanderson): We are not agreed, sir. One of the jurors insists on a verdict of "Death from visitation by the act of God."

IV

But Sandy Sanderson's burning solicitude to fix the crime flickered out in the face of opposition, and in the end he bowed his head to the inevitable "open verdict." Then the floodgates of inkland were opened, and the deluge pattered for nine days on the deaf coffin where the poor idealist mouldered. The tongues of the Press were loosened, and the leader-writers revelled in recapitulating the circumstances of "The Big Bow Mystery," though they could contribute nothing but adjectives to the solution. The papers teemed with letters—it was a kind of Indian summer of the silly season. But the editors could not keep them out, nor cared to. The mystery was the one topic of conversation everywhere—it was on the carpet and the bare boards alike, in the kitchen and the drawing-room. It was discussed with science or stupidity, with aspirates or without. It came up for breakfast with the rolls, and was swept off the supper-table with the last crumbs.

No. 11 Glover Street, Bow, remained for days a shrine of pilgrimage. The once sleepy little street buzzed from morning till night. From all parts of the town people came to stare up at the bedroom window and wonder with a foolish face of horror. The pavement was often blocked for hours together, and itinerant vendors of refreshment made it a new market centre, while vocalists hastened thither to sing the delectable ditty of the deed without having any voice in the matter. It was a pity the Government did not erect a toll-gate at either end of the street. But Chancellors of the Exchequer rarely avail themselves of the more obvious expedients for paying off the National Debt.

Finally, familiarity bred contempt, and the wits grew facetious at the expense of the Mystery. Jokes on the subject appeared even in the comic papers.

To the proverb, "You must not say Bo to a goose," one added, "or else she will explain you the Mystery." The name of the gentleman who asked whether the Bow Mystery was not 'arrowing shall not be divulged. There was more point in "Dagonet's" remark that, if he had been one of the unhappy jurymen, he should have been driven to "suicide." A professional paradox-monger pointed triumphantly to the somewhat similar situation in "the murder in the Rue Morgue," and said that Nature had been plagiarising again—like the monkey she was—and he recommended Poe's publishers to apply for an injunction. More seriously, Poe's solution was re-suggested by "Constant Reader" as an original idea. He thought that a small organ-grinder's monkey might have got down the chimney with its master's razor, and, after attempting to shave the occupant of the bed, have returned the way it came. This idea created considerable sensation, but a correspondent with a long train of letters draggling after his name pointed out that a monkey small enough to get down so narrow a flue would not be strong enough to inflict so deep a wound. This was disputed by a third writer, and the contest raged so keenly about the power of monkeys' muscles that it was almost taken for granted that a monkey was the guilty party. The bubble was pricked by the pen of "Common Sense," who laconically remarked that no traces of soot or blood had been discovered on the floor, or on the nightshirt, or the counterpane. The Lancet's leader on the Mystery was awaited with interest. It said: "We cannot join in the praises that have been showered upon the coroner's summing up. It shows again the evils resulting from having coroners who are not medical men. He seems to have appreciated but inadequately the significance of the medical evidence. He should certainly have directed the jury to return a verdict of murder on that. What was it to do with him that he could see no way by which the wound could have been inflicted by an outside agency? It was for the police to find how that was done. Enough that it was impossible for the unhappy young man to have inflicted such a wound, and then to have strength and will power enough to hide the instrument and to remove perfectly every trace of his having left the bed for the purpose." It is impossible to enumerate all the theories propounded by the amateur detectives, while Scotland Yard religiously held its tongue. Ultimately the interest on the subject became confined to a few papers which had received the best letters. Those papers that couldn't get interesting letters stopped the correspondence and sneered at the "sensationalism" of those that could. Among the mass of fantasy there were not a few notable solutions, which failed brilliantly, like rockets posing as fixed stars. One was that in the obscurity of the fog the murderer had ascended to the window of the bedroom by means of a ladder from the pavement. He had then with a diamond cut one of the panes away, and effected an entry through the aperture. On leaving he fixed in the pane of glass again (or another which he had brought with him) and thus the room remained with its bolts and locks untouched. On its being pointed out that the panes were too small, a third correspondent showed that that didn't matter, as it was only necessary to insert the hand and undo the fastening, when the entire window could be opened, the process being reversed by the murderer on leaving. This pretty edifice of glass was smashed by a glazier, who wrote to say that a pane could hardly be fixed in from only one side of a window frame, that it would fall out when touched, and that in any case the wet putty could not have escaped detection. A door panel sliced out and replaced was also put forward, and as many trap-doors and secret passages were ascribed to No. 11 Glover Street, as if it were a mediæval castle. Another of these clever theories was that the murderer was in the room the whole time the police were there—hidden in the wardrobe. Or he had got behind the door when Grodman broke it open, so that he was not noticed in the excitement of the discovery, and escaped with his weapon at the moment when Grodman and Mrs. Drabdump were examining the window fastenings.

Scientific explanations also were to hand to explain how the assassin locked and bolted the door behind him. Powerful magnets outside the door had been used to turn the key and push the bolt within. Murderers armed with magnets loomed on the popular imagination like a new microbe. There was only one defect in this ingenious theory—the thing could not be done. A physiologist recalled the conjurers who swallow swords—by an anatomical peculiarity of the throat—and said that the deceased might have swallowed the weapon after cutting his own throat. This was too much for the public to swallow. As for the idea that the suicide had been effected with a penknife or its blade, or a bit of steel, which had then got buried in the wound, not even the quotation of Shelley's line:—

"Makes such a wound, the knife is lost in it,"

could secure it a moment's acceptance. The same reception was accorded to the idea that the cut had been made with a candle-stick (or other harmless necessary bedroom article) constructed like a sword stick. Theories of this sort caused a humorist to explain that the deceased had hidden the razor in his hollow tooth! Some kind friend of Messrs. Maskelyne and Cook suggested that they were the only persons who could have done the deed, as no one else could get out of a locked cabinet. But perhaps the most brilliant of these flashes of false fire was the facetious, yet probably half-seriously meant letter that appeared in the Pell Mell Press under the heading of

"THE BIG BOW MYSTERY SOLVED

"Sir,—You will remember that when the Whitechapel murders were agitating the universe, I suggested that the district coroner was the assassin. My suggestion has been disregarded. The coroner is still at large. So is the Whitechapel murderer. Perhaps this suggestive coincidence will incline the authorities to pay more attention to me this time. The problem seems to be this. The deceased could not have cut his own throat. The deceased could not have had his throat cut for him. As one of the two must have happened, this is obvious nonsense. As this is obvious nonsense I am justified in disbelieving it. As this obvious nonsense was primarily put in circulation by Mrs. Drabdump and Mr. Grodman, I am justified in disbelieving them. In short, sir, what guarantee have we that the whole tale is not a cock-and-bull story, invented by the two persons who first found the body? What proof is there that the deed was not done by these persons themselves, who then went to work to smash the door and break the locks and the bolts, and fasten up all the windows before they called the police in?—I enclose my card, and am, sir, yours truly,

"ONE WHO LOOKS THROUGH HIS OWN SPECTACLES."

"[Our correspondent's theory is not so audaciously original as he seems to imagine. Has he not looked through the spectacles of the people who persistently suggested that the Whitechapel murderer was invariably the policeman who found the body? Somebody must find the body, if it is to be found at all.— Ed. P.M.P.]"

The editor had reason to be pleased that he inserted this letter, for it drew the following interesting communication from the great detective himself:—

"THE BIG BOW MYSTERY SOLVED

"Sir,—I do not agree with you that your correspondent's theory lacks originality. On the contrary, I think it is delightfully original. In fact it has given me an idea. What that idea is I do not yet propose to say, but if 'One who looks through his own spectacles' will favour me with his name and address I shall be happy to inform him a little before the rest of the world whether his germ has borne any fruit. I feel he is a kindred spirit, and take this opportunity of saying publicly that I was extremely disappointed at the unsatisfactory verdict. The thing was a palpable assassination; an open verdict has a tendency to relax the exertions of Scotland Yard. I hope I shall not be accused of immodesty, or of making personal reflections, when I say that the Department has had several notorious failures of late. It is not what it used to be. Crime is becoming impertinent. It no longer knows its place, so to speak. It throws down the gauntlet where once it used to cower in its fastnesses. I repeat, I make these remarks solely in the interest of law and order. I do not for one moment believe that Arthur Constant killed himself, and if Scotland Yard satisfies itself with that explanation, and turns on its other side and goes to sleep again, then, sir, one of the foulest and most horrible crimes of the century will for ever go unpunished. My acquaintance with the unhappy victim was but recent; still, I saw and knew enough of the man to be certain (and I hope I have seen and known enough of other men to judge) that he was a man constitutionally incapable of committing an act of violence, whether against himself or anybody else. He would not hurt a fly, as the saying goes. And a man of that gentle stamp always lacks the active energy to lay hands on himself. He was a man to be esteemed in no common degree, and I feel proud to be able to say that he considered me a friend. I am hardly at the time of life at which a man cares to put on his harness again; but, sir, it is impossible that I should ever know a day's rest till the perpetrator of this foul deed is discovered. I have already put myself in communication with the family of the victim, who, I am pleased to say, have every confidence in me, and look to me to clear the name of their unhappy relative from the semi-imputation of suicide. I shall be pleased if any one who shares my distrust of the authorities, and who has any clue whatever to this terrible mystery or any plausible suggestion to offer, if, in brief, any 'One who looks through his own spectacles' will communicate with me. If I were asked to indicate the direction in which new clues might be most usefully sought, I should say, in the first instance, anything is valuable that helps us to piece together a complete picture of the manifold activities of the man in the East-end. He entered one way or another into the lives of a good many people; is it true that he nowhere made enemies? With the best intentions a man may wound or offend; his interference may be resented; he may even excite jealousy. A young man like the late Mr. Constant could not have had as much practical sagacity as he had goodness. Whose corns did he tread on? The more we know of the last few months of his life the more we shall know of the manner of his death.

Thanking you by anticipation for the insertion of this letter in your valuable columns, I am, sir, yours truly,

"George Grodman.

"46 Glover Street, Bow.

"P. S.—Since writing the above lines, I have, by the kindness of Miss Brent, been placed in possession of a most valuable letter, probably the last letter written by the unhappy gentleman. It is dated Monday, 3 December, the very eve of the murder, and was addressed to her at Florence, and has now, after some delay, followed her back to London where the sad news unexpectedly brought her. It is a letter couched, on the whole, in the most hopeful spirit, and speaks in detail of his schemes. Of course there are things in it not meant for the ears of the public, but there can be no harm in transcribing an important passage:—

"'You seem to have imbibed the idea that the East-end is a kind of Golgotha, and this despite that the books out of which you probably got it are carefully labelled "Fiction." Lamb says somewhere that we think of the "Dark Ages" as literally without sunlight, and so I fancy people like you, dear, think of the "East-end" as a mixture of mire, misery, and murder. How's that for alliteration? Why, within five minutes' walk of me there are the loveliest houses, with gardens back and front, inhabited by very fine people and furniture. Many of my university friends' mouths would water if they knew the income of some of the shopkeepers in the High Road.

"'The rich people about here may not be so fashionable as those in Kensington and Bayswater, but they are every bit as stupid and materialistic. I don't deny, Lucy, I do have my black moments, and I do sometimes pine to get away from all this to the lands of sun and lotus-eating. But, on the whole, I am too busy even to dream of dreaming. My real black moments are when I doubt if I am really doing any good. But yet on the whole my conscience or my self-conceit tells me that I am. If one cannot do much with the mass, there is at least the consolation of doing good to the individual. And, after all, is it not enough to have been an influence for good over one or two human souls? There are quite fine characters hereabout—especially in the women—natures capable not only of self-sacrifice, but of delicacy of sentiment. To have learnt to know of such, to have been of service to one or two of such—is not this ample return? I could not get to St. James's Hall to hear your friend's symphony at the Henschel concert. I have been reading Mme. Blavatsky's latest book, and getting quite interested in occult philosophy. Unfortunately I have to do all my reading in bed, and I don't find the book as soothing a soporific as most new books. For keeping one awake I find Theosophy as bad as toothache....'"

"The Big Bow Mystery Solved

"Sir,—I wonder if any one besides myself has been struck by the incredible bad taste of Mr. Grodman's letter in your last issue. That he, a former servant of the Department, should publicly insult and run it down can only be charitably explained by the supposition that his judgment is failing him in his old age. In view of this letter, are the relatives of the deceased justified in entrusting him with any private documents? It is, no doubt, very good of him to undertake to avenge one whom he seems snobbishly anxious to claim as a friend; but, all things considered, should not his letter have been headed 'The Big Bow Mystery Shelved'? I enclose my card, and am, sir,

"Your obedient servant,

"Scotland Yard."

George Grodman read this letter with annoyance, and crumpling up the paper, murmured scornfully, "Edward Wimp!"

V

"Yes, but what will become of the Beautiful?" said Denzil Cantercot.

"Hang the Beautiful!" said Peter Crowl, as if he were on the committee of the Academy. "Give me the True."

Denzil did nothing of the sort. He didn't happen to have it about him.

Denzil Cantercot stood smoking a cigarette in his landlord's shop, and imparting an air of distinction and an agreeable aroma to the close leathery atmosphere. Crowl cobbled away, talking to his tenant without raising his eyes. He was a small, big-headed, sallow, sad-eyed man, with a greasy apron. Denzil was wearing a heavy overcoat with a fur collar. He was never seen without it in public during the winter. In private he removed it and sat in his shirt sleeves. Crowl was a thinker, or thought he was—which seems to involve original thinking anyway. His hair was thinning rapidly at the top, as if his brain was struggling to get as near as possible to the realities of things. He prided himself on having no fads. Few men are without some foible or hobby; Crowl felt almost lonely at times in his superiority. He was a Vegetarian, a Secularist, a Blue Ribbonite, a Republican, and an Anti-tobacconist. Meat was a fad. Drink was a fad. Religion was a fad. Monarchy was a fad. Tobacco was a fad. "A plain man like me," Crowl used to say, "can live without fads." "A plain man" was Crowl's catchword. When of a Sunday morning he stood on Mile-end Waste, which was opposite his shop—and held forth to the crowd on the evils of kings, priests, and mutton chops, the "plain man" turned up at intervals like the "theme" of a symphonic movement. "I am only a plain man and I want to know." It was a phrase that sabred the spider-webs of logical refinement, and held them up scornfully on the point. When Crowl went for a little recreation in Victoria Park on Sunday afternoons, it was with this phrase that he invariably routed the supernaturalists. Crowl knew his Bible better than most ministers, and always carried a minutely printed copy in his pocket, dog's-eared to mark contradictions in the text. The second chapter of Jeremiah says one thing; the first chapter of Corinthians says another. Two contradictory statements may both be true, but "I am only a plain man, and I want to know." Crowl spent a large part of his time in setting "the word against the word." Cock-fighting affords its votaries no acuter pleasure than Crowl derived from setting two texts by the ears. Crowl had a metaphysical genius which sent his Sunday morning disciples frantic with admiration, and struck the enemy dumb with dismay. He had discovered, for instance, that the Deity could not move, owing to already filling all space. He was also the first to invent, for the confusion of the clerical, the crucial case of a saint dying at the Antipodes contemporaneously with another in London. Both went skyward to heaven, yet the two travelled in directly opposite directions. In all eternity they would never meet. Which, then, got to heaven? Or was there no such place? "I am only a plain man, and I want to know."

Preserve us our open spaces; they exist to testify to the incurable interest of humanity in the Unknown and the Misunderstood. Even 'Arry is capable of five minutes' attention to speculative theology, if 'Arriet isn't in a 'urry.

Peter Crowl was not sorry to have a lodger like Denzil Cantercot, who, though a man of parts and thus worth powder and shot, was so hopelessly wrong on all subjects under the sun. In only one point did Peter Crowl agree with Denzil Cantercot—he admired Denzil Cantercot secretly. When he asked him for the True—which was about twice a day on the average—he didn't really expect to get it from him. He knew that Denzil was a poet.

"The Beautiful," he went on, "is a thing that only appeals to men like you. The True is for all men. The majority have the first claim. Till then you poets must stand aside. The True and the Useful—that's what we want. The Good of Society is the only test of things. Everything stands or falls by the Good of Society."

"The Good of Society!" echoed Denzil, scornfully. "What's the good of Society? The Individual is before all. The mass must be sacrificed to the Great Man. Otherwise the Great Man will be sacrificed to the mass. Without great men there would be no art. Without art life would be a blank."

"Ah, but we should fill it up with bread and butter," said Peter Crowl.

"Yes, it is bread and butter that kills the Beautiful," said Denzil Cantercot, bitterly. "Many of us start by following the butterfly through the verdant meadows, but we turn aside—"

"To get the grub," chuckled Peter, cobbling away.

"Peter, if you make a jest of everything, I'll not waste my time on you."

Denzil's wild eyes flashed angrily. He shook his long hair. Life was very serious to him. He never wrote comic verse intentionally.

There are three reasons why men of genius have long hair. One is, that they forget it is growing. The second is, that they like it. The third is, that it comes cheaper; they wear it long for the same reason that they wear their hats long.

Owing to this peculiarity of genius, you may get quite a reputation for lack of twopence. The economic reason did not apply to Denzil, who could always get credit with the profession on the strength of his appearance. Therefore, when street arabs vocally commanded him to get his hair cut, they were doing no service to barbers. Why does all the world watch over barbers and conspire to promote their interests? Denzil would have told you it was not to serve the barbers, but to gratify the crowd's instinctive resentment of originality. In his palmy days Denzil had been an editor, but he no more thought of turning his scissors against himself than of swallowing his paste. The efficacy of hair has changed since the days of Samson, otherwise Denzil would have been a Hercules instead of a long, thin, nervous man, looking too brittle and delicate to be used even for a pipe-cleaner. The narrow oval of his face sloped to a pointed, untrimmed beard. His linen was reproachable, his dingy boots were down at heel, and his cocked hat was drab with dust. Such are the effects of a love for the Beautiful.

Peter Crowl was impressed with Denzil's condemnation of flippancy, and he hastened to turn off the joke.

"I'm quite serious," he said. "Butterflies are no good to nothing or nobody; caterpillars at least save the birds from starving."

"Just like your view of things, Peter," said Denzil. "Good morning, madam." This to Mrs. Crowl, to whom he removed his hat with elaborate courtesy.

Mrs. Crowl grunted and looked at her husband with a note of interrogation in each eye. For some seconds Crowl stuck to his last, endeavouring not to see the question. He shifted uneasily on his stool. His wife coughed grimly. He looked up, saw her towering over him, and helplessly shook his head in a horizontal direction. It was wonderful how Mrs. Crowl towered over Mr. Crowl, even when he stood up in his shoes. She measured half an inch less. It was quite an optical illusion.

"Mr. Crowl," said Mrs. Crowl, "then I'll tell him."

"No, no, my dear, not yet," faltered Peter, helplessly; "leave it to me."

"I've left it to you long enough. You'll never do nothing. If it was a question of provin' to a lot of chuckleheads that Jollygee and Genesis, or some other dead and gone Scripture folk that don't consarn no mortal soul, used to contradict each other, your tongue'ud run thirteen to the dozen. But when it's a matter of takin' the bread out o' the mouths o' your own children, you ain't got no more to say for yourself than a lamp-post. Here's a man stayin' with you for weeks and weeks—eatin' and drinkin' the flesh off your bones—without payin' a far—"

"Hush, hush, mother; it's all right," said poor Crowl, red as fire.

Denzil looked at her dreamily. "Is it possible you are alluding to me, Mrs. Crowl?" he said.

"Who then should I be alludin' to, Mr. Cantercot? Here's seven weeks come and gone, and not a blessed 'aypenny have I—"

"My dear Mrs. Crowl," said Denzil, removing his cigarette from his mouth with a pained air, "why reproach me for your neglect?"

"My neglect! I like that!"

"I don't," said Denzil more sharply. "If you had sent me in the bill you would have had the money long ago. How do you expect me to think of these details?"

"We ain't so grand down here. People pays their way—they don't get no bills" said Mrs. Crowl, accentuating the word with infinite scorn.

Peter hammered away at a nail, as though to drown his spouse's voice.

"It's three pounds fourteen and eightpence, if you're so anxious to know," Mrs. Crowl resumed. "And there ain't a woman in the Mile End Road as 'ud a-done it cheaper, with bread at fourpence threefarden a quartern and landlords clamburin' for rent every Monday morning almost afore the sun's up and folks draggin' and slidderin' on till their shoes is only fit to throw after brides and Christmas comin' and sevenpence a week for schoolin'!"

Peter winced under the last item. He had felt it coming—like Christmas. His wife and he parted company on the question of Free Education. Peter felt that, having brought nine children into the world, it was only fair he should pay a penny a week for each of those old enough to bear educating. His better half argued that, having so many children, they ought in reason to be exempted. Only people who had few children could spare the penny. But the one point on which the cobbler-sceptic of the Mile End Road got his way was this of the fees. It was a question of conscience, and Mrs. Crowl had never made application for their remission, though she often slapped her children in vexation instead. They were used to slapping, and when nobody else slapped them they slapped one another. They were bright, ill-mannered brats, who pestered their parents and worried their teachers, and were as happy as the Road was long.

"Bother the school fees!" Peter retorted, vexed. "Mr. Cantercot's not responsible for your children."

"I should hope not, indeed, Mr. Crowl," Mrs. Crowl said sternly. "I'm ashamed of you." And with that she flounced out of the shop into the back parlour.

"It's all right," Peter called after her soothingly. "The money'll be all right, mother."

In lower circles it is customary to call your wife your mother; in somewhat superior circles it is the fashion to speak of her as "the wife," as you speak of "the Stock Exchange," or "the Thames," without claiming any peculiar property. Instinctively men are ashamed of being moral and domesticated.

Denzil puffed his cigarette, unembarrassed. Peter bent attentively over his work, making nervous stabs with his awl. There was a long silence. An organ-grinder played a waltz outside, unregarded; and, failing to annoy anybody, moved on. Denzil lit another cigarette. The dirty-faced clock on the wall chimed twelve.

"What do you think," said Crowl, "of Republics?"

"They are low," Denzil replied. "Without a Monarch there is no visible incarnation of Authority."

"What! do you call Queen Victoria visible?"

"Peter, do you want to drive me from the house? Leave frivolousness to women, whose minds are only large enough for domestic difficulties. Republics are low. Plato mercifully kept the poets out of his. Republics are not congenial soil for poetry."

"What nonsense! If England dropped its fad of Monarchy and became a Republic to-morrow, do you mean to say that—?"

"I mean to say there would be no Poet Laureate to begin with."

"Who's fribbling now, you or me, Cantercot? But I don't care a button-hook about poets, present company always excepted. I'm only a plain man, and I want to know where's the sense of givin' any one person authority over everybody else?"

"Ah, that's what Tom Mortlake used to say. Wait till you're in power, Peter, with trade-union money to control, and working men bursting to give you flying angels and to carry you aloft, like a banner, huzzahing."

"Ah, that's because he's head and shoulders above 'em already," said Crowl, with a flash in his sad grey eyes. "Still, it don't prove that I'd talk any different. And I think you're quite wrong about his being spoilt. Tom's a fine fellow—a man every inch of him, and that's a good many. I don't deny he has his weaknesses, and there was a time when he stood in this very shop and denounced that poor dead Constant. 'Crowl,' said he, 'that man'll do mischief. I don't like these kid-glove philanthropists mixing themselves up in practical labour disputes they don't understand.'"

Denzil whistled involuntarily. It was a piece of news.

"I dare say," continued Crowl, "he's a bit jealous of anybody's interference with his influence. But in this case the jealousy did wear off, you see, for the poor fellow and he got quite pals, as everybody knows. Tom's not the man to hug a prejudice. However, all that don't prove nothing against Republics. Look at the Czar and the Jews. I'm only a plain man, but I wouldn't live in Russia not for—not for all the leather in it! An Englishman, taxed as he is to keep up his Fad of Monarchy, is at least king in his own castle, whoever bosses it at Windsor. Excuse me a minute, the missus is callin'."

"Excuse me a minute. I'm going, and I want to say before I go—I feel it only right you should know at once—that after what has passed to-day I can never be on the same footing here as in the—shall I say pleasant?—days of yore."

"Oh, no, Cantercot. Don't say that; don't say that!" pleaded the little cobbler.

"Well, shall I say unpleasant, then?"

"No, no, Cantercot. Don't misunderstand me. Mother has been very much put to it lately to rub along. You see she has such a growing family. It grows—daily. But never mind her. You pay whenever you've got the money."

Denzil shook his head. "It cannot be. You know when I came here first I rented your top room and boarded myself. Then I learnt to know you. We talked together. Of the Beautiful. And the Useful. I found you had no soul. But you were honest, and I liked you. I went so far as to take my meals with your family. I made myself at home in your back parlour. But the vase has been shattered (I do not refer to that on the mantel-piece), and though the scent of the roses may cling to it still, it can be pieced together—nevermore." He shook his hair sadly and shambled out of the shop. Crowl would have gone after him, but Mrs. Crowl was still calling, and ladies must have the precedence in all polite societies.

Cantercot went straight—or as straight as his loose gait permitted—to 46 Glover Street, and knocked at the door. Grodman's factotum opened it. She was a pock-marked person, with a brickdust complexion and a coquettish manner.

"Oh! Here we are again!" she said vivaciously.

"Don't talk like a clown," Cantercot snapped. "Is Mr. Grodman in?"

"No, you've put him out," growled the gentleman himself, suddenly appearing in his slippers. "Come in. What the devil have you been doing with yourself since the inquest? Drinking again?"

"I've sworn off. Haven't touched a drop since—"

"The murder?"

"Eh?" said Denzil Cantercot, startled. "What do you mean?"

"What I say. Since December 4. I reckon everything from that murder, now, as they reckon longitude from Greenwich."

"Oh," said Denzil Cantercot.

"Let me see. Nearly a fortnight. What a long time to keep away from Drink—and Me."

"I don't know which is worse," said Denzil, irritated. "You both steal away my brains."

"Indeed?" said Grodman, with an amused smile. "Well, it's only petty pilfering, after all. What's put salt on your wounds?"

"The twenty-fourth edition of my book."

"Whose book?"

"Well, your book. You must be making piles of money out of Criminals I have Caught."

"'Criminals I have Caught,'" corrected Grodman. "My dear Denzil, how often am I to point out that I went through the experiences that make the backbone of my book, not you? In each case I cooked the criminal's goose. Any journalist could have supplied the dressing."

"The contrary. The journeymen of journalism would have left the truth naked. You yourself could have done that—for there is no man to beat you at cold, lucid, scientific statement. But I idealised the bare facts and lifted them into the realm of poetry and literature. The twenty-fourth edition of the book attests my success."

"Rot! The twenty-fourth edition was all owing to the murder. Did you do that?"

"You take one up so sharply, Mr. Grodman," said Denzil, changing his tone.

"No—I've retired," laughed Grodman.

Denzil did not reprove the ex-detective's flippancy. He even laughed a little.

"Well, give me another fiver, and I'll cry 'quits.' I'm in debt."

"Not a penny. Why haven't you been to see me since the murder? I had to write that letter to the Pell Mell Press myself. You might have earned a crown."

"I've had writer's cramp, and couldn't do your last job. I was coming to tell you so on the morning of the—"

"Murder. So you said at the inquest."

"It's true."

"Of course. Weren't you on your oath? It was very zealous of you to get up so early to tell me. In which hand did you have this cramp?"

"Why, in the right of course."

"And you couldn't write with your left?"

"I don't think I could even hold a pen."

"Or any other instrument, mayhap. What had you been doing to bring it on?"

"Writing too much. That is the only possible cause."

"Oh! I didn't know. Writing what?"

Denzil hesitated. "An epic poem."

"No wonder you're in debt. Will a sovereign get you out of it?"

"No; it wouldn't be the least use to me."

"Here it is, then."

Denzil took the coin and his hat.

"Aren't you going to earn it, you beggar? Sit down and write something for me."

Denzil got pen and paper, and took his place.

"What do you want me to write?"

"Your Epic Poem."

Denzil started and flushed. But he set to work. Grodman leaned back in his arm-chair and laughed, studying the poet's grave face.

Denzil wrote three lines and paused.

"Can't remember any more? Well, read me the start."

Denzil read:—

"Of man's first disobedience and the fruit
Of that forbidden tree whose mortal taste
Brought death into the world—"

"Hold on!" cried Grodman. "What morbid subjects you choose, to be sure!"

"Morbid! Why, Milton chose the same subject!"

"Blow Milton. Take yourself off—you and your Epics."

Denzil went. The pock-marked person opened the street door for him.

"When am I to have that new dress, dear?" she whispered coquettishly.

"I have no money, Jane," he said shortly.

"You have a sovereign."

Denzil gave her the sovereign, and slammed the door viciously. Grodman overheard their whispers, and laughed silently. His hearing was acute. Jane had first introduced Denzil to his acquaintance about two years ago, when he spoke of getting an amanuensis, and the poet had been doing odd jobs for him ever since. Grodman argued that Jane had her reasons. Without knowing them, he got a hold over both. There was no one, he felt, he could not get a hold over. All men—and women—have something to conceal, and you have only to pretend to know what it is. Thus Grodman, who was nothing if not scientific.

Denzil Cantercot shambled home thoughtfully, and abstractedly took his place at the Crowl dinner-table.

VI

Mrs. Crowl surveyed Denzil Cantercot so stonily and cut him his beef so savagely that he said grace when the dinner was over. Peter fed his metaphysical genius on tomatoes. He was tolerant enough to allow his family to follow their Fads; but no savoury smells ever tempted him to be false to his vegetable loves. Besides, meat might have reminded him too much of his work. There is nothing like leather, but Bow beefsteaks occasionally come very near it.

After dinner Denzil usually indulged in poetic reverie. But to-day he did not take his nap. He went out at once to "raise the wind." But there was a dead calm everywhere. In vain he asked for an advance at the office of the Mile End Mirror, to which he contributed scathing leaderettes about vestrymen. In vain he trudged to the City and offered to write the Ham and Eggs Gazette an essay on the modern methods of bacon-curing. Denzil knew a great deal about the breeding and slaughtering of pigs, smoke-lofts and drying processes, having for years dictated the policy of the New Pork Herald in these momentous matters. Denzil also knew a great deal about many other esoteric matters, including weaving machines, the manufacture of cabbage leaves and snuff, and the inner economy of drain-pipes. He had written for the trade papers since boyhood. But there is great competition on these papers. So many men of literary gifts know all about the intricate technicalities of manufactures and markets, and are eager to set the trade right. Grodman perhaps hardly allowed sufficiently for the step backwards that Denzil made when he devoted his whole time for months to Criminals I have Caught. It was as damaging as a debauch. For when your rivals are pushing forwards, to stand still is to go back.

In despair Denzil shambled toilsomely to Bethnal Green. He paused before the window of a little tobacconist's shop, wherein was displayed a placard announcing

"PLOTS FOR SALE."

The announcement went on to state that a large stock of plots was to be obtained on the premises—embracing sensational plots, humorous plots, love plots, religious plots, and poetic plots; also complete manuscripts, original novels, poems, and tales. Apply within.

It was a very dirty-looking shop, with begrimed bricks and blackened woodwork. The window contained some musty old books, an assortment of pipes and tobacco, and a large number of the vilest daubs unhung, painted in oil on Academy boards, and unframed. These were intended for landscapes, as you could tell from the titles. The most expensive was "Chingford Church," and it was marked IS. 9d. The others ran from 6d. to IS. 3d., and were mostly representations of Scottish scenery—a loch with mountains in the background, with solid reflections in the water and a tree in the foreground. Sometimes the tree would be in the background. Then the loch would be in the foreground. Sky and water were intensely blue in all. The name of the collection was "Original oil-paintings done by hand." Dust lay thick upon everything, as if carefully shovelled on; and the proprietor looked as if he slept in his shop-window at night without taking his clothes off. He was a gaunt man with a red nose, long but scanty black locks covered by a smoking-cap, and a luxuriant black moustache. He smoked a long clay pipe, and had the air of a broken-down operatic villain.

"Ah, good afternoon, Mr. Cantercot," he said, rubbing his hands, half from cold, half from usage; "what have you brought me?"

"Nothing," said Denzil, "but if you will lend me a sovereign I'll do you a stunner."

The operatic villain shook his locks, his eyes full of pawky cunning. "If you did it after that, it would be a stunner."

What the operatic villain did with these plots, and who bought them, Cantercot never knew nor cared to know. Brains are cheap to-day, and Denzil was glad enough to find a customer.

"Surely you've known me long enough to trust me," he cried.

"Trust is dead," said the operatic villain, puffing away.

"So is Queen Anne," cried the irritated poet. His eyes took a dangerous hunted look. Money he must have. But the operatic villain was inflexible. No plot, no supper.

Poor Denzil went out flaming. He knew not where to turn. Temporarily he turned on his heel again and stared despairingly at the shop-window. Again he read the legend

"PLOTS FOR SALE."

He stared so long at this that it lost its meaning. When the sense of the words suddenly flashed upon him again, they bore a new significance. He went in meekly, and borrowed fourpence of the operatic villain. Then he took the 'bus for Scotland Yard. There was a not ill-looking servant girl in the 'bus. The rhythm of the vehicle shaped itself into rhymes in his brain. He forgot all about his situation and his object. He had never really written an epic—except "Paradise Lost"—but he composed lyrics about wine and women and often wept to think how miserable he was. But nobody ever bought anything of him, except articles on bacon-curing or attacks on vestrymen. He was a strange, wild creature, and the wench felt quite pretty under his ardent gaze. It almost hypnotised her, though, and she looked down at her new French kid boots to escape it.

At Scotland Yard Denzil asked for Edward Wimp. Edward Wimp was not on view. Like kings and editors, detectives are difficult of approach—unless you are a criminal, when you cannot see anything of them at all. Denzil knew of Edward Wimp, principally because of Grodman's contempt for his successor. Wimp was a man of taste and culture. Grodman's interests were entirely concentrated on the problems of logic and evidence. Books about these formed his sole reading; for belles lettres he cared not a straw. Wimp, with his flexible intellect, had a great contempt for Grodman and his slow, laborious, ponderous, almost Teutonic methods. Worse, he almost threatened to eclipse the radiant tradition of Grodman by some wonderfully ingenious bits of workmanship. Wimp was at his greatest in collecting circumstantial evidence; in putting two and two together to make five. He would collect together a number of dark and disconnected data and flash across them the electric light of some unifying hypothesis in a way which would have done credit to a Darwin or a Faraday. An intellect which might have served to unveil the secret workings of nature was subverted to the protection of a capitalistic civilisation.

By the assistance of a friendly policeman, whom the poet magnetised into the belief that his business was a matter of life and death, Denzil obtained the great detective's private address. It was near King's Cross. By a miracle Wimp was at home in the afternoon. He was writing when Denzil was ushered up three pairs of stairs into his presence, but he got up and flashed the bull's-eye of his glance upon the visitor.

"Mr. Denzil Cantercot, I believe," said Wimp.

Denzil started. He had not sent up his name, merely describing himself as a gentleman.

"That is my name," he murmured.

"You were one of the witnesses at the inquest on the body of the late Arthur Constant. I have your evidence there." He pointed to a file. "Why have you come to give fresh evidence?"

Again Denzil started, flushing in addition this time. "I want money," he said, almost involuntarily.

"Sit down." Denzil sat. Wimp stood.

Wimp was young and fresh-coloured. He had a Roman nose, and was smartly dressed. He had beaten Grodman by discovering the wife Heaven meant for him. He had a bouncing boy, who stole jam out of the pantry without any one being the wiser. Wimp did what work he could do at home in a secluded study at the top of the house. Outside his chamber of horrors he was the ordinary husband of commerce. He adored his wife, who thought poorly of his intellect but highly of his heart. In domestic difficulties Wimp was helpless. He could not tell even whether the servant's "character" was forged or genuine. Probably he could not level himself to such petty problems. He was like the senior wrangler who has forgotten how to do quadratics, and has to solve equations of the second degree by the calculus.

"How much money do you want?" he asked.

"I do not make bargains," Denzil replied, his calm come back by this time. "I came here to tender you a suggestion. It struck me that you might offer me a fiver for my trouble. Should you do so, I shall not refuse it."

"You shall not refuse it—if you deserve it."

"Good. I will come to the point at once. My suggestion concerns—Tom Mortlake."

Denzil threw out the name as if it were a torpedo. Wimp did not move.

"Tom Mortlake," went on Denzil, looking disappointed, "had a sweetheart." He paused impressively.

Wimp said, "Yes?"

"Where is that sweetheart now?"

"Where, indeed?"

"You know about her disappearance?"

"You have just informed me of it."

"Yes, she is gone—without a trace. She went about a fortnight before Mr. Constant's murder."

"Murder? How do you know It was murder?"

"Mr. Grodman says so," said Denzil, startled again.

"H'm! Isn't that rather a proof that it was suicide? Well, go on."

"About a fortnight before the suicide, Jessie Dymond disappeared. So they tell me in Stepney Green, where she lodged and worked."

"What was she?"

"She was a dressmaker. She had a wonderful talent. Quite fashionable ladies got to know of it. One of her dresses was presented at Court. I think the lady forgot to pay for it; so Jessie's landlady said."

"Did she live alone?"

"She had no parents, but the house was respectable."

"Good-looking, I suppose?"

"As a poet's dream."

"As yours, for instance?"

"I am a poet; I dream."

"You dream you are a poet. Well, well! She was engaged to Mortlake?"

"Oh, yes! They made no secret of it. The engagement was an old one. When he was earning 36s. a week as a compositor, they were saving up to buy a home. He worked at Railton and Hockes who print the New Pork Herald. I used to take my 'copy' into the comps' room, and one day the Father of the Chapel told me all about 'Mortlake and his young woman.' Ye gods! How times are changed! Two years ago Mortlake had to struggle with my calligraphy—now he is in with all the nobs, and goes to the 'At Homes' of the aristocracy."

"Radical M.P.'s," murmured Wimp, smiling.

"While I am still barred from the dazzling drawing-rooms, where beauty and intellect foregather. A mere artisan! A manual labourer!" Denzil's eyes flashed angrily. He rose with excitement. "They say he always was a jabberer in the composing-room, and he has jabbered himself right out of it and into a pretty good thing. He didn't have much to say about the crimes of capital when he was set up to second the toast of 'Railton and Hockes' at the beanfeast."

"Toast and butter, toast and butter," said Wimp, genially. "I shouldn't blame a man for serving the two together, Mr. Cantercot."

Denzil forced a laugh. "Yes; but consistency's my motto. I like to see the royal soul immaculate, unchanging, immovable by fortune. Anyhow, when better times came for Mortlake the engagement still dragged on. He did not visit her so much. This last autumn he saw very little of her."

"How do you know?"

"I—I was often in Stepney Green. My business took me past the house of an evening. Sometimes there was no light in her room. That meant she was downstairs gossiping with the landlady."

"She might have been out with Tom?"

"No, sir; I knew Tom was on the platform somewhere or other. He was working up to all hours organising the eight hours' working movement."

"A very good reason for relaxing his sweethearting."

"It was. He never went to Stepney Green on a week night."

"But you always did."

"No—not every night."

"You didn't go in?"

"Never. She wouldn't permit my visits. She was a girl of strong character. She always reminded me of Flora Macdonald."

"Another lady of your acquaintance?"

"A lady I know better than the shadows who surround me, who is more real to me than the women who pester me for the price of apartments. Jessie Dymond, too, was of the race of heroines. Her eyes were clear blue, two wells with Truth at the bottom of each. When I looked into those eyes my own were dazzled. They were the only eyes I could never make dreamy." He waved his hand as if making a pass with it. "It was she who had the influence over me."

"You knew her, then?"

"Oh, yes. I knew Tom from the old New Pork Herald days, and when I first met him with Jessie hanging on his arm he was quite proud to introduce her to a poet. When he got on he tried to shake me off."

"You should have repaid him what you borrowed."

"It—it—was only a trifle," stammered Denzil.

"Yes, but the world turns on trifles," said the wise Wimp.

"The world is itself a trifle," said the pensive poet. "The Beautiful alone is deserving of our regard."

"And when the Beautiful was not gossiping with her landlady, did she gossip with you as you passed the door?"

"Alas, no! She sat in her room reading, and cast a shadow—"

"On your life?"

"No; on the blind."

"Always one shadow?"

"No, sir. Once or twice, two."

"Ah, you had been drinking."

"On my life, not. I have sworn off the treacherous wine-cup."

"That's right. Beer is bad for poets. It makes their feet shaky. Whose was the second shadow?"

"A man's."

"Naturally. Mortlake's, perhaps."

"Impossible. He was still striking eight hours."

"You found out whose shadow? You didn't leave a shadow of doubt?"

"No; I waited till the substance came out."

"It was Arthur Constant."

"You are a magician! You—you terrify me. Yes, it was he."

"Only once or twice, you say?"

"I didn't keep watch over them."

"No, no, of course not. You only passed casually. I understand you thoroughly."

Denzil did not feel comfortable at the assertion.

"What did he go there for?" Wimp went on.

"I don't know. I'd stake my soul on Jessie's honour."

"You might double your stake without risk."

"Yes, I might! I would! You see her with my eyes."

"For the moment they are the only ones available. When was the last time you saw the two together?"

"About the middle of November."

"Mortlake knew nothing of the meetings?"

"I don't know. Perhaps he did. Mr. Constant had probably enlisted her in his social mission work. I knew she was one of the attendants at the big children's tea in the Great Assembly Hall early in November. He treated her quite like a lady. She was the only attendant who worked with her hands."

"The others carried the cups on their feet, I suppose."

"No; how could that be? My meaning is that all the other attendants were real ladies, and Jessie was only an amateur, so to speak. There was no novelty for her in handing kids cups of tea. I dare say she had helped her landlady often enough at that—there's quite a bushel of brats below stairs. It's almost as bad as at friend Crowl's. Jessie was a real brick. But perhaps Tom didn't know her value. Perhaps he didn't like Constant to call on her, and it led to a quarrel. Anyhow, she's disappeared, like the snowfall on the river. There's not a trace. The landlady, who was such a friend of hers that Jessie used to make up her stuff into dresses for nothing, tells me that she's dreadfully annoyed at not having been left the slightest clue to her late tenant's whereabouts."

"You have been making inquiries on your own account apparently?"

"Only of the landlady. Jessie never even gave her the week's notice, but paid her in lieu of it, and left immediately. The landlady told me I could have knocked her down with a feather. Unfortunately, I wasn't there to do it, or I should certainly have knocked her down for not keeping her eyes open better. She says if she had only had the least suspicion beforehand that the minx (she dared to call Jessie a minx) was going, she'd have known where, or her name would have been somebody else's. And yet she admits that Jessie was looking ill and worried. Stupid old hag!"

"A woman of character," murmured the detective.

"Didn't I tell you so?" cried Denzil, eagerly. "Another girl would have let out that she was going. But no, not a word. She plumped down the money and walked out. The landlady ran upstairs. None of Jessie's things were there. She must have quietly sold them off, or transferred them to the new place. I never in my life met a girl who so thoroughly knew her own mind or had a mind so worth knowing. She always reminded me of the Maid of Saragossa."

"Indeed! And when did she leave?"

"On the l9th of November."

"Mortlake of course knows where she is?"

"I can't say. Last time I was at the house to inquire—it was at the end of November—he hadn't been seen there for six weeks. He wrote to her, of course, sometimes—the landlady knew his writing."

Wimp looked Denzil straight in the eyes, and said, "You mean, of course, to accuse Mortlake of the murder of Mr. Constant?"

"N-n-no, not at all," stammered Denzil, "only you know what Mr. Grodman wrote to the Pell Mell. The more we know about Mr. Constant's life the more we shall know about the manner of his death. I thought my information would be valuable to you, and I brought it."

"And why didn't you take it to Mr. Grodman?"

"Because I thought it wouldn't be valuable to me."

"You wrote Criminals I have Caught?"

"How—how do you know that?" Wimp was startling him to-day with a vengeance.

"Your style, my dear Mr. Cantercot. The unique, noble style."

"Yes, I was afraid it would betray me," said Denzil. "And since you know, I may tell you that Grodman's a mean curmudgeon. What does he want with all that money and those houses—a man with no sense of the Beautiful? He'd have taken my information, and given me more kicks than ha'pence for it, so to speak."

"Yes, he is a shrewd man after all. I don't see anything valuable in your evidence against Mortlake."

"No!" said Denzil in a disappointed tone, and fearing he was going to be robbed. "Not when Mortlake was already jealous of Mr. Constant, who was a sort of rival organiser, unpaid! A kind of blackleg doing the work cheaper—nay, for nothing."

"Did Mortlake tell you he was jealous?" said Wimp, a shade of sarcastic contempt piercing through his tones.

"Oh, yes! He said to me, 'That man will work mischief. I don't like your kid-glove philanthropists meddling in matters they don't understand.'"

"Those were his very words?"

"His ipsissima verba."

"Very well. I have your address in my files. Here is a sovereign for you."

"Only one sovereign! It's not the least use to me."

"Very well. It's of great use to me. I have a wife to keep."

"I haven't," said Denzil, with a sickly smile, "so perhaps I can manage on it after all." He took his hat and the sovereign.

Outside the door he met a rather pretty servant just bringing in some tea to her master. He nearly upset her tray at sight of her. She seemed more amused at the rencontre than he.

"Good afternoon, dear," she said coquettishly. "You might let me have that sovereign. I do so want a new Sunday bonnet."

Denzil gave her the sovereign, and slammed the hall-door viciously when he got to the bottom of the stairs. He seemed to be walking arm-in-arm with the long arm of coincidence. Wimp did not hear the duologue. He was already busy on his evening's report to headquarters. The next day Denzil had a body-guard wherever he went. It might have gratified his vanity had he known it. But to-night he was yet unattended, so no one noted that he went to 46 Glover Street, after the early Crowl supper. He could not help going. He wanted to get another sovereign. He also itched to taunt Grodman. Not succeeding in the former object, he felt the road open for the second.

"Do you still hope to discover the Bow murderer?" he asked the old bloodhound.

"I can lay my hand on him now," Grodman announced curtly.

Denzil hitched his chair back involuntarily. He found conversation with detectives as lively as playing at skittles with bombshells. They got on his nerves terribly, these undemonstrative gentlemen with no sense of the Beautiful.

"But why don't you give him up to justice?" he murmured.

"Ah—it has to be proved yet. But it is only a matter of time."

"Oh!" said Denzil, "and shall I write the story for you?"

"No. You will not live long enough."

Denzil turned white. "Nonsense! I am years younger than you," he gasped.

"Yes," said Grodman, "but you drink so much."

VII

When Wimp invited Grodman to eat his Christmas plum-pudding at King's Cross, Grodman was only a little surprised. The two men were always overwhelmingly cordial when they met, in order to disguise their mutual detestation. When people really like each other, they make no concealment of their mutual contempt. In his letter to Grodman, Wimp said that he thought it might be nicer for him to keep Christmas in company than in solitary state. There seems to be a general prejudice in favour of Christmas numbers, and Grodman yielded to it. Besides, he thought that a peep at the Wimp domestic interior would be as good as a pantomime. He quite enjoyed the fun that was coming, for he knew that Wimp had not invited him out of mere "peace and goodwill."

There was only one other guest at the festive board. This was Wimp's wife's mother's mother, a lady of sweet seventy. Only a minority of mankind can obtain a grandmother-in-law by marrying, but Wimp was not unduly conceited. The old lady suffered from delusions. One of them was that she was a centenarian. She dressed for the part. It is extraordinary what pains ladies will take to conceal their age. Another of Wimp's grandmother-in-law's delusions was that Wimp had married to get her into the family. Not to frustrate his design, she always gave him her company on high-days and holidays. Wilfred Wimp—the little boy who stole the jam—was in great form at the Christmas dinner. The only drawback to his enjoyment was that its sweets needed no stealing. His mother presided over the platters, and thought how much cleverer Grodman was than her husband. When the pretty servant who waited on them was momentarily out of the room, Grodman had remarked that she seemed very inquisitive. This coincided with Mrs. Wimp's own convictions, though Mr. Wimp could never be brought to see anything unsatisfactory or suspicious about the girl, not even though there were faults in spelling in the "character" with which her last mistress had supplied her.

It was true that the puss had pricked up her ears when Denzil Cantercot's name was mentioned. Grodman saw it, and watched her, and fooled Wimp to the top of his bent. It was, of course, Wimp who introduced the poet's name, and he did it so casually that Grodman perceived at once that he wished to pump him. The idea that the rival bloodhound should come to him for confirmation of suspicions against his own pet jackal was too funny. It was almost as funny to Grodman that evidence of some sort should be obviously lying to hand in the bosom of Wimp's hand-maiden; so obviously that Wimp could not see it. Grodman enjoyed his Christmas dinner, secure that he had not found a successor after all. Wimp, for his part, contemptuously wondered at the way Grodman's thought hovered about Denzil without grazing the truth. A man constantly about him, too!

"Denzil is a man of genius," said Grodman. "And as such comes under the heading of Suspicious Characters. He has written an Epic Poem and read it to me. It is morbid from start to finish. There is 'death' in the third line. I dare say you know he polished up my book?" Grodman's artlessness was perfect.

"No. You surprise me," Wimp replied. "I'm sure he couldn't have done much to it. Look at your letter in the Pell Mell. Who wants more polish and refinement than that showed?"

"Ah, I didn't know you did me the honour of reading that."

"Oh, yes; we both read it," put in Mrs. Wimp. "I told Mr. Wimp it was very clever and cogent. After that quotation from the letter to the poor fellow's fiancée there could be no more doubt but that it was murder. Mr. Wimp was convinced by it too, weren't you, Edward?"

Edward coughed uneasily. It was a true statement, and therefore an indiscreet. Grodman would plume himself terribly. At this moment Wimp felt that Grodman had been right in remaining a bachelor. Grodman perceived the humour of the situation, and wore a curious, sub-mocking smile.

"On the day I was born," said Wimp's grand-mother-in-law, "over a hundred years ago, there was a babe murdered."—Wimp found himself wishing it had been she. He was anxious to get back to Cantercot. "Don't let us talk shop on Christmas Day," he said, smiling at Grodman. "Besides, murder isn't a very appropriate subject."

"No, it ain't," said Grodman. "How did we get on to it? Oh, yes—Denzil Cantercot. Ha! ha! ha! That's curious, for since Denzil revised Criminals I have Caught, his mind's running on nothing but murders. A poet's brain is easily turned."

Wimp's eye glittered with excitement and contempt for Grodman's blindness. In Grodman's eye there danced an amused scorn of Wimp; to the outsider his amusement appeared at the expense of the poet.

Having wrought his rival up to the highest pitch, Grodman slyly and suddenly unstrung him.

"How lucky for Denzil!" he said, still in the same naive, facetious Christmasy tone, "that he can prove an alibi in this Constant affair."

"An alibi!" gasped Wimp. "Really?"

"Oh, yes. He was with his wife, you know. She's my woman of all work, Jane. She happened to mention his being with her."

Jane had done nothing of the kind. After the colloquy he had overheard, Grodman had set himself to find out the relation between his two employees. By casually referring to Denzil as "your husband," he so startled the poor woman that she did not attempt to deny the bond. Only once did he use the two words, but he was satisfied. As to the alibi, he had not yet troubled her; but to take its existence for granted would upset and discomfort Wimp. For the moment that was triumph enough for Wimp's guest.

"Par," said Wilfred Wimp, "what's a alleybi? A marble?"

"No, my lad," said Grodman, "it means being somewhere else when you're supposed to be somewhere."

"Ah, playing truant," said Wilfred, self-consciously; his schoolmaster had often proved an alibi against him. "Then Denzil will be hanged."

Was it a prophecy? Wimp accepted it as such; as an oracle from the gods bidding him mistrust Grodman. Out of the mouths of little children issueth wisdom; sometimes even when they are not saying their lessons.

"When I was in my cradle, a century ago," said Wimp's grandmother-in-law, "men were hanged for stealing horses."

They silenced her with snapdragon performances.

Wimp was busy thinking how to get at Grodman's factotum.

Grodman was busy thinking how to get at Wimp's domestic.

Neither received any of the usual messages from the Christmas Bells.

The next day was sloppy and uncertain. A thin rain drizzled languidly. One can stand that sort of thing on a summer Bank Holiday; one expects it. But to have a bad December Bank Holiday is too much of a bad thing. Some steps should surely be taken to confuse the weather clerk's chronology. Once let him know that Bank Holiday is coming, and he writes to the company for more water. To-day his stock seemed low, and he was dribbling it out; at times the wintry sun would shine in a feeble, diluted way, and though the holiday-makers would have preferred to take their sunshine neat, they swarmed forth in their myriads whenever there was a ray of hope. But it was only dodging the raindrops; up went the umbrellas again, and the streets became meadows of ambulating mushrooms.

Denzil Cantercot sat in his fur overcoat at the open window, looking at the landscape in watercolours. He smoked an after-dinner cigarette, and spoke of the Beautiful. Crowl was with him. They were in the first floor front, Crowl's bedroom, which, from its view of the Mile End Road, was livelier than the parlour with its outlook on the backyard. Mrs. Crowl was an anti-tobacconist as regards the best bedroom; but Peter did not like to put the poet or his cigarette out. He felt there was something in common between smoke and poetry, over and above their being both Fads. Besides, Mrs. Crowl was sulking in the kitchen. She had been arranging for an excursion with Peter and the children to Victoria Park. (She had dreamed of the Crystal Palace, but Santa Claus had put no gifts in the cobbler's shoes.) Now she could not risk spoiling the feather in her bonnet. The nine brats expressed their disappointment by slapping one another on the staircases. Peter felt that Mrs. Crowl connected him in some way with the rainfall, and was unhappy. Was it not enough that he had been deprived of the pleasure of pointing out to a superstitious majority the mutual contradictions of Leviticus and the Song of Solomon? It was not often that Crowl could count on such an audience.

"And you still call Nature Beautiful?" he said to Denzil, pointing to the ragged sky and the dripping eaves. "Ugly old scare-crow!"

"Ugly she seems to-day," admitted Denzil. "But what is Ugliness but a higher form of Beauty? You have to look deeper into it to see it; such vision is the priceless gift of the few. To me this wan desolation of sighing rain is lovely as the sea-washed ruins of cities."

"Ah, but you wouldn't like to go out into it," said Peter Crowl. As he spoke the drizzle suddenly thickened into a torrent.

"We do not always kiss the woman we love."

"Speak for yourself, Denzil. I'm only a plain man, and I want to know if Nature isn't a Fad. Hallo, there goes Mortlake! Lord, a minute of this will soak him to the skin."

The labour leader was walking along with bowed head. He did not seem to mind the shower. It was some seconds before he even heard Crowl's invitation to him to take shelter. When he did hear it he shook his head.

"I know I can't offer you a drawing-room with duchesses stuck about it," said Peter, vexed.

Tom turned the handle of the shop door and went in. There was nothing in the world which now galled him more than the suspicion that he was stuck-up and wished to cut old friends. He picked his way through the nine brats who clung affectionately to his wet knees, dispersing them finally by a jet of coppers to scramble for. Peter met him on the stairs and shook his hand lovingly and admiringly, and took him into Mrs. Crowl's bedroom.

"Don't mind what I say, Tom. I'm only a plain man, and my tongue will say what comes uppermost! But it ain't from the soul, Tom, it ain't from the soul," said Peter, punning feebly, and letting a mirthless smile play over his sallow features. "You know Mr. Cantercot, I suppose? The Poet."

"Oh, yes; how do you do, Tom?" cried the Poet. "Seen the New Pork Herald lately? Not bad, those old times, eh?"

"No," said Tom, "I wish I was back in them."

"Nonsense, nonsense," said Peter, in much concern. "Look at the good you are doing to the working man. Look how you are sweeping away the Fads. Ah, it's a grand thing to be gifted, Tom. The idea of your chuckin' yourself away on a composin'-room! Manual labour is all very well for plain men like me, with no gift but just enough brains to see into the realities of things—to understand that we've got no soul and no immortality, and all that—and too selfish to look after anybody's comfort but my own and mother's and the kids'. But men like you and Cantercot—it ain't right that you should be peggin' away at low material things. Not that I think Cantercot's gospel any value to the masses. The Beautiful is all very well for folks who've got nothing else to think of, but give me the True. You're the man for my money, Mortlake. No reference to the funds, Tom, to which I contribute little enough, Heaven knows; though how a place can know anything, Heaven alone knows. You give us the Useful, Tom; that's what the world wants more than the Beautiful."

"Socrates said that the Useful is the Beautiful," said Denzil.

"That may be," said Peter, "but the Beautiful ain't the Useful."

"Nonsense!" said Denzil. "What about Jessie—I mean Miss Dymond? There's a combination for you. She always reminds me of Grace Darling. How is she, Tom?"

"She's dead!" snapped Tom.

"What?" Denzil turned as white as a Christmas ghost.

"It was in the papers," said Tom; "all about her and the lifeboat."

"Oh, you mean Grace Darling," said Denzil, visibly relieved. "I meant Miss Dymond."

"You needn't be so interested in her," said Tom surlily. "She don't appreciate it. Ah, the shower is over. I must be going."

"No, stay a little longer, Tom," pleaded Peter.

"I see a lot about you in the papers, but very little of your dear old phiz now. I can't spare the time to go and hear you. But I really must give myself a treat. When's your next show?"

"Oh, I am always giving shows," said Tom, smiling a little. "But my next big performance is on the twenty-first of January, when that picture of poor Mr. Constant is to be unveiled at the Bow Break o' Day Club. They have written to Gladstone and other big pots to come down. I do hope the old man accepts. A non-political gathering like this is the only occasion we could both speak at, and I have never been on the same platform with Gladstone."

He forgot his depression and ill-temper in the prospect, and spoke with more animation.

"No, I should hope not, Tom," said Peter. "What with his Fads about the Bible being a Rock, and Monarchy being the right thing, he is a most dangerous man to lead the Radicals. He never lays his axe to the root of anything—except oak trees."

"Mr. Cantycot!" It was Mrs. Crowl's voice that broke in upon the tirade. "There's a gentleman to see you." The astonishment Mrs. Crowl put into the "gentleman" was delightful. It was almost as good as a week's rent to her to give vent to her feelings. The controversial couple had moved away from the window when Tom entered, and had not noticed the immediate advent of another visitor who had spent his time profitably in listening to Mrs. Crowl before asking to see the presumable object of his visit.

"Ask him up if it's a friend of yours, Cantercot," said Peter. It was Wimp. Denzil was rather dubious as to the friendship, but he preferred to take Wimp diluted. "Mortlake's upstairs," he said; "will you come up and see him?"

Wimp had intended a duologue, but he made no objection, so he, too, stumbled through the nine brats to Mrs. Crowl's bedroom. It was a queer quartette. Wimp had hardly expected to find anybody at the house on Boxing Day, but he did not care to waste a day. Was not Grodman, too, on the track? How lucky it was that Denzil had made the first overtures, so that he could approach him without exciting suspicion.

Mortlake scowled when he saw the detective. He objected to the police—on principle. But Crowl had no idea who the visitor was, even when told his name. He was rather pleased to meet one of Denzil's high-class friends, and welcomed him warmly. Probably he was some famous editor, which would account for his name stirring vague recollections. He summoned the eldest brat and sent him for beer (people would have their Fads), and not without trepidation called down to "Mother" for glasses. "Mother" observed at night (in the same apartment) that the beer money might have paid the week's school fees for half the family.

"We were just talking of poor Mr. Constant's portrait, Mr. Wimp," said the unconscious Crowl; "they're going to unveil it, Mortlake tells me, on the twenty-first of next month at the Bow Break o' Day Club."

"Ah," said Wimp, elate at being spared the trouble of manoeuvring the conversation; "mysterious affair that, Mr. Crowl."

"No; it's the right thing," said Peter. "There ought to be some memorial of the man in the district where he worked and where he died, poor chap." The cobbler brushed away a tear.

"Yes, it's only right," echoed Mortlake, a whit eagerly. "He was a noble fellow, a true philanthropist—the only thoroughly unselfish worker I've ever met."

"He was that," said Peter; "and it's a rare pattern is unselfishness. Poor fellow, poor fellow. He preached the Useful, too. I've never met his like. Ah, I wish there was a heaven for him to go to!" He blew his nose violently with a red pocket-handkerchief.

"Well, he's there, if there is," said Tom.

"I hope he is," added Wimp, fervently; "but I shouldn't like to go there the way he did."

"You were the last person to see him, Tom, weren't you?" said Denzil.

"Oh, no," answered Tom, quickly. "You remember he went out after me; at least, so Mrs. Drabdump said at the inquest."

"That last conversation he had with you, Tom," said Denzil. "He didn't say anything to you that would lead you to suppose—"

"No, of course not!" interrupted Mortlake, impatiently.

"Do you really think he was murdered, Tom?" said Denzil.

"Mr. Wimp's opinion on that point is more valuable than mine," replied Tom, testily. "It may have been suicide. Men often get sick of life—especially if they are bored," he added meaningly.

"Ah, but you were the last person known to be with him," said Denzil.

Crowl laughed. "Had you there, Tom."

But they did not have Tom there much longer, for he departed, looking even worse-tempered than when he came. Wimp went soon after, and Crowl and Denzil were left to their interminable argumentation concerning the Useful and the Beautiful.

Wimp went West. He had several strings (or cords) to his bow, and he ultimately found himself at Kensal Green Cemetery. Being there, he went down the avenues of the dead to a grave to note down the exact date of a death. It was a day on which the dead seemed enviable. The dull, sodden sky, the dripping, leafless trees, the wet, spongy soil, the reeking grass—everything combined to make one long to be in a warm, comfortable grave away from the leaden ennuis of life. Suddenly the detective's keen eye caught sight of a figure that made his heart throb with sudden excitement. It was that of a woman in a grey shawl and a brown bonnet, standing before a railed-in grave. She had no umbrella. The rain plashed mournfully upon her, but left no trace on her soaking garments. Wimp crept up behind her, but she paid no heed to him. Her eyes were lowered to the grave, which seemed to be drawing them towards it by some strange morbid fascination. His eyes followed hers. The simple headstone bore the name, "Arthur Constant."

Wimp tapped her suddenly on the shoulder.

"How do you do, Mrs. Drabdump?"

Mrs. Drabdump went deadly white. She turned round, staring at Wimp without any recognition.

"You remember me, surely," he said; "I've been down once or twice to your place about that poor gentleman's papers." His eye indicated the grave.

"Lor! I remember you now," said Mrs. Drabdump.

"Won't you come under my umbrella? You must be drenched to the skin."

"It don't matter, sir. I can't take no hurt. I've had the rheumatics this twenty year."

Mrs. Drabdump shrank from accepting Wimp's attentions, not so much perhaps because he was a man as because he was a gentleman. Mrs. Drabdump liked to see the fine folks keep their place, and not contaminate their skirts by contact with the lower castes. "It's set wet, it'll rain right into the new year," she announced. "And they say a bad beginnin' makes a worse endin'." Mrs. Drabdump was one of those persons who give you the idea that they just missed being born barometers.

"But what are you doing in this miserable spot, so far from home?" queried the detective.

"It's Bank Holiday," Mrs. Drabdump reminded him in tones of acute surprise. "I always make a hexcursion on Bank Holiday."

The New Year drew Mrs. Drabdump a new lodger. He was an old gentleman with a long grey beard. He rented the rooms of the late Mr. Constant, and lived a very retired life. Haunted rooms—or rooms that ought to be haunted if the ghosts of those murdered in them had any self-respect—are supposed to fetch a lower rent in the market. The whole Irish problem might be solved if the spirits of "Mr. Balfour's victims" would only depreciate the value of property to a point consistent with the support of an agricultural population. But Mrs. Drabdump's new lodger paid so much for his rooms that he laid himself open to a suspicion of a special interest in ghosts. Perhaps he was a member of the Psychical Society. The neighbourhood imagined him another mad philanthropist, but as he did not appear to be doing any good to anybody it relented and conceded his sanity. Mortlake, who occasionally stumbled across him in the passage, did not trouble himself to think about him at all. He was too full of other troubles and cares. Though he worked harder than ever, the spirit seemed to have gone out of him. Sometimes he forgot himself in a fine rapture of eloquence—lashing himself up into a divine resentment of injustice or a passion of sympathy with the sufferings of his brethren—but mostly he plodded on in dull, mechanical fashion. He still made brief provincial tours, starring a day here and a day there, and everywhere his admirers remarked how jaded and overworked he looked. There was talk of starting a subscription to give him a holiday on the Continent—a luxury obviously unobtainable on the few pounds allowed him per week. The new lodger would doubtless have been pleased to subscribe, for he seemed quite to like occupying Mortlake's chamber the nights he was absent, though he was thoughtful enough not to disturb the hard-worked landlady in the adjoining room by unseemly noise. Wimp was always a quiet man.

Meantime the twenty-first of the month approached, and the East-end was in excitement. Mr. Gladstone had consented to be present at the ceremony of unveiling the portrait of Arthur Constant, presented by an unknown donor to the Bow Break o' Day Club, and it was to be a great function. The whole affair was outside the lines of party politics, so that even Conservatives and Socialists considered themselves justified in pestering the committee for tickets. To say nothing of ladies! As the committee desired to be present themselves, nine-tenths of the applications for admission had to be refused, as is usual on these occasions. The committee agreed among themselves to exclude the fair sex altogether as the only way of disposing of their womankind, who were making speeches as long as Mr. Gladstone's. Each committeeman told his sisters, female cousins, and aunts, that the other committeemen had insisted on divesting the function of all grace; and what could a man do when he was in a minority of one?

Crowl, who was not a member of the Break o' Day Club, was particularly anxious to hear the great orator whom he despised; fortunately Mortlake remembered the cobbler's anxiety to hear himself, and on the eve of the ceremony sent him a ticket. Crowl was in the first flush of possession when Denzil Cantercot returned, after a sudden and unannounced absence of three days. His clothes were muddy and tattered, his cocked hat was deformed, his cavalier beard was matted, and his eyes were bloodshot. The cobbler nearly dropped the ticket at the sight of him. "Hallo, Cantercot!" he gasped. "Why, where have you been all these days?"

"Terribly busy!" said Denzil. "Here, give me a glass of water. I'm dry as the Sahara."

Crowl ran inside and got the water, trying hard not to inform Mrs. Crowl of their lodger's return. "Mother" had expressed herself freely on the subject of the poet during his absence, and not in terms which would have commended themselves to the poet's fastidious literary sense. Indeed, she did not hesitate to call him a sponger and a low swindler, who had run away to avoid paying the piper. Her fool of a husband might be quite sure he would never set eyes on the scoundrel again. However, Mrs. Crowl was wrong. Here was Denzil back again. And yet Mr. Crowl felt no sense of victory. He had no desire to crow over his partner and to utter that "See! didn't I tell you so?" which is a greater consolation than religion in most of the misfortunes of life. Unfortunately, to get the water, Crowl had to go to the kitchen; and as he was usually such a temperate man, this desire for drink in the middle of the day attracted the attention of the lady in possession. Crowl had to explain the situation. Mrs. Crowl ran into the shop to improve it. Mr. Crowl followed in dismay, leaving a trail of spilt water in his wake.

"You good-for-nothing, disreputable scare-crow, where have—"

"Hush, mother. Let him drink. Mr. Cantercot is thirsty."

"Does he care if my children are hungry?"

Denzil tossed the water greedily down his throat almost at a gulp, as if it were brandy.

"Madam," he said, smacking his lips, "I do care. I care intensely. Few things in life would grieve me more deeply than to hear that a child, a dear little child—the Beautiful in a nutshell—had suffered hunger. You wrong me." His voice was tremulous with the sense of injury. Tears stood in his eyes.

"Wrong you? I've no wish to wrong you," said Mrs. Crowl. "I should like to hang you."

"Don't talk of such ugly things," said Denzil, touching his throat nervously.

"Well, what have you been doin' all this time?"

"Why, what should I be doing?"

"How should I know what became of you? I thought it was another murder."

"What!" Denzil's glass dashed to fragments on the floor. "What do you mean?"

But Mrs. Crowl was glaring too viciously at Mr. Crowl to reply. He understood the message as if it were printed. It ran. "You have broken one of my best glasses. You have annihilated threepence, or a week's school fees for half the family." Peter wished she would turn the lightning upon Denzil, a conductor down whom it would run innocuously. He stooped down and picked up the pieces as carefully as if they were cuttings from the Koh-i-noor. Thus the lightning passed harmlessly over his head and flew towards Cantercot.

"What do I mean?" Mrs. Crowl echoed, as if there had been no interval. "I mean that it would be a good thing if you had been murdered."

"What unbeautiful ideas you have to be sure!" murmured Denzil.

"Yes; but they'd be useful," said Mrs. Crowl, who had not lived with Peter all these years for nothing. "And if you haven't been murdered, what have you been doing?"

"My dear, my dear," put in Crowl, deprecatingly, looking up from his quadrupedal position like a sad dog, "you are not Cantercot's keeper."

"Oh, ain't I?" flashed his spouse. "Who else keeps him, I should like to know?"

Peter went on picking up the pieces of the Koh-i-noor.

"I have no secrets from Mrs. Crowl," Denzil explained courteously. "I have been working day and night bringing out a new paper. Haven't had a wink of sleep for three nights."

Peter looked up at his bloodshot eyes with respectful interest.

"The capitalist met me in the street—an old friend of mine—I was overjoyed at the rencontre and told him the idea I'd been brooding over for months, and he promised to stand all the racket."

"What sort of a paper?" said Peter.

"Can you ask? To what do you think I've been devoting my days and nights but to the cultivation of the Beautiful?"

"Is that what the paper will be devoted to?"

"Yes. To the Beautiful."

"I know," snorted Mrs. Crowl, "with portraits of actresses."

"Portraits? Oh, no!" said Denzil. "That would be the True, not the Beautiful."

"And what's the name of the paper?" asked Crowl.

"Ah, that's a secret, Peter. Like Scott, I prefer to remain anonymous."

"Just like your Fads. I'm only a plain man, and I want to know where the fun of anonymity comes in. If I had any gifts, I should like to get the credit. It's a right and natural feeling to my thinking."

"Unnatural, Peter; unnatural. We're all born anonymous, and I'm for sticking close to Nature. Enough for me that I disseminate the Beautiful. Any letters come during my absence, Mrs. Crowl?"

"No," she snapped. "But a gent named Grodman called. He said you hadn't been to see him for some time, and looked annoyed to hear you'd disappeared. How much have you let him in for?"

"The man's in my debt," said Denzil, annoyed. "I wrote a book for him and he's taken all the credit for it, the rogue! My name doesn't appear even in the Preface. What's that ticket you're looking so lovingly at, Peter?"

"That's for to-night—the unveiling of Constant's portrait. Gladstone speaks. Awful demand for places."

"Gladstone!" sneered Denzil. "Who wants to hear Gladstone? A man who's devoted his life to pulling down the pillars of Church and State."

"A man who's devoted his whole life to propping up the crumbling Fads of Religion and Monarchy. But, for all that, the man has his gifts, and I'm burnin' to hear him."

"I wouldn't go out of my way an inch to hear him," said Denzil; and went up to his room, and when Mrs. Crowl sent him up a cup of nice strong tea at tea-time, the brat who bore it found him lying dressed on the bed, snoring unbeautifully.

The evening wore on. It was fine frosty weather. The Whitechapel Road swarmed with noisy life, as though it were a Saturday night. The stars flared in the sky like the lights of celestial costermongers. Everybody was on the alert for the advent of Mr. Gladstone. He must surely come through the Road on his journey from the West Bow-wards. But nobody saw him or his carriage, except those about the Hall. Probably he went by tram most of the way. He would have caught cold in an open carriage, or bobbing his head out of the window of a closed.

"If he had only been a German prince, or a cannibal king," said Crowl, bitterly, as he plodded towards the Club, "we should have disguised Mile End in bunting and blue fire. But perhaps it's a compliment. He knows his London, and it's no use trying to hide the facts from him. They must have queer notions of cities, those monarchs. They must fancy everybody lives in a flutter of flags and walks about under triumphal arches, like as if I were to stitch shoes in my Sunday clothes." By a defiance of chronology Crowl had them on to-day, and they seemed to accentuate the simile.

"And why shouldn't life be fuller of the Beautiful?" said Denzil. The poet had brushed the reluctant mud off his garments to the extent it was willing to go, and had washed his face, but his eyes were still bloodshot from the cultivation of the Beautiful. Denzil was accompanying Crowl to the door of the Club out of good fellowship. Denzil was himself accompanied by Grodman, though less obtrusively. Least obtrusively was he accompanied by his usual Scotland Yard shadows, Wimp's agents. There was a surging nondescript crowd about the Club, so that the police, and the doorkeeper, and the stewards could with difficulty keep out the tide of the ticketless, through which the current of the privileged had equal difficulty in permeating. The streets all around were thronged with people longing for a glimpse of Gladstone. Mortlake drove up in a hansom (his head a self-conscious pendulum of popularity, swaying and bowing to right and left) and received all the pent-up enthusiasm.

"Well, good-by, Cantercot," said Crowl.

"No, I'll see you to the door, Peter."

They fought their way shoulder to shoulder.

Now that Grodman had found Denzil he was not going to lose him again. He had only found him by accident, for he was himself bound to the unveiling ceremony, to which he had been invited in view of his known devotion to the task of unveiling the Mystery. He spoke to one of the policemen about, who said, "Ay, ay, sir," and he was prepared to follow Denzil, if necessary, and to give up the pleasure of hearing Gladstone for an acuter thrill. The arrest must be delayed no longer.

But Denzil seemed as if he were going in on the heels of Crowl. This would suit Grodman better. He could then have the two pleasures. But Denzil was stopped halfway through the door.

"Ticket, sir!"

Denzil drew himself up to his full height.

"Press," he said majestically. All the glories and grandeurs of the Fourth Estate were concentrated in that haughty monosyllable. Heaven itself is full of journalists who have overawed St. Peter. But the doorkeeper was a veritable dragon.

"What paper, sir?"

"New York Herald" said Denzil, sharply. He did not relish his word being distrusted.

"New York Herald" said one of the bystanding stewards, scarce catching the sounds. "Pass him in."

And in the twinkling of an eye Denzil had eagerly slipped inside.

But during the brief altercation Wimp had come up. Even he could not make his face quite impassive, and there was a suppressed intensity in the eyes and a quiver about the mouth. He went in on Denzil's heels, blocking up the doorway with Grodman. The two men were so full of their coming coups that they struggled for some seconds, side by side, before they recognised each other. Then they shook hands heartily.

"That was Cantercot just went in, wasn't it, Grodman?" said Wimp.

"I didn't notice," said Grodman, in tones of utter indifference.

At bottom Wimp was terribly excited. He felt that his coup was going to be executed under very sensational circumstances. Everything would combine to turn the eyes of the country upon him—nay, of the world, for had not the Big Bow Mystery been discussed in every language under the sun? In these electric times the criminal receives a cosmopolitan reputation. It is a privilege he shares with few other artists. This time Wimp would be one of them. And he felt deservedly so. If the criminal had been cunning to the point of genius in planning the murder, he had been acute to the point of divination in detecting it. Never before had he pieced together so broken a chain. He could not resist the unique opportunity of setting a sensational scheme in a sensational framework. The dramatic instinct was strong in him; he felt like a playwright who has constructed a strong melodramatic plot, and has the Drury Lane stage suddenly offered him to present it on. It would be folly to deny himself the luxury, though the presence of Mr. Gladstone and the nature of the ceremony should perhaps have given him pause. Yet, on the other hand, these were the very factors of the temptation. Wimp went in and took a seat behind Denzil. All the seats were numbered, so that everybody might have the satisfaction of occupying somebody else's. Denzil was in the special reserved places in the front row just by the central gangway; Crowl was squeezed into a corner behind a pillar near the back of the hall. Grodman had been honoured with a seat on the platform, which was accessible by steps on the right and left, but he kept his eye on Denzil. The picture of the poor idealist hung on the wall behind Grodman's head, covered by its curtain of brown holland. There was a subdued buzz of excitement about the hall, which swelled into cheers every now and again as some gentleman known to fame or Bow took his place upon the platform. It was occupied by several local M.P.'s of varying politics, a number of other Parliamentary satellites of the great man, three or four labour leaders, a peer or two of philanthropic pretensions, a sprinkling of Toynbee and Oxford Hall men, the president and other honorary officials, some of the family and friends of the deceased, together with the inevitable percentage of persons who had no claim to be there save cheek. Gladstone was late—later than Mortlake, who was cheered to the echo when he arrived, some one starting "For He's a Jolly Good Fellow," as if it were a political meeting. Gladstone came in just in time to acknowledge the compliment. The noise of the song, trolled out from iron lungs, had drowned the huzzahs heralding the old man's advent. The convivial chorus went to Mortlake's head, as if champagne had really preceded it. His eyes grew moist and dim. He saw himself swimming to the Millennium on waves of enthusiasm. Ah, how his brother toilers should be rewarded for their trust in him!

With his usual courtesy and consideration, Mr. Gladstone had refused to perform the actual unveiling of Arthur Constant's portrait. "That," he said in his postcard, "will fall most appropriately to Mr. Mortlake, a gentleman who has, I am given to understand, enjoyed the personal friendship of the late Mr. Constant, and has cooperated with him in various schemes for the organisation of skilled and unskilled classes of labour, as well as for the diffusion of better ideals—ideals of self-culture and self-restraint—among the working men of Bow, who have been fortunate, so far as I can perceive, in the possession (if in one case unhappily only temporary possession) of two such men of undoubted ability and honesty to direct their divided counsels and to lead them along a road, which, though I cannot pledge myself to approve of it in all its turnings and windings, is yet not unfitted to bring them somewhat nearer to goals to which there are few of us but would extend some measure of hope that the working classes of this great Empire may in due course, yet with no unnecessary delay, be enabled to arrive."

Mr. Gladstone's speech was an expansion of his postcard, punctuated by cheers. The only new thing in it was the graceful and touching way in which he revealed what had been a secret up till then—that the portrait had been painted and presented to the Bow Break o' Day Club, by Lucy Brent, who in the fulness of time would have been Arthur Constant's wife. It was a painting for which he had sat to her while alive, and she had stifled yet pampered her grief by working hard at it since his death. The fact added the last touch of pathos to the occasion. Crowl's face was hidden behind his red handkerchief; even the fire of excitement in Wimp's eye was quenched for a moment by a teardrop, as he thought of Mrs. Wimp and Wilfred. As for Grodman, there was almost a lump in his throat. Denzil Cantercot was the only unmoved man in the room. He thought the episode quite too Beautiful, and was already weaving it into rhyme.

At the conclusion of his speech Mr. Gladstone called upon Tom Mortlake to unveil the portrait. Tom rose, pale and excited. He faltered as he touched the cord. He seemed overcome with emotion. Was it the mention of Lucy Brent that had moved him to his depths?

The brown holland fell away—the dead stood revealed as he had been in life. Every feature, painted by the hand of Love, was instinct with vitality: the fine, earnest face, the sad kindly eyes, the noble brow, seeming still a-throb with the thought of Humanity. A thrill ran through the room—there was a low, undefinable murmur. Oh, the pathos and the tragedy of it! Every eye was fixed, misty with emotion, upon the dead man in the picture, and the living man who stood, pale and agitated, and visibly unable to commence his speech, at the side of the canvas. Suddenly a hand was laid upon the labour leader's shoulder, and there rang through the hall in Wimp's clear, decisive tones the words—"Tom Mortlake, I arrest you for the murder of Arthur Constant!"

For a moment there was an acute, terrible silence. Mortlake's face was that of a corpse; the face of the dead man at his side was flushed with the hues of life. To the overstrung nerves of the onlookers, the brooding eyes of the picture seemed sad and stern with menace, and charged with the lightnings of doom.

It was a horrible contrast. For Wimp, alone, the painted face had fuller, more tragical meanings. The audience seemed turned to stone. They sat or stood—in every variety of attitude—frozen, rigid. Arthur Constant's picture dominated the scene, the only living thing in a hall of the dead.

But only for a moment. Mortlake shook off the detective's hand.

"Boys!" he cried, in accents of infinite indignation, "this is a police conspiracy."

His words relaxed the tension. The stony figures were agitated. A dull excited hubbub answered him. The little cobbler darted from behind his pillar, and leapt upon a bench. The cords of his brow were swollen with excitement. He seemed a giant overshadowing the hall.

"Boys!" he roared, in his best Victoria Park voice, "listen to me. This charge is a foul and damnable lie."

"Bravo!" "Hear, hear!" "Hooray!" "It is!" was roared back at him from all parts of the room. Everybody rose and stood in tentative attitudes, excited to the last degree.

"Boys!" Peter roared on, "you all know me. I'm a plain man, and I want to know if it's likely a man would murder his best friend."

"No!" in a mighty volume of sound.

Wimp had scarcely calculated upon Mortlake's popularity. He stood on the platform, pale and anxious as his prisoner.

"And if he did, why didn't they prove it the first time?"

"Hear, Hear!"

"And if they want to arrest him, why couldn't they leave it till the ceremony was over? Tom Mortlake's not the man to run away."

"Tom Mortlake! Tom Mortlake! Three cheers for Tom Mortlake!" "Hip, hip, hip, hooray!"

"Three groans for the police!" "Hoo! Oo! Oo!"

Wimp's melodrama was not going well. He felt like the author to whose ears is borne the ominous sibilance of the pit. He almost wished he had not followed the curtain-raiser with his own stronger drama. Unconsciously the police, scattered about the hall, drew together. The people on the platform knew not what to do. They had all risen and stood in a densely packed mass. Even Mr. Gladstone's speech failed him in circumstances so novel. The groans died away; the cheers for Mortlake rose and swelled and fell and rose again. Sticks and umbrellas were banged and rattled, handkerchiefs were waved, the thunder deepened. The motley crowd still surging about the hall took up the cheers, and for hundreds of yards around people were going black in the face out of mere irresponsible enthusiasm. At last Tom waved his hand—the thunder dwindled, died. The prisoner was master of the situation.

Grodman stood on the platform, grasping the back of his chair, a curious mocking Mephistophelian glitter about his eyes, his lips wreathed into a half smile. There was no hurry for him to get Denzil Cantercot arrested now. Wimp had made an egregious, a colossal blunder. In Grodman's heart there was a great, glad calm as of a man who has strained his sinews to win in a famous match, and has heard the judge's word. He felt almost kindly to Denzil now.

Tom Mortlake spoke. His face was set and stony. His tall figure was drawn up haughtily to its full height. He pushed the black mane back from his forehead with a characteristic gesture. The fevered audience hung upon his lips—the men at the back leaned eagerly forward—the reporters were breathless with fear lest they should miss a word. What would the great labour leader have to say at this supreme moment?

"Mr. Chairman and gentlemen. It is to me a melancholy pleasure to have been honoured with the task of unveiling to-night this portrait of a great benefactor to Bow and a true friend to the labouring classes. Except that he honoured me with his friendship while living, and that the aspirations of my life have, in my small and restricted way, been identical with his, there is little reason why this honourable duty should have fallen upon me. Gentlemen, I trust that we shall all find an inspiring influence in the daily vision of the dead, who yet liveth in our hearts and in this noble work of art—wrought, as Mr. Gladstone has told us, by the hand of one who loved him." The speaker paused a moment, his low vibrant tones faltering into silence. "If we humble working men of Bow can never hope to exert individually a tithe of the beneficial influence wielded by Arthur Constant, it is yet possible for each of us to walk in the light he has kindled in our midst—a perpetual lamp of self-sacrifice and brotherhood."

That was all. The room rang with cheers. Tom Mortlake resumed his seat. To Wimp the man's audacity verged on the Sublime; to Denzil on the Beautiful. Again there was a breathless hush. Mr. Gladstone's mobile face was working with excitement. No such extraordinary scene had occurred in the whole of his extraordinary experience. He seemed about to rise. The cheering subsided to a painful stillness. Wimp cut the situation by laying his hand again upon Tom's shoulder.

"Come quietly with me," he said. The words were almost a whisper, but in the supreme silence they travelled to the ends of the hall.

"Don't you go, Tom!" The trumpet tones were Peter's. The call thrilled an answering chord of defiance in every breast, and a low ominous murmur swept through the hall.

Tom rose, and there was silence again. "Boys," he said, "let me go. Don't make any noise about it. I shall be with you again to-morrow."

But the blood of the Break o' Day boys was at fever heat. A hurtling mass of men struggled confusedly from their seats. In a moment all was chaos. Tom did not move. Half-a-dozen men headed by Peter scaled the platform. Wimp was thrown to one side, and the invaders formed a ring round Tom's chair. The platform people scampered like mice from the centre. Some huddled together in the corners, others slipped out at the rear. The committee congratulated themselves on having had the self-denial to exclude ladies. Mr. Gladstone's satellites hurried the old man off and into his carriage, though the fight promised to become Homeric. Grodman stood at the side of the platform secretly more amused than ever, concerning himself no more with Denzil Cantercot, who was already strengthening his nerves at the bar upstairs. The police about the hall blew their whistles, and policemen came rushing in from outside and the neighbourhood. An Irish M.P. on the platform was waving his gingham like a shillelagh in sheer excitement, forgetting his new-found respectability and dreaming himself back at Donnybrook Fair. Him a conscientious constable floored with a truncheon. But a shower of fists fell on the zealot's face, and he tottered back bleeding. Then the storm broke in all its fury. The upper air was black with staves, sticks, and umbrellas, mingled with the pallid hailstones of knobby fists. Yells, and groans, and hoots, and battle-cries blent in grotesque chorus, like one of Dvorák's weird diabolical movements. Mortlake stood impassive, with arms folded, making no further effort, and the battle raged round him as the water swirls round some steadfast rock. A posse of police from the back fought their way steadily towards him, and charged up the heights of the platform steps, only to be sent tumbling backwards, as their leader was hurled at them like a battering-ram. Upon the top of the heap he fell, surmounting the strata of policemen. But others clambered upon them, escalading the platform. A moment more and Mortlake would have been taken. Then the miracle happened.

As when of old a reputable goddess ex machinâ saw her favourite hero in dire peril, straightway she drew down a cloud from the celestial stores of Jupiter and enveloped her fondling in kindly night, so that his adversary strove with the darkness, so did Crowl, the cunning cobbler, the much-daring, essay to ensure his friend's safety. He turned off the gas at the meter.

An Arctic night—unpreceded by twilight—fell, and there dawned the sabbath of the witches. The darkness could be felt—and it left blood and bruises behind it. When the lights were turned on again, Mortlake was gone. But several of the rioters were arrested, triumphantly.

And through all, and over all, the face of the dead man, who had sought to bring peace on earth, brooded.

Crowl sat meekly eating his supper of bread and cheese, with his head bandaged, while Denzil Cantercot told him the story of how he had rescued Tom Mortlake. He had been among the first to scale the height, and had never budged from Tom's side or from the forefront of the battle till he had seen him safely outside and into a by-street.

"I am so glad you saw that he got away safely," said Crowl, "I wasn't quite sure he would."

"Yes; but I wish some cowardly fool hadn't turned off the gas. I like men to see that they are beaten."

"But it seemed—easier," faltered Crowl.

"Easier!" echoed Denzil, taking a deep draught of bitter. "Really, Peter, I'm sorry to find you always will take such low views. It may be easier, but it's shabby. It shocks one's sense of the Beautiful."

Crowl ate his bread and cheese shamefacedly.

"But what was the use of breaking your head to save him?" said Mrs. Crowl, with an unconscious pun. "He must be caught."

"Ah, I don't see how the Useful does come in, now," said Peter, thoughtfully. "But I didn't think of that at the time."

He swallowed his water quickly, and it went the wrong way and added to his confusion. It also began to dawn upon him that he might be called to account. Let it be said at once that he wasn't. He had taken too prominent a part.

Meantime, Mrs. Wimp was bathing Mr. Wimp's eye, and rubbing him generally with arnica. Wimp's melodrama had been, indeed, a sight for the gods. Only virtue was vanquished and vice triumphant. The villain had escaped, and without striking a blow.

X

There was matter and to spare for the papers the next day. The striking ceremony—Mr. Gladstone's speech—the sensational arrest—these would of themselves have made excellent themes for reports and leaders. But the personality of the man arrested, and the Big Bow Mystery Battle—as it came to be called—gave additional piquancy to the paragraphs and the posters. The behaviour of Mortlake put the last touch to the picturesqueness of the position. He left the hall when the lights went out, and walked unnoticed and unmolested through pleiads of policemen to the nearest police station, where the superintendent was almost too excited to take any notice of his demand to be arrested. But to do him justice, the official yielded as soon as he understood the situation. It seems inconceivable that he did not violate some red-tape regulation in so doing. To some this self-surrender was limpid proof of innocence; to others it was the damning token of despairing guilt.

The morning papers were pleasant reading for Grodman, who chuckled as continuously over his morning egg, as if he had laid it. Jane was alarmed for the sanity of her saturnine master. As her husband would have said, Grodman's grins were not Beautiful. But he made no effort to suppress them. Not only had Wimp perpetrated a grotesque blunder, but the journalists to a man were down on his great sensation tableau, though their denunciations did not appear in the dramatic columns. The Liberal papers said that he had endangered Mr. Gladstone's life; the Conservative that he had unloosed the raging elements of Bow blackguardism, and set in motion forces which might have easily swelled to a riot, involving severe destruction of property. But "Tom Mortlake" was, after all, the thought swamping every other. It was, in a sense, a triumph for the man.

But Wimp's turn came when Mortlake, who reserved his defence, was brought up before a magistrate, and by force of the new evidence, fully committed for trial on the charge of murdering Arthur Constant. Then men's thoughts centred again on the Mystery, and the solution of the inexplicable problem agitated mankind from China to Peru.

In the middle of February, the great trial befell. It was another of the opportunities which the Chancellor of the Exchequer neglects. So stirring a drama might have easily cleared its expenses—despite the length of the cast, the salaries of the stars, and the rent of the house—in mere advance booking. For it was a drama which (by the rights of Magna Charta) could never be repeated; a drama which ladies of fashion would have given their earrings to witness, even with the central figure not a woman. And there was a woman in it anyhow, to judge by the little that had transpired at the magisterial examination, and the fact that the country was placarded with bills offering a reward for information concerning a Miss Jessie Dymond. Mortlake was defended by Sir Charles Brown-Harland, Q.C., retained at the expense of the Mortlake Defence Fund (subscriptions to which came also from Australia and the Continent), and set on his mettle by the fact that he was the accepted labour candidate for an East-end constituency. Their Majesties, Victoria and the Law, were represented by Mr. Robert Spigot, Q.C.

Mr. SPIGOT, Q.C, in presenting his case, said: "I propose to show that the prisoner murdered his friend and fellow-lodger, Mr. Arthur Constant, in cold blood, and with the most careful premeditation; premeditation so studied, as to leave the circumstances of the death an impenetrable mystery for weeks to all the world, though, fortunately, without altogether baffling the almost superhuman ingenuity of Mr. Edward Wimp, of the Scotland Yard Detective Department. I propose to show that the motives of the prisoner were jealousy and revenge; jealousy, not only of his friend's superior influence over the working men he himself aspired to lead, but the more commonplace animosity engendered by the disturbing element of a woman having relations to both. If, before my case is complete, it will be my painful duty to show that the murdered man was not the saint the world has agreed to paint him, I shall not shrink from unveiling the truer picture, in the interests of justice, which cannot say nil nisi bonum even of the dead. I propose to show that the murder was committed by the prisoner shortly before half-past six on the morning of December 4th, and that the prisoner having, with the remarkable ingenuity which he has shown throughout, attempted to prepare an alibi by feigning to leave London by the first train to Liverpool, returned home, got in with his latch-key through the street door, which he had left on the latch, unlocked his victim's bedroom with a key which he possessed, cut the sleeping man's throat, pocketed his razor, locked the door again, and gave it the appearance of being bolted, went downstairs, unslipped the bolt of the big lock, closed the door behind him, and got to Euston in time for the second train to Liverpool. The fog helped his proceedings throughout." Such was in sum the theory of the prosecution. The pale, defiant figure in the dock winced perceptibly under parts of it.

Mrs. Drabdump was the first witness called for the prosecution. She was quite used to legal inquisitiveness by this time, but did not appear in good spirits.

"On the night of December 3rd, you gave the prisoner a letter?"

"Yes, your ludship."

"How did he behave when he read it?"

"He turned very pale and excited. He went up to the poor gentleman's room, and I'm afraid he quarrelled with him. He might have left his last hours peaceful." (Amusement.)

"What happened then?"

"Mr. Mortlake went out in a passion, and came in again in about an hour."

"He told you he was going away to Liverpool very early the next morning?"

"No, your ludship, he said he was going to Devonport." (Sensation.)

"What time did you get up the next morning?"

"Half-past six."

"That is not your usual time?"

"No, I always get up at six."

"How do you account for the extra sleepiness?"

"Misfortunes will happen."

"It wasn't the dull, foggy weather?"

"No, my lud, else I should never get up early." (Laughter.)

"You drink something before going to bed?"

"I like my cup o' tea. I take it strong, without sugar. It always steadies my nerves."

"Quite so. Where were you when the prisoner told you he was going to Devonport?"

"Drinkin' my tea in the kitchen."

"What should you say if prisoner dropped something in it to make you sleep late?"

WITNESS (startled): "He ought to be shot."

"He might have done it without your noticing it, I suppose?"

"If he was clever enough to murder the poor gentleman, he was clever enough to try and poison me."

The JUDGE: "The witness in her replies must confine herself to the evidence."

Mr. SPIGOT, Q.C.: "I must submit to your lordship that it is a very logical answer, and exactly illustrates the interdependence of the probabilities. Now, Mrs. Drabdump, let us know what happened when you awoke at half-past six the next morning." Thereupon Mrs. Drabdump recapitulated the evidence (with new redundancies, but slight variations) given by her at the inquest. How she became alarmed—how she found the street door locked by the big lock—how she roused Grodman, and got him to burst open the door—how they found the body—all this with which the public was already familiar ad nauseam was extorted from her afresh.

"Look at this key (key passed to witness). Do you recognise it?"

"Yes; how did you get it? It's the key of my first-floor front. I am sure I left it sticking in the door."

"Did you know a Miss Dymond?"

"Yes, Mr. Mortlake's sweetheart. But I knew he would never marry her, poor thing." (Sensation.)

"Why not?"

"He was getting too grand for her." (Amusement.)

"You don't mean anything more than that?"

"I don't know; she only came to my place once or twice. The last time I set eyes on her must have been in October."

"How did she appear?"

"She was very miserable, but she wouldn't let you see it." (Laughter.)

"How has the prisoner behaved since the murder?"

"He always seemed very glum and sorry for it."

Cross-examined: "Did not the prisoner once occupy the bedroom of Mr. Constant, and give it up to him, so that Mr. Constant might have the two rooms on the same floor?"

"Yes, but he didn't pay as much."

"And, while occupying this front bedroom, did not the prisoner once lose his key and have another made?"

"He did; he was very careless."

"Do you know what the prisoner and Mr. Constant spoke about on the night of December 3rd?"

"No; I couldn't hear."

"Then how did you know they were quarrelling?"

"They were talkin' so loud."

Sir CHARLES BROWN-HARLAND, Q.C. (sharply): "But I'm talking loudly to you now. Should you say I was quarrelling?"

"It takes two to make a quarrel." (Laughter.)

"Was prisoner the sort of man who, in your opinion, would commit a murder?"

"No, I never should ha' guessed it was him."

"He always struck you as a thorough gentleman?"

"No, my lud. I knew he was only a comp."

"You say the prisoner has seemed depressed since the murder. Might not that have been due to the disappearance of his sweetheart?"

"No, he'd more likely be glad to get rid of her."

"Then he wouldn't be jealous if Mr. Constant took her off his hands?" (Sensation.)

"Men are dog-in-the-mangers."

"Never mind about men, Mrs. Drabdump. Had the prisoner ceased to care for Miss Dymond?"

"He didn't seem to think of her, my lud. When he got a letter in her handwriting among his heap he used to throw it aside till he'd torn open the others."

BROWN-HARLAND, Q.C. (with a triumphant ring in his voice): "Thank you, Mrs. Drabdump. You may sit down."

SPIGOT, Q.C.: "One moment, Mrs. Drabdump. You say the prisoner had ceased to care for Miss Dymond. Might not this have been in consequence of his suspecting for some time that she had relations with Mr. Constant?"

The JUDGE: "That is not a fair question."

SPIGOT, Q.C.: "That will do, thank you, Mrs. Drabdump."

BROWN-HARLAND, Q.C.: "No; one question more, Mrs. Drabdump. Did you ever see anything—say, when Miss Dymond came to your house—to make you suspect anything between Mr. Constant and the prisoner's sweetheart?"

"She did meet him once when Mr. Mortlake was out." (Sensation.)

"Where did she meet him?"

"In the passage. He was going out when she knocked and he opened the door." (Amusement.)

"You didn't hear what they said?"

"I ain't a eavesdropper. They spoke friendly and went away together."

Mr. GEORGE GRODMAN was called, and repeated his evidence at the inquest. Cross-examined, he testified to the warm friendship between Mr. Constant and the prisoner. He knew very little about Miss Dymond, having scarcely seen her. Prisoner had never spoken to him much about her. He should not think she was much in prisoner's thoughts. Naturally the prisoner had been depressed by the death of his friend. Besides, he was overworked. Witness thought highly of Mortlake's character. It was incredible that Constant had had improper relations of any kind with his friend's promised wife. Grodman's evidence made a very favourable impression on the jury; the prisoner looked his gratitude; and the prosecution felt sorry it had been necessary to call this witness.

Inspector HOWLETT and Sergeant RUNNYMEDE had also to repeat their evidence. Dr. ROBINSON, police surgeon, likewise retendered his evidence as to the nature of the wound, and the approximate hour of death. But this time he was much more severely examined. He would not bind himself down to state the time within an hour or two. He thought life had been extinct two or three hours when he arrived, so that the deed had been committed between seven and eight. Under gentle pressure from the prosecuting counsel, he admitted that it might possibly have been between six and seven. Cross-examined, he reiterated his impression in favour of the later hour.

Supplementary evidence from medical experts proved as dubious and uncertain as if the court had confined itself to the original witness. It seemed to be generally agreed that the data for determining the time of death of any body were too complex and variable to admit of very precise inference; rigor mortis and other symptoms setting in within very wide limits and differing largely in different persons. All agreed that death from such a cut must have been practically instantaneous, and the theory of suicide was rejected by all. As a whole the medical evidence tended to fix the time of death, with a high degree of probability, between the hours of six and half-past eight. The efforts of the prosecution were bent upon throwing back the time of death to as early as possible after about half-past five. The defence spent all its strength upon pinning the experts to the conclusion that death could not have been earlier than seven. Evidently the prosecution was going to fight hard for the hypothesis that Mortlake had committed the crime in the interval between the first and second trains for Liverpool; while the defence was concentrating itself on an alibi, showing that the prisoner had travelled by the second train which left Euston Station at a quarter-past seven, so that there could have been no possible time for the passage between Bow and Euston. It was an exciting struggle. As yet the contending forces seemed equally matched. The evidence had gone as much for as against the prisoner. But everybody knew that worse lay behind.

"Call Edward Wimp."

The story EDWARD WIMP had to tell began tamely enough with thrice-threshed-out facts. But at last the new facts came.

"In consequence of suspicions that had formed in your mind you took up your quarters, disguised, in the late Mr. Constant's rooms?"

"I did; at the commencement of the year. My suspicions had gradually gathered against the occupants of No. 11 Glover Street, and I resolved to quash or confirm these suspicions once for all."

"Will you tell the jury what followed?"

"Whenever the prisoner was away for the night I searched his room. I found the key of Mr. Constant's bedroom buried deeply in the side of prisoner's leather sofa. I found what I imagine to be the letter he received on December 3rd, in the pages of a 'Bradshaw' lying under the same sofa. There were two razors about."

Mr. SPIGOT, Q.C., said: "The key has already been identified by Mrs. Drabdump. The letter I now propose to read."

It was undated, and ran as follows:—

"Dear Tom,—This is to bid you farewell. It is best for us all. I am going a long way, dearest. Do not seek to find me, for it will be useless. Think of me as one swallowed up by the waters, and be assured that it is only to spare you shame and humiliation in the future that I tear myself from you and all the sweetness of life. Darling, there is no other way. I feel you could never marry me now. I have felt it for months. Dear Tom, you will understand what I mean. We must look facts in the face. I hope you will always be friends with Mr. Constant. Good-by, dear. God bless you! May you always be happy, and find a worthier wife than I. Perhaps when you are great, and rich, and famous, as you deserve, you will sometimes think not unkindly of one who, however faulty and unworthy of you, will at least love you till the end.—Yours, till death,

"JESSIE."

By the time this letter was finished numerous old gentlemen, with wigs or without, were observed to be polishing their glasses. Mr. Wimp's examination was resumed.

"After making these discoveries what did you do?"

"I made inquiries about Miss Dymond, and found Mr. Constant had visited her once or twice in the evening. I imagined there would be some traces of a pecuniary connection. I was allowed by the family to inspect Mr. Constant's cheque-book, and found a paid cheque made out for £25 in the name of Miss Dymond. By inquiry at the Bank, I found it had been cashed on November l2th of last year. I then applied for a warrant against the prisoner."

Cross-examined: "Do you suggest that the prisoner opened Mr. Constant's bedroom with the key you found?"

"Certainly."

BROWN-HARLAND, Q.C. (sarcastically): "And locked the door from within with it on leaving?"

"Certainly."

"Will you have the goodness to explain how the trick was done?"

"It wasn't done. (Laughter.) The prisoner probably locked the door from the outside. Those who broke it open naturally imagined it had been locked from the inside when they found the key inside. The key would, on this theory, be on the floor as the outside locking could not have been effected if it had been in the lock. The first persons to enter the room would naturally believe it had been thrown down in the bursting of the door. Or it might have been left sticking very loosely inside the lock so as not to interfere with the turning of the outside key, in which case it would also probably have been thrown to the ground."

"Indeed. Very ingenious. And can you also explain how the prisoner could have bolted the door within from the outside?"

"I can. (Renewed sensation.) There is only one way in which it was possible—and that was, of course, a mere conjurer's illusion. To cause a locked door to appear bolted in addition, it would only be necessary for the person on the inside of the door to wrest the staple containing the bolt from the woodwork. The bolt in Mr. Constant's bedroom worked perpendicularly. When the staple was torn off, it would simply remain at rest on the pin of the bolt instead of supporting it or keeping it fixed. A person bursting open the door and finding the staple resting on the pin and torn away from the lintel of the door, would, of course, imagine he had torn it away, never dreaming the wresting off had been done beforehand." (Applause in court, which was instantly checked by the ushers.) The counsel for the defence felt he had been entrapped in attempting to be sarcastic with the redoubtable detective. Grodman seemed green with envy. It was the one thing he had not thought of.

Mrs. Drabdump, Grodman, Inspector Howlett, and Sergeant Runnymede were recalled and reëxammed by the embarrassed Sir Charles Brown-Harland as to the exact condition of the lock and the bolt and the position of the key. It turned out as Wimp had suggested; so prepossessed were the witnesses with the conviction that the door was locked and bolted from the inside when it was burst open that they were a little hazy about the exact details. The damage had been repaired, so that it was all a question of precise past observation. The inspector and the sergeant testified that the key was in the lock when they saw it, though both the mortice and the bolt were broken. They were not prepared to say that Wimp's theory was impossible; they would even admit it was quite possible that the staple of the bolt had been torn off beforehand. Mrs. Drabdump could give no clear account of such petty facts in view of her immediate engrossing interest in the horrible sight of the corpse. Grodman alone was positive that the key was in the door when he burst it open. No, he did not remember picking it up from the floor and putting it in. And he was certain that the staple of the bolt was not broken, from the resistance he experienced in trying to shake the upper panels of the door.

By the Prosecution: "Don't you think, from the comparative ease with which the door yielded to your onslaught, that it is highly probable that the pin of the bolt was not in a firmly fixed staple, but in one already detached from the woodwork of the lintel?"

"The door did not yield so easily."

"But you must be a Hercules."

"Not quite; the bolt was old, and the woodwork crumbling; the lock was new and shoddy. But I have always been a strong man."

"Very well, Mr. Grodman. I hope you will never appear at the music-halls." (Laughter.)

Jessie Dymond's landlady was the next witness for the prosecution. She corroborated Wimp's statements as to Constant's occasional visits, and narrated how the girl had been enlisted by the dead philanthropist as a collaborator in some of his enterprises. But the most telling portion of her evidence was the story of how, late at night, on December 3rd, the prisoner called upon her and inquired wildly about the whereabouts of his sweetheart. He said he had just received a mysterious letter from Miss Dymond saying she was gone. She (the landlady) replied that she could have told him that weeks ago, as her ungrateful lodger was gone now some three weeks without leaving a hint behind her. In answer to his most ungentlemanly raging and raving, she told him it served him right, as he should have looked after her better, and not kept away for so long. She reminded him that there were as good fish in the sea as ever came out, and a girl of Jessie's attractions need not pine away (as she had seemed to be pining away) for lack of appreciation. He then called her a liar and left her, and she hoped never to see his face again, though she was not surprised to see it in the dock.

Mr. FITZJAMES MONTGOMERY, a bank clerk, remembered cashing the cheque produced. He particularly remembered it, because he paid the money to a very pretty girl. She took the entire amount in gold. At this point the case was adjourned.

DENZIL CANTERCOT was the first witness called for the prosecution on the resumption of the trial. Pressed as to whether he had not told Mr. Wimp that he had overheard the prisoner denouncing Mr. Constant, he could not say. He had not actually heard the prisoner's denunciations; he might have given Mr. Wimp a false impression, but then Mr. Wimp was so prosaically literal. (Laughter.) Mr. Crowl had told him something of the kind. Cross-examined, he said Jessie Dymond was a rare spirit and she always reminded him of Joan of Arc.

Mr. CROWL, being called, was extremely agitated. He refused to take the oath, and informed the court that the Bible was a Fad. He could not swear by anything so self-contradictory. He would affirm. He could not deny—though he looked like wishing to—that the prisoner had at first been rather mistrustful of Mr. Constant, but he was certain that the feeling had quickly worn off. Yes, he was a great friend of the prisoner, but he didn't see why that should invalidate his testimony, especially as he had not taken an oath. Certainly the prisoner seemed rather depressed when he saw him on Bank Holiday, but it was overwork on behalf of the people and for the demolition of the Fads.

Several other familiars of the prisoner gave more or less reluctant testimony as to his sometime prejudice against the amateur rival labour leader. His expressions of dislike had been strong and bitter. The prosecution also produced a poster announcing that the prisoner would preside at a great meeting of clerks on December 4th. He had not turned up at this meeting nor sent any explanation. Finally, there was the evidence of the detectives who originally arrested him at Liverpool Docks in view of his suspicious demeanour. This completed the case for the prosecution.

Sir CHARLES BROWN-HARLAND, Q.C., rose with a swagger and a rustle of his silk gown, and proceeded to set forth the theory of the defence. He said he did not purpose to call many witnesses. The hypothesis of the prosecution was so inherently childish and inconsequential, and so dependent upon a bundle of interdependent probabilities that it crumbled away at the merest touch. The prisoner's character was of unblemished integrity, his last public appearance had been made on the same platform with Mr. Gladstone, and his honesty and highmindedness had been vouched for by statesmen of the highest standing. His movements could be accounted for from hour to hour—and those with which the prosecution credited him rested on no tangible evidence whatever. He was also credited with superhuman ingenuity and diabolical cunning of which he had shown no previous symptom. Hypothesis was piled on hypothesis, as in the old Oriental legend, where the world rested on the elephant and the elephant on the tortoise. It might be worth while, however, to point out that it was at least quite likely that the death of Mr. Constant had not taken place before seven, and as the prisoner left Euston Station at 7.15 A.M. for Liverpool, he could certainly not have got there from Bow in the time; also that it was hardly possible for the prisoner, who could prove being at Euston Station at 5.25 A.M., to travel backwards and forwards to Glover Street and commit the crime all within less than two hours. "The real facts," said Sir Charles, impressively, "are most simple. The prisoner, partly from pressure of work, partly (he had no wish to conceal) from worldly ambition, had begun to neglect Miss Dymond, to whom he was engaged to be married. The man was but human, and his head was a little turned by his growing importance. Nevertheless, at heart he was still deeply attached to Miss Dymond. She, however, appears to have jumped to the conclusion that he had ceased to love her, that she was unworthy of him, unfitted by education to take her place side by side with him in the new spheres to which he was mounting— that, in short, she was a drag on his career. Being, by all accounts, a girl of remarkable force of character, she resolved to cut the Gordian knot by leaving London, and, fearing lest her affianced husband's conscientiousness should induce him to sacrifice himself to her; dreading also, perhaps, her own weakness, she made the parting absolute, and the place of her refuge a mystery. A theory has been suggested which drags an honoured name in the mire—a theory so superflous that I shall only allude to it. That Arthur Constant could have seduced, or had any improper relations with his friend's betrothed is a hypothesis to which the lives of both give the lie. Before leaving London—or England—Miss Dymond wrote to her aunt in Devonport—her only living relative in this country—asking her as a great favour to forward an addressed letter to the prisoner, a fortnight after receipt. The aunt obeyed implicitly. This was the letter which fell like a thunderbolt on the prisoner on the night of December 3rd. All his old love returned—he was full of self-reproach and pity for the poor girl. The letter read ominously. Perhaps she was going to put an end to herself. His first thought was to rush up to his friend, Constant, to seek his advice. Perhaps Constant knew something of the affair. The prisoner knew the two were in not infrequent communication. It is possible—my lord and gentlemen of the jury, I do not wish to follow the methods of the prosecution and confuse theory with fact, so I say it is possible—that Mr. Constant had supplied her with the £25 to leave the country. He was like a brother to her, perhaps even acted imprudently in calling upon her, though neither dreamed of evil. It is possible that he may have encouraged her in her abnegation and in her altruistic aspirations, perhaps even without knowing their exact drift, for does he not speak in his very last letter of the fine female characters he was meeting, and the influence for good he had over individual human souls? Still, this we can now never know, unless the dead speak or the absent return. It is also not impossible that Miss Dymond was entrusted with the £25 for charitable purposes. But to come back to certainties. The prisoner consulted Mr. Constant about the letter. He then ran to Miss Dymond's lodgings in Stepney Green, knowing beforehand his trouble would be futile. The letter bore the postmark of Devonport. He knew the girl had an aunt there; possibly she might have gone to her. He could not telegraph, for he was ignorant of the address. He consulted his 'Bradshaw,' and resolved to leave by the 5.30 A.M. from Paddington, and told his landlady so. He left the letter in the 'Bradshaw,' which ultimately got thrust among a pile of papers under the sofa, so that he had to get another. He was careless and disorderly, and the key found by Mr. Wimp in his sofa, which he was absurdly supposed to have hidden there after the murder, must have lain there for some years, having been lost there in the days when he occupied the bedroom afterwards rented by Mr. Constant. For it was his own sofa, removed from that room, and the suction of sofas was well known. Afraid to miss his train, he did not undress on that distressful night. Meantime the thought occurred to him that Jessie was too clever a girl to leave so easy a trail, and he jumped to the conclusion that she would be going to her married brother in America, and had gone to Devonport merely to bid her aunt farewell. He determined therefore to get to Liverpool, without wasting time at Devonport, to institute inquiries. Not suspecting the delay in the transit of the letter, he thought he might yet stop her, even at the landing-stage or on the tender. Unfortunately his cab went slowly in the fog, he missed the first train, and wandered about brooding disconsolately in the mist till the second. At Liverpool his suspicious, excited demeanour procured his momentary arrest. Since then the thought of the lost girl has haunted and broken him. That is the whole, the plain, and the sufficing story."

The effective witnesses for the defence were, indeed, few. It is so hard to prove a negative. There was Jessie's aunt, who bore out the statement of the counsel for the defence. There were the porters who saw him leave Euston by the 7.15 train for Liverpool, and arrive just too late for the 5.15; there was the cabman (2138), who drove him to Euston just in time, he (witness) thought, to catch the 5.15 A.M. Under cross-examination, the cabman got a little confused; he was asked whether, if he really picked up the prisoner at Bow Railway Station at about 4.30, he ought not to have caught the first train at Euston. He said the fog made him drive rather slowly, but admitted the mist was transparent enough to warrant full speed. He also admitted being a strong trade unionist, SPIGOT, Q.C., artfully extorting the admission as if it were of the utmost significance. Finally, there were numerous witnesses—of all sorts and conditions—to the prisoner's high character, as well as to Arthur Constant's blameless and moral life.

In his closing speech on the third day of the trial, Sir CHARLES pointed out with great exhaustiveness and cogency the flimsiness of the case for the prosecution, the number of hypotheses it involved, and their mutual interdependence. Mrs. Drabdump was a witness whose evidence must be accepted with extreme caution. The jury must remember that she was unable to dissociate her observations from her inferences, and thought that the prisoner and Mr. Constant were quarrelling merely because they were agitated. He dissected her evidence, and showed that it entirely bore out the story of the defence. He asked the jury to bear in mind that no positive evidence (whether of cabmen or others) had been given of the various and complicated movements attributed to the prisoner on the morning of December 4th, between the hours of 5.25 and 7.15 A.M., and that the most important witness on the theory of the prosecution—he meant, of course, Miss Dymond—had not been produced. Even if she were dead, and her body were found, no countenance would be given to the theory of the prosecution, for the mere conviction that her lover had deserted her would be a sufficient explanation of her suicide. Beyond the ambiguous letter, no tittle of evidence of her dishonour—on which the bulk of the case against the prisoner rested—had been adduced. As for the motive of political jealousy that had been a mere passing cloud. The two men had become fast friends. As to the circumstances of the alleged crime, the medical evidence was on the whole in favour of the time of death being late; and the prisoner had left London at a quarter-past seven. The drugging theory was absurd, and as for the too clever bolt and lock theories, Mr. Grodman, a trained scientific observer, had pooh-poohed them. He would solemnly exhort the jury to remember that if they condemned the prisoner they would not only send an innocent man to an ignominious death on the flimsiest circumstantial evidence, but they would deprive the working men of this country of one of their truest friends and their ablest leader.

The conclusion of Sir Charles's vigorous speech was greeted with irrepressible applause.

Mr. SPIGOT, Q.C., in closing the case for the prosecution, asked the jury to return a verdict against the prisoner for as malicious and premeditated a crime as ever disgraced the annals of any civilised country. His cleverness and education had only been utilised for the devil's ends, while his reputation had been used as a cloak. Everything pointed strongly to the prisoner's guilt. On receiving Miss Dymond's letter announcing her shame, and (probably) her intention to commit suicide, he had hastened upstairs to denounce Constant. He had then rushed to the girl's lodgings, and, finding his worst fears confirmed, planned at once his diabolically ingenious scheme of revenge. He told his landlady he was going to Devonport, so that if he bungled, the police would be put temporarily off his track. His real destination was Liverpool, for he intended to leave the country. Lest, however, his plan should break down here, too, he arranged an ingenious alibi by being driven to Euston for the 5.15 train to Liverpool. The cabman would not know he did not intend to go by it, but meant to return to 11 Glover Street, there to perpetrate this foul crime, interruption to which he had possibly barred by drugging his landlady. His presence at Liverpool (whither he really went by the second train) would corroborate the cabman's story. That night he had not undressed nor gone to bed; he had plotted out his devilish scheme till it was perfect; the fog came as an unexpected ally to cover his movements. Jealousy, outraged affection, the desire for revenge, the lust for political power—these were human. They might pity the criminal, they could not find him innocent of the crime.

Mr. Justice CROGIE, summing up, began dead against the prisoner. Reviewing the evidence, he pointed out that plausible hypotheses neatly dove-tailed did not necessarily weaken one another, the fitting so well together of the whole rather making for the truth of the parts. Besides, the case for the prosecution was as far from being all hypothesis as the case for the defence was from excluding hypotheses. The key, the letter, the reluctance to produce the letter, the heated interview with Constant, the misstatement about the prisoner's destination, the flight to Liverpool, the false tale about searching for a "him," the denunciations of Constant, all these were facts. On the other hand, there were various lacunæ and hypotheses in the case for the defence. Even conceding the somewhat dubious alibi afforded by the prisoner's presence at Euston at 5.25 A.M., there was no attempt to account for his movements between that and 7.15 A.M. It was as possible that he returned to Bow as that he lingered about Euston. There was nothing in the medical evidence to make his guilt impossible. Nor was there anything inherently impossible in Constant's yielding to the sudden temptation of a beautiful girl, nor in a working girl deeming herself deserted, temporarily succumbing to the fascinations of a gentleman and regretting it bitterly afterwards. What had become of the girl was a mystery. Hers might have been one of those nameless corpses which the tide swirls up on slimy river banks. The jury must remember, too, that the relation might not have actually passed into dishonour, it might have been just grave enough to smite the girl's conscience, and to induce her to behave as she had done. It was enough that her letter should have excited the jealousy of the prisoner. There was one other point which he would like to impress on the jury, and which the counsel for the prosecution had not sufficiently insisted upon. This was that the prisoner's guiltiness was the only plausible solution that had ever been advanced of the Bow Mystery. The medical evidence agreed that Mr. Constant did not die by his own hand. Some one must therefore have murdered him. The number of people who could have had any possible reason or opportunity to murder him was extremely small. The prisoner had both reason and opportunity. By what logicians called the method of exclusion, suspicion would attach to him on even slight evidence. The actual evidence was strong and plausible, and now that Mr. Wimp's ingenious theory had enabled them to understand how the door could have been apparently locked and bolted from within, the last difficulty and the last argument for suicide had been removed. The prisoner's guilt was as clear as circumstantial evidence could make it. If they let him go free, the Bow Mystery might henceforward be placed among the archives of unavenged assassinations. Having thus well-nigh hung the prisoner, the judge wound up by insisting on the high probability of the story for the defence, though that, too, was dependent in important details upon the prisoner's mere private statements to his counsel. The jury, being by this time sufficiently muddled by his impartiality, were dismissed, with the exhortation to allow due weight to every fact and probability in determining their righteous verdict.

The minutes ran into hours, but the jury did not return. The shadows of night fell across the reeking, fevered court before they announced their verdict—

"Guilty!"

The judge put on his black cap.

The great reception arranged outside was a fiasco; the evening banquet was indefinitely postponed. Wimp had won; Grodman felt like a whipped cur.

XI

"So you were right," Denzil could not help saying as he greeted Grodman a week afterwards. "I shall not live to tell the story of how you discovered the Bow murderer."

"Sit down," growled Grodman; "perhaps you will after all." There was a dangerous gleam in his eyes. Denzil was sorry he had spoken.

"I sent for you," Grodman said, "to tell you that on the night Wimp arrested Mortlake I had made preparations for your arrest."

Denzil gasped, "What for?"

"My dear Denzil, there is a little law in this country invented for the confusion of the poetic. The greatest exponent of the Beautiful is only allowed the same number of wives as the greengrocer. I do not blame you for not being satisfied with Jane—she is a good servant but a bad mistress—but it was cruel to Kitty not to inform her that Jane had a prior right in you, and unjust to Jane not to let her know of the contract with Kitty."

"They both know it now well enough, curse 'em," said the poet.

"Yes; your secrets are like your situations—you can't keep 'em long. My poor poet, I pity you—betwixt the devil and the deep sea."

"They're a pair of harpies, each holding over me the Damocles sword of an arrest for bigamy. Neither loves me."

"I should think they would come in very useful to you. You plant one in my house to tell my secrets to Wimp, and you plant one in Wimp's house to tell Wimp's secrets to me, I suppose. Out with some, then."

"Upon my honour, you wrong me. Jane brought me here, not I Jane. As for Kitty, I never had such a shock in my life as at finding her installed in Wimp's house."

"She thought it safer to have the law handy for your arrest. Besides, she probably desired to occupy a parallel position to Jane's. She must do something for a living; you wouldn't do anything for hers. And so you couldn't go anywhere without meeting a wife! Ha! ha! ha! Serve you right, my polygamous poet."

"But why should you arrest me?"

"Revenge, Denzil. I have been the best friend you ever had in this cold, prosaic world. You have eaten my bread, drunk my claret, written my book, smoked my cigars, and pocketed my money. And yet, when you have an important piece of information bearing on a mystery about which I am thinking day and night, you calmly go and sell it to Wimp."

"I did-didn't," stammered Denzil.

"Liar! Do you think Kitty has any secrets from me? As soon as I discovered your two marriages I determined to have you arrested for—your treachery. But when I found you had, as I thought, put Wimp on the wrong scent, when I felt sure that by arresting Mortlake he was going to make a greater ass of himself than even nature had been able to do, then I forgave you. I let you walk about the earth—and drink—freely. Now it is Wimp who crows—everybody pats him on the back—they call him the mystery man of the Scotland Yard tribe. Poor Tom Mortlake will be hanged, and all through your telling Wimp about Jessie Dymond!"

"It was you yourself," said Denzil, sullenly. "Everybody was giving it up. But you said 'Let us find out all that Arthur Constant did in the last few months of his life.' Wimp couldn't miss stumbling on Jessie sooner or later. I'd have throttled Constant, if I had known he'd touched her," he wound up with irrelevant indignation.

Grodman winced at the idea that he himself had worked ad majorem gloriam of Wimp. And yet, had not Mrs. Wimp let out as much at the Christmas dinner?

"What's past is past," he said gruffly. "But if Tom Mortlake hangs, you go to Portland."

"How can I help Tom hanging?"

"Help the agitation as much as you can. Write letters under all sorts of names to all the papers. Get everybody you know to sign the great petition. Find out where Jessie Dymond is—the girl who holds the proof of Mortlake's innocence."

"You really believe him innocent?"

"Don't be satirical, Denzil. Haven't I taken the chair at all the meetings? Am I not the most copious correspondent of the Press?"

"I thought it was only to spite Wimp."

"Rubbish. It's to save poor Tom. He no more murdered Arthur Constant than—you did!" He laughed an unpleasant laugh.

Denzil bade him farewell, frigid with fear.

Grodman was up to his ears in letters and telegrams. Somehow he had become the leader of the rescue party—suggestions, subscriptions came from all sides. The suggestions were burnt, the subscriptions acknowledged in the papers and used for hunting up the missing girl. Lucy Brent headed the list with a hundred pounds. It was a fine testimony to her faith in her dead lover's honour.

The release of the Jury had unloosed "The Greater Jury," which always now sits upon the smaller. Every means was taken to nullify the value of the "palladium of British liberty." The foreman and the jurors were interviewed, the judge was judged, and by those who were no judges. The Home Secretary (who had done nothing beyond accepting office under the Crown) was vituperated, and sundry provincial persons wrote confidentially to the Queen. Arthur Constant's backsliding cheered many by convincing them that others were as bad as themselves; and well-to-do tradesmen saw in Mortlake's wickedness the pernicious effects of Socialism. A dozen new theories were afloat. Constant had committed suicide by Esoteric Buddhism, as witness his devotion to Mme. Blavatsky, or he had been murdered by his Mahatma or victimised by Hypnotism, Mesmerism, Somnambulism, and other weird abstractions. Grodman's great point was—Jessie Dymond must be produced, dead or alive. The electric current scoured the civilised world in search of her. What wonder if the shrewder sort divined that the indomitable detective had fixed his last hope on the girl's guilt? If Jessie had wrongs why should she not have avenged them herself? Did she not always remind the poet of Joan of Arc?

Another week passed; the shadow of the gallows crept over the days; on, on, remorselessly drawing nearer, as the last ray of hope sank below the horizon. The Home Secretary remained inflexible; the great petitions discharged their signatures at him in vain. He was a Conservative, sternly conscientious; and the mere insinuation that his obstinacy was due to the politics of the condemned only hardened him against the temptation of a cheap reputation for magnanimity. He would not even grant a respite, to increase the chances of the discovery of Jessie Dymond. In the last of the three weeks there was a final monster meeting of protest. Grodman again took the chair, and several distinguished faddists were present, as well as numerous respectable members of society. The Home Secretary acknowledged the receipt of their resolutions. The Trade Unions were divided in their allegiance; some whispered of faith and hope, others of financial defalcations. The former essayed to organise a procession and an indignation meeting on the Sunday preceding the Tuesday fixed for the execution, but it fell through on a rumour of confession. The Monday papers contained a last masterly letter from Grodman exposing the weakness of the evidence, but they knew nothing of a confession. The prisoner was mute and disdainful, professing little regard for a life empty of love and burdened with self-reproach. He refused to see clergymen. He was accorded an interview with Miss Brent in the presence of a gaoler, and solemnly asseverated his respect for her dead lover's memory. Monday buzzed with rumours; the evening papers chronicled them hour by hour. A poignant anxiety was abroad. The girl would be found. Some miracle would happen. A reprieve would arrive. The sentence would be commuted. But the short day darkened into night even as Mortlake's short day was darkening. And the shadow of the gallows crept on and on, and seemed to mingle with the twilight.

Crowl stood at the door of his shop, unable to work. His big grey eyes were heavy with unshed tears. The dingy wintry road seemed one vast cemetery; the street lamps twinkled like corpse-lights. The confused sounds of the street life reached his ear as from another world. He did not see the people who flitted to and fro amid the gathering shadows of the cold, dreary night. One ghastly vision flashed and faded and flashed upon the background of the duskiness.

Denzil stood beside him, smoking in silence. A cold fear was at his heart. That terrible Grodman! As the hangman's cord was tightening round Mortlake, he felt the convict's chains tightening round himself. And yet there was one gleam of hope, feeble as the yellow flicker of the gas-lamp across the way. Grodman had obtained an interview with the condemned late that afternoon, and the parting had been painful, but the evening paper, that in its turn had obtained an interview with the ex-detective, announced on its placard

"GRODMAN STILL CONFIDENT"

and the thousands who yet pinned their faith on this extraordinary man refused to extinguish the last sparks of hope. Denzil had bought the paper and scanned it eagerly, but there was nothing save the vague assurance that the indefatigable Grodman was still almost pathetically expectant of the miracle. Denzil did not share the expectation; he meditated flight.

"Peter," he said at last, "I'm afraid it's all over."

Crowl nodded, heart-broken. "All over!" he repeated, "and to think that he dies—and it is—all over!"

He looked despairingly at the blank winter sky, where leaden clouds shut out the stars. "Poor, poor young fellow! To-night alive and thinking. To-morrow night a clod, with no more sense or motion than a bit of leather! No compensation nowhere for being cut off innocent in the pride of youth and strength!

A man who has always preached the Useful day and night, and toiled and suffered for his fellows. Where's the justice of it, where's the justice of it?" he demanded fiercely. Again his wet eyes wandered upwards towards heaven, that heaven away from which the soul of a dead saint at the Antipodes was speeding into infinite space.

"Well, where was the justice for Arthur Constant if he, too, was innocent?" said Denzil. "Really, Peter, I don't see why you should take it for granted that Tom is so dreadfully injured. Your horny-handed labour leaders are, after all, men of no aesthetic refinement, with no sense of the Beautiful; you cannot expect them to be exempt from the coarser forms of crime. Humanity must look to far other leaders—to the seers and the poets!"

"Cantercot, if you say Tom's guilty I'll knock you down." The little cobbler turned upon his tall friend like a roused lion. Then he added, "I beg your pardon, Cantercot, I don't mean that. After all, I've no grounds. The judge is an honest man, and with gifts I can't lay claim to. But I believe in Tom with all my heart. And if Tom is guilty I believe in the Cause of the People with all my heart all the same. The Fads are doomed to death, they may be reprieved, but they must die at last."

He drew a deep sigh, and looked along the dreary Road. It was quite dark now, but by the light of the lamps and the gas in the shop windows the dull, monotonous Road lay revealed in all its sordid, familiar outlines; with its long stretches of chill pavement, its unlovely architecture, and its endless stream of prosaic pedestrians.

A sudden consciousness of the futility of his existence pierced the little cobbler like an icy wind. He saw his own life, and a hundred million lives like his, swelling and breaking like bubbles on a dark ocean, unheeded, uncared for.

A newsboy passed along, clamouring "The Bow murderer, preparaitions for the hexecution!"

A terrible shudder shook the cobbler's frame. His eyes ranged sightlessly after the boy; the merciful tears filled them at last.

"The Cause of the People," he murmured brokenly, "I believe in the Cause of the People. There is nothing else."

"Peter, come in to tea, you'll catch cold," said Mrs. Crowl.

Denzil went in to tea and Peter followed.

Meantime, round the house of the Home Secretary, who was in town, an ever-augmenting crowd was gathered, eager to catch the first whisper of a reprieve.

The house was guarded by a cordon of police, for there was no inconsiderable danger of a popular riot. At times a section of the crowd groaned and hooted. Once a volley of stones was discharged at the windows. The newsboys were busy vending their special editions, and the reporters struggled through the crowd, clutching descriptive pencils, and ready to rush off to telegraph offices should anything "extra special" occur. Telegraph boys were coming up every now and again with threats, messages, petitions, and exhortations from all parts of the country to the unfortunate Home Secretary, who was striving to keep his aching head cool as he went through the voluminous evidence for the last time and pondered over the more important letters which "The Greater Jury" had contributed to the obscuration of the problem. Grodman's letter in that morning's paper shook him most; under his scientific analysis the circumstantial chain seemed forged of painted cardboard. Then the poor man read the judge's summing up, and the chain became tempered steel. The noise of the crowd outside broke upon his ear in his study like the roar of a distant ocean. The more the rabble hooted him, the more he essayed to hold scrupulously the scales of life and death. And the crowd grew and grew, as men came away from their work. There were many that loved the man who lay in the jaws of death, and a spirit of mad revolt surged in their breasts. And the sky was grey, and the bleak night deepened, and the shadow of the gallows crept on.

Suddenly a strange inarticulate murmur spread through the crowd, a vague whisper of no one knew what. Something had happened. Somebody was coming. A second later and one of the outskirts of the throng was agitated, and a convulsive cheer went up from it, and was taken up infectiously all along the street. The crowd parted—a hansom dashed through the centre. "Grodman! Grodman!" shouted those who recognised the occupant. "Grodman! Hurrah!" Grodman was outwardly calm and pale, but his eyes glittered; he waved his hand encouragingly as the hansom dashed up to the door, cleaving the turbulent crowd as a canoe cleaves the waters. Grodman sprang out, the constables at the portal made way for him respectfully. He knocked imperatively, the door was opened cautiously; a boy rushed up and delivered a telegram; Grodman forced his way in, gave his name, and insisted on seeing the Home Secretary on a matter of life and death. Those near the door heard his words and cheered, and the crowd divined the good omen, and the air throbbed with cannonades of joyous sound. The cheers rang in Grodman's ears as the door slammed behind him. The reporters struggled to the front. An excited knot of working men pressed round the arrested hansom; they took the horse out. A dozen enthusiasts struggled for the honour of placing themselves between the shafts. And the crowd awaited Grodman.

XII

Grodman was ushered into the conscientious Minister's study. The doughty chief of the agitation was, perhaps, the one man who could not be denied. As he entered, the Home Secretary's face seemed lit up with relief. At a sign from his master, the amanuensis who had brought in the last telegram took it back with him into the outer room where he worked. Needless to say not a tithe of the Minister's correspondence ever came under his own eyes.

"You have a valid reason for troubling me, I suppose, Mr. Grodman?" said the Home Secretary, almost cheerfully. "Of course it is about Mortlake?"

"It is; and I have the best of all reasons."

"Take a seat. Proceed."

"Pray do not consider me impertinent, but have you ever given any attention to the science of evidence?"

"How do you mean?" asked the Home Secretary, rather puzzled, adding, with a melancholy smile, "I have had to lately. Of course, I've never been a criminal lawyer, like some of my predecessors. But I should hardly speak of it as a science; I look upon it as a question of common-sense."

"Pardon me, sir. It is the most subtle and difficult of all the sciences. It is, indeed, rather the science of the sciences. What is the whole of Inductive Logic, as laid down, say, by Bacon and Mill, but an attempt to appraise the value of evidence, the said evidence being the trails left by the Creator, so to speak? The Creator has—I say it in all reverence—drawn a myriad red herrings across the track, but the true scientist refuses to be baffled by superficial appearances in detecting the secrets of Nature. The vulgar herd catches at the gross apparent fact, but the man of insight knows that what lies on the surface does lie."

"Very interesting, Mr. Grodman, but really—"

"Bear with me, sir. The science of evidence being thus so extremely subtle, and demanding the most acute and trained observation of facts, the most comprehensive understanding of human psychology, is naturally given over to professors who have not the remotest idea that 'things are not what they seem,' and that everything is other than it appears; to professors, most of whom by their year-long devotion to the shop-counter or the desk, have acquired an intimate acquaintance with all the infinite shades and complexities of things and human nature. When twelve of these professors are put in a box, it is called a jury. When one of these professors is put in a box by himself, he is called a witness. The retailing of evidence—the observation of the facts—is given over to people who go through their lives without eyes; the appreciation of evidence—the judging of these facts—is surrendered to people who may possibly be adepts in weighing out pounds of sugar. Apart from their sheer inability to fulfil either function—to observe, or to judge—their observation and their judgment alike are vitiated by all sorts of irrelevant prejudices."

"You are attacking trial by jury."

"Not necessarily. I am prepared to accept that scientifically, on the ground that, as there are, as a rule, only two alternatives, the balance of probability is slightly in favour of the true decision being come to. Then, in cases where experts like myself have got up the evidence, the jury can be made to see through trained eyes."

The Home Secretary tapped impatiently with his foot.

"I can't listen to abstract theorising," he said. "Have you any fresh concrete evidence?"

"Sir, everything depends on our getting down to the root of the matter. What percentage of average evidence should you think is thorough, plain, simple, unvarnished fact, 'the truth, the whole truth, and nothing but the truth'?"

"Fifty?" said the Minister, humouring him a little.

"Not five. I say nothing of lapses of memory, of inborn defects of observational power—though the suspiciously precise recollection of dates and events possessed by ordinary witnesses in important trials taking place years after the occurrences involved, is one of the most amazing things in the curiosities of modern jurisprudence. I defy you, sir, to tell me what you had for dinner last Monday, or what exactly you were saying and doing at five o'clock last Tuesday afternoon. Nobody whose life does not run in mechanical grooves can do anything of the sort; unless, of course, the facts have been very impressive. But this by the way. The great obstacle to veracious observation is the element of prepossession in all vision. Has it ever struck you, sir, that we never see any one more than once, if that? The first time we meet a man we may possibly see him as he is; the second time our vision is coloured and modified by the memory of the first. Do our friends appear to us as they appear to strangers? Do our rooms, our furniture, our pipes strike our eye as they would strike the eye of an outsider, looking on them for the first time? Can a mother see her babe's ugliness, or a lover his mistress's shortcomings, though they stare everybody else in the face? Can we see ourselves as others see us? No; habit, prepossession changes all. The mind is a large factor of every so-called external fact. The eye sees, sometimes, what it wishes to see, more often what it expects to see. You follow me, sir?"

The Home Secretary nodded his head less impatiently. He was beginning to be interested. The hubbub from without broke faintly upon their ears.

"To give you a definite example. Mr. Wimp says that when I burst open the door of Mr. Constant's room on the morning of December 4th, and saw that the staple of the bolt had been wrested by the pin from the lintel, I jumped at once to the conclusion that I had broken the bolt. Now I admit that this was so, only in things like this you do not seem to conclude, you jump so fast that you see, or seem to. On the other hand, when you see a standing ring of fire produced by whirling a burning stick, you do not believe in its continuous existence. It is the same when witnessing a legerdemain performance. Seeing is not always believing, despite the proverb; but believing is often seeing. It is not to the point that in that little matter of the door Wimp was as hopelessly and incurably wrong as he has been in everything all along. The door was securely bolted. Still I confess that I should have seen that I had broken the bolt in forcing the door, even if it had been broken beforehand. Never once since December 4th did this possibility occur to me, till Wimp with perverted ingenuity suggested it. If this is the case with a trained observer, one moreover fully conscious of this ineradicable tendency of the human mind, how must it be with an untrained observer?"

"Come to the point, come to the point," said the Home Secretary, putting out his hand as if it itched to touch the bell on the writing-table.

"Such as," went on Grodman, imperturbably, "such as—Mrs. Drabdump. That worthy person is unable, by repeated violent knocking, to arouse her lodger who yet desires to be aroused; she becomes alarmed, she rushes across to get my assistance; I burst open the door—what do you think the good lady expected to see?"

"Mr. Constant murdered, I suppose," murmured the Home Secretary, wonderingly.

"Exactly. And so she saw it. And what should you think was the condition of Arthur Constant when the door yielded to my violent exertions and flew open?"

"Why, was he not dead?" gasped the Home Secretary, his heart fluttering violently.

"Dead? A young, healthy fellow like that! When the door flew open, Arthur Constant was sleeping the sleep of the just. It was a deep, a very deep sleep, of course, else the blows at his door would long since have awakened him. But all the while Mrs. Drabdump's fancy was picturing her lodger cold and stark, the poor young fellow was lying in bed in a nice warm sleep."

"You mean to say you found Arthur Constant alive?"

"As you were last night."

The Minister was silent, striving confusedly to take in the situation. Outside the crowd was cheering again. It was probably to pass the time.

"Then, when was he murdered?"

"Immediately afterwards."

"By whom?"

"Well, that is, if you will pardon me, not a very intelligent question. Science and common-sense are in accord for once. Try the method of exhaustion. It must have been either by Mrs. Drabdump or myself."

"You mean to say that Mrs. Drabdump—!"

"Poor dear Mrs. Drabdump, you don't deserve this of your Home Secretary! The idea of that good lady!"

"It was you!"

"Calm yourself, my dear Home Secretary. There is nothing to be alarmed at. It was a solitary experiment, and I intend it to remain so." The noise without grew louder. "Three cheers for Grodman! Hip, hip, hip, hooray," fell faintly on their ears.

But the Minister, pallid and deeply moved, touched the bell. The Home Secretary's home secretary appeared. He looked at the great man's agitated face with suppressed surprise.

"Thank you for calling in your amanuensis," said Grodman. "I intended to ask you to lend me his services. I suppose he can write shorthand."

The Minister nodded, speechless.

"That is well. I intend this statement to form the basis of an appendix to the twenty-fifth edition—sort of silver wedding—of my book, Criminals I have Caught. Mr. Denzil Cantercot, who, by the will I have made to-day, is appointed my literary executor, will have the task of working it up with literary and dramatic touches after the model of the other chapters of my book. I have every confidence he will be able to do me as much justice, from a literary point of view, as you, sir, no doubt will from a legal. I feel certain he will succeed in catching the style of the other chapters to perfection."

"Templeton," whispered the Home Secretary, "this man may be a lunatic. The effort to solve the Big Bow Mystery may have addled his brain. Still," he added aloud, "it will be as well for you to take down his statement in shorthand."

"Thank you, sir," said Grodman, heartily. "Ready, Mr. Templeton? Here goes. My career till I left the Scotland Yard Detective Department is known to all the world. Is that too fast for you, Mr. Templeton? A little? Well, I'll go slower; but pull me up if I forget to keep the brake on. When I retired, I discovered that I was a bachelor. But it was too late to marry. Time hung heavy on my hands. The preparation of my book, Criminals I have Caught, kept me occupied for some months. When it was published, I had nothing more to do but think. I had plenty of money, and it was safely invested; there was no call for speculation. The future was meaningless to me; I regretted I had not elected to die in harness. As idle old men must, I lived in the past. I went over and over again my ancient exploits; I re-read my book. And as I thought and thought, away from the excitement of the actual hunt, and seeing the facts in a truer perspective, so it grew daily clearer to me that criminals were more fools than rogues. Every crime I had traced, however cleverly perpetrated, was from the point of view of penetrability a weak failure. Traces and trails were left on all sides—ragged edges, rough-hewn corners; in short, the job was botched, artistic completeness unattained. To the vulgar, my feats might seem marvellous—the average man is mystified to grasp how you detect the letter 'e' in a simple cryptogram—to myself they were as commonplace as the crimes they unveiled. To me now, with my lifelong study of the science of evidence, it seemed possible to commit not merely one but a thousand crimes that should be absolutely undiscoverable. And yet criminals would go on sinning, and giving themselves away, in the same old grooves—no originality, no dash, no individual insight, no fresh conception! One would imagine there were an Academy of crime with forty thousand armchairs. And gradually, as I pondered and brooded over the thought, there came upon me the desire to commit a crime that should baffle detection. I could invent hundreds of such crimes, and please myself by imagining them done; but would they really work out in practice? Evidently the sole performer of my experiment must be myself; the subject—whom or what? Accident should determine. I itched to commence with murder—to tackle the stiffest problems first, and I burned to startle and baffle the world—especially the world of which I had ceased to be. Outwardly I was calm, and spoke to the people about me as usual. Inwardly I was on fire with a consuming scientific passion. I sported with my pet theories, and fitted them mentally on every one I met. Every friend or acquaintance I sat and gossiped with, I was plotting how to murder without leaving a clue. There is not one of my friends or acquaintances I have not done away with in thought. There is no public man—have no fear, my dear Home Secretary—I have not planned to assassinate secretly, mysteriously, unintelligibly, undiscoverably. Ah, how I could give the stock criminals points—with their second-hand motives, their conventional conceptions, their commonplace details, their lack of artistic feeling and restraint."

The crowd had again started cheering. Impatient as the watchers were, they felt that no news was good news. The longer the interview accorded by the Home Secretary to the chairman of the Defence Committee, the greater the hope his obduracy was melting. The idol of the people would be saved, and "Grodman" and "Tom Mortlake" were mingled in the exultant plaudits.

"The late Arthur Constant," continued the great criminologist, "came to live nearly opposite me. I cultivated his acquaintance—he was a lovable young fellow, an excellent subject for experiment. I do not know when I have ever taken to a man more. From the moment I first set eyes on him, there was a peculiar sympathy between us. We were drawn to each other. I felt instinctively he would be the man. I loved to hear him speak enthusiastically of the Brotherhood of Man—I, who knew the brotherhood of man was to the ape, the serpent, and the tiger—and he seemed to find a pleasure in stealing a moment's chat with me from his engrossing self-appointed duties. It is a pity humanity should have been robbed of so valuable a life. But it had to be. At a quarter to ten on the night of December 3rd he came to me. Naturally I said nothing about this visit at the inquest or the trial. His object was to consult me mysteriously about some girl. He said he had privately lent her money—which she was to repay at her convenience. What the money was for he did not know, except that it was somehow connected with an act of abnegation in which he had vaguely encouraged her. The girl had since disappeared, and he was in distress about her. He would not tell me who it was—of course now, sir, you know as well as I it was Jessie Dymond—but asked for advice as to how to set about finding her. He mentioned that Mortlake was leaving for Devonport by the first train on the next day. Of old I should have connected these two facts and sought the thread; now, as he spoke, all my thoughts were dyed red. He was suffering perceptibly from toothache, and in answer to my sympathetic inquiries told me it had been allowing him very little sleep. Everything combined to invite the trial of one of my favourite theories. I spoke to him in a fatherly way, and when I had tendered some vague advice about the girl, I made him promise to secure a night's rest (before he faced the arduous tram-men's meeting in the morning) by taking a sleeping draught. I gave him a quantity of sulfonal in a phial. It is a new drug, which produces protracted sleep without disturbing digestion, and which I use myself. He promised faithfully to take the draught; and I also exhorted him earnestly to bolt and bar and lock himself in so as to stop up every chink or aperture by which the cold air of the winter's night might creep into the room. I remonstrated with him on the careless manner he treated his body, and he laughed in his good-humoured, gentle way, and promised to obey me in all things. And he did. That Mrs. Drabdump, failing to rouse him, would cry 'Murder!' I took for certain. She is built that way. As even Sir Charles Brown-Harland remarked, she habitually takes her prepossessions for facts, her inferences for observations. She forecasts the future in grey. Most women of Mrs. Drabdump's class would have behaved as she did. She happened to be a peculiarly favourable specimen for working on by 'suggestion,' but I would have undertaken to produce the same effect on almost any woman. The key to the Big Bow Mystery is feminine psychology. The only uncertain link in the chain was, Would Mrs. Drabdump rush across to get me to break open the door? Women always rush for a man. I was well-nigh the nearest, and certainly the most authoritative man in the street, and I took it for granted she would."

"But suppose she hadn't?" the Home Secretary could not help asking.

"Then the murder wouldn't have happened, that's all. In due course Arthur Constant would have awoke, or somebody else breaking open the door would have found him sleeping; no harm done, nobody any the wiser. I could hardly sleep myself that night. The thought of the extraordinary crime I was about to commit—a burning curiosity to know whether Wimp would detect the modus operandi—the prospect of sharing the feelings of murderers with whom I had been in contact all my life without being in touch with the terrible joys of their inner life—the fear lest I should be too fast asleep to hear Mrs. Drabdump's knock—these things agitated me and disturbed my rest. I lay tossing on my bed, planning every detail of poor Constant's end. The hours dragged slowly and wretchedly on towards the misty dawn. I was racked with suspense. Was I to be disappointed after all? At last the welcome sound came—the rat-tat-tat of murder. The echoes of that knock are yet in my ear. 'Come over and kill him!' I put my night-capped head out of the window and told her to wait for me. I dressed hurriedly, took my razor, and went across to 11 Glover Street. As I broke open the door of the bedroom in which Arthur Constant lay sleeping, his head resting on his hands, I cried, 'My God!' as if I saw some awful vision. A mist as of blood swam before Mrs. Drabdump's eyes. She cowered back, for an instant (I divined rather than saw the action) she shut off the dreaded sight with her hands. In that instant I had made my cut—precisely, scientifically—made so deep a cut and drawn out the weapon so sharply that there was scarce a drop of blood on it; then there came from the throat a jet of blood which Mrs. Drabdump, conscious only of the horrid gash, saw but vaguely. I covered up the face quickly with a handkerchief to hide any convulsive distortion. But as the medical evidence (in this detail accurate) testified, death was instantaneous. I pocketed the razor and the empty sulfonal phial. With a woman like Mrs. Drabdump to watch me, I could do anything I pleased. I got her to draw my attention to the fact that both the windows were fastened. Some fool, by the by, thought there was a discrepancy in the evidence because the police found only one window fastened, forgetting that, in my innocence I took care not to refasten the window I had opened to call for aid. Naturally I did not call for aid before a considerable time had elapsed. There was Mrs. Drabdump to quiet, and the excuse of making notes—as an old hand. My object was to gain time. I wanted the body to be fairly cold and stiff before being discovered, though there was not much danger here; for, as you saw by the medical evidence, there is no telling the time of death to an hour or two. The frank way in which I said the death was very recent disarmed all suspicion, and even Dr. Robinson was unconsciously worked upon, in adjudging the time of death, by the knowledge (query here, Mr. Templeton) that it had preceded my advent on the scene.

"Before leaving Mrs. Drabdump, there is just one point I should like to say a word about. You have listened so patiently, sir, to my lectures on the science of sciences that you will not refuse to hear the last. A good deal of importance has been attached to Mrs. Drabdump's oversleeping herself by half an hour. It happens that this (like the innocent fog which has also been made responsible for much) is a purely accidental and irrelevant circumstance. In all works on inductive logic it is thoroughly recognised that only some of the circumstances of a phenomenon are of its essence and casually interconnected; there is always a certain proportion of heterogeneous accompaniments which have no intimate relation whatever with the phenomenon. Yet, so crude is as yet the comprehension of the science of evidence, that every feature of the phenomenon under investigation is made equally important, and sought to be linked with the chain of evidence. To attempt to explain everything is always the mark of the tyro. The fog and Mrs. Drabdump's oversleeping herself were mere accidents. There are always these irrelevant accompaniments, and the true scientist allows for this element of (so to speak) chemically unrelated detail. Even I never counted on the unfortunate series of accidental phenomena which have led to Mortlake's implication in a network of suspicion. On the other hand, the fact that my servant, Jane, who usually goes about ten, left a few minutes earlier on the night of December 3rd, so that she didn't know of Constant's visit, was a relevant accident. In fact, just as the art of the artist or the editor consists largely in knowing what to leave out, so does the art of the scientific detector of crime consist in knowing what details to ignore. In short, to explain everything is to explain too much. And too much is worse than too little.

"To return to my experiment. My success exceeded my wildest dreams. None had an inkling of the truth. The insolubility of the Big Bow Mystery teased the acutest minds in Europe and the civilised world. That a man could have been murdered in a thoroughly inaccessible room savoured of the ages of magic. The redoubtable Wimp, who had been blazoned as my successor, fell back on the theory of suicide. The mystery would have slept till my death, but—I fear—for my own ingenuity. I tried to stand outside myself, and to look at the crime with the eyes of another, or of my old self. I found the work of art so perfect as to leave only one sublimely simple solution. The very terms of the problem were so inconceivable that, had I not been the murderer, I should have suspected myself, in conjunction, of course, with Mrs. Drabdump. The first persons to enter the room would have seemed to me guilty. I wrote at once (in a disguised hand and over the signature of 'One who looks through his own spectacles') to the Pell Mell Press to suggest this. By associating myself thus with Mrs. Drabdump I made it difficult for people to dissociate the two who entered the room together. To dash a half-truth in the world's eyes is the surest way of blinding it altogether. This pseudonymous letter of mine I contradicted (in my own name) the next day, and in the course of the long letter which I was tempted to write, I adduced fresh evidence against the theory of suicide. I was disgusted with the open verdict, and wanted men to be up and doing and trying to find me out. I enjoyed the hunt more.

"Unfortunately, Wimp, set on the chase again by my own letter, by dint of persistent blundering, blundered into a track which—by a devilish tissue of coincidences I had neither foreseen nor dreamt of—seemed to the world the true. Mortlake was arrested and condemned. Wimp had apparently crowned his reputation. This was too much. I had taken all this trouble merely to put a feather in Wimp's cap, whereas I had expected to shake his reputation by it. It was bad enough that an innocent man should suffer; but that Wimp should achieve a reputation he did not deserve, and over-shadow all his predecessors by dint of a colossal mistake, this seemed to me intolerable. I have moved heaven and earth to get the verdict set aside, and to save the prisoner; I have exposed the weakness of the evidence; I have had the world searched for the missing girl; I have petitioned and agitated. In vain. I have failed. Now I play my last card. As the overweening Wimp could not be allowed to go down to posterity as the solver of this terrible mystery, I decided that the condemned man might just as well profit by his exposure. That is the reason I make the exposure to-night, before it is too late to save Mortlake."

"So that is the reason?" said the Home Secretary, with a suspicion of mockery in his tones.

"The sole reason."

Even as he spoke, a deeper roar than ever penetrated the study.

"A Reprieve! Hooray! Hooray!" The whole street seemed to rock with earthquake and the names of Grodman and Mortlake to be thrown up in a fiery jet. "A Reprieve! A Reprieve!" And then the very windows rattled with cheers for the Minister. And even above that roar rose the shrill voices of the newsboys, "Reprieve of Mortlake! Mortlake Reprieved!" Grodman looked wonderingly towards the street. "How do they know?" he murmured.

"Those evening papers are amazing," said the Minister, drily. "But I suppose they had everything ready in type for the contingency." He turned to his secretary.

"Templeton, have you got down every word of Mr. Grodman's confession?"

"Every word, sir."

"Then bring in the cable you received just as Mr. Grodman entered the house."

Templeton went back into the outer room and brought back the cablegram that had been lying on the Minister's writing-table when Grodman came in. The Home Secretary silently handed it to his visitor. It was from the Chief of Police of Melbourne, announcing that Jessie Dymond had just arrived in that city in a sailing vessel, ignorant of all that had occurred, and had been immediately despatched back to England, having made a statement entirely corroborating the theory of the defence.

"Pending further inquiries into this," said the Home Secretary, not without appreciation of the grim humour of the situation as he glanced at Grodman's ashen cheeks, "I have reprieved the prisoner. Mr. Templeton was about to despatch the messenger to the governor of Newgate as you entered this room. Mr. Wimp's card-castle would have tumbled to pieces without your assistance. Your still undiscoverable crime would have shaken his reputation as you intended."

A sudden explosion shook the room and blent with the cheers of the populace. Grodman had shot himself—very scientifically—in the heart. He fell at the Home Secretary's feet, stone dead.

Some of the working men who had been standing waiting by the shafts of the hansom helped to bear the stretcher.

I

Sometimes Lancelot's bell rang up Mrs. Leadbatter herself, but far more often merely Mary Ann.

The first time Lancelot saw Mary Ann she was cleaning the steps. He avoided treading upon her, being kind to animals. For the moment she was merely a quadruped, whose head was never lifted to the stars. Her faded print dress showed like the quivering hide of some crouching animal. There were strange irregular splashes of pink in the hide, standing out in bright contrast with the neutral background. These were scraps of the original material neatly patched in.

The cold, damp steps gave Lancelot a shudder, for the air was raw. He passed by the prostrate figure as quickly as he could, and hastened to throw himself into the easy chair before the red fire.

There was a lamp-post before the door, so he knew the house from its neighbours. Baker's Terrace as a whole was a defeated aspiration after gentility. The more auspicious houses were marked by white stones, the steps being scrubbed and hearth-stoned almost daily; the gloomier doorsteps were black, except on Sundays. Thus variety was achieved by houses otherwise as monotonous and prosaic as a batch of fourpenny loaves. This was not the reason why the little South London side-street was called Baker's Terrace, though it might well seem so; for Baker was the name of the builder, a worthy gentleman whose years and virtues may still be deciphered on a doddering, round-shouldered stone in a deceased cemetery not far from the scene of his triumphs.

The second time Lancelot saw Mary Ann he did not remember having seen her before. This time she was a biped, and wore a white cap. Besides, he hardly glanced at her. He was in a bad temper, and Beethoven was barking terribly at the intruder who stood quaking in the doorway, so that the crockery clattered on the tea-tray she bore. With a smothered oath Lancelot caught up the fiery little spaniel and rammed him into the pocket of his dressing-gown, where he quivered into silence like a struck gong. While the girl was laying his breakfast, Lancelot, who was looking moodily at the pattern of the carpet as if anxious to improve upon it, was vaguely conscious of relief in being spared his landlady's conversation. For Mrs. Leadbatter was a garrulous body, who suffered from the delusion that small-talk is a form of politeness, and that her conversation was part of the "all inclusive" her lodgers stipulated for. The disease was hereditary, her father having been a barber, and remarkable for the coolness with which, even as a small boy whose function was lathering and nothing more, he exchanged views about the weather with his victims.

The third time Lancelot saw Mary Ann he noticed that she was rather pretty. She had a slight, well-built figure, not far from tall, small shapely features, and something of a complexion. This did not displease him: she was a little aesthetic touch amid the depressing furniture.

"Don't be afraid, Polly," he said more kindly. "The little devil won't bite. He's all bark. Call him Beethoven and throw him a bit of sugar."

The girl threw Beethoven the piece of sugar, but did not venture on the name. It seemed to her a long name for such a little dog. As she timidly took the sugar from the basin by the aid of the tongs, Lancelot saw how coarse and red her hand was. It gave him the same sense of repugnance and refrigescence as the cold, damp steps. Something he was about to say froze on his lips. He did not look at Mary Ann for some days; by which time Beethoven had conquered his distrust of her, though she was still distrustful of Beethoven, drawing her skirts tightly about her as if he were a rat. What forced Mary Ann again upon Lancelot's morose consciousness was a glint of winter sunshine that settled on her light brown hair. He said, "By the way, Susan, tell your mistress—or is it your mother?"

Mary Ann shook her head but did not speak.

"Oh, you are not Miss Leadbatter?"

"No; Mary Ann."

She spoke humbly; her eyes were shy and would not meet his. He winced as he heard the name, though her voice was not unmusical.

"Ah, Mary Ann! and I've been calling you Jane all along, Mary Ann what?"

She seemed confused and flushed a little.

"Mary Ann!" she murmured.

"Merely Mary Ann?"

"Yessir."

He smiled. "Seems a sort of white Topsy," he was thinking.

She stood still, holding in her hand the table-cloth she had just folded. Her eyes were downcast, and the glint of sunshine had leapt upon the long lashes.

"Well, Mary Ann, tell your mistress there is a piano coming. It will stand over there—you'll have to move the sideboard somewhere else."

"A piano!" Mary Ann opened her eyes, and Lancelot saw that they were large and pathetic. He could not see the colour for the glint of sunshine that touched them with false fire.

"Yes; I suppose it will have to come up through the window, these staircases are so beastly narrow. Do you never have a stout person in the house, I wonder?"

"Oh, yes, sir. We had a lodger here last year as was quite a fat man."

"And did he come up through the window by a pulley?"

He smiled at the image, and expected to see Mary Ann smile in response. He was disappointed when she did not; it was not only that her stolidity made his humour seem feeble—he half wanted to see how she looked when she smiled.

"Oh, dear, no," said Mary Ann; "he lived on the ground floor!"

"Oh!" murmured Lancelot, feeling the last sparkle taken from his humour. He was damped to the skin by Mary Ann's platitudinarian style of conversation. Despite its prettiness, her face was dulness incarnate.

"Anyhow, remember to take in the piano if I'm out," he said tartly. "I suppose you've seen a piano—you'll know it from a kangaroo?"

"Yessir," breathed Mary Ann.

"Oh, come, that's something. There is some civilisation in Baker's Terrace after all. But are you quite sure?" he went on, the teasing instinct getting the better of him. "Because, you know, you've never seen a kangaroo."

Mary Ann's face lit up a little. "Oh, yes, I have, sir; it came to the village fair when I was a girl."

"Oh, indeed!" said Lancelot, a little staggered; "what did it come there for—to buy a new pouch?"

"No, sir; in a circus."

"Ah, in a circus. Then, perhaps, you can play the piano, too."

Mary Ann got very red. "No, sir; missus never showed me how to do that."

Lancelot surrendered himself to a roar of laughter. "This is a real original," he said to himself, just a touch of pity blending with his amusement.

"I suppose, though, you'd be willing to lend a hand occasionally?" he could not resist saying.

"Missus says I must do anything I'm asked," she said, in distress, the tears welling to her eyes. And a merciless bell mercifully sounding from an upper room, she hurried out.

How much Mary Ann did, Lancelot never rightly knew, any more than he knew the number of lodgers in the house, or who cooked his chops in the mysterious regions below stairs. Sometimes he trod on the toes of boots outside doors and vaguely connected them with human beings, peremptory and exacting as himself. To Mary Ann each of those pairs of boots was a personality, with individual hours of rising and retiring, breakfasting and supping, going out and coming in, and special idiosyncrasies of diet and disposition. The population of 5 Baker's Terrace was nine, mostly bell-ringers. Life was one ceaseless round of multifarious duties; with six hours of blessed unconsciousness, if sleep were punctual. All the week long Mary Ann was toiling up and down the stairs or sweeping them, making beds or puddings, polishing boots or fire-irons. Holidays were not in Mary Ann's calendar; and if Sunday ever found her on her knees, it was only when she was scrubbing out the kitchen. All work and no play makes Jack a dull boy; it had not, apparently, made Mary Ann a bright girl.

The piano duly came in through the window like a burglar. It was a good instrument, but hired. Under Lancelot's fingers it sang like a bird and growled like a beast. When the piano was done growling Lancelot usually started. He paced up and down the room, swearing audibly. Then he would sit down at the table and cover ruled paper with hieroglyphics for hours together. His movements were erratic to the verge of mystery. He had no fixed hours for anything; to Mary Ann he was hopeless. At any given moment he might be playing on the piano, or writing on the curiously ruled paper, or stamping about the room, or sitting limp with despair in the one easy chair, or drinking whisky and water, or smoking a black meerschaum, or reading a book, or lying in bed, or driving away in a hansom, or walking about Heaven alone knew where or why. Even Mrs. Leadbatter, whose experience of life was wider than Mary Ann's, considered his vagaries almost unchristian, though to the highest degree gentlemanly. Sometimes, too, he sported the swallow-tail and the starched breast-plate, which was a wonder to Mary Ann, who knew that waiters were connected only with the most stylish establishments. Baker's Terrace did not wear evening dress.

Mary Ann liked him best in black and white. She thought he looked like the pictures in the young ladies' novelettes, which sometimes caught her eye as she passed newsvendors' shops on errands. Not that she was read in this literature—she had no time for reading. But, even when clothed in rough tweeds, Lancelot had for Mary Ann an aristocratic halo; in his dressing-gown he savoured of the grand Turk. His hands were masterful: the fingers tapering, the nails pedantically polished. He had fair hair, with moustache to match; his brow was high and white, and his grey eyes could flash fire. When he drew himself up to his full height, he threatened the gas globes. Never had No. 5 Baker's Terrace boasted of such a tenant. Altogether, Lancelot loomed large to Mary Ann; she dazzled him with his own boots in humble response, and went about sad after a reprimand for putting his papers in order. Her whole theory of life oscillated in the presence of a being whose views could so run counter to her strongest instincts. And yet, though the universe seemed tumbling about her ears when he told her she must not move a scrap of manuscript, howsoever wildly it lay about the floor or under the bed, she did not for a moment question his sanity. She obeyed him like a dog; uncomprehending, but trustful. But, after all, this was only of a piece with the rest of her life. There was nothing she questioned. Life stood at her bedside every morning in the cold dawn, bearing a day heaped high with duties; and she jumped cheerfully out of her warm bed and took them up one by one, without question or murmur. They were life. Life had no other meaning any more than it has for the omnibus hack, which cannot conceive existence outside shafts, and devoid of the intermittent flick of a whip point. The comparison is somewhat unjust; for Mary Ann did not fare nearly so well as the omnibus hack, having to make her meals off such scraps as even the lodgers sent back. Mrs. Leadbatter was extremely economical, as much so with the provisions in her charge as with those she bought for herself. She sedulously sent up remainders till they were expressly countermanded. Less economical by nature, and hungrier by habit, Mary Ann had much trouble in restraining herself from surreptitious pickings. Her conscience was rarely worsted; still there was a taint of dishonesty in her soul, else had the stairs been less of an ethical battle-ground for her. Lancelot's advent only made her hungrier; somehow the thought of nibbling at his provisions was too sacrilegious to be entertained. And yet—so queerly are we and life compounded—she was probably less unhappy at this period than Lancelot, who would come home in the vilest of tempers, and tramp the room with thunder on his white brow. Sometimes he and the piano and Beethoven would all be growling together, at other times they would all three be mute; Lancelot crouching in the twilight with his head in his hands, and Beethoven moping in the corner, and the closed piano looming in the background like a coffin of dead music.

One February evening—an evening of sleet and mist—Lancelot, who had gone out in evening dress, returned unexpectedly, bringing with him for the first time a visitor. He was so perturbed that he forgot to use his latch-key, and Mary Ann, who opened the door, heard him say angrily, "Well, I can't slam the door in your face, but I will tell you in your face I don't think it at all gentlemanly of you to force yourself upon me like this."

"My dear Lancelot, when did I ever set up to be a gentleman? You know that was always your part of the contract." And a swarthy, thick-set young man with a big nose lowered the dripping umbrella he had been holding over Lancelot, and stepped from the gloom of the street into the fuscous cheerfulness of the ill-lit passage.

By this time Beethoven, who had been left at home, was in full ebullition upstairs, and darted at the intruder the moment his calves appeared. Beethoven barked with short sharp snaps, as became a bilious liver-coloured Blenheim spaniel.

"Like master like dog," said the swarthy young man, defending himself at the point of the umbrella. "Really your animal is more intelligent than the over-rated common or garden dog, which makes no distinction between people calling in the small hours and people calling in broad daylight under the obvious patronage of its own master. This beast of yours is evidently more in sympathy with its liege lord. Down, Fido, down! I wonder they allow you to keep such noisy creatures—but stay! I was forgetting you keep a piano. After that, I suppose, nothing matters."

Lancelot made no reply, but surprised Beethoven into silence by kicking him out of the way. He lit the gas with a neatly written sheet of music which he rammed into the fire Mary Ann had been keeping up, then as silently he indicated the easy chair.

"Thank you," said the swarthy young man, taking it. "I would rather see you in it, but as there's only one I know you wouldn't be feeling a gentleman; and that would make us both uncomfortable."

"'Pon my word, Peter," Lancelot burst forth, "you're enough to provoke a saint."

"'Pon my word, Lancelot," replied Peter, imperturbably, "you're more than enough to provoke a sinner. Why, what have you to be ashamed of? You've got one of the cosiest dens in London and one of the comfortablest chairs. Why, it's twice as jolly as the garret we shared at Leipsic—up the ninety stairs."

"We're not in Germany now. I don't want to receive visitors," answered Lancelot, sulkily.

"A visitor! you call me a visitor! Lancelot, it's plain you were not telling the truth when you said just now you had forgiven me."

"I had forgiven—and forgotten you."

"Come, that's unkind. It's scarcely three years since I threw up my career as a genius, and you know why I left you, old man. When the first fever of youthful revolt was over, I woke to see things in their true light. I saw how mean it was of me to help to eat up your wretched thousand pounds. Neither of us saw the situation nakedly at first—it was sicklied o'er with Quixotic foolishness. You see, you had the advantage of me. Your governor was a gentleman. He says: 'Very well, if you won't go to Cambridge, if you refuse to enter the Church as the younger son of a blue-blooded but impecunious baronet should, and to step into the living which is fattening for you, then I must refuse to take any further responsibility for your future. Here is a thousand pounds; it is the money I had set aside for your college course. Use it for your musical tomfoolery if you insist, and then—get what living you can.' Which was severe but dignified, unpaternal yet patrician. But what does my governor do? That cantankerous, pig-headed old Philistine—God bless him!—he's got no sense of the respect a father owes to his offspring. Not an atom. You're simply a branch to be run on the lines of the old business or be shut up altogether. And, by the way, Lancelot, he hasn't altered a jot since those days when—as you remember—the City or starvation was his pleasant alternative. Of course I preferred starvation—one usually does at nineteen; especially if one knows there's a scion of aristocracy waiting outside to elope with him to Leipsic."

"But you told me you were going back to your dad, because you found you had mistaken your vocation."

"Gospel truth also! My Heavens, shall I ever forget the blank horror that grew upon me when I came to understand that music was a science more barbarous than the mathematics that floored me at school, that the life of a musical student, instead of being a delicious whirl of waltz tunes, was 'one dem'd grind,' that seemed to grind out all the soul of the divine art and leave nothing but horrid technicalities about consecutive fifths and suspensions on the dominant? I dare say most people still think of the musician as a being who lives in an enchanted world of sound, rather than as a person greatly occupied with tedious feats of penmanship; just as I myself still think of a prima ballerina not as a hard-working gymnast but as a fairy, whose existence is all bouquets and lime-light."

"But you had a pretty talent for the piano," said Lancelot, in milder accents. "No one forced you to learn composition. You could have learnt anything for the paltry fifteen pounds exacted by the Conservatoire—from the German flute to the grand organ; from singing to scoring band parts."

"No, thank you. Aut Cæsar aut nihil. You remember what I always used to say, 'Either Beethoven—' (The spaniel pricked up his ears)—'or bust.' If I could not be a great musician it was hardly worth while enduring the privations of one, especially at another man's expense. So I did the Prodigal Son dodge, as you know, and out of the proceeds sent you my year's exes in that cheque you with your damnable pride sent me back again. And now, old fellow, that I have you face to face at last, can you offer the faintest scintilla of a shadow of a reason for refusing to take that cheque? No, you can't! Nothing but simple beastly stuckuppishness. I saw through you at once; all your heroics were a fraud. I was not your friend, but your protégé—something to practise your chivalry on. You dropped your cloak, and I saw your feet of clay. Well, I tell you straight, I made up my mind at once to be bad friends with you for life; only when I saw your fiery old phiz at Brahmson's I felt a sort of something tugging inside my greatcoat like a thief after my pocket-book, and I kinder knew, as the Americans say, that in half an hour I should be sitting beneath your hospitable roof."

"I beg your pardon—you will have some whisky?" He rang the bell violently.

"Don't be a fool—you know I didn't mean that. Well, don't let us quarrel. I have forgiven you for your youthful bounty, and you have forgiven me for chucking it up; and now we are going to drink to the Vaterland," he added, as Mary Ann appeared with suspicious alacrity.

"Do you know," he went on, when they had taken the first sip of renewed amity dissolved in whisky, "I think I showed more musical soul than you in refusing to trammel my inspiration with the dull rules invented by fools. I suppose you have mastered them all, eh?" He picked up some sheets of manuscript. "Great Scot! How you must have schooled yourself to scribble all this—you, with your restless nature— full scores, too! I hope you don't offer this sort of thing to Brahmson."

"I certainly went there with that intention," admitted Lancelot. "I thought I'd catch Brahmson himself in the evening—he's never in when I call in the morning."

Peter groaned.

"Quixotic as ever! You can't have been long in London then?"

"A year."

"I suppose you'd jump down my throat if I were to ask you how much is left of that—" he hesitated, then turned the sentence facetiously—"of those twenty thousand shillings you were cut off with?"

"Let this vile den answer."

"Don't disparage the den; it's not so bad."

"You are right—I may come to worse. I've been an awful ass. You know how lucky I was while at the Conservatoire—no, you don't. How should you? Well, I carried off some distinctions and a lot of conceit, and came over here thinking Europe would be at my feet in a month. I was only sorry my father died before I could twit him with my triumph. That's candid, isn't it?"

"Yes; you're not such a prig after all," mused Peter. "I saw the old man's death in the paper—your brother Lionel became the bart."

"Yes, poor beggar, I don't hate him half so much as I did. He reminds me of a man invited to dinner which is nothing but flowers and serviettes and silver plate."

"I'd pawn the plate, anyhow," said Peter, with a little laugh.

"He can't touch anything, I tell you; everything's tied up."

"Ah, well, he'll get tied up, too. He'll marry an American heiress."

"Confound him! I'd rather see the house extinct first."

"Hoity, toity! She'll be quite as good as any of you."

"I can't discuss this with you, Peter," said Lancelot, gently but firmly. "If there is a word I hate more than the word heiress, it is the word American."

"But why? They're both very good words and better things."

"They both smack of the most vulgar thing in the world—money," said Lancelot, walking hotly about the room. "In America there's no other standard. To make your pile, to strike ile—oh, how I shudder to hear these idioms! And can any one hear the word heiress without immediately thinking of matrimony? Phaugh! It's a prostitution."

"What is? You're not very coherent, my friend."

"Very well, I am incoherent. If a great old family can only bolster up its greatness by alliances with the daughters of oil-strikers, then let the family perish with honour."

"But the daughters of oil-strikers are sometimes very charming creatures. They are polished with their fathers' oil."

"You are right. They reek of it. Pah! I pray to Heaven Lionel will either wed a lady or die a bachelor."

"Yes; but what do you call a lady?" persisted Peter.

Lancelot uttered an impatient snarl, and rang the bell violently. Peter stared in silence. Mary Ann appeared.

"How often am I to tell you to leave my matches on the mantel-shelf?" snapped Lancelot. "You seem to delight to hide them away, as if I had time to play parlour games with you."

Mary Ann silently went to the mantel-piece, handed him the matches, and left the room without a word.

"I say, Lancelot, adversity doesn't seem to have agreed with you," said Peter, severely. "That poor girl's eyes were quite wet when she went out. Why didn't you speak? I could have given you heaps of lights, and you might even have sacrificed another scrap of that precious manuscript."

"Well, she has got a knack of hiding my matches all the same," said Lancelot, somewhat shamefacedly. "Besides, I hate her for being called Mary Ann. It's the last terror of cheap apartments. If she only had another name like a human being, I'd gladly call her Miss something. I went so far as to ask her, and she stared at me in a dazed, stupid, silly way, as if I'd asked her to marry me. I suppose the fact is she's been called Mary Ann so long and so often that she's forgotten her father's name—if she ever had any. I must do her the justice, though, to say she answers to the name of Mary Ann in every sense of the phrase."

"She didn't seem at all bad-looking, anyway," said Peter.

"Every man to his taste!" growled Lancelot. "She's as platt and uninteresting as a wooden sabot."

"There's many a pretty foot in a sabot," retorted Peter, with an air of philosophy.

"You think that's clever, but it's simply silly. How does that fact affect this particular sabot?"

"I've put my foot in it," groaned Peter, comically.

"Besides, she might be a houri from heaven," said Lancelot; "but a houri in a patched print frock—" He shuddered and struck a match.

"I don't know exactly what houris from heaven are, but I have a kind of feeling any sort of frock would be out of harmony—!"

Lancelot lit his pipe.

"If you begin to say that sort of thing we must smoke," he said, laughing between the puffs. "I can offer you lots of tobacco—I'm sorry I've got no cigars. Wait till you see Mrs. Leadbatter—my landlady—then you'll talk about houris. Poverty may not be a crime, but it seems to make people awful bores. Wonder if it'll have that effect on me? Ach Himmel! how that woman bores me. No, there's no denying it—there's my pouch, old man—I hate the poor; their virtues are only a shade more vulgar than their vices. This Leadbatter creature is honest after her lights—she sends me up the most ridiculous leavings—and I only hate her the more for it."

"I suppose she works Mary Ann's fingers to the bone from the same mistaken sense of duty," said Peter, acutely. "Thanks; think I'll try one of my cigars. I filled my case, I fancy, before I came out. Yes, here it is; won't you try one?"

"No, thanks, I prefer my pipe."

"It's the same old meerschaum, I see," said Peter.

"The same old meerschaum," repeated Lancelot, with a little sigh.

Peter lit a cigar, and they sat and puffed in silence.

"Dear me!" said Peter, suddenly; "I can almost fancy we're back in our German garret, up the ninety stairs, can't you?"

"No," said Lancelot, sadly, looking round as if in search of something; "I miss the dreams."

"And I," said Peter, striving to speak cheerfully, "I see a dog too much."

"Yes," said Lancelot, with a melancholy laugh. "When you funked becoming a Beethoven, I got a dog and called him after you."

"What? you called him Peter?"

"No, Beethoven!"

"Beethoven! Really?"

"Really. Here, Beethoven!"

The spaniel shook himself, and perked his wee nose up wistfully towards Lancelot's face.

Peter laughed, with a little catch in his voice. He didn't know whether he was pleased, or touched, or angry.

"You started to tell me about those twenty thousand shillings," he said.

"Didn't I tell you? On the expectations of my triumph, I lived extravagantly, like a fool, joined a club, and took up my quarters there. When I began to realise the struggle that lay before me, I took chambers; then I took rooms; now I'm in lodgings. The more I realised it, the less rent I paid. I only go to the club for my letters now. I won't have them come here. I'm living incognito."

"That's taking fame by the forelock, indeed! Then by what name must I ask for you next time? For I'm not to be shaken off."

"Lancelot."

"Lancelot what?"

"Only Lancelot! Mr. Lancelot."

"Why, that's like your Mary Ann!"

"So it is!" he laughed, more bitterly than cordially; "it never struck me before. Yes, we are a pair."

"How did you stumble on this place?"

"I didn't stumble. Deliberate, intelligent selection. You see, it's the next best thing to Piccadilly. You just cross Waterloo Bridge, and there you are at the centre, five minutes from all the clubs. The natives have not yet risen to the idea."

"You mean the rent," laughed Peter. "You're as canny and careful as a Scotch professor. I think it's simply grand the way you've beaten out those shillings, in defiance of your natural instincts. I should have melted them years ago. I believe you have got some musical genius after all."

"You over-rate my abilities," said Lancelot, with the whimsical expression that sometimes flashed across his face even in his most unamiable moments. "You must deduct the thalers I made in exhibitions. As for living in cheap lodgings, I am not at all certain it's an economy, for every now and again it occurs to you that you are saving an awful lot, and you take a hansom on the strength of it."

"Well, I haven't torn up that cheque yet—"

"Peter!" said Lancelot, his flash of gaiety dying away, "I tell you these things as a friend, not as a beggar. If you look upon me as the second, I cease to be the first."

"But, man, I owe you the money; and if it will enable you to hold out a little longer—why, in Heaven's name, shouldn't you—?"

"You don't owe me the money at all; I made no bargain with you; I am not a moneylender."

"Pack dick sum Henker!" growled Peter, with a comical grimace. "Was für a casuist! What a swindler you'd make! I wonder you have the face to deny the debt. Well, and how did you leave Frau Sauer-Kraut?" he said, deeming it prudent to sheer off the subject.

"Fat as a Christmas turkey."

"Or a German sausage. The extraordinary things that woman stuffed herself with!—chunks of fat, stewed apples, Kartoffel salad—all mixed up in one plate, as in a dustbin."

"Don't! You make my gorge rise. Ach Himmel! to think that this nation should be musical! O Music, heavenly maid, how much garlic I have endured for thy sake!"

"Ha! ha! ha!" laughed Peter, putting down his whisky that he might throw himself freely back in the easy chair and roar.

"O that garlic!" he said, panting. "No wonder they smoked so much in Leipsic. Even so they couldn't keep the reek out of the staircases. Still, it's a great country is Germany. Our house does a tremendous business in German patents."

"A great country? A land of barbarians rather. How can a people be civilised that eats jam with its meat?"

"Bravo, Lancelot! You're in lovely form to-night. You seem to go a hundred miles out of your way to come the truly British. First it was oil—now it's jam. There was that aristocratic flash in your eye, too, that look of supreme disdain which brings on riots in Trafalgar Square. Behind the patriotic, the national note, 'How can a people be civilised that eats jam with its meat?' I heard the deeper, the oligarchic accent, 'How can a people be enfranchised that eats meat with its fingers?' Ah, you are right! How you do hate the poor! What bores they are! You aristocrats—the products of centuries of culture, comfort, and cocksureness—will never rid yourselves of your conviction that you are the backbone of England— no, not though that backbone were picked clean of every scrap of flesh by the rats of Radicalism."

"What in the devil are you talking about now?" demanded Lancelot. "You seem to me to go a hundred miles out of your way to twit me with my poverty and my breeding. One would almost think you were anxious to convince me of the poverty of your breeding."

"Oh, a thousand pardons!" ejaculated Peter, blushing violently. "But good heavens, old chap! There's your hot temper again. You surely wouldn't suspect me, of all people in the world, of meaning anything personal? I'm talking of you as a class. Contempt is in your blood—and quite right! We're such snobs, we deserve it. Why d'ye think I ever took to you as a boy at school? Was it because you scribbled inaccurate sonatas and I had myself a talent for knocking tunes off the piano? Not a bit of it. I thought it was, perhaps, but that was only one of my many youthful errors. No, I liked you because your father was an old English baronet, and mine was a merchant who trafficked mainly in things Teutonic. And that's why I like you still. 'Pon my soul it is. You gratify my historic sense—like an old building. You are picturesque. You stand to me for all the good old ideals—including the pride which we are beginning to see is deuced unchristian. Mind you, it's a curious kind of pride when one looks into it. Apparently it's based on the fact that your family has lived on the nation for generations. And yet you won't take my cheque—which is your own. Now don't swear—I know one mustn't analyse things, or the world would come to pieces, so I always vote Tory."

"Then I shall have to turn Radical," grumbled Lancelot.

"Certainly you will, when you have had a little more experience of poverty," retorted Peter. "There, there, old man! forgive me. I only do it to annoy you. Fact is, your outbursts of temper attract me. They are pleasant to look back upon when the storm is over. Yes, my dear Lancelot, you are like the king you look—you can do no wrong. You are picturesque. Pass the whisky."

Lancelot smiled, his handsome brow serene once more. He murmured, "Don't talk rot," but inwardly he was not displeased at Peter's allegiance, half mocking though he knew it.

"Therefore, my dear chap," resumed Peter, sipping his whisky and water, "to return to our lambs, I bow to your patrician prejudices in favour of forks. But your patriotic prejudices are on a different level. There, I am on the same ground as you, and I vow I see nothing inherently superior in the British combination of beef and beetroot, to the German amalgam of lamb and jam."

"Damn lamb and jam!" burst forth Lancelot, adding, with his whimsical look: "There's rhyme, as well as reason. How on earth did we get on this tack?"

"I don't know," said Peter, smiling. "We were talking about Frau Sauer-Kraut, I think. And did you board with her all the time?"

"Yes, and I was always hungry. Till the last, I never learnt to stomach her mixtures. But it was really too much trouble to go down the ninety stairs to a restaurant. It was much easier to be hungry."

"And did you ever get a reform in the hours of washing the floor?"

"Ha! ha! ha! No, they always waited till I was going to bed. I suppose they thought I liked damp. They never got over my morning tub, you know. And that, too, sprang a leak after you left, and helped spontaneously to wash the floor."

"Shows the fallacy of cleanliness," said Peter, "and the inferiority of British ideals. They never bathed in their lives, yet they looked the pink of health."

"Yes,—their complexion was high,—like the fish."

"Ha! ha! Yes, the fish! That was a great luxury, I remember. About once a month."

"Of course, the town is so inland," said Lancelot.

"I see—it took such a long time coming. Ha! ha! ha! And the Herr Professor—is he still a bachelor?"

As the Herr Professor was a septuagenarian and a misogamist, even in Peter's time, his question tickled Lancelot. Altogether the two young men grew quite jolly, recalling a hundred oddities, and reknitting their friendship at the expense of the Fatherland.

"But was there ever a more madcap expedition than ours?" exclaimed Peter. "Most boys start out to be pirates—"

"And some do become music-publishers," Lancelot finished grimly, suddenly reminded of a grievance.

"Ha! ha! ha! Poor fellow!" laughed Peter. "Then you have found them out already."

"Does any one ever find them in?" flashed Lancelot. "I suppose they do exist and are occasionally seen of mortal eyes. I suppose wives and friends and mothers gaze on them with no sense of special privilege, unconscious of their invisibility to the profane eyes of mere musicians."

"My dear fellow, the mere musicians are as plentiful as niggers on the sea-shore. A publisher might spend his whole day receiving regiments of unappreciated geniuses. Bond Street would be impassable. You look at the publisher too much from your own standpoint."

"I tell you I don't look at him from any standpoint. That's what I complain of. He's encircled with a prickly hedge of clerks. 'You will hear from us.' 'It shall have our best consideration. We have no knowledge of the Ms. in question.' Yes, Peter, two valuable quartets have I lost, messing about with these villains."

"I tell you what. I'll give you an introduction to Brahmson. I know him—privately."

"No, thank you, Peter."

"Why not?"

"Because you know him."

"I couldn't give you an introduction if I didn't. This is silly of you, Lancelot."

"If Brahmson can't see any merits in my music, I don't want you to open his eyes. I'll stand on my own bottom. And what's more, Peter, I tell you once for all"—his voice was low and menacing—"if you try any anonymous deus ex machinâ tricks on me in some sly, roundabout fashion, don't you flatter yourself I shan't recognise your hand. I shall, and, by God, it shall never grasp mine again."

"I suppose you think that's very noble and sublime," said Peter, coolly. "You don't suppose if I could do you a turn I'd hesitate for fear of excommunication? I know you're like Beethoven there—your bark is worse than your bite."

"Very well; try. You'll find my teeth nastier than you bargain for."

"I'm not going to try. If you want to go to the dogs—go. Why should I put out a hand to stop you?"

These amenities having reëstablished them in their mutual esteem, they chatted lazily and spasmodically till past midnight, with more smoke than fire in the conversation.

At last Peter began to go, and in course of time actually did take up his umbrella. Not long after, Lancelot conducted him softly down the dark, silent stairs, holding his bedroom candle-stick in his hand, for Mrs. Leadbatter always turned out the hall lamp on her way to bed. The old phrases came to the young men's lips as their hands met in a last hearty grip.

"Lebt wohl!" said Lancelot.

"Auf Wiedersehen!" replied Peter, threateningly.

Lancelot stood at the hall door looking for a moment after his friend—the friend he had tried to cast out of his heart as a recreant. The mist had cleared—the stars glittered countless in the frosty heaven; a golden crescent-moon hung low; the lights and shadows lay almost poetically upon the little street. A rush of tender thoughts whelmed the musician's soul. He saw again the dear old garret, up the ninety stairs, in the Hotel Cologne, where he had lived with his dreams; he heard the pianos and violins going in every room in happy incongruity, publishing to all the prowess of the players; dirty, picturesque old Leipsic rose before him; he was walking again in the Hainstrasse, in the shadow of the quaint, tall houses. Yes, life was sweet after all; he was a coward to lose heart so soon; fame would yet be his; fame and love—the love of a noble woman that fame earns; some gracious creature, breathing sweet refinements, cradled in an ancient home, such as he had left for ever.

The sentimentality of the Fatherland seemed to have crept into his soul; a divinely sweet, sad melody was throbbing in his brain. How glad he was he had met Peter again!

From a neighbouring steeple came a harsh, resonant clang, "One."

It roused him from his dream. He shivered a little, closed the door, bolted it and put up the chain, and turned, half sighing, to take up his bedroom candle again. Then his heart stood still for a moment. A figure—a girl's figure—was coming towards him from the kitchen stairs. As she came into the dim light he saw that it was merely Mary Ann.

She looked half drowsed. Her cap was off, her hair tangled loosely over her forehead. In her disarray she looked prettier than he had ever remembered her. There was something provoking about the large, dreamy eyes, the red lips that parted at the unexpected sight of him.

"Good heavens!" he cried. "Not gone to bed yet?"

"No, sir. I had to stay up to wash up a lot of crockery. The second floor front had some friends to supper late. Missus says she won't stand it again."

"Poor thing!" He patted her soft cheek—it grew hot and rosy under his fingers, but was not withdrawn. Mary Ann made no sign of resentment. In his mood of tenderness to all creation his rough words to her recurred to him.

"You mustn't mind what I said about the matches," he murmured. "When I am in a bad temper I say anything. Remember now for the future, will you?"

"Yessir."

Her face—its blushes flickered over strangely by the candle-light—seemed to look up at him invitingly.

"That's a good girl." And bending down he kissed her on the lips.

"Good night," he murmured.

Mary Ann made some startled, gurgling sound in reply.

Five minutes afterwards Lancelot was in bed, denouncing himself as a vulgar beast.

"I must have drunk too much whisky," he said to himself, angrily. "Good heavens! Fancy sinking to Mary Ann. If Peter had only seen—There was infinitely more poetry in that red-cheeked Mädchen, and yet I never—It is true-there is something sordid about the atmosphere that subtly permeates you, that drags you down to it. Mary Ann! A transpontine drudge! whose lips are fresh from the coalman's and the butcher's. Phaugh!"

The fancy seized hold of his imagination. He could not shake it off, he could not sleep till he had got out of bed and sponged his lips vigorously.

Meanwhile Mary Ann was lying on her bed, dressed, doing her best to keep her meaningless, half-hysterical sobs from her mistress's keen ear.

II

It was a long time before Mary Ann came so prominently into the centre of Lancelot's consciousness again. She remained somewhere in the outer periphery of his thought—nowhere near the bull's-eye, so to speak—as a vague automaton that worked when he pulled a bell-rope. Infinitely more important things were troubling him; the visit of Peter had somehow put a keener edge on his blunted self-confidence; he had started a grand opera, and worked at it furiously in all the intervals left him by his engrossing pursuit after a publisher. Sometimes he would look up from his hieroglyphics and see Mary Ann at his side surveying him curiously, and then he would start, and remember he had rung her up, and try to remember what for. And Mary Ann would turn red, as if the fault was hers.

But the publisher was the one thing that was never out of Lancelot's mind, though he drove Lancelot himself nearly out of it. He was like an arrow stuck in the aforesaid bull's-eye, and, the target being conscious, he rankled sorely. Lancelot discovered that the publisher kept a "musical adviser," whose advice appeared to consist of the famous monosyllable, "Don't." The publisher generally published all the musical adviser's own works, his advice having apparently been neglected when it was most worth taking; at least so Lancelot thought, when he had skimmed through a set of Lancers by one of these worthies.

"I shall give up being a musician," he said to himself, grimly. "I shall become a musical adviser."

Once, half by accident, he actually saw a publisher. "My dear sir," said the great man, "what is the use of bringing quartets and full scores to me? You should have taken them to Brahmson; he's the very man you want. You know his address, of course—just down the street."

Lancelot did not like to say that it was Brahmson's clerks that had recommended him here; so he replied, "But you publish operas, oratorios, cantatas!"

"Ah, yes!—h'm—things that have been played at the big Festivals—composers of prestige—quite a different thing, sir, quite a different thing. There's no sale for these things—none at all, sir—public never heard of you. Now, if you were to write some songs—nice catchy tunes—high class, you know, with pretty words—"

Now Lancelot by this time was aware of the publisher's wily ways; he could almost have constructed an Ollendorffian dialogue, entitled "Between a Music Publisher and a Composer." So he opened his portfolio again and said, "I have brought some."

"Well, send—send them in," stammered the publisher, almost disconcerted. "They shall have our best consideration."

"Oh, but you might just as well look over them at once," said Lancelot, firmly, uncoiling them. "It won't take you five minutes—just let me play one to you. The tunes are rather more original than the average, I can promise you; and yet I think they have a lilt that—"

"I really can't spare the time now. If you leave them, we will do our best."

"Listen to this bit!" said Lancelot, desperately. And dashing at a piano that stood handy, he played a couple of bars. "That's quite a new modulation."

"That's all very well," said the publisher; "but how do you suppose I'm going to sell a thing with an accompaniment like that? Look here, and here! Why, it's all accidentals."

"That's the best part of the song," explained Lancelot; "a sort of undercurrent of emotion that brings out the full pathos of the words. Note the elegant and novel harmonies." He played another bar or two, singing the words softly.

"Yes; but if you think you'll get young ladies to play that, you've got a good deal to learn," said the publisher, gruffly. "This is the sort of accompaniment that goes down," and seating himself at the piano for a moment (somewhat to Lancelot's astonishment, for he had gradually formed a theory that music publishers did not really know the staff from a five-barred gate), he rattled off the melody with his right hand, pounding away monotonously with his left at a few elementary chords.

Lancelot looked dismayed.

"That's the kind of thing you'll have to produce, young man," said the publisher, feeling that he had at last resumed his natural supremacy, "if you want to get your songs published. Elegant harmonies are all very well, but who's to play them?"

"And do you mean to say that a musician in this God-forsaken country must have no chords but tonics and dominants?" ejaculated Lancelot, hotly.

"The less he has of any other the better," said the great man, drily. "I haven't said a word about the melody itself, which is quite out of the ordinary compass, and makes demands upon the singer's vocalisation which are not likely to make a demand for the song. What you have to remember, my dear sir, if you wish to achieve success, is that music, if it is to sell, must appeal to the average amateur young person. The average amateur young person is the main prop of music in this country."

Lancelot snatched up his song and tied the strings of his portfolio very tightly, as if he were clenching his lips.

"If I stay here any longer I shall swear," he said. "Good afternoon."

He went out with a fire at his heart that made him insensitive to the frost without. He walked a mile out of his way mechanically, then, perceiving his stupidity, avenged it by jumping into a hansom. He dared not think how low his funds were running. When he got home he forgot to have his tea, crouching in dumb misery in his easy chair, while the coals in the grate faded like the sunset from red to grey, and the dusk of twilight deepened into the gloom of night, relieved only by a gleam from the street lamp.

The noise of the door opening made him look up.

"Beg pardon, sir. I didn't yer ye come in."

It was Mary Ann's timid accents. Lancelot's head drooped again on his breast. He did not answer.

"You've bin and let your fire go out, sir."

"Don't bother!" he grumbled. He felt a morbid satisfaction in this aggravation of discomfort, almost symbolic as it was of his sunk fortunes.

"Oh, but it'll freeze 'ard to-night, sir. Let me make it up." Taking his sullen silence for consent she ran downstairs and reappeared with some sticks. Soon there were signs of life, which Mary Ann assiduously encouraged by blowing at the embers with her mouth. Lancelot looked on in dull apathy, but as the fire rekindled and the little flames leapt up and made Mary Ann's flushed face the one spot of colour and warmth in the cold dark room, Lancelot's torpidity vanished suddenly. The sensuous fascination seized him afresh, and ere he was aware of it he was lifting the pretty face by the chin.

"I'm so sorry to be so troublesome, Mary Ann. There, you shall give me a kiss to show you bear no malice."

The warm lips obediently met his, and for a moment Lancelot forgot his worries while he held her soft cheek against his.

This time the shock of returning recollection was not so violent as before. He sat up in his chair, but his right arm still twined negligently round her neck, the fingers patting the warm face. "A fellow must have something to divert his mind," he thought, "or he'd go mad. And there's no harm done—the poor thing takes it as a kindness, I'm sure. I suppose her life's dull enough. We're a pair." He felt her shoulders heaving a little, as if she were gulping down something. At last she said: "You ain't troublesome. I ought to ha' yerd ye come in."

He released her suddenly. Her words broke the spell. The vulgar accent gave him a shudder.

"Don't you hear a bell ringing?" he said with dual significance.

"Nosir," said Mary Ann, ingenuously. "I'd yer it in a moment if there was. I yer it in my dreams, I'm so used to it. One night I dreamt the missus was boxin' my yers and askin' me if I was deaf and I said to 'er—"

"Can't you say 'her'?" cried Lancelot, cutting her short impatiently.

"Her," said Mary Ann.

"Then why do you say ''er'?"

"Missus told me to. She said my own way was all wrong."

"Oh, indeed!" said Lancelot. "It's missus that has corrupted you, is it? And pray what used you to say?"

"She," said Mary Ann.

Lancelot was taken aback. "She!" he repeated.

"Yessir," said Mary Ann, with a dawning suspicion that her own vocabulary was going to be vindicated; "whenever I said 'she' she made me say ''er,' and whenever I said 'her' she made me say 'she.' When I said 'her and me' she made me say 'me and she,' and when I said 'I got it from she,' she made me say 'I got it from "er.'"

"Bravo! A very lucid exposition," said Lancelot, laughing. "Did she set you right in any other particulars?"

"Eessir—I mean yessir," replied Mary Ann, the forbidden words flying to her lips like prisoned skylarks suddenly set free. "I used to say, 'Gie I thek there broom, oo't?' 'Arten thee goin' to?' 'Her did say to I.' 'I be goin' on to bed.' 'Look at—'"

"Enough! Enough! What a memory you've got! Now I understand. You're a country girl."

"Eessir," said Mary Ann, her face lighting up. "I mean yessir."

"Well, that redeems you a little," thought Lancelot, with his whimsical look. "So it's missus, is it, who's taught you Cockneyese? My instinct was not so unsound, after all. I dare say you'll turn out something nobler than a Cockney drudge." He finished aloud, "I hope you went a-milking."

"Eessir, sometimes; and I drove back the milk-trunk in the cart, and I rode down on a pony to the second pasture to count the sheep and the heifers."

"Then you are a farmer's daughter?"

"Eessir. But my feyther—I mean my father—had only two little fields when he was alive, but we had a nice garden, with plum trees, and rose bushes, and gillyflowers—"

"Better and better," murmured Lancelot, smiling. And, indeed, the image of Mary Ann skimming the meads on a pony in the sunshine, was more pleasant to contemplate than that of Mary Ann whitening the wintry steps. "What a complexion you must have had to start with!" he cried aloud, surveying the not unenviable remains of it. "Well, and what else did you do?"

Mary Ann opened her lips. It was delightful to see how the dull veil, as of London fog, had been lifted from her face; her eyes sparkled.

Then, "Oh, there's the ground-floor bell," she cried, moving instinctively toward the door.

"Nonsense; I hear no bell," said Lancelot.

"I told you I always hear it," said Mary Ann, hesitating and blushing delicately before the critical word.

"Oh, well, run along then. Stop a moment—I must give you another kiss for talking so nicely. There! And—stop a moment—bring me up some coffee, please, when the ground floor is satisfied."

"Eessir—I mean yessir. What must I say?" she added, pausing troubled on the threshold.

"Say, 'Yes, Lancelot,'" he answered recklessly.

"Yessir," and Mary Ann disappeared.

It was ten endless minutes before she reappeared with the coffee. The whole of the second five minutes Lancelot paced his room feverishly, cursing the ground floor, and stamping as if to bring down its ceiling. He was curious to know more of Mary Ann's history.

But it proved meagre enough. Her mother died when Mary Ann was a child; her father when she was still a mere girl. His affairs were found in hopeless confusion, and Mary Ann was considered lucky to be taken into the house of the well-to-do Mrs. Leadbatter, of London, the elder sister of a young woman who had nursed the vicar's wife. Mrs. Leadbatter had promised the vicar to train up the girl in the way a domestic should go.

"And when I am old enough she is going to pay me wages as well," concluded Mary Ann, with an air of importance.

"Indeed—how old were you when you left the village?"

"Fourteen."

"And how old are you now?"

Mary Ann looked confused. "I don't quite know," she murmured.

"Oh, come," said Lancelot laughingly; "is this your country simplicity? You're quite young enough to tell how old you are."

The tears came into Mary Ann's eyes.

"I can't, Mr. Lancelot," she protested earnestly; "I forgot to count—I'll ask missus."

"And whatever she tells you, you'll be," he said, amused at her unshakable loyalty.

"Yessir," said Mary Ann.

"And so you are quite alone in the world?"

"Yessir—but I've got my canary. They sold everything when my father died, but the vicar's wife she bought my canary back for me because I cried so. And I brought it to London and it hangs in my bedroom. And the vicar, he was so kind to me, he did give me a lot of advice, and Mrs. Amersham, who kept the chandler's shop, she did give me ninepence, all in threepenny bits."

"And you never had any brothers or sisters?"

"There was our Sally, but she died before mother."

"Nobody else?"

"There's my big brother Tom—but I mustn't tell you about him."

"Mustn't tell me about him? Why not?"

"He's so wicked."

The answer was so unexpected that Lancelot could not help laughing, and Mary Ann flushed to the roots of her hair.

"Why, what has he done?" said Lancelot, composing his mouth to gravity.

"I don't know; I was only six. Father told me it was something very dreadful, and Tom had to run away to America, and I mustn't mention him any more. And mother was crying, and I cried because Tom used to give me tickey-backs and go black-berrying with me and our little Sally; and everybody else in the village they seemed glad, because they had said so all along, because Tom would never go to church, even when a little boy."

"I suppose then you went to church regularly?"

"Yessir. When I was at home, I mean."

"Every Sunday?"

Mary Ann hung her head. "Once I went meechin'," she said in low tones. "Some boys and girls they wanted me to go nutting, and I wanted to go too, but I didn't know how to get away, and they told me to cough very loud when the sermon began, so I did, and coughed on and on till at last the vicar glowed at father, and father had to send me out of church."

Lancelot laughed heartily. "Then you didn't like the sermon."

"It wasn't that, sir. The sun was shining that beautiful outside, and I never minded the sermon, only I did get tired of sitting still. But I never done it again—our little Sally, she died soon after."

Lancelot checked his laughter. "Poor little fool!" he thought. Then to brighten her up again he asked cheerily, "And what else did you do on the farm?"

"Oh, please sir, missus will be wanting me now."

"Bother missus. I want some more milk," he said, emptying the milk-jug into the slop-basin. "Run down and get some."

Mary Ann was startled by the splendour of the deed. She took the jug silently and disappeared.

When she returned he said: "Well, you haven't told me half yet. I suppose you kept bees?"

"Oh, yes, and I fed the pigs."

"Hang the pigs! Let's hear something more romantic."

"There was the calves to suckle sometimes, when the mother died or was sold."

"Calves! H'm! H'm! Well, but how could you do that?"

"Dipped my fingers in milk, and let the calves suck 'em. The silly creatures thought it was their mother's teats. Like this."

With a happy inspiration she put her fingers into the slop-basin, and held them up dripping.

Lancelot groaned. It was not only that his improved Mary Ann was again sinking to earth, unable to soar in the romantic æther where he would fain have seen her volant; it was not only that the coarseness of her nature had power to drag her down, it was the coarseness of her red, chapped hands that was thrust once again and violently upon his reluctant consciousness.

Then, like Mary Ann, he had an inspiration.

"How would you like a pair of gloves, Mary Ann?"

He had struck the latent feminine. Her eyes gleamed. "Oh, sir!" was all she could say. Then a swift shade of disappointment darkened the eager little face.

"But I never goes out," she cried.

"I never go out," he corrected, shuddering.

"I never go out," said Mary Ann, her lip twitching.

"That doesn't matter. I want you to wear them indoors."

"But there's nobody to see 'em indoors!"

"I shall see them," he reminded her.

"But they'll get dirty."

"No they won't. You shall only wear them when you come to me. If I buy you a nice pair of gloves, will you promise to put them on every time I ring for you?"

"But what'll missus say?"

"Missus won't see them. The moment you come in, you'll put them on, and just before going out—you'll take them off! See!"

"Yessir. Then nobody'll see me looking so grand but you."

"That's it. And wouldn't you rather look grand for me than for anybody else?"

"Of course I would, sir," said Mary Ann, earnestly, with a grateful little sigh.

So Lancelot measured her wrist, feeling her pulse beat madly. She really had a very little hand, though to his sensitive vision the roughness of the skin seemed to swell it to a size demanding a boxing glove. He bought her six pairs of tan kid, in a beautiful cardboard box. He could ill afford the gift, and made one of his whimsical grimaces when he got the bill. The young lady who served him looked infinitely more genteel than Mary Ann. He wondered what she would think if she knew for whom he was buying these dainty articles. Perhaps her feelings would be so outraged she would refuse to participate in the transaction. But the young lady was happily unconscious; she had her best smile for the handsome, aristocratic young gentleman, and mentioned his moustache later to her bosom-friend in the next department.

And thus Mary Ann and Lancelot became the joint owners of a secret, and coplayers in a little comedy. When Mary Ann came into the room, she would put whatever she was carrying on a chair, gravely extract her gloves from her pocket, and draw them on, Lancelot pretending not to know she was in the room, though he had just said, "Come in." After allowing her a minute he would look up. In the course of a week this became mechanical, so that he lost the semi-ludicrous sense of secrecy which he felt at first, as well as the little pathetic emotion inspired by her absolute unconsciousness that the performance was not intended for her own gratification. Nevertheless, though he could now endure to see Mary Ann handling the sugar tongs, he remained cold to her for some weeks. He had kissed her again in the flush of her joy at the sight of the gloves, but after that there was a reaction. He rarely went to the club now (there was no one with whom he was in correspondence except music publishers, and they didn't reply), but he dropped in there once soon after the glove episode, looked over the papers in the smoking-room, and chatted with a popular composer and one or two men he knew. It was while the waiter was holding out the coffee-tray to him that Mary Ann flashed upon his consciousness. The thought of her seemed so incongruous with the sober magnificence, the massive respectability that surrounded him, the cheerful, marble hearth reddened with leaping flame, the luxurious lounges, the well-groomed old gentlemen smoking eighteenpenny cheroots, the suave, noiseless satellites, that Lancelot felt a sudden pang of bewildered shame. Why, the very waiter who stood bent before him would disdain her. He took his coffee hastily, with a sense of personal unworthiness. This feeling soon evaporated, but it left less of resentment against Mary Ann which made him inexplicable to her. Fortunately, her habit of acceptance saved her some tears, though she shed others. And there remained always the gloves. When she was putting them on she always felt she was slipping her hands in his.

And then there was yet a further consolation.

For the gloves had also a subtle effect on Lancelot. They gave him a sense of responsibility. Vaguely resentful as he felt against Mary Ann (in the intervals of his more definite resentment against publishers), he also felt that he could not stop at the gloves. He had started refining her, and he must go on till she was, so to speak, all gloves. He must cover up her coarse speech, as he had covered up her coarse hands. He owed that to the gloves; it was the least he could do for them. So, whenever Mary Ann made a mistake, Lancelot corrected her. He found these grammatical dialogues not uninteresting, and a vent for his ill-humour against publishers to boot. Very often his verbal corrections sounded astonishingly like reprimands. Here, again, Mary Ann was forearmed by her feeling that she deserved them. She would have been proud had she known how much Mr. Lancelot was satisfied with her aspirates, which came quite natural. She had only dropped her "h's" temporarily, as one drops country friends in coming to London. Curiously enough, Mary Ann did not regard the new locutions and pronunciations as superseding the old. They were a new language; she knew two others, her mother-tongue and her missus's tongue. She would as little have thought of using her new linguistic acquirements in the kitchen as of wearing her gloves there. They were for Lancelot's ears only, as her gloves were for his eyes.

All this time Lancelot was displaying prodigious musical activity, so much so that the cost of ruled paper became a consideration. There was no form of composition he did not essay, none by which he made a shilling. Once he felt himself the prey of a splendid inspiration, and sat up all night writing at fever pitch, surrounded with celestial harmonies, audible to him alone; the little room resounded with the thunder of a mighty orchestra, in which every instrument sang to him individually—the piccolo, the flute, the oboes, the clarionets, filling the air with a silver spray of notes; the drums throbbing, the trumpets shrilling, the four horns pealing with long stately notes, the trombones and bassoons vibrating, the violins and violas sobbing in linked sweetness, the 'cello and the contra-bass moaning their under-chant. And then, in the morning, when the first rough sketch was written, the glory faded. He threw down his pen, and called himself an ass for wasting his time on what nobody would ever look at. Then he laid his head on the table, overwrought, full of an infinite pity for himself. A sudden longing seized him for some one to love him, to caress his hair, to smooth his hot forehead. This mood passed too; he smoothed the slumbering Beethoven instead. After a while he went into his bedroom, and sluiced his face and hands in ice-cold water, and rang the bell for breakfast.

There was a knock at the door in response.

"Come in!" he said gently—his emotions had left him tired to the point of tenderness. And then he waited a minute while Mary Ann was drawing on her gloves.

"Did you ring, sir?" said a wheezy voice, at last. Mrs. Leadbatter had got tired of waiting.

Lancelot started violently—Mrs. Leadbatter had latterly left him entirely to Mary Ann. "It's my hastmer," she had explained to him apologetically, meeting him casually in the passage. "I can't trollop up and down stairs as I used to when I fust took this house five-an'-twenty year ago, and pore Mr. Leadbatter—" and here followed reminiscences long since in their hundredth edition.

"Yes; let me have some coffee—very hot—please," said Lancelot, less gently. The woman's voice jarred upon him; and her features were not redeeming.

"Lawd, sir, I 'ope that gas 'asn't been burnin' all night, sir," she said, as she was going out.

"It has," he said shortly.

"You'll hexcoose me, sir, but I didn't bargen for that. I'm only a pore, honest, 'ard-workin' widder, and I noticed the last gas bill was 'eavier then hever since that black winter that took pore Mr. Leadbatter to 'is grave. Fair is fair, and I shall 'ave to reckon it a hextry, with the rate gone up sevenpence a thousand

and my Rosie leavin' a fine nurse-maid's place in Bayswater at the end of the month to come 'ome and 'elp 'er mother, 'cos my hastmer—"

"Will you please shut the door after you?" interrupted Lancelot, biting his lip with irritation. And Mrs. Leadbatter, who was standing in the aperture with no immediate intention of departing, could find no repartee beyond slamming the door as hard as she could.

This little passage of arms strangely softened Lancelot to Mary Ann. It made him realise faintly what her life must be.

"I should go mad and smash all the crockery!" he cried aloud. He felt quite tender again towards the uncomplaining girl.

Presently there was another knock. Lancelot growled, half prepared to renew the battle, and to give Mrs. Leadbatter a piece of his mind on the subject. But it was merely Mary Ann.

Shaken in his routine, he looked on steadily while Mary Ann drew on her gloves; and this in turn confused Mary Ann. Her hand trembled.

"Let me help you," he said.

And there was Lancelot buttoning Mary Ann's glove just as if her name were Guinevere! And neither saw the absurdity of wasting time upon an operation which would have to be undone in two minutes. Then Mary Ann, her eyes full of soft light, went to the sideboard and took out the prosaic elements of breakfast.

When she returned, to put them back, Lancelot was astonished to see her carrying a cage—a plain square cage, made of white tin wire.

"What's that?" he gasped.

"Please, Mr. Lancelot, I want to ask you to do me a favour." She dropped her eyelashes timidly.

"Yes, Mary Ann," he said briskly. "But what have you got there?"

"It's only my canary, sir. Would you—please, sir, would you mind?"—then desperately, "I want to hang it up here, sir!"

"Here?" he repeated in frank astonishment. "Why?"

"Please, sir, I—I—it's sunnier here, sir, and I—I think it must be pining away. It hardly ever sings in my bedroom."

"Well, but," he began—then seeing the tears gathering on her eyelids, he finished with laughing good-nature—"as long as Mrs. Leadbatter doesn't reckon it an extra."

"Oh, no, sir," said Mary Ann, seriously. "I'll tell her. Besides, she will be glad, because she don't like the canary—she says its singing disturbs her. Her room is next to mine, you know, Mr. Lancelot."

"But you said it doesn't sing much."

"Please, sir, I—I mean in summer," explained Mary Ann, in rosy confusion; "and—and—it'll soon be summer, sir."

"Sw—e-e-t!" burst forth the canary, suddenly, as if encouraged by Mary Ann's opinion.

It was a pretty little bird—one golden yellow from beak to tail, as though it had been dipped in sunshine.

"You see, sir," she cried eagerly, "it's beginning already."

"Yes," said Lancelot, grimly; "but so is Beethoven."

"I'll hang it high up—in the window," said Mary Ann, "where the dog can't get at it."

"Well, I won't take any responsibilities," murmured Lancelot, resignedly.

"No, sir, I'll attend to that," said Mary Ann, vaguely.

After the installation of the canary Lancelot found himself slipping more and more into a continuous matter-of-course flirtation; more and more forgetting the slavey in the candid young creature who had, at moments, strange dancing lights in her awakened eyes, strange flashes of witchery in her ingenuous expression. And yet he made a desultory struggle against what a secret voice was always whispering was a degradation. He knew she had no real place in his life; he scarce thought of her save when she came bodily before his eyes with her pretty face and her trustful glance.

He felt no temptation to write sonatas on her eyebrow—to borrow Peter's variation, for the use of musicians, of Shakespeare's "write sonnets on his mistress's eyebrow"—and, indeed, he knew she could be no fit mistress for him—this starveling drudge, with passive passions, meek, accepting, with well-nigh every spark of spontaneity choked out of her. The women of his dreams were quite other—beautiful, voluptuous, full of the joy of life, tremulous with poetry and lofty thought, with dark amorous orbs that flashed responsive to his magic melodies. They hovered about him as he wrote and played—Venuses rising from the seas of his music. And then—with his eyes full of the divine tears of youth, with his brain a hive of winged dreams—he would turn and kiss merely Mary Ann! Such is the pitiful breed of mortals.

And after every such fall, he thought more contemptuously of Mary Ann. Idealise her as he might, see all that was best in her as he tried to, she remained common and commonplace enough. Her ingenuousness, while from one point of view it was charming, from another was but a pleasant synonym for silliness. And it might not be ingenuousness—or silliness—after all! For, was Mary Ann as innocent as she looked? The guilelessness of the dove might very well cover the wisdom of the serpent. The instinct—the repugnance that made him sponge off her first kiss from his lips—was probably a true instinct. How was it possible a girl of that class should escape the sordid attentions of street swains? Even when she was in the country she was well-nigh of wooable age, the likely cynosure of neighbouring ploughboys' eyes. And what of the other lodgers!

A finer instinct—that of a gentleman—kept him from putting any questions to Mary Ann. Indeed, his own delicacy repudiated the images that strove to find entry in his brain, even as his fastidiousness shrank from realising the unlovely details of Mary Ann's daily duties—these things disgusted him more with himself than with her. And yet he found himself acquiring a new and illogical interest in the boots he met outside doors. Early one morning he went halfway up the second flight of stairs—a strange region where his own boots had never before trod—but came down ashamed and with fluttering heart as if he had gone up to steal boots instead of to survey them. He might have asked Mary Ann or her "missus" who the other tenants were, but he shrank from the topic. Their hours were not his, and he only once chanced on a fellow-man in the passage, and then he was not sure it was not the tax-collector. Besides, he was not really interested—it was only a flicker of idle curiosity as to the actual psychology of Mary Ann. That he did not really care he proved to himself by kissing her next time. He accepted her as she was—because she was there. She brightened his troubled life a little, and he was quite sure he brightened hers. So he drifted on, not worrying himself to mean any definite harm to her. He had quite enough worry with those music publishers.

The financial outlook was, indeed, becoming terrifying. He was glad there was nobody to question him, for he did not care to face the facts. Peter's threat of becoming a regular visitor had been nullified by his father despatching him to Germany to buy up some more Teutonic patents. "Wonderful are the ways of Providence!" he had written to Lancelot. "If I had not flown in the old man's face and picked up a little German here years ago, I should not be half so useful to him now.... I shall pay a flying visit to Leipsic—not on business."

But at last Peter returned, Mrs. Leadbatter panting to the door to let him in one afternoon without troubling to ask Lancelot if he was "at home." He burst upon the musician, and found him in the most undisguisable dumps.

"Why didn't you answer my letter, you impolite old bear?" Peter asked, warding off Beethoven with his umbrella.

"I was busy," Lancelot replied pettishly.

"Busy writing rubbish. Haven't you got 'Ops.' enough? I bet you haven't had anything published yet."

"I am working at a grand opera," he said in dry, mechanical tones. "I have hopes of getting it put on. Gasco, the impresario, is a member of my club, and he thinks of running a season in the autumn. I had a talk with him yesterday."

"I hope I shall live to see it," said Peter, sceptically.

"I hope you will," said Lancelot, sharply.

"None of my family ever lived beyond ninety," said Peter, shaking his head dolefully; "and then, my heart is not so good as it might be."

"It certainly isn't!" cried poor Lancelot. "But everybody hits a chap when he's down."

He turned his head away, striving to swallow the lump that would rise to his throat. He had a sense of infinite wretchedness and loneliness.

"Oh, poor old chap; is it so bad as all that?" Peter's somewhat strident voice had grown tender as a woman's. He laid his hand affectionately on Lancelot's tumbled hair. "You know I believe in you with all my soul. I never doubted your genius for a moment. Don't I know too well that's what keeps you back? Come, come, old fellow. Can't I persuade you to write rot? One must keep the pot boiling, you know. You turn out a dozen popular ballads, and the coin'll follow your music as the rats did the pied piper's. Then, if you have any ambition left, you kick away the ladder by which you mounted, and stand on the heights of art."

"Never!" cried Lancelot. "It would degrade me in my own eyes. I'd rather starve; and you can't shake them off—the first impression is everything; they would always be remembered against me," he added after a pause.

"Motives mixed," reflected Peter. "That's a good sign." Aloud he said, "Well, you think it over. This is a practical world, old man; it wasn't made for dreamers. And one of the first dreams that you've got to wake from is the dream that anybody connected with the stage can be relied on from one day to the next. They gas for the sake of gassing, or they tell you pleasant lies out of mere goodwill, just as they call for your drinks. Their promises are beautiful bubbles, on a basis of soft soap, and made to 'bust.'"

"You grow quite eloquent," said Lancelot, with a wan smile.

"Eloquent! There's more in me than you've yet found out. Now then! Give us your hand that you'll chuck art, and we'll drink to your popular ballad—hundredth thousand edition, no drawing-room should be without it."

Lancelot flushed. "I was just going to have some tea. I think it's five o'clock," he murmured.

"The very thing I'm dying for," cried Peter, energetically; "I'm as parched as a pea." Inwardly he was shocked to find the stream of whisky run dry.

So Lancelot rang the bell, and Mary Ann came up with the tea-tray in the twilight.

"We'll have a light," cried Peter, and struck one of his own with a shadowy underthought of saving Mary Ann from a possible scolding, in case Lancelot's matches should be again unapparent. Then he uttered a comic exclamation of astonishment. Mary Ann was putting on a pair of gloves! In his surprise he dropped the match.

Mary Ann was equally startled by the unexpected sight of a stranger, but when he struck his second match her hands were bare and red.

"What in Heaven's name were you putting on gloves for, my girl?" said Peter, amused.

Lancelot stared fixedly at the fire, trying to keep the blood from flooding his cheeks. He wondered that the ridiculousness of the whole thing had never struck him in its full force before. Was it possible he could have made such an ass of himself?

"Please, sir, I've got to go out, and I'm in a hurry," said Mary Ann.

Lancelot felt intense relief. An instant after his brow wrinkled itself. "Oho!" he thought. "So this is Miss Simpleton, is it?"

"Then why did you take them off again?" retorted Peter.

Mary Ann's repartee was to burst into tears and leave the room.

"Now I've offended her," said Peter. "Did you see how she tossed her pretty head?"

"Ingenious minx," thought Lancelot.

"She's left the tray on a chair by the, door," went on Peter. "What an odd girl! Does she always carry on like this?"

"She's got such a lot to do. I suppose she sometimes gets a bit queer in her head," said Lancelot, conceiving he was somehow safeguarding Mary Ann's honour by the explanation.

"I don't think that," answered Peter. "She did seem dull and stupid when I was here last. But I had a good stare at her just now, and she seems rather bright. Why, her accent is quite refined—she must have picked it up from you."

"Nonsense, nonsense," exclaimed Lancelot, testily.

The little danger—or rather the great danger of being made to appear ridiculous—which he had just passed through, contributed to rouse him from his torpor. He exerted himself to turn the conversation, and was quite lively over tea.

"Sw—eet! Sw—w—w—w—eet!" suddenly broke into the conversation.

"More mysteries!" cried Peter. "What's that?"

"Only a canary."

"What, another musical instrument! Isn't Beethoven jealous? I wonder he doesn't consume his rival in his wrath. But I never knew you liked birds."

"I don't particularly. It isn't mine."

"Whose is it?"

Lancelot answered briskly: "Mary Ann's. She asked to be allowed to keep it here. It seems it won't sing in her attic; it pines away."

"And do you believe that?"

"Why not? It doesn't sing much even here."

"Let me look at it—ah, it's a plain Norwich yellow. If you wanted a singing canary you should have come to me; I'd have given you one 'made in Germany'—one of our patents—they train them to sing tunes and that puts up the price."

"Thank you, but this one disturbs me sufficiently."

"Then why do you put up with it?"

"Why do I put up with that Christmas number supplement over the mantel-piece? It's part of the furniture. I was asked to let it be here and I couldn't be rude."

"No, it's not in your nature. What a bore it must be to feed it! Let me see, I suppose you give it canary seed biscuits—I hope you don't give it butter."

"Don't be an ass!" roared Lancelot. "You don't imagine I bother my head whether it eats butter or—or marmalade."

"Who feeds it then?"

"Mary Ann, of course."

"She comes in and feeds it?"

"Certainly."

"Several times a day?"

"I suppose so."

"Lancelot," said Peter, solemnly. "Mary Ann's mashed on you."

Lancelot shrank before Peter's remark as a burglar from a policeman's bull's-eye. The bull's-eye seemed to cast a new light on Mary Ann, too, but he felt too unpleasantly dazzled to consider that for the moment; his whole thought was to get out of the line of light.

"Nonsense!" he answered; "why, I'm hardly ever in when she feeds it, and I believe it eats all day long—gets supplied in the morning like a coal-scuttle. Besides, she comes in to dust and all that when she pleases. And I do wish you wouldn't use that word 'mashed.' I loathe it."

Indeed, he writhed under the thought of being coupled with Mary Ann. The thing sounded so ugly—so squalid. In the actual, it was not so unpleasant, but looked at from the outside—unsympathetically—it was hopelessly vulgar, incurably plebeian. He shuddered.

"I don't know," said Peter. "It's a very expressive word, is 'mashed.' But I will make allowance for your poetical feelings and give up the word—except in its literal sense, of course. I'm sure you wouldn't object to mashing a music publisher!"

Lancelot laughed with false heartiness. "Oh, but if I'm to write those popular ballads, you say he'll become my best friend."

"Of course he will," cried Peter, eagerly sniffing at the red herring Lancelot had thrown across the track. "You stand out for a royalty on every copy, so that if you strike ile—oh, I beg your pardon, that's another of the phrases you object to, isn't it?"

"Don't be a fool," said Lancelot, laughing on. "You know I only object to that in connection with English peers marrying the daughters of men who have done it."

"Oh, is that it? I wish you'd publish an expurgated dictionary with most of the words left out, and exact definitions of the conditions under which one may use the remainder. But I've got on a siding. What was I talking about?"

"Royalty," muttered Lancelot, languidly.

"Royalty? No. You mentioned the aristocracy, I think." Then he burst into a hearty laugh. "Oh, yes—on that ballad. Now, look here! I've brought a ballad with me, just to show you—a thing that is going like wildfire."

"Not Good-night and Good-by, I hope," laughed Lancelot.

"Yes—the very one!" cried Peter, astonished.

"Himmel!" groaned Lancelot, in comic despair.

"You know it already?" inquired Peter, eagerly.

"No; only I can't open a paper without seeing the advertisement and the sickly sentimental refrain."

"You see how famous it is, anyway," said Peter. "And if you want to strike—er—to make a hit you'll just take that song and do a deliberate imitation of it."

"Wha-a-a-t!" gasped Lancelot.

"My dear chap, they all do it. When the public cotton to a thing, they can't have enough of it."

"But I can write my own rot, surely."

"In the face of all this litter of 'Ops.' I daren't dispute that for a moment. But it isn't enough to write rot—the public want a particular kind of rot. Now just play that over—oblige me." He laid both hands on Lancelot's shoulders in amicable appeal.

Lancelot shrugged them, but seated himself at the piano, played the introductory chords, and commenced singing the words in his pleasant baritone.

Suddenly Beethoven ran towards the door, howling.

Lancelot ceased playing and looked approvingly at the animal.

"By Jove! he wants to go out. What an ear for music that animal's got."

Peter smiled grimly. "It's long enough. I suppose that's why you call him Beethoven."

"Not at all. Beethoven had no ear—at least not in his latest period—he was deaf. Lucky devil! That is, if this sort of thing was brought round on barrel-organs."

"Never mind, old man! Finish the thing."

"But consider Beethoven's feelings!"

"Hang Beethoven!"

"Poor Beethoven. Come here, my poor maligned musical critic! Would they give you a bad name and hang you? Now you must be very quiet. Put your paws into those lovely long ears of yours, if it gets too horrible. You have been used to high-class music, I know, but this is the sort of thing that England expects every man to do, so the sooner you get used to it, the better." He ran his fingers along the keys. "There, Peter, he's growling already. I'm sure he'll start again, the moment I strike the theme."

"Let him! We'll take it as a spaniel obligato."

"Oh, but his accompaniments are too staccato. He has no sense of time."

"Why don't you teach him, then, to wag his tail like the pendulum of a metronome? He'd be more use to you that way than setting up to be a musician, which Nature never meant him for—his hair's not long enough. But go ahead, old man, Beethoven's behaving himself now."

Indeed, as if he were satisfied with his protest, the little beast remained quiet, while his lord and master went through the piece. He did not even interrupt at the refrain:—

"Kiss me, good-night, dear love,
Dream of the old delight;
My spirit is summoned above,
Kiss me, dear love, good-night."

"I must say it's not so awful as I expected," said Lancelot, candidly; "it's not at all bad—for a waltz."

"There, you see!" cried Peter, eagerly; "the public are not such fools after all."

"Still, the words are the most maudlin twaddle!" said Lancelot, as if he found some consolation in the fact.

"Yes, but I didn't write them!" replied Peter, quickly. Then he grew red and laughed an embarrassed laugh. "I didn't mean to tell you, old man. But there—the cat's out. That's what took me to Brahmson's that afternoon we met! And I harmonised it myself, mind you, every crotchet. I picked up enough at the Conservatoire for that. You know lots of fellows only do the tune—they give out all the other work."

"So you are the great Keeley Lesterre, eh?" said Lancelot, in amused astonishment.

"Yes; I have to do it under another name. I don't want to grieve the old man. You see, I promised him to reform, when he took me back to his heart and business."

"Is that strictly honourable, Peter?" said Lancelot, shaking his head.

"Oh, well! I couldn't give it up altogether, but I do practically stick to the contract—it's all overtime, you know. It doesn't interfere a bit with business. Besides, as you'd say, it isn't music," he said slyly. "And just because I don't want it I make a heap of coin out of it—that's why I'm so vexed at your keeping me still in your debt."

Lancelot frowned. "Then you had no difficulty in getting published?" he asked.

"I don't say that. It was bribery and corruption so far as my first song was concerned. I tipped a professional to go down and tell Brahmson he was going to take it up. You know, of course, well-known singers get half-a-guinea from the publisher every time they sing a song."

"No; do they?" said Lancelot. "How mean of them!"

"Business, my boy. It pays the publisher to give it them. Look at the advertisement!"

"But suppose a really fine song was published, and the publisher refused to pay this blood-money?"

"Then I suppose they'd sing some other song, and let that moulder on the foolish publisher's shelves."

"Great Heavens!" said Lancelot, jumping up from the piano in wild excitement. "Then a musician's reputation is really at the mercy of a mercenary crew of singers, who respect neither art nor themselves. Oh, yes, we are indeed a musical people!"

"Easy there! Several of 'em are pals of mine, and I'll get them to take up those ballads of yours as soon as you write 'em."

"Let them go to the devil with their ballads!" roared Lancelot, and with a sweep of his arm whirled Good-night and Good-by into the air. Peter picked it up and wrote something on it with a stylographic pen which he produced from his waistcoat pocket.

"There!" he said, "that'll make you remember it's your own property—and mine—that you are treating so disrespectfully."

"I beg your pardon, old chap," said Lancelot, rebuked and remorseful.

"Don't mention it," replied Peter. "And whenever you decide to become rich and famous—there's your model."

"Never! Never! Never!" cried Lancelot, when Peter went at ten. "My poor Beethoven! What you must have suffered! Never mind, I'll play you your moonlight sonata."

He touched the keys gently and his sorrows and his temptations faded from him. He glided into Bach, and then into Chopin and Mendelssohn, and at last drifted into dreamy improvisation, his fingers moving almost of themselves, his eyes half closed, seeing only inward visions.

And then, all at once, he awoke with a start, for Beethoven was barking towards the door, with pricked-up ears and rigid tail.

"Sh! You little beggar," he murmured, becoming conscious that the hour was late, and that he himself had been noisy at unbeseeming hours. "What's the matter with you?" And, with a sudden thought, he threw open the door.

It was merely Mary Ann.

Her face—flashed so unexpectedly upon him—had the piquancy of a vision, but its expression was one of confusion and guilt; there were tears on her cheeks; in her hand was a bedroom candle-stick.

She turned quickly, and began to mount the stairs. Lancelot put his hand on her shoulder, and turned her face towards him and said in an imperious whisper:—

"Now then, what's up? What are you crying about?"

"I ain't—I mean I'm not crying," said Mary Ann, with a sob in her breath.

"Come, come, don't fib. What's the matter?"

"I'm not crying, it's only the music," she murmured.

"The music," he echoed, bewildered.

"Yessir. The music always makes me cry—but you can't call it crying—it feels so nice."

"Oh, then you've been listening!"

"Yessir." Her eyes drooped in humiliation.

"But you ought to have been in bed," he said. "You get little enough sleep as it is."

"It's better than sleep," she answered.

The simple phrase vibrated through him, like a beautiful minor chord. He smoothed her hair tenderly.

"Poor child!" he said.

There was an instant's silence. It was past midnight, and the house was painfully still. They stood upon the dusky landing, across which a bar of light streamed from his half-open door, and only Beethoven's eyes were upon them. But Lancelot felt no impulse to fondle her, only just to lay his hand on her hair, as in benediction and pity.

"So you liked what I was playing," he said, not without a pang of personal pleasure.

"Yessir; I never heard you play that before."

"So you often listen!"

"I can hear you, even in the kitchen. Oh, it's just lovely! I don't care what I have to do then, if it's grates or plates or steps. The music goes and goes, and I feel back in the country again, and standing, as I used to love to stand of an evening, by the stile, under the big elm, and watch how the sunset did redden the white birches, and fade in the water. Oh, it was so nice in the springtime, with the hawthorn that grew on the other bank, and the bluebells—"

The pretty face was full of dreamy tenderness, the eyes lit up witchingly. She pulled herself up suddenly, and stole a shy glance at her auditor.

"Yes, yes, go on," he said; "tell me all you feel about the music."

"And there's one song you sometimes play that makes me feel floating on and on like a great white swan."

She hummed a few bars of the Gondel-Lied—flawlessly.

"Dear me! you have an ear!" he said, pinching it. "And how did you like what I was playing just now?" he went on, growing curious to know how his own improvisations struck her.

"Oh, I liked it so much," she whispered back, enthusiastically; "because it reminded me of my favourite one—every moment I did think—I thought—you were going to come into that."

The whimsical sparkle leapt into his eyes. "And I thought I was so original," he murmured.

"But what I liked best," she began, then checked herself, as if suddenly remembering she had never made a spontaneous remark before, and lacking courage to establish a precedent.

"Yes—what you liked best?" he said encouragingly.

"That song you sang this afternoon," she said shyly.

"What song? I sang no song," he said, puzzled for a moment.

"Oh, yes! That one about—

"'Kiss me, dear love, good-night.'

"I was going upstairs but it made me stop just here—and cry."

He made his comic grimace.

"So it was you Beethoven was barking at! And I thought he had an ear! And I thought you had an ear! But no! You're both Philistines after all. Heigho!"

She looked sad. "Oughtn't I to ha' liked it?" she asked anxiously.

"Oh, yes," he said reassuringly; "it's very popular. No drawing-room is without it."

She detected the ironic ring in his voice. "It wasn't so much the music," she began apologetically.

"Now—now you're going to spoil yourself," he said. "Be natural."

"But it wasn't," she protested. "It was the words—"

"That's worse," he murmured below his breath.

"They reminded me of my mother as she laid dying."

"Ah!" said Lancelot.

"Yes, sir, mother was a long time dying—it was when I was a little girl and I used to nurse her—I fancy it was our little Sally's death that killed her, she took to her bed after the funeral and never left it till she went to her own," said Mary Ann, with unconscious flippancy. "She used to look up to the ceiling and say that she was going to little Sallie, and I remember I was such a silly then, I brought mother flowers and apples and bits of cake to take to Sally with my love. I put them on her pillow, but the flowers faded and the cake got mouldy—mother was such a long time dying—and at last I ate the apples myself, I was so tired of waiting. Wasn't I silly?" And Mary Ann laughed a little laugh with tears in it. Then growing grave again, she added: "And at last, when mother was really on the point of death, she forgot all about little Sally and said she was going to meet Tom. And I remember thinking she was going to America—I didn't know people talk nonsense before they die."

"They do—a great deal of it, unfortunately," said Lancelot, lightly, trying to disguise from himself that his eyes were moist. He seemed to realise now what she was—a child; a child who, simpler than most children to start with, had grown only in body, whose soul had been stunted by uncounted years of dull and monotonous drudgery. The blood burnt in his veins as he thought of the cruelty of circumstance and the heartless honesty of her mistress. He made up his mind for the second time to give Mrs. Leadbatter a piece of his mind in the morning.

"Well, go to bed now, my poor child," he said, "or you'll get no rest at all."

"Yessir."

She went obediently up a couple of stairs, then turned her head appealingly towards him. The tears still glimmered on her eyelashes. For an instant he thought she was expecting her kiss, but she only wanted to explain anxiously once again, "That was why I liked that song, 'Kiss me, good-night, dear love.' It was what my mother—"

"Yes, yes, I understand," he broke in, half amused, though somehow the words did not seem so full of maudlin pathos to him now. "And there—" he drew her head towards him—"Kiss me, good-night—"

He did not complete the quotation; indeed, her lips were already drawn too close to his. But, ere he released her, the long-repressed thought had found expression.

"You don't kiss anybody but me?" he said half playfully.

"Oh, no, sir," said Mary Ann, earnestly.

"What!" more lightly still. "Haven't you got half a dozen young men?"

Mary Ann shook her head, more regretfully than resentfully. "I told you I never go out—except for little errands."

She had told him, but his attention had been so concentrated on the ungrammatical form in which she had conveyed the information, that the fact itself had made no impression. Now his anger against Mrs. Leadbatter dwindled. After all, she was wise in not giving Mary Ann the run of the London streets.

"But"—he hesitated. "How about the—the milkman—and the—the other gentlemen?"

"Please, sir," said Mary Ann, "I don't like them."

After that no man could help expressing his sense of her good taste.

"Then you won't kiss anybody but me," he said, as he let her go for the last time. He had a Quixotic sub-consciousness that he was saving her from his kind by making her promise formally.

"How could I, Mr. Lancelot?" And the brimming eyes shone with soft light. "I never shall—never."

It sounded like a troth.

He went back to the room and shut the door, but could not shut out her image. The picture she had unwittingly supplied of herself took possession of his imagination: he saw her almost as a dream-figure—the virginal figure he knew—standing by the stream in the sunset, amid the elms and silver birches, with daisies in her hands and bluebells at her feet, inhaling the delicate scent that wafted from the white hawthorn bushes, and watching the water glide along till it seemed gradually to wash away the fading colours of the sunset that glorified it. And as he dwelt on the vision he felt harmonies and phrases stirring and singing in his brain, like a choir of awakened birds. Quickly he seized paper and wrote down the theme that flowed out at the point of his pen—a reverie full of the haunting magic of quiet waters and woodland sunsets and the gracious innocence of maidenhood. When it was done he felt he must give it a distinctive name. He cast about for one, pondering and rejecting titles innumerable. Countless lines of poetry ran through his head, from which he sought to pick a word or two as one plucks a violet from a posy. At last a half-tender, half-whimsical look came into his face, and picking his pen out of his hair, he wrote merely—"Marianne."

It was only natural that Mary Ann should be unable to maintain herself—or be maintained—at this idyllic level. But her fall was aggravated by two circumstances, neither of which had any particular business to occur. The first was an intimation from the misogamist German Professor that he had persuaded another of his old pupils to include a prize-symphony by Lancelot in the programme of a

Crystal Palace Concert. This was of itself sufficient to turn Lancelot's head away from all but thoughts of Fame, even if Mary Ann had not been luckless enough to be again discovered cleaning the steps—and without gloves. Against such a spectacle the veriest idealist is powerless. If Mary Ann did not immediately revert to the category of quadrupeds in which she had started, it was only because of Lancelot's supplementary knowledge of the creature. But as he passed her by, solicitous as before not to tread upon her, he felt as if all the cold water in her pail were pouring down the back of his neck.

Nevertheless, the effect of both of these turns of fortune was transient. The symphony was duly performed, and dismissed in the papers as promising, if over-ambitious; the only tangible result was a suggestion from the popular composer, who was a member of his club, that Lancelot should collaborate with him in a comic opera, for the production of which he had facilities. The composer confessed he had a fluent gift of tune, but had no liking for the drudgery of orchestration, and, as Lancelot was well up in these tedious technicalities, the two might strike a partnership to mutual advantage.

Lancelot felt insulted, but retained enough mastery of himself to reply that he would think it over. As he gave no signs of life or thought, the popular composer then wrote to him at length on the subject, offering him fifty pounds for the job, half of it on account. Lancelot was in sore straits when he got the letter, for his stock of money was dwindling to vanishing point, and he dallied with the temptation sufficiently to take the letter home with him. But his spirit was not yet broken, and the letter, crumpled like a rag, was picked up by Mary Ann and straightened out, and carefully placed upon the mantel-shelf.

Time did something of a similar service for Mary Ann herself, picking her up from the crumpled attitude in which Lancelot had detected her on the doorstep, straightening her out again, and replacing her upon her semi-poetic pedestal. But, as with the cream-laid note-paper, the wrinklings could not be effaced entirely; which was more serious for Mary Ann.

Not that Mary Ann was conscious of these diverse humours in Lancelot. Unconscious of changes in herself she could not conceive herself related to his variations of mood; still less did she realise the inward struggle, of which she was the cause. She was vaguely aware that he had external worries, for all his grandeur, and if he was by turns brusque, affectionate, indifferent, playful, brutal, charming, callous, demonstrative, she no more connected herself with these vicissitudes than with the caprices of the weather. If her sun smiled once a day it was enough. How should she know that his indifference was often a victory over himself, as his amativeness was a defeat?

If any excuse could be found for Lancelot, it would be that which he administered to his conscience morning and evening like a soothing syrup. His position was grown so desperate that Mary Ann almost stood between him and suicide. Continued disappointment made his soul sick; his proud heart fed on itself. He would bite his lips till the blood came, vowing never to give in. And not only would he not move an inch from his ideal, he would rather die than gratify Peter by falling back on him; he would never even accept that cheque which was virtually his own.

It was wonderful how, in his stoniest moments, the sight of Mary Ann's candid face, eloquent with dumb devotion, softened and melted him. He would take her gloved hand and press it silently. And Mary Ann never knew one iota of his inmost thought! He could not bring himself to that; indeed, she never for a moment appeared to him in the light of an intelligent being; at her best she was a sweet, simple, loving child. And he scarce spoke to her at all now—theirs was a silent communion—he had no heart to converse with her as he had done. The piano too was almost silent; the canary sang less and less, though spring was coming, and glints of sunshine stole between the wires of its cage; even Beethoven sometimes failed to bark when there was a knock at the street door.

And at last there came a day when—for the first time in his life—Lancelot inspected his wardrobe, and hunted together his odds and ends of jewelry. From this significant task he was aroused by hearing Mrs. Leadbatter coughing in his sitting-room.

He went in with an interrogative look.

"Oh, my chest!" said Mrs. Leadbatter, patting it. "It's no use my denyin' of it, sir, I'm done up. It's as much as I can do to crawl up to the top to bed. I'm thinkin' I shall have to make up a bed in the kitchen. It only shows 'ow right I was to send for my Rosie, though quite the lady, and where will you find a nattier nursemaid in all Bayswater?"

"Nowhere," assented Lancelot, automatically.

"Oh, I didn't know you'd noticed her running in to see 'er pore old mother of a Sunday arternoon," said Mrs. Leadbatter, highly gratified. "Well, sir, I won't say anything about the hextry gas, though a poor widder and sevenpence hextry on the thousand, but I'm thinkin' if you would give my Rosie a lesson once a week on that there pianner, it would be a kind of set-off, for you know, sir, the policeman tells me your winder is a landmark to 'im on the foggiest nights."

Lancelot flushed, then wrinkled his brows. This was a new idea altogether. Mrs. Leadbatter stood waiting for his reply, with a deferential smile tempered by asthmatic contortions.

"But have you got a piano of your own?"

"Oh, no, sir," cried Mrs. Leadbatter, almost reproachfully.

"Well; but how is your Rosie to practise? One lesson a week is of very little use anyway, but unless she practises a good deal it'll only be a waste of time."

"Ah, you don't know my Rosie," said Mrs. Leadbatter, shaking her head with sceptical pride. "You mustn't judge by other gels—the way that gel picks up things is—well, I'll just tell you what 'er school-teacher, Miss Whiteman said. She says—"

"My good lady," interrupted Lancelot, "I practised six hours a day myself."

"Yes, but it don't come so natural to a man," said Mrs. Leadbatter, unshaken. "And it don't look natural neither to see a man playin' the pianner—it's like seein' him knittin'."

But Lancelot was knitting his brows in a way that was exceedingly natural. "I may as well tell you at once that what you propose is impossible. First of all, because I am doubtful whether I shall remain in these rooms; and secondly, because I am giving up the piano immediately. I only have it on hire, and I—I—" He felt himself blushing.

"Oh, what a pity!" interrupted Mrs. Leadbatter. "You might as well let me go on payin' the hinstalments, instead of lettin' all you've paid go for nothing. Rosie ain't got much time, but I could allow 'er a 'our a day if it was my own pianner."

Lancelot explained "hire" did not mean the "hire system." But the idea of acquiring the piano, having once fired Mrs. Leadbatter's brain, could not be extinguished. The unexpected conclusion arrived at was that she was to purchase the piano on the hire system, allowing it to stand in Lancelot's room, and that five shillings a week should be taken off his rent in return for six lessons of an hour each, one of the hours counterbalancing the gas grievance. Reviewing the bargain, when Mrs. Leadbatter was gone, Lancelot did not think it at all bad for him.

"Use of the piano. Gas," he murmured, with a pathetic smile, recalling the advertisements he had read before lighting on Mrs. Leadbatter's. "And five shillings a week—it's a considerable relief! There's no loss of dignity either—for nobody will know. But I wonder what the governor would have said!"

The thought shook him with silent laughter; a spectator might have fancied he was sobbing.

But, after the lessons began, it might almost be said it was only when a spectator was present that he was not sobbing. For Rosie, who was an awkward, ungraceful young person, proved to be the dullest and most butter-fingered pupil ever invented for the torture of teachers; at least, so Lancelot thought, but then he had never had any other pupils, and was not patient. It must be admitted, though, that Rosie giggled perpetually, apparently finding endless humour in her own mistakes. But the climax of the horror was the attendance of Mrs. Leadbatter at the lessons, for, to Lancelot's consternation, she took it for granted that her presence was part of the contract. She marched into the room in her best cap, and sat, smiling, in the easy chair, wheezing complacently and beating time with her foot. Occasionally she would supplement Lancelot's critical observations.

"It ain't as I fears to trust 'er with you, sir," she also remarked about three times a week, "for I knows, sir, you're a gentleman. But it's the neighbours; they never can mind their own business. I told 'em you was going to give my Rosie lessons, and you know, sir, that they will talk of what don't concern 'em. And, after all, sir, it's an hour, and an hour is sixty minutes, ain't it, sir?"

And Lancelot, groaning inwardly, and unable to deny this chronometry, felt that an ironic Providence was punishing him for his attentions to Mary Ann.

And yet he only felt more tenderly towards Mary Ann. Contrasted with these two vulgar females, whom he came to conceive as her oppressors, sitting in gauds and finery, and taking lessons which had better befitted their Cinderella—the figure of Mary Ann definitely reassumed some of its antediluvian poetry, if we may apply the adjective to that catastrophic washing of the steps. And Mary Ann herself had grown gloomier—once or twice he thought she had been crying, though he was too numbed and apathetic to ask, and was incapable of suspecting that Rosie had anything to do with her tears. He hardly noticed that Rosie had taken to feeding the canary; the question of how he should feed himself was becoming every day more and more menacing. He saw starvation slowly closing in upon him like the walls of a torture-chamber. He had grown quite familiar with the pawn-shop now, though he still slipped in as though his goods were stolen.

And at last there came a moment when Lancelot felt he could bear it no longer. And then he suddenly saw daylight. Why should he teach only Rosie? Nay, why should he teach Rosie at all? If he was reduced to giving lessons—and after all it was no degradation to do so, no abandonment of his artistic ideal, rather a solution of the difficulty so simple that he wondered it had not occurred to him before—why should he give them at so wretched a price? He would get another pupil, other pupils, who would enable him to dispense with the few shillings he made by Rosie. He would not ask anybody to recommend him pupils—there was no need for his acquaintances to know, and if he asked Peter, Peter would probably play him some philanthropic trick. No, he would advertise.

After he had spent his last gold breast-pin in advertisements, he realised that to get pianoforte pupils in London was as easy as to get songs published. By the time he quite realised it, it was May, and then he sat down to realise his future.

The future was sublimely simple—as simple as his wardrobe had grown. All his clothes were on his back. In a week or two he would be on the streets; for a poor widow could not be expected to lodge, partially board (with use of the piano, gas), an absolutely penniless young gentleman, though he combined the blood of twenty county families with the genius of a pleiad of tone poets.

There was only one bright spot in the prospect. Rosie's lessons would come to an end.

What he would do when he got on the streets was not so clear as the rest of this prophetic vision. He might take to a barrel-organ—but that would be a cruel waste of his artistic touch. Perhaps he would die on a doorstep, like the professor of many languages, whose starvation was recorded in that very morning's paper.

Thus, driven by the saturnine necessity that sneers at our puny resolutions, Lancelot began to meditate surrender. For surrender of some sort must be—either of life or ideal. After so steadfast and protracted a struggle—oh, it was cruel, it was terrible; how noble, how high-minded he had been; and this was how the fates dealt with him—but at that moment—

"Sw—eet," went the canary, and filled the room with its rapturous demi-semi-quavers, its throat swelling, its little body throbbing with joy of the sunshine. And then Lancelot remembered—not the joy of the sunshine, not the joy of life—no, merely Mary Ann.

Noble! high-minded! No, let Peter think that, let posterity think that. But he could not cozen himself thus! He had fallen—horribly, vulgarly. How absurd of him to set himself up as a saint, a martyr, an idealist! He could not divide himself into two compartments like that and pretend that only one counted in his character. Who was he to talk of dying for art? No, he was but an everyday man. He wanted Mary Ann—yes, he might as well admit that to himself now. It was no use humbugging himself any longer. Why should he give her up? She was his discovery, his treasure-trove, his property.

And if he could stoop to her, why should he not stoop to popular work, to devilling, to anything that would rid him of these sordid cares? Bah! away with all pretences!

Was not this shamefaced pawning as vulgar, as wounding to the artist's soul as the turning out of tawdry melodies?

Yes, he would escape from Mrs. Leadbatter and her Rosie; he would write to that popular composer—he had noticed his letter lying on the mantel-piece the other day—and accept the fifty pounds, and whatever he did he could do anonymously, so that Peter wouldn't know, after all; he would escape from this wretched den and take a flat far away, somewhere where nobody knew him, and there he would sit and work, with Mary Ann for his housekeeper. Poor Mary Ann! How glad she would be when he told her! The tears came into his eyes as he thought of her naïve delight. He would rescue her from this horrid, monotonous slavery, and—happy thought—he would have her to give lessons to instead of Rosie.

Yes, he would refine her; prune away all that reminded him of her wild growth, so that it might no longer humiliate him to think to what a companion he had sunk. How happy they would be! Of course the world would censure him if it knew, but the world was stupid and prosaic, and measured all things by its coarse rule of thumb. It was the best thing that could happen to Mary Ann—the best thing in the world. And then the world wouldn't know.

"Sw—eet," went the canary. "Sw—eet."

This time the joy of the bird penetrated to his own soul—the joy of life, the joy of the sunshine. He rang the bell violently, as though he were sounding a clarion of defiance, the trumpet of youth.

Mary Ann knocked at the door, came in, and began to draw on her gloves.

He was in a mad mood—the incongruity struck him so that he burst into a roar of laughter.

Mary Ann paused, flushed, and bit her lip. The touch of resentment he had never noted before gave her a novel charm, spicing her simplicity.

He came over to her and took her half-bare hands. No, they were not so terrible, after all. Perhaps she had awakened to her iniquities, and had been trying to wash them white. His last hesitation as to her worthiness to live with him vanished.

"Mary Ann," he said, "I'm going to leave these rooms."

The flush deepened, but the anger faded. She was a child again—her big eyes full of tears. He felt her hands tremble in his.

"Mary Ann," he went on, "how would you like me to take you with me?"

"Do you mean it, sir?" she asked eagerly.

"Yes, dear." It was the first time he had used the word. The blood throbbed madly in her ears. "If you will come with me—and be my little housekeeper—we will go away to some nice spot, and be quite alone together—in the country if you like, amid the foxglove and the meadowsweet, or by the green waters, where you shall stand in the sunset and dream; and I will teach you music and the piano"—her eyes dilated—"and you shall not do any of this wretched nasty work any more. What do you say?"

"Sw—eet, sw—eet," said the canary, in thrilling jubilation.

Her happiness was choking her—she could not speak.

"And we will take the canary, too—unless I say good-by to you as well."

"Oh, no, you mustn't leave us here!"

"And then," he said slowly, "it will not be good-by—nor good-night. Do you understand?"

"Yes, yes," she breathed, and her face shone.

"But think, think, Mary Ann," he said, a sudden pang of compunction shooting through his breast. He released her hands. "Do you understand?"

"I understand—I shall be with you, always."

He replied uneasily, "I shall look after you—always."

"Yes, yes," she breathed. Her bosom heaved. "Always."

Then his very first impression of her as "a sort of white Topsy" recurred to him suddenly and flashed into speech.

"Mary Ann, I don't believe you know how you came into the world. I dare say you 'specs you growed."

"No, sir," said Mary Ann, gravely; "God made me."

That shook him strangely for a moment. But the canary sang on:—

"Sw-eet. Sw-w-w-w-w-eet."

III

And so it was settled. He wrote the long-delayed answer to the popular composer, found him still willing to give out his orchestration, and they met by appointment at the club.

"I've got hold of a splendid book," said the popular composer. "Awfully clever; jolly original. Bound to go—from the French, you know. Haven't had time to set to work on it—old engagement to run over to Monte Carlo for a few days—but I'll leave you the book; you might care to look over it. And—I say—if any catchy tunes suggest themselves as you go along, you might just jot them down, you know. Not worth while losing an idea; eh, my boy! Ha! ha! ha! Well, good-by. See you again when I come back; don't suppose I shall be away more than a month. Good-by!" And, having shaken his hand with tremendous cordiality, the popular composer rushed downstairs and into a hansom.

Lancelot walked home with the libretto and the five five-pound notes. He asked for Mrs. Leadbatter, and gave her a week's notice. He wanted to drop Rosie immediately, on the plea of pressure of work, but her mother received the suggestion with ill grace, and said that Rosie should come up and practise on her own piano all the same, so he yielded to the complexities of the situation, and found hope a wonderful sweetener of suffering. Despite Rosie and her giggling, and Mrs. Leadbatter and her best cap and her asthma, the week went by almost cheerfully. He worked regularly at the comic opera, nearly as happy as the canary which sang all day long, and, though scarcely a word more passed between him and Mary Ann, their eyes met ever and anon in the consciousness of a sweet secret.

It was already Friday afternoon. He gathered together his few personal belongings—his books, his manuscripts, opera innumerable. There was room in his portmanteau for everything—now he had no clothes. On the Monday the long nightmare would be over. He would go down to some obscure seaside nook and live very quietly for a few weeks, and gain strength and calm in the soft spring airs, and watch hand-in-hand with Mary Ann the rippling scarlet trail of the setting sun fade across the green waters. Life, no doubt, would be hard enough still. Struggles and trials enough were yet before him, but he would not think of that now—enough that for a month or two there would be bread and cheese and kisses. And then, in the midst of a tender reverie, with his hand on the lid of his portmanteau, he was awakened by ominous sounds of objurgation from the kitchen.

His heart stood still. He went down a few stairs and listened.

"Not another stroke of work do you do in my house, Mary Ann!" Then there was silence, save for the thumping of his own heart. What had happened?

He heard Mrs. Leadbatter mounting the kitchen stairs, wheezing and grumbling, "Well, of all the sly little things!"

Mary Ann had been discovered. His blood ran cold at the thought. The silly creature had been unable to keep the secret.

"Not a word about 'im all this time. Oh, the sly little thing! Who would hever a-believed it?"

And then, in the intervals of Mrs. Leadbatter's groanings, there came to him the unmistakable sound of Mary Ann sobbing—violently, hysterically. He turned from cold to hot in a fever of shame and humiliation. How had it all come about? Oh, yes, he could guess. The gloves! What a fool he had been! Mrs. Leadbatter had unearthed the box. Why did he give her more than the pair that could always be kept hidden in her pocket? Yes, it was the gloves. And then there was the canary. Mrs. Leadbatter had suspected he was leaving her for a reason. She had put two and two together, she had questioned Mary Ann, and the ingenuous little idiot had naively told her he was going to take her with him. It didn't really matter, of course; he didn't suppose Mrs. Leadbatter could exercise any control over Mary Ann, but it was horrible to be discussed by her and Rosie; and then there was that meddlesome vicar, who might step in and make things nasty.

Mrs. Leadbatter's steps and wheezes and grumblings had arrived in the passage, and Lancelot hastily stole back into his room, his heart continuing to flutter painfully.

He heard the complex noises reach his landing, pass by, and move up higher. She wasn't coming in to him then; he could endure the suspense no longer. He threw open his door and said, "Is there anything the matter?"

Mrs. Leadbatter paused and turned her head.

"His there anything the matter!" she echoed, looking down upon him. "A nice thing when a woman's troubled with hastmer and brought 'ome 'er daughter to take 'er place, that she should 'ave to start 'untin' afresh!"

"Why, is Rosie going away?" he said, immeasurably relieved.

"My Rosie! She's the best girl breathing. It's that there Mary Ann!"

"Wh-a-t!" he stammered. "Mary Ann leaving you?"

"Well, you don't suppose," replied Mrs. Leadbatter, angrily, "as I can keep a gel in my kitchen as is a-goin' to 'ave 'er own nors-end-kerridge!"

"Her own horse and carriage!" repeated Lancelot, utterly dazed. "Whatever are you talking about?"

"Well—there's the letter!" exclaimed Mrs. Leadbatter, indignantly. "See for yourself if you don't believe me. I don't know how much two and a 'arf million dollars is—but it sounds unkimmonly like a nors-end-kerridge—and never said a word about 'im the whole time, the sly little thing!"

The universe seemed oscillating so that he grasped at the letter like a drunken man. It was from the vicar. He wrote:—

"I have much pleasure in informing you that our dear Mary Ann is the fortunate inheritress of two and a half million dollars by the death of her brother Tom, who, as I learn from the lawyers who have applied to me for news of the family, has just died in America, leaving his money to his surviving relatives. He was rather a wild young man, but it seems he became the lucky possessor of some petroleum wells which made him wealthy in a few months. I pray God Mary Ann may make a better use of the money than he would have done. I want you to break the news to her, please, and to prepare her for my visit. As I have to preach on Sunday, I cannot come to town before, but on Monday (D.V.) I shall run up and shall probably take her back with me, as I desire to help her through the difficulties that will attend her entry into the new life. How pleased you will be to think of the care you took of the dear child during these last five years. I hope she is well and happy; I think you omitted to write to me last Christmas on the subject. Please give her my kindest regards and best wishes and say I shall be with her (D.V.) on Monday."

The words swam uncertainly before Lancelot's eyes, but he got through them all at last. He felt chilled and numbed. He averted his face as he handed the letter back to Mary Ann's "missus."

"What a fortunate girl!" he said in a low, stony voice.

"Fortunate ain't the word for it! The mean, sly little cat! Fancy never telling me a word about 'er brother all these years—me as 'as fed her, and clothed her, and lodged her, and kepper out of all mischief, as if she'd bin my own daughter; never let her go out Bankhollidayin' in loose company—as you can bear witness yourself, sir—and eddicated 'er out of 'er country talk and rough ways, and made 'er the smart young woman she is, fit to wait on the most troublesome of gentlemen. And now she'll go away and say I used 'er 'arsh, and overworked 'er, and Lord knows what, don't tell me! Oh, my poor chest!"

"I think you may make your mind quite easy," said Lancelot, grimly. "I'm sure Mary Ann is perfectly satisfied with your treatment."

"But she ain't—there, listen! don't you hear her going on?" Poor Mary Ann's sobs were still audible, though exhaustion was making them momently weaker. "She's been going on like that ever since I broke the news to 'er and gave her a piece of my mind—the sly little cat! She wanted to go on scrubbing the kitchen, and I had to take the brush away by main force. A nice thing, indeed! A gel as can keep a nors-end-kerridge down on the cold kitchen stones! 'Twasn't likely I could allow that. 'No, Mary Ann,' says I, firmly, 'you're a lady, and if you don't know what's proper for a lady, you'd best listen to them as does. You go and buy yourself a dress and a jacket to be ready for that vicar who's been a real good kind friend to you; he's coming to take you away on Monday, he is, and how will you look in that dirty print? Here's a suvrin,' says I, 'out of my 'ard-earned savin's—and get a pair o' boots, too: you can git a sweet pair for 2s. 11d. at Rackstraw's afore the sale closes,' and with that I shoves the suvrin into 'er hand instead o' the scrubbin' brush, and what does she do? Why, busts out a-cryin' and sits on the damp stones, and sobs, and sulks, and stares at the suvrin in her hand as if I'd told her of a funeral instead of a fortune!" concluded Mrs. Leadbatter, alliteratively.

"But you did—her brother's death," said Lancelot. "That's what she's crying about."

Mrs. Leadbatter was taken aback by this obverse view of the situation; but recovering herself, she shook her head. "I wouldn't cry for no brother that lef me to starve when he was rollin' in two and a 'arf million dollars," she said sceptically. "And I'm sure my Rosie wouldn't. But she never 'ad nobody to leave her money, poor dear child, except me, please Gaud. It's only the fools as 'as the luck in this world." And having thus relieved her bosom, she resumed her panting progress upwards.

The last words rang on in Lancelot's ears long after he had returned to his room. In the utter breakdown and confusion of his plans and his ideas, it was the one definite thought he clung to, as a swimmer in a whirlpool clings to a rock. His brain refused to concentrate itself on any other aspect of the situation—he could not, would not, dared not, think of anything else. He knew vaguely he ought to rejoice with her over her wonderful stroke of luck, that savoured of the fairy-story, but everything was swamped by that one almost resentful reflection. Oh, the irony of fate! Blind fate showering torrents of gold upon this foolish, babyish household drudge, who was all emotion and animal devotion, without the intellectual outlook of a Hottentot, and leaving men of genius to starve, or sell their souls for a handful of it! How was the wisdom of the ages justified! Verily did fortune favour fools. And Tom—the wicked—he had flourished as the wicked always do, like the green bay tree, as the Psalmist discovered ever so many centuries ago.

But gradually the wave of bitterness waned. He found himself listening placidly and attentively to the joyous trills and roulades of the canary, till the light faded and the grey dusk crept into the room and stilled the tiny winged lover of the sunshine. Then Beethoven came and rubbed himself against his master's leg, and Lancelot got up, as one wakes from a dream, and stretched his cramped limbs dazedly, and rang the bell mechanically for tea. He was groping on the mantel-piece for the matches when the knock at the door came, and he did not turn round till he had found them. He struck a light, expecting to see Mrs. Leadbatter or Rosie. He started to find it was merely Mary Ann.

But she was no longer merely Mary Ann, he remembered with another shock. She loomed large to him in the match-light—he seemed to see her through a golden haze. Tumultuous images of her glorified gilded future rose and mingled dizzily in his brain.

And yet, was he dreaming? Surely it was the same Mary Ann, with the same winsome face and the same large pathetic eyes, ringed though they were with the shadow of tears. Mary Ann, in her neat white cap—yes—and in her tan kid gloves. He rubbed his eyes. Was he really awake? Or—a thought still more dizzying—had he been dreaming? He had fallen asleep and reinless fancy had played him the fantastic trick, from which, cramped and dazed, he had just awakened to the old sweet reality.

"Mary Ann!" he cried wildly. The lighted match fell from his fingers and burnt itself out unheeded on the carpet.

"Yessir."

"Is it true"—his emotion choked him—"is it true you've come into two and a half million dollars?"

"Yessir, and I've brought you some tea."

The room was dark, but darkness seemed to fall on it as she spoke.

"But why are you waiting on me, then?" he said slowly. "Don't you know that you—that you—"

"Please, Mr. Lancelot, I wanted to come in and see you."

He felt himself trembling.

"But Mrs. Leadbatter told me she wouldn't let you do any more work."

"I told missus that I must; I told her she couldn't get another girl before Monday, if then, and if she didn't let me I wouldn't buy a new dress and a pair of boots with her sovereign—it isn't suvrin, is it, sir?"

"No," murmured Lancelot, smiling in spite of himself.

"With her sovereign. And I said I would be all dirty on Monday."

"But what can you get for a sovereign?" he asked irrelevantly. He felt his mind wandering away from him.

"Oh, ever such a pretty dress!"

The picture of Mary Ann in a pretty dress painted itself upon the darkness. How lovely the child would look in some creamy white evening dress with a rose in her hair. He wondered that in all his thoughts of their future he had never dressed her up thus in fancy, to feast his eyes on the vision.

"And so the vicar will find you in a pretty dress," he said at last.

"No, sir."

"But you promised Mrs. Leadbatter to—"

"I promised to buy a dress with her sovereign. But I shan't be here when the vicar comes. He can't come till the afternoon."

"Why, where will you be?" he said, his heart beginning to beat fast.

"With you," she replied, with a faint accent of surprise.

He steadied himself against the mantel-piece.

"But—" he began, and ended, "is that honest?"

He dimly descried her lips pouting. "We can always send her another when we have one," she said.

He stood there, dumb, glad of the darkness.

"I must go down now," she said. "I mustn't stay long."

"Why?" he articulated.

"Rosie," she replied briefly.

"What about Rosie?"

"She watches me—ever since she came. Don't you understand?"

This time he was the dullard. He felt an extra quiver of repugnance for Rosie, but said nothing, while Mary Ann briskly lit the gas, and threw some coals on the decaying fire. He was pleased she was going down; he was suffocating; he did not know what to say to her. And yet, as she was disappearing through the doorway, he had a sudden feeling things couldn't be allowed to remain an instant in this impossible position.

"Mary Ann!" he cried.

"Yessir."

She turned back—her face wore merely the expectant expression of a summoned servant. The childishness of her behaviour confused him, irritated him.

"Are you foolish?" he cried suddenly; half regretting the phrase the instant he had uttered it.

Her lip twitched.

"No, Mr. Lancelot!" she faltered.

"But you talk as if you were," he said less roughly. "You mustn't run away from the vicar just when he is going to take you to the lawyer's to certify who you are, and see that you get your money."

"But I don't want to go with the vicar—I want to go with you. You said you would take me with you." She was almost in tears now.

"Yes—but don't you—don't you understand that—that," he stammered; then, temporising, "but I can wait."

"Can't the vicar wait?" said Mary Ann. He had never known her show such initiative.

He saw that it was hopeless—that the money had made no more dint upon her consciousness than some vague dream, that her whole being was set towards the new life with him, and shrank in horror from the menace of the vicar's withdrawal of her in the opposite direction. If joy and redemption had not already lain in the one quarter, the advantages of the other might have been more palpably alluring. As it was, her consciousness was "full up" in the matter, so to speak. He saw that he must tell her plain and plump, startle her out of her simple confidence.

"Listen to me, Mary Ann."

"Yessir."

"You are a young woman—not a baby. Strive to grasp what I am going to tell you."

"Yessir," in a half sob, that vibrated with the obstinate resentment of a child that knows it is to be argued out of its instincts by adult sophistry. What had become of her passive personality?

"You are now the owner of two and a half million dollars—that is about five hundred thousand pounds. Five—hundred thousand—pounds. Think of ten sovereigns—ten golden sovereigns like that Mrs. Leadbatter gave you. Then ten times as much as that, and ten times as much as all that"—he spread his arms wider and wider—"and ten times as much as all that, and then"—here his arms were prematurely horizontal, so he concluded hastily but impressively,—"and then FIFTY times as much as all that. Do you understand how rich you are?"

"Yessir." She was fumbling nervously at her gloves, half drawing them off.

"Now all this money will last forever. For you invest it—if only at three per cent.—never mind what that is—and then you get fifteen thousand a year—fifteen thousand golden sovereigns to spend every—"

"Please, sir, I must go now. Rosie!"

"Oh, but you can't go yet. I have lots more to tell you."

"Yessir; but can't you ring for me again?"

In the gravity of the crisis, the remark tickled him; he laughed with a strange ring in his laughter.

"All right; run away, you sly little puss."

He smiled on as he poured out his tea; finding a relief in prolonging his sense of the humour of the suggestion, but his heart was heavy, and his brain a-whirl. He did not ring again till he had finished tea.

She came in, and took her gloves out of her pocket.

"No! no!" he cried, strangely exasperated. "An end to this farce! Put them away. You don't need gloves any more."

She squeezed them into her pocket nervously, and began to clear away the things, with abrupt movements, looking askance every now and then at the overcast handsome face.

At last he nerved himself to the task and said: "Well, as I was saying, Mary Ann, the first thing for you to think of is to make sure of all this money—this fifteen thousand pounds a year. You see you will be able to live in a fine manor house—such as the squire lived in in your village—surrounded by a lovely park with a lake in it for swans and boats—"

Mary Ann had paused in her work, slop-basin in hand. The concrete details were beginning to take hold of her imagination.

"Oh, but I should like a farm better," she said. "A large farm with great pastures and ever so many cows and pigs and outhouses, and a—oh, just like Atkinson's farm. And meat every day, with pudding on Sundays! Oh, if father was alive, wouldn't he be glad!"

"Yes, you can have a farm—anything you like."

"Oh, how lovely! A piano?"

"Yes—six pianos."

"And you will learn me?"

He shuddered and hesitated.

"Well—I can't say, Mary Ann."

"Why not? Why won't you? You said you would! You learn Rosie."

"I may not be there, you see," he said, trying to put a spice of playfulness into his tones.

"Oh, but you will," she said feverishly. "You will take me there. We will go there instead of where you said—instead of the green waters." Her eyes were wild and witching.

He groaned inwardly.

"I cannot promise you now," he said slowly. "Don't you see that everything is altered?"

"What's altered? You are here and here am I." Her apprehension made her almost epigrammatic.

"Ah, but you are quite different now, Mary Ann."

"I'm not—I want to be with you just the same."

He shook his head. "I can't take you with me," he said decisively.

"Why not?" She caught hold of his arm entreatingly.

"You are not the same Mary Ann—to other people. You are a somebody. Before, you were a nobody. Nobody cared or bothered about you—you were no more than a dead leaf whirling in the street."

"Yes, you cared and bothered about me," she cried, clinging to him.

Her gratitude cut him like a knife. "The eyes of the world are on you now," he said. "People will talk about you if you go away with me now."

"Why will they talk about me? What harm shall I do them?"

Her phrases puzzled him.

"I don't know that you will harm them," he said slowly, "but you will harm yourself."

"How will I harm myself?" she persisted.

"Well, one day, you will want a—a husband. With all that money it is only right and proper you should marry—"

"No, Mr. Lancelot, I don't want a husband. I don't want to marry. I should never want to go away from you."

There was another painful silence. He sought refuge in a brusque playfulness.

"I see you understand I'm not going to marry you."

"Yessir."

He felt a slight relief.

"Well, then," he said, more playfully still. "Suppose I wanted to go away from you, Mary Ann?"

"But you love me," she said, unaffrighted.

He started back perceptibly.

After a moment, he replied, still playfully, "I never said so."

"No, sir; but—but—" she lowered her eyes; a coquette could not have done it more artlessly—"but I—know it."

The accusation of loving her set all his suppressed repugnances and prejudices bristling in contradiction. He cursed the weakness that had got him into this soul-racking situation. The silence clamoured for him to speak—to do something.

"What—what were you crying about before?" he said abruptly.

"I—I don't know, sir," she faltered.

"Was it Tom's death?"

"No, sir, not much. I did think of him black-berrying with me and our little Sally—but then he was so wicked! It must have been what missus said; and I was frightened because the vicar was coming to take me away—away from you; and then—oh, I don't know—I felt—I couldn't tell you—I felt I must cry and cry, like that night when—" she paused suddenly and looked away.

"When," he said encouragingly.

"I must go—Rosie," she murmured, and took up the tea-tray.

"That night when—" he repeated tenaciously.

"When you first kissed me," she said.

He blushed. "That—that made you cry!" he stammered. "Why?"

"Please, sir, I don't know."

"Mary Ann," he said gravely, "don't you see that when I did that I was—like your brother Tom?"

"No, sir. Tom didn't kiss me like that."

"I don't mean that, Mary Ann, I mean I was wicked."

Mary Ann stared at him.

"Don't you think so, Mary Ann?"

"Oh, no, sir. You were very good."

"No, no, Mary Ann. Don't say good."

"Ever since then I have been so happy," she persisted.

"Oh, that was because you were wicked too," he explained grimly. "We have both been very wicked, Mary Ann; and so we had better part now, before we get more wicked."

She stared at him plaintively, suspecting a lurking irony, but not sure.

"But you didn't mind being wicked before!" she protested.

"I'm not so sure I mind now. It's for your sake, Mary Ann, believe me, my dear." He took her bare hand kindly and felt it burning. "You're a very simple, foolish little thing, yes, you are. Don't cry. There's no harm in being simple. Why, you told me yourself how silly you were once when you brought your dying mother cakes and flowers to take to your dead little sister. Well, you're just as foolish and childish now, Mary Ann, though you don't know it any more than you did then. After all you're only nineteen—I found it out from the vicar's letter. But a time will come—yes, I'll warrant in only a few months' time you'll see how wise I am and how sensible you have been to be guided by me. I never wished you any harm, Mary Ann, believe me, my dear, I never did. And I hope, I do hope so much that this money will make you happy. So you see you mustn't go away with me now—you don't want everybody to talk of you as they did of your brother Tom, do you, dear? Think what the vicar would say."

But Mary Ann had broken down under the touch of his hand and the gentleness of his tones.

"I was a dead leaf so long, I don't care!" she sobbed passionately. "Nobody never bothered to call me wicked then. Why should I bother now?"

Beneath the mingled emotions her words caused him was a sense of surprise at her recollection of his metaphor.

"Hush! You're a silly little child," he repeated sternly. "Hush! or Mrs. Leadbatter will hear you." He went to the door and closed it tightly. "Listen, Mary Ann! Let me tell you once for all that even if you were fool enough to be willing to go with me, I wouldn't take you with me. It would be doing you a terrible wrong."

She interrupted him quietly.

"Why more now than before?"

He dropped her hand as if stung, and turned away. He knew he could not answer that to his own satisfaction, much less to hers.

"You're a silly little baby," he repeated resentfully. "I think you had better go down now. Missus will be wondering."

Mary Ann's sobs grew more spasmodic. "You are going away without me," she cried hysterically.

He went to the door again, as if apprehensive of an eavesdropper. The scene was becoming terrible. The passive personality had developed with a vengeance.

"Hush, hush!" he cried imperatively.

"You are going away without me. I shall never see you again."

"Be sensible, Mary Ann. You will be—"

"You won't take me with you."

"How can I take you with me?" he cried brutally, losing every vestige of tenderness for this distressful vixen. "Don't you understand that it's impossible—unless I marry you," he concluded contemptuously.

Mary Ann's sobs ceased for a moment.

"Can't you marry me, then?" she said plaintively.

"You know it is impossible," he replied curtly.

"Why is it impossible?" she breathed.

"Because—" He saw her sobs were on the point of breaking out, and had not the courage to hear them afresh. He dared not wound her further by telling her straight out that, with all her money, she was ridiculously unfit to bear his name—that it was already a condescension for him to have offered her his companionship on any terms.

He resolved to temporise again.

"Go downstairs now, there's a good girl; and I'll tell you in the morning. I'll think it over. Go to bed early and have a long, nice sleep—missus will let you—now. It isn't Monday yet; we have plenty of time to talk it over."

She looked up at him with large appealing eyes, uncertain, but calming down.

"Do, now, there's a dear." He stroked her wet cheek soothingly.

"Yessir," and almost instinctively she put up her lips for a good-night kiss. He brushed them hastily with his. She went out softly, drying her eyes. His own grew moist—he was touched by the pathos of her implicit trust. The soft warmth of her lips still thrilled him. How sweet and loving she was! The little dialogue rang in his brain.

"Can't you marry me, then?"

"You know it is impossible."

"Why is it impossible?"

"Because—"

"Because what?" an audacious voice whispered. Why should he not? He stilled the voice but it refused to be silent—was obdurate, insistent, like Mary Ann herself. "Because—oh, because of a hundred things," he told it. "Because she is no fit mate for me—because she would degrade me, make me ridiculous—an unfortunate fortune-hunter, the butt of the witlings. How could I take her about as my wife? How could she receive my friends? For a housekeeper—a good, loving housekeeper—she is perfection, but for a wife—my wife—the companion of my soul—impossible!"

"Why is it impossible?" repeated the voice, catching up the cue. And then, from that point, the dialogue began afresh.

"Because this, and because that, and because the other—in short, because I am Lancelot and she is merely Mary Ann."

"But she is not merely Mary Ann any longer," urged the voice.

"Yes, for all her money, she is merely Mary Ann. And am I to sell myself for her money—I who have stood out so nobly, so high-mindedly, through all these years of privation and struggle? And her money is all in dollars. Pah! I smell the oil. Struck ile! Of all things in the world, her brother should just go and strike ile!" A great shudder traversed his form. "Everything seems to have been arranged out of pure cussedness, just to spite me. She would have been happier without the money, poor child—without the money, but with me. What will she do with all her riches? She will only be wretched—like me."

"Then why not be happy together?"

"Impossible."

"Why is it impossible?"

"Because her dollars would stick in my throat—the oil would make me sick. And what would Peter say, and my brother (not that I care what he says), and my acquaintances?"

"What does that matter to you? While you were a dead leaf nobody bothered to talk about you; they let you starve—you, with your genius—now you can let them talk—you, with your heiress. Five hundred thousand pounds. More than you will make with all your operas if you live a century. Fifteen thousand a year. Why, you could have all your works performed at your own expense, and for your own sole pleasure if you chose, as the King of Bavaria listened to Wagner's operas. You could devote your life to the highest art—nay, is it not a duty you owe to the world? Would it not be a crime against the future to draggle your wings with sordid cares, to sink to lower aims by refusing this Heaven-sent boon?"

The thought clung to him. He rose and laid out heaps of muddled manuscript—opera disjecta—and turned their pages.

"Yes—yes—give us life!" they seemed to cry to him. "We are dead drops of ink, wake us to life and beauty. How much longer are we to lie here, dusty in death? We have waited so patiently—have pity on us, raise us up from our silent tomb, and we will fly abroad through the whole earth, chanting your glory; yea, the world shall be filled to eternity with the echoes of our music and the splendour of your name."

But he shook his head and sighed, and put them back in their niches, and placed the comic opera he had begun in the centre of the table.

"There lie the only dollars that will ever come my way," he said aloud. And, humming the opening bars of a lively polka from the manuscript, he took up his pen and added a few notes. Then he paused; the polka would not come—the other voice was louder.

"It would be a degradation," he repeated, to silence it. "It would be merely for her money. I don't love her."

"Are you so sure of that?"

"If I really loved her I shouldn't refuse to marry her."

"Are you so sure of that?"

"What's the use of all this wire-drawing?—the whole thing is impossible."

"Why is it impossible?"

He shrugged his shoulders impatiently, refusing to be drawn back into the eddy, and completed the bar of the polka.

Then he threw down his pen, rose and paced the room in desperation.

"Was ever any man in such a dilemma?" he cried aloud.

"Did ever any man get such a chance?" retorted his silent tormentor.

"Yes, but I mustn't seize the chance—it would be mean."

"It would be meaner not to. You're not thinking of that poor girl—only of yourself. To leave her now would be more cowardly than to have left her when she was merely Mary Ann. She needs you even more now that she will be surrounded by sharks and adventurers. Poor, poor Mary Ann! It is you who have the right to protect her now; you were kind to her when the world forgot her. You owe it to yourself to continue to be good to her."

"No, no, I won't humbug myself. If I married her it would only be for her money."

"No, no, don't humbug yourself. You like her. You care for her very much. You are thrilling at this very moment with the remembrance of her lips to-night. Think of what life will be with her—life full of all that is sweet and fair—love and riches, and leisure for the highest art, and fame and the promise of immortality. You are irritable, sensitive, delicately organised; these sordid, carking cares, these wretched struggles, these perpetual abasements of your highest self—a few more years of them—they will wreck and ruin you, body and soul. How many men of genius have married their housekeepers even—good, clumsy, homely bodies, who have kept their husband's brain calm and his pillow smooth. And again, a man of genius is the one man who can marry anybody. The world expects him to be eccentric. And Mary Ann is no coarse city weed, but a sweet country bud. How splendid will be her blossoming under the sun! Do not fear that she will ever shame you; she will look beautiful, and men will not ask her to talk. Nor will you want her to talk. She will sit silent in the cosy room where you are working, and every now and again you will glance up from your work at her and draw inspiration from her sweet presence. So pull yourself together, man; your troubles are over, and life henceforth one long blissful dream. Come, burn me that tinkling, inglorious comic opera, and let the whole sordid past mingle with its ashes."

So strong was the impulse—so alluring the picture—that he took up the comic opera and walked towards the fire, his finger itching to throw it in. But he sat down again after a moment and went on with his work. It was imperative he should make progress with it; he could not afford to waste his time—which was money—because another person—Mary Ann to wit—had come into a superfluity of both. In spite of which the comic opera refused to advance; somehow he did not feel in the mood for gaiety; he threw down his pen in despair and disgust. But the idea of not being able to work rankled in him. Every hour seemed suddenly precious—now that he had resolved to make money in earnest—now that for a year or two he could have no other aim or interest in life. Perhaps it was that he wished to overpower the din of contending thoughts. Then a happy thought came to him. He rummaged out Peter's ballad. He would write a song on the model of that, as Peter had recommended—something tawdry and sentimental, with a cheap accompaniment. He placed the ballad on the rest and started going through it to get himself in the vein. But to-night the air seemed to breathe an ineffable melancholy, the words—no longer mawkish—had grown infinitely pathetic:—

"Kiss me, good-night, dear love,
Dream of the old delight;
My spirit is summoned above,
Kiss me, dear love, good-night!"

The hot tears ran down his cheeks, as he touched the keys softly and lingeringly. He could go no farther than the refrain; he leant his elbows on the keyboard, and dropped his head upon his arms. The clashing notes jarred like a hoarse cry, then vibrated slowly away into a silence that was broken only by his sobs.

He rose late the next day, after a sleep that was one prolonged nightmare, full of agonised, abortive striving after something that always eluded him, he knew not what. And when he woke—after a momentary breath of relief at the thought of the unreality of these vague horrors—he woke to the heavier nightmare of reality. Oh, those terrible dollars!

He drew the blind, and saw with a dull acquiescence that the brightness of May had fled. The wind was high—he heard it fly past, moaning. In the watery sky, the round sun loomed silver-pale and blurred. To his fevered eye it looked like a worn dollar.

He turned away, shivering, and began to dress. He opened the door a little, and pulled in his lace-up boots, which were polished in the highest style of art. But when he tried to put one on, his toes stuck fast in the opening, and refused to advance. Annoyed, he put his hand in, and drew out a pair of tan gloves, perfectly new. Astonished, he inserted his hand again and drew out another pair, then another. Reddening uncomfortably, for he divined something of the meaning, he examined the left boot, and drew out three more pairs of gloves, two new and one slightly soiled.

He sank down, half dressed, on the bed with his head on his breast, leaving his boots and Mary Ann's gloves scattered about the floor. He was angry, humiliated; he felt like laughing, and he felt like sobbing.

At last he roused himself, finished dressing, and rang for breakfast. Rosie brought it up.

"Hullo! Where's Mary Ann?" he said lightly.

"She's above work now," said Rosie, with an unamiable laugh. "You know about her fortune."

"Yes; but your mother told me she insisted on going about her work till Monday."

"So she said yesterday—silly little thing! But to-day she says she'll only help mother in the kitchen—and do all the boots of a morning. She won't do any more waiting."

"Ah!" said Lancelot, crumbling his toast.

"I don't believe she knows what she wants," concluded Rosie, turning to go.

"Then I suppose she's in the kitchen now?" he said, pouring out his coffee down the side of his cup.

"No, she's gone out now, sir."

"Gone out!" He put down the coffee-pot—his saucer was full. "Gone out where?"

"Only to buy things. You know her vicar is coming to take her away the day after to-morrow, and mother wanted her to look tidy enough to travel with the vicar; so she gave her a sovereign."

"Ah, yes; your mother said something about it."

"And yet she won't answer the bells," said Rosie, "and mother's asthma is worse, so I don't know whether I shall be able to take my lesson to-day, Mr. Lancelot. I'm so sorry, because it's the last."

Rosie probably did not intend the ambiguity of the phrase. There was real regret in her voice.

"Do you like learning, then?" said Lancelot, softened, for the first time, towards his pupil. His nerves seemed strangely flaccid to-day. He did not at all feel the relief he should have felt at forgoing his daily infliction.

"Ever so much, sir. I know I laugh too much, sometimes; but I don't mean it, sir. I suppose I couldn't go on with the lessons after you leave here?" She looked at him wistfully.

"Well"—he had crumbled the toast all to little pieces now—"I don't quite know. Perhaps I shan't go away after all."

Rosie's face lit up. "Oh, I'll tell mother," she exclaimed joyously.

"No, don't tell her yet; I haven't quite settled. But if I stay—of course the lessons can go on as before."

"Oh, I do hope you'll stay," said Rosie, and went out of the room with airy steps, evidently bent on disregarding his prohibition, if, indeed, it had penetrated to her consciousness.

Lancelot made no pretence of eating breakfast; he had it removed, and then fished out his comic opera. But nothing would flow from his pen; he went over to the window, and stood thoughtfully drumming on the panes with it, and gazing at the little drab-coloured street, with its high roof of mist; along which the faded dollar continued to spin imperceptibly. Suddenly he saw Mary Ann turn the corner, and come along towards the house, carrying a big parcel and a paper bag in her ungloved hands. How buoyantly she walked! He had never before seen her move in free space, nor realised how much of the grace of a sylvan childhood remained with her still. What a pretty colour there was on her cheeks, too!

He ran down to the street door and opened it before she could knock. The colour on her cheeks deepened at the sight of him, but now that she was near he saw her eyes were swollen with crying.

"Why do you go out without gloves, Mary Ann?" he inquired sternly. "Remember you're a lady now."

She started and looked down at his boots, then up at his face.

"Oh, yes, I found them, Mary Ann. A nice graceful way of returning me my presents, Mary Ann. You might at least have waited till Christmas. Then I should have thought Santa Claus sent them."

"Please, sir, I thought it was the surest way for me to send them back."

"But what made you send them back at all?"

Mary Ann's lip quivered, her eyes were cast down. "Oh—Mr. Lancelot—you know," she faltered.

"But I don't know," he said sharply.

"Please let me go downstairs, Mr. Lancelot. Missus must have heard me come in."

"You shan't go downstairs till you've told me what's come over you. Come upstairs to my room."

"Yessir."

She followed him obediently. He turned round brusquely, "Here, give me your parcels." And almost snatching them from her, he carried them upstairs and deposited them on his table on top of the comic opera.

"Now, then, sit down. You can take off your hat and jacket."

"Yessir."

He helped her to do so.

"Now, Mary Ann, why did you return me those gloves?"

"Please, sir, I remember in our village when—when"—she felt a diffidence in putting the situation into words and wound up quickly, "something told me I ought to."

"I don't understand you," he grumbled, comprehending only too well. "But why couldn't you come in and give them to me instead of behaving in that ridiculous way?"

"I didn't want to see you again," she faltered.

He saw her eyes were welling over with tears.

"You were crying again last night," he said sharply.

"Yessir."

"But what did you have to cry about now? Aren't you the luckiest girl in the world?"

"Yessir."

As she spoke a flood of sunlight poured suddenly into the room; the sun had broken through the clouds, the worn dollar had become a dazzling gold-piece. The canary stirred in its cage.

"Then what were you crying about?"

"I didn't want to be lucky."

"You silly girl—I have no patience with you. And why didn't you want to see me again?"

"Please, Mr. Lancelot, I knew you wouldn't like it."

"Whatever put that into your head?"

"I knew it, sir," said Mary Ann, firmly. "It came to me when I was crying. I was thinking of all sorts of things—of my mother and our Sally, and the old pig that used to get so savage, and about the way the organ used to play in church, and then all at once somehow I knew it would be best for me to do what you told me—to buy my dress and go back with the vicar, and be a good girl, and not bother you, because you were so good to me, and it was wrong for me to worry you and make you miserable."

"Tw-oo! Tw-oo!" It was the canary starting on a preliminary carol.

"So I thought it best," she concluded tremulously, "not to see you again. It would only be two days, and after that it would be easier. I could always be thinking of you just the same, Mr. Lancelot, always. That wouldn't annoy you, sir, would it? Because you know, sir, you wouldn't know it."

Lancelot was struggling to find a voice. "But didn't you forget something you had to do, Mary Ann?" he said in hoarse accents.

She raised her eyes swiftly a moment, then lowered them again.

"I don't know; I didn't mean to," she said apologetically.

"Didn't you forget that I told you to come to me and get my answer to your question?"

"No, sir, I didn't forget. That was what I was thinking of all night."

"About your asking me to marry you?"

"Yessir."

"And my saying it was impossible?"

"Yessir, and I said, 'Why is it impossible?' and you said, 'Because—' and then you left off; but please, Mr. Lancelot, I didn't want to know the answer this morning."

"But I want to tell you. Why don't you want to know?"

"Because I found out for myself, Mr. Lancelot. That's what I found out when I was crying—but there was nothing to find out, sir. I knew it all along. It was silly of me to ask you—but you know I am silly sometimes, sir, like I was when my mother was dying. And that was why I made up my mind not to bother you any more, Mr. Lancelot, I knew you wouldn't like to tell me straight out."

"And what was the answer you found out? Ah, you won't speak. It looks as if you don't like to tell me straight out. Come, come, Mary Ann, tell me why—why—it is impossible."

She looked up at last and said slowly and simply, "Because I am not good enough for you, Mr. Lancelot."

He put his hands suddenly to his eyes. He did not see the flood of sunlight—he did not hear the mad jubilance of the canary.

"No, Mary Ann," his voice was low and trembling. "I will tell you why it is impossible, I didn't know last night, but I know now. It is impossible, because—you are right, I don't like to tell you straight out."

She opened her eyes wide, and stared at him in puzzled expectation.

"Mary Ann," he bent his head, "it is impossible—because I am not good enough for you."

Mary Ann grew scarlet. Then she broke into a little nervous laugh. "Oh, Mr. Lancelot, don't make fun of me."

"Believe me, my dear," he said tenderly, raising his head; "I wouldn't make fun of you for two million million dollars. It is the truth—the bare, miserable, wretched truth. I am not worthy of you, Mary Ann."

"I don't understand you, sir," she faltered.

"Thank Heaven for that!" he said with the old whimsical look. "If you did you would think meanly of me ever after. Yes, that is why, Mary Ann. I am a selfish brute—selfish to the last beat of my heart, to the inmost essence of my every thought. Beethoven is worth two of me, aren't you, Beethoven?" The spaniel, thinking himself called, trotted over. "He never calculates—he just comes and licks my hand— don't look at me as if I were mad, Mary Ann. You don't understand me—thank Heaven again. Come now! Does it never strike you that if I were to marry you now, it would be only for your two and a half million dollars?"

"No, sir," faltered Mary Ann.

"I thought not," he said triumphantly. "No, you will always remain a fool, I am afraid, Mary Ann."

She met his contempt with an audacious glance.

"But I know it wouldn't be for that, Mr. Lancelot."

"No, no, of course it wouldn't be, not now. But it ought to strike you just the same. It doesn't make you less a fool, Mary Ann. There! There! I don't mean to be unkind, and, as I think I told you once before, it's not so very dreadful to be a fool. A rogue is a worse thing, Mary Ann. All I want to do is to open your eyes. Two and a half million dollars are an awful lot of money—a terrible lot of money. Do you know how long it will be before I make two million dollars, Mary Ann?"

"No, sir." She looked at him wonderingly.

"Two million years. Yes, my child, I can tell you now. You thought I was rich and grand, I know, but all the while I was nearly a beggar. Perhaps you thought I was playing the piano—yes, and teaching Rosie—for my amusement; perhaps you thought I sat up writing half the night out of—sleeplessness," he smiled at the phrase, "or a wanton desire to burn Mrs. Leadbatter's gas. No, Mary Ann, I have to get my own living by hard work—by good work if I can, by bad work if I must—but always by hard work. While you will have fifteen thousand pounds a year, I shall be glad, overjoyed, to get fifteen hundred. And while I shall be grinding away body and soul for my fifteen hundred, your fifteen thousand will drop into your pockets, even if you keep your hands there all day. Don't look so sad, Mary Ann. I'm not blaming you. It's not your fault in the least. It's only one of the many jokes of existence. The only reason I want to drive this into your head is to put you on your guard. Though I don't think myself good enough to marry you, there are lots of men who will think they are ... though they don't know you. It is you, not me, who are grand and rich, Mary Ann ... beware of men like me—poor and selfish. And when you do marry—"

"Oh, Mr. Lancelot!" cried Mary Ann, bursting into tears at last, "why do you talk like that? You know I shall never marry anybody else."

"Hush, hush! Mary Ann! I thought you were going to be a good girl and never cry again. Dry your eyes now, will you?"

"Yessir."

"Here, take my handkerchief."

"Yessir ... but I won't marry anybody else."

"You make me smile, Mary Ann. When you brought your mother that cake for Sally you didn't know a time would come when—"

"Oh, please, sir, I know that. But you said yesterday I was a young woman now. And this is all different to that."

"No, it isn't, Mary Ann. When they've put you to school, and made you a Ward in Chancery, or something, and taught you airs, and graces, and dressed you up"—a pang traversed his heart, as the picture of her in the future flashed for a moment upon his inner eye—"why, by that time, you'll be a different Mary Ann, outside and inside. Don't shake your head; I know better than you. We grow and become different. Life is full of chances, and human beings are full of changes, and nothing remains fixed."

"Then, perhaps"—she flushed up, her eyes sparkled—"perhaps"—she grew dumb and sad again.

"Perhaps what?"

He waited for her thought. The rapturous trills of the canary alone possessed the silence.

"Perhaps you'll change, too." She flashed a quick deprecatory glance at him—her eyes were full of soft light.

This time he was dumb.

"Sw—eet!" trilled the canary, "sw—eet!" though Lancelot felt the throbbings of his heart must be drowning its song.

"Acutely answered," he said at last. "You're not such a fool after all, Mary Ann. But I'm afraid it will never be, dear. Perhaps if I also made two million dollars, and if I felt I had grown worthy of you, I might come to you and say—two and two are four—let us go into partnership. But then, you see," he went on briskly, "the odds are I may never even have two thousand. Perhaps I'm as much a duffer in music as in other things. Perhaps you'll be the only person in the world who has ever heard my music, for no one will print it, Mary Ann. Perhaps I shall be that very common thing—a complete failure—and be worse off than even you ever were, Mary Ann."

"Oh, Mr. Lancelot, I'm so sorry." And her eyes filled again with tears.

"Oh, don't be sorry for me. I'm a man. I dare say I shall pull through. Just put me out of your mind, dear. Let all that happened at Baker's Terrace be only a bad dream—a very bad dream, I am afraid I must call it. Forget me, Mary Ann. Everything will help you to forget me, thank Heaven, it'll be the best thing for you. Promise me now."

"Yessir ... if you will promise me."

"Promise you what?"

"To do me a favour."

"Certainly, dear, if I can."

"You have the money, Mr. Lancelot, instead of me—I don't want it, and then you could—"

"Now, now, Mary Ann," he interrupted, laughing nervously, "you're getting foolish again, after talking so sensibly."

"Oh, but why not?" she said plaintively.

"It is impossible," he said curtly.

"Why is it impossible?" she persisted.

"Because—," he began, and then he realised with a start that they had come back again to that same old mechanical series of questions—if only in form.

"Because there is only one thing I could ever bring myself to ask you for in this world," he said slowly.

"Yes; what is that?" she said flutteringly.

He laid his hand tenderly on her hair.

"Merely Mary Ann."

She leapt up: "Oh, Mr. Lancelot, take me, take me! You do love me! You do love me!"

He bit his lip. "I am a fool," he said roughly. "Forget me. I ought not to have said anything. I spoke only of what might be—in the dim future—if the—chances and changes of life bring us together again—as they never do. No! You were right, Mary Ann. It is best we should not meet again. Remember your resolution last night."

"Yessir." Her submissive formula had a smack of sullenness, but she regained her calm, swallowing the lump in her throat that made her breathing difficult.

"Good-by, then, Mary Ann," he said, taking her hard red hands in his.

"Good-by, Mr. Lancelot." The tears she would not shed were in her voice. "Please, sir—could you—couldn't you do me a favour?—Nothing about money, sir."

"Well, if I can," he said kindly.

"Couldn't you just play Good-night and Good-by, for the last time? You needn't sing it—only play it."

"Why, what an odd girl you are!" he said with a strange, spasmodic laugh. "Why, certainly! I'll do both, if it will give you any pleasure."

And, releasing her hands, he sat down to the piano, and played the introduction softly. He felt a nervous thrill going down his spine as he plunged into the mawkish words. And when he came to the refrain, he had an uneasy sense that Mary Ann was crying—he dared not look at her. He sang on bravely:—

"Kiss me, good-night, dear love,
Dream of the old delight;
My spirit is summoned above,
Kiss me, dear love, good-night."

He couldn't go through another verse—he felt himself all a-quiver, every nerve shattered. He jumped up. Yes, his conjecture had been right. Mary Ann was crying. He laughed spasmodically again. The thought had occurred to him how vain Peter would be if he could know the effect of his commonplace ballad.

"There, I'll kiss you too, dear!" he said huskily, still smiling. "That'll be for the last time."

Their lips met, and then Mary Ann seemed to fade out of the room in a blur of mist.

An instant after there was a knock at the door.

"Forgot her parcels after a last good-by," thought Lancelot, and continued to smile at the comicality of the new episode.

He cleared his throat.

"Come in," he cried, and then he saw that the parcels were gone, too, and it must be Rosie.

But it was merely Mary Ann.

"I forgot to tell you, Mr. Lancelot," she said—her accents were almost cheerful—"that I'm going to church to-morrow morning."

"To church!" he echoed.

"Yes, I haven't been since I left the village, but missus says I ought to go in case the vicar asks me what church I've been going to."

"I see," he said, smiling on.

She was closing the door when it opened again, just revealing Mary Ann's face.

"Well?" he said, amused.

"But I'll do your boots all the same, Mr. Lancelot." And the door closed with a bang.

They did not meet again. On the Monday afternoon the vicar duly came and took Mary Ann away. All Baker's Terrace was on the watch, for her story had now had time to spread. The weather remained bright. It was cold but the sky was blue. Mary Ann had borne up wonderfully, but she burst into tears as she got into the cab.

"Sweet, sensitive little thing!" said Baker's Terrace.

"What a good woman you must be, Mrs. Leadbatter," said the vicar, wiping his spectacles.

As part of Baker's Terrace, Lancelot witnessed the departure from his window, for he had not left after all.

Beethoven was barking his short snappy bark the whole time at the unwonted noises and the unfamiliar footsteps; he almost extinguished the canary, though that was clamorous enough.

"Shut up, you noisy little devils!" growled Lancelot. And taking the comic opera he threw it on the dull fire. The thick sheets grew slowly blacker and blacker, as if with rage; while Lancelot thrust the five five-pound notes into an envelope addressed to the popular composer, and scribbled a tiny note:—

"Dear Peter,—If you have not torn up that cheque I shall be glad of it by return. Yours,

"LANCELOT.

"P.S.—I send by this post a Reverie, called Marianne, which is the best thing I have done, and should be glad if you could induce Brahmson to look at it."

A big, sudden blaze, like a jubilant bonfire, shot up in the grate and startled Beethoven into silence.

But the canary took it for an extra flood of sunshine, and trilled and demi-semi-quavered like mad.

"Sw—eet! Sweet!"

"By Jove!" said Lancelot, starting up, "Mary Ann's left her canary behind!"

Then the old whimsical look came over his face.

"I must keep it for her," he murmured. "What a responsibility! I suppose I oughtn't to let Rosie look after it any more. Let me see, what did Peter say? Canary seed, biscuits ... yes, I must be careful not to give it butter.... Curious I didn't think of her canary when I sent back all those gloves ... but I doubt if I could have squeezed it in—my boots are only sevens after all—to say nothing of the cage."

THE SERIO-COMIC GOVERNESS

I

Nelly O'Neill had her day in those earlier and quieter reaches of the Victorian era when the privilege of microscopic biography was reserved for the great and the criminal classes, and when the Bohemian celebrity (who is perhaps a cross between the two) was permitted to pass—like a magic-lantern slide—from obscurity to oblivion through an illuminated moment.

Thus even her real name has not hitherto leaked out, and to this day the O'Keeffes are unaware of their relative's reputation and believe their one connection with the stage to be a dubious and undesirable consanguinity with O'Keeffe, the actor and fertile farce-writer whose Wild Oats made a sensation at Covent Garden at the end of the eighteenth century. To her many brothers and sisters, Eileen was just the baby, and always remained so, even in the eyes of the eminent civil engineer who was only her senior by a year. Among the peasantry—subtly prescient of her freakish destinies—she was dubbed "a fairy child": which was by no means a compliment. A bad uncanny creature for all the colleen's winsome looks. The later London whispers of a royal origin had a travestied germ of truth in her father's legendary descent from Brian Boru. He himself seemed scarcely less legendary, this highly coloured squire of the old Irish school, surviving into the Victorian era, like a Georgian caricature; still inhabiting a turreted castle romantically out of repair, infested with ragged parasites: still believing in high living and deep drinking: still receiving the reverence if not the rent of a feudal tenantry, and the affection of a horsey and bibulous countryside. When in liquor there was nothing the O'Keeffe might not do except pay off his mortgages. "He looked like an elephant when he put his trousers on wrong—you know elephants have their knees the wrong way," Eileen once told the public in a patter-song. She did not tell the public it was her father, but like a true artist she learned in suffering what she taught in song. One of her childish memories was to be stood in a row of brothers and sisters against a background of antlers, fishing-rods, and racing prints, and solemnly sworn at for innumerability by a ruddy-faced giant in a slovenly surtout. "Bad luck to ye, ye gomerals, make up your minds whether ye're nine or eleven," he would say. "A man ought to know the size of his family: Mother in heaven, I never thought mine was half so large!" These attempts to take a census of his children generally occurred after a peasant had brought him up the drive—"hat in one hand, and Squire in the other," as the patter-song had it. At the moment of assisted entry his paternal dignity was always at its stateliest, and it was not till he had gravely hung his cocked hat upon an imaginary door-peg in the middle of the hall and seen it flop floorward that he lost his calm. "Blood and 'ouns, ye've the door taken away again."

Sometimes—though this was scarcely a relief—another befuddled gentleman would be left at the uninhabited lodge in his stead. That was chiefly after hunt dinners or card and claret parties, when a new coachman would take a quartet of gentry home, all clouded as to their identities. "Arrah now! they've got thimselves mixed! let thim sort thimselves." And the coachman would grab at the nearest limb, extricate it and its belongings from the tangle, and prop the total mass against the first gate he passed. And so with the rest.

Eileen's mother, who was as remarkable for her microscopic piety as for the beauty untarnished by a copious maternity, figured in the child's memories as a stout saint who moved with a rustle of silken skirts and heaved an opulent black silk bosom relieved by a silver cross.

"Who are you?" her spouse would inquire with an oath.

"It's your wife I am, Bagenal dear," she would reply cheerfully. For she had grown up in the four-bottle tradition, and intoxication appeared as natural for the superior sex as sleep. Both were temporary phases, and did not prevent men from being the best of husbands and creatures when clear. And when the marketwomen or the beggarwomen respectfully inquired of her, "How is your good provider?" she made her reply with no sense of irony, though she had been long paying the piper herself. And the piper figured literally in the household accounts, as well as the fiddler, for the O'Keeffe was what the mud cabins called a "ginthleman to the backbone."

II

Family tradition necessitated that Eileen should at least complete her education at a convent in the outskirts of Paris, and her first communion was delayed till she should "make" it in that more pious atmosphere. The O'Keeffe convoyed her across the two Channels, and took the opportunity of visiting a "variety" theatre in Montmartre, where he was delighted to find John Bull and his inelegant womenkind so faithfully delineated. So exhilarated was he by this excellent take-off and a few bocks on the Boulevard, that he refused to get down from the omnibus at its terminus.

"Jamais je ne descendrai, jamais," he vociferated. Eileen was, however, spared the sight of this miniature French revolution. She was lying sleepless in the strange new dormitory, watching the nun walking up and down in the dim weird room reading her breviary, now lost in deep shadow with the remoter beds, now lucidly outlined in purple dress with creamy cross as she came under the central night-light. Eileen wondered how she could see to read, and if she were not just posing picturesquely, but from the fervency with which she occasionally kissed the crucifix hanging to the rosary at her side Eileen concluded she must know the office by heart. Her own Irish home seemed on another planet, and her turret-bedroom was already far more shadowy than this: presently both were swallowed up into nothingness.

She commenced her convent career characteristically enough by making a sensation. For on rising in the morning she felt ineffably feeble and forlorn; she seemed to have scarcely closed her eyes, when she must be up and doing. The tiny hand-basin scarcely held enough water to cool her brow, still giddy from the sea-passage; to do her hair she had to borrow a minute hand-glass from her neighbour, and when after early mass in the chapel she found other prayers postponing breakfast, she fainted most alarmingly and dramatically. She was restored and refreshed with balm-mint water, but it took some days to reconcile her to the rigid life. To some aspects of it, indeed, she was never reconciled. The atmosphere of suspicious supervision was asphyxiating, after the disorderliness and warm humanity of her Irish home, after the run of the stables and the kennels, and the freedom of the village, after the chats with the pedlars and the beggars, and the borrowing and blowing of the postman's bugle, after the queenship of a host of barefooted gossoons, her loyal messenger-boys. Now her mere direct glance under reproof was considered "hardi." "Droop your eyes, you bold child," said the shocked Madame Agathe. A fancy she took to a French girl was checked. "On defend les amities particulières," she was told to her astonishment. But on this one point Eileen was recalcitrant. She would even walk with her arm in Marcelle's, and somehow her will prevailed. Perhaps Eileen was trusted as a foreigner: perhaps Marcelle, being a day-boarder, weighed less upon the convent's conscience. There came a time when even their desks adjoined and were not put asunder. For by this time Madame La Supèrieure herself, at the monthly reading of the marks, had often beamed upon Eileen. The maîtresse de classe had permitted her to kiss her crucifix, and the music-mistress was enchanted with her skill upon the piano and her rich contralto voice, such a godsend for the choir. In her very first term she was allowed to run up to the dormitory for something, unescorted by an Enfant de Marie. "Ascend, my child," said Madame Agathe, smiling sweetly, for Eileen had outstripped all her classmates that morning in geography, and Eileen, with a prim "Oui, ma mere," rose and sailed with drooping eyelashes to the other end of the schoolroom, and courtesied herself out of the door, knowing herself the focus of envy and humorously conscious of her goodness. She had learned to love this soothing sensation of goodness, as she sat in her blue pelerine on a hard tabouret before her desk, her hands folded in front of her, her little feet demurely crossed. The sweeping courtesy of entrance and exit dramatised this pleasant sense of virtue. Later her aspirant's ribbon painted it in purple.

She worked hard for her examinations. "Elle est si sage, cet enfant," she heard Madame Ursule say to Madame Hortense, and she had a delicious sense of overwork. But she was not always sage. Once when her school desk was ransacked in her absence—one of the many forms of espionage—she refused to rearrange its tumbled contents, and when she was given a bad mark for disorder, she cried defiantly, "It is Madame Rosaline who deserves that bad mark." And the pleasure of seeing herself as rebel and phrasemaker was no less keen than the pleasure of goodness.

One other institution found her regularly rebellious, and that was the pious reading which came punctually at half-past eight every morning. She was bored by all the holy heroines who seemed to have taken vows of celibacy at the age of four. "Devil take them all," she thought whimsically one morning. "But I dare say these good little people have no more reality than our 'little good people' who dance reels with the dead on November Eve. I wish Dan O'Leary had taught them all to shake their feet," and at the picture of jiggling little saints Eileen nearly gave herself away by a peal of laughter. For she had learned to conceal her unshared contempt for the holy heroines, and found a compensating pleasure in the sense of amused superiority, and the secret duality which it gave to her consciousness. She even went so far as to ransack the library for these beatific biographies, and when she found herself rewarded for "diligent reading" her amusement was at its apogee. And thus, when the first awe and interest of the strange life receded, Eileen was left standing apart as on a little rock, criticising, satirising, and even circulating verses among the few cronies who were not sneaks. The dowerless "sisters" who scrubbed the floors, the portioned Mesdames, with their more dignified humility, the Refectory readers, the Father Confessors, the little Enfants de Jésus, the big Enfants de Marie, who sometimes owed their blue ribbon to their birth or their money rather than to their exemplary behaviour, all had their humours, and all figured in Eileen's French couplets. The difficulty of passing these from hand to hand only made the reading—and the writing—the spicier. Literature did not interfere with lessons, for Eileen composed not during "preparation," but while she sat embroidering handkerchiefs, as demure as a sleeping kitten.

When the kitten was not thus occupied, she was playing with skeins of logic and getting herself terribly tangled.

She put her difficulties to her favourite nun as they walked in the quaint arcades of the lovely old garden, and their talk was punctuated by the flippant click of croquet-balls in the courtyard beyond.

"Madame Agathe is pleased with me to-day," said Eileen. "To-morrow she will be displeased. But how can I help the colour of my soul any more than the colour of my hair?"

"Hush, my child; if you talk like that you will lose your faith. Nobody is pleased or vexed with anybody for the colour of their hair."

"Yes, where I come from a peasant girl suffers a little for having red hair. Also a man with a hump, he cannot marry unless he owns many pigs."

"Eileen! Who has put such dreadful thoughts into your head?"

"That is what I ask myself, ma mère. Many things are done to me and I sit in the centre looking on, like the weathercock on our castle at home, who sees himself turning this way and that way and can only creak."

"A weathercock is dead—you are alive."

"Not at night, ma mère. At home in my bedroom I used to put out my candle every night by clapping the extinguisher upon it. Who is it puts the extinguisher upon me?"

The good sister almost wished it could be she.

But she replied gently, "It is God who gives us sleep—we can't be always awake."

"Then I am not responsible for my dreams anyhow?"

"I hope you don't have bad dreams," said the nun, affrighted.

"Oh, I dream—what do I not dream? Sometimes I fly—oh, so high, and all the people look up at me, they marvel. But I laugh and kiss my hand to them down there."

"Well, there's no harm in flying," said the nun. "The angels fly."

"Oh, but I am not always an angel in my dreams. Is it God who sends these bad dreams, too?"

"No—that is the devil."

"Then it is sometimes he who puts the extinguisher on?"

"That is when you have not said your prayers properly."

Eileen opened wide eyes of protest. "Oh, but, dear mother, I always say my prayers properly."

"You think so? That is already a sin in you—the sin of spiritual pride."

"But, ma mere, devil-dreams or angel-dreams—it is always the same in the morning. Every morning one finds oneself ready on the pillow, like a clock that has been wound up. One did not make the works."

"But one can keep them clean."

Eileen burst into a peal of laughter.

"Qu'avez-vous donc?" said the good creature in vexation.

"I thought of a clock washing its face with its hands."

"You are a naughty child—one cannot talk seriously to you."

"Oh, dear mother, I am just as serious when I am laughing as when I am crying."

"My child, we must never cultivate the mocking spirit. Leave me. I am vexed with you."

As her first communion approached, however, all these simmerings of scepticism and revolt died down into the recommended recueillement. Her days of retreat, passed in holy exercises, were an ecstasy of absorption into the divine, and the pious readings began to assume a truer complexion as the experiences of sister-souls, deep crying unto deep. Oh, how she yearned to take the vows, to leave the trivial distracting life of the outer world for the peace of self-sacrificial love!

As she sat in the chapel, all white muslin and white veil, her hair braided under a little cap, the new rosary of amethyst—a gift from home—at her side, her hands clasped, exalted by incense and flowers and the sweet voices of the choir, chanting Gounod's Canticle, "Le Ciel a visité la terre," she felt that never more would she let this celestial visitant go. When after the communion she pulled the last piece of veiling over her face, she felt that it was for ever between her and the crude world of sense; the "Hymn of Thanksgiving" was the apt expression of her emotions.

But next time she came under these aesthetic, devotional influences—even as her own voice was soaring heavenward in the choir—she thought to herself, "How delicious to have an emotion which you feel will last for ever and which you know won't!" And a gleam of amusement flitted over her rapt features.

III

When Eileen returned to the Convent after her first summer vacation in Ireland she was richer by a surreptitious correspondent. He wrote to her, care of Marcelle, who had a careless mother. He was a young officer from the neighbouring barracks who, invited to make merry with the hospitable O'Keeffe, had fallen a victim to Eileen's girlish charms and mature appearance, for Eileen carried herself as if her years were three more and her inches six higher. Her face had the winsome Irish sweetness; it, too, looked lovelier than a scientific survey would have determined. Her nose was straightish, her mouth small, her lashes were long and dark and conspired with her dark hair to trick a casual observer into thinking her eyes dark, but they were grey with little flecks of golden light if you looked closelier than you should. Her hands were large but finely shaped, with long fingers somewhat turned back at the tips, and pretty pink nails—the hands were especially noticeable, because even when Eileen was not playing the pianoforte, she was prone to extend her thumb as though stretching an octave and to flick it as though striking a note.

It was not love-letters, though, that Lieutenant Doherty sent Eileen, for the schoolgirl had always taken him in a motherly way, and indeed signed herself "Your Mother-Confessor." But the mystery and difficulty of smuggling the letters to and fro lent colour to the drab Convent days, far vivider colour than the whilom passing of verses. So long as Marcelle's desk remained next to Eileen's it was comparatively easy—though still risky—while one's head was studiously buried in "Greek roots," for one's automatic hand to pass or receive the letter beneath the desks through the dangerous space of daylight between the two. "Let not your right hand know what your left hand doeth," Eileen once quoted when Marcelle's conscience pricked. For Marcelle imagined an amour of the darkest dye, and could not understand Eileen's calmness any more than Eileen could understand Marcelle's romantic palpitations alternating with suggestive sniggerings.

But when Marcelle was at length separated from Eileen by a suspicious management, a much more breathless plan was necessary. For Marcelle would deposit the Doherty letter in Eileen's compartment in the curtained row of little niches—where one kept one's work-bag, atlas, and other educational reserves—or Eileen would slip the reply into Marcelle's, and there it would lie, exposed to inspectorial ransacking, till such times as Eileen or Marcelle could transfer it to her bosom. Poor Marcelle lived with her heart in her mouth, trembling, at every rustle of the curtain, for her purple ribbon. However, luck favoured the bold, while the only bad moment in which Eileen was on the verge of detection she surmounted by a stroke of genius.

"What are you hiding there?" said the music-mistress, more sharply than she was wont to address her pet pupil. Eileen put her hand to her bosom. 'Twas as if she were protecting the young lieutenant from pursuing foes, and he became romantically dear to her in that perilous moment, pregnant with swift invention.

She looked round with dramatic mysteriousness. "Hush, ma mère," she breathed; "the Mother Superior might hear."

"Ah, it concerns the Reverend Mother's fête," cried the music-mistress, falling into the trap and even saving Eileen from the lie direct. "Good, my child," and she smiled tenderly upon her. For the birthday of the Lady Superior which was imminent was heralded by infinite mysteriousness. The Reverend Mother was taken by surprise, regularly and punctually. The girls all subscribed, their parents were invited to send plants and flowers. The air vibrated with sublime secrecy, amid which the Reverend Mother walked guilelessly. And when the great day came and the fête was duly sprung upon her, and the pupils all dressed in white overwhelmed her with bouquets and courtesies, how exquisite was her pleased astonishment! That night talking was allowed in the Refectory, and how the girls jabbered! It was like the rolling of ceaseless thunder—one would have thought they had never talked before and never would talk again, and that they were anxious to unload themselves once for all.

"How the ordinary becomes the extraordinary by being forbidden," philosophised Eileen. "At the Castle I can do a hundred things, which here become enormous privileges, even if I am allowed to do them at all. Is it so with everything they say is wrong? Is all sin artificial, and do people sin so zestfully only because they are cramped? Or is there a residue of real wickedness?" Thus she thought, struggling against the obsession of an inquisitorial system which merely clouded her perceptions of real right and wrong. And alone she ate silently, a saintly figure amid the laughing, chattering crew.

She wrote her maternal admonitions to young Doherty during the preparation-time, and far keener than her sense of the lively, good-looking young officer was her sense of the double life she led through him in this otherwise monotonous Convent. When she achieved the blue ribbon of the Enfants de Marie, for which she had worked with true devotion, it added poignancy to her pious pleasure to think that one false step in her secret life would have marred her overt life.

IV

As the end of her conventual period drew nigh Eileen resolved never to go back to the spotted world, but to ask her father to pay her dowry as Bride to the Church, and she had just placed in Marcelle's niche the letter informing Lieutenant Doherty of her call to the higher life (and pointing out how apter than ever his confessions would now be) when Marcelle's signal warned her to look in her own niche. There she found a letter which she could not read till bread-and-chocolate time, but which then took the flavour out of these refreshments. Her lover—he leaped to that verbal position in her thought in this moment of crisis—was ordered off in haste to Afghanistan. The geographical proficiency which had won her so many marks served her only too well, but she hastened to extract her atlas from the fatal niche, and to pore over her geographical misery. She felt she ought to withdraw her own letter for revision, but she could not get at Marcelle or even make her understand. In her perturbation she gave Cabul and Candahar as Kings of Navarre, and Marcelle, implacable as a pillar-box, went away in the evening like a mail-cart.

But the very same night the Superior handed Eileen an opened cablegram which banished Lieutenant Doherty much farther than Afghanistan. Her father was very ill, and called her to his bedside. Things had a way of happening simultaneously to Eileen, these coincidences dogged her life, so that she came to think of them as the rival threads of her life getting tangled at certain points and then going off separately again. After all, if you have several strings to your life, she told herself, it would be more improbable that they should always remain separate than that they should sometimes intertwine.

Eileen reached the Castle through a tossing avenue of villagers, weeping and blessing, and divined from their torment of sympathy that "his honour" was already in his grave. Poor feckless father, how she had loved him spite all his rollicking ways, or perhaps because of them. Through her tears she saw him counting—on his entry into Paradise—the children who had preceded him, and more than ever fuzzled by the flapping of their wings. Oh, poor dearest, how unhomely it would all be to him, this other world where his jovial laugh would shock the nun-like spirits, where there was no more claret, cold, mulled, or buttered, and no sound of horn or tally-ho.

Perhaps it was as well that so many of his brood had gone before him, for with his departure the Castle fell metaphorically about the ears of the survivors. Creditors gave quarter no longer, and Mrs. O'Keeffe found herself reduced to a modest red-gabled farmhouse, with nothing saved from the crash save that part of her dowry which was invested in trustees for the education of her boys. There was no question of Eileen returning to the Convent as a pupil: her desire to take the veil failed at the thought that now she could only be a dowerless working-sister, not a teacher. And for teaching, especially music-teaching, she felt she had a real gift. By a natural transition arose the idea of becoming a music-teacher or a governess outside a Convent, and since her stay at home only helped to diminish her mother's resources, she resolved to augment them by leaving her. Family pride forbade the neighbourhood witnessing a deeper decline. The O'Keeffes were still "the Quality"; it would be better to seek her fortunes outside Ireland and retain her prestige at home. The dual existence would give relish and variety.

Eileen's mind worked so quickly that she communicated these ideas to her mother, ere that patient lady had quite realised that never more would she say, "It's your wife I am, Bagenal dear."

"No, no, you are not to be going away," cried Mrs. O'Keeffe, in alarm.

"Why wouldn't I?" asked Eileen.

Mrs. O'Keeffe could not tell, but looked mysterious meanings. This excited Eileen, so that the poor woman had no rest till she answered plainly, "Because, mavourneen, it's married you are going to be, please the saints."

"Married! Me!"

"It was your father's dying wish, God keep his soul."

"But to whom?"

"You should be asking the priest how good he is. Didn't you notice that the chapel is being white-washed afresh and how clear the Angelus bell rings? Not that it matters much to him, for he has lashings of money as well as a heart of gold."

"Hasn't he a name, too?"

"Don't jump down my throat, Eileen darling. I shouldn't be thinking of O'Flanagan if your father—"

"O'Flanagan! Do you mean the man that bought our Castle at the auction?"

"And isn't it beautifully repaired he's having it for you? He saw you when you were home for the holidays, and he asked us for your hand, all so humble, but your father told him he must wait till you came home for good."

"O'Flanagan!" Eileen flicked him away with her thumb. "A half-mounted gentleman like that."

"Eileen aroon, beggars can't be choosers."

Eileen flushed all over her body. "No more can beggars on horseback."

"Your father will be sorry you take it like that, mavourneen." And the stout saint burst into tears.

Eileen winced. She could almost have flung her arms round her mother and promised to think of it. Suddenly she remembered Lieutenant Doherty. How dared they tear her away from the man she loved! They had not even consulted her. She flicked her thumb agitatedly on the back of her mother's chair. Let her weep! Did they want to sell her, to exchange her for a castle, as if she were a chess-piece? The thought made her smile again.

Her mother said no more, but she could not have employed a more convincing eloquence. The reticence wrought upon Eileen's nerves. After a couple of months of maternal meekness and family poverty, the suggested sacrifice began to appeal to her. A letter from Doherty on his steamer (forwarded to her from Paris by Marcelle), passionately protesting against her intention to take the vows, came to remind her that sacrifice was what she yearned for. The coming of the letter was providential, she told herself: if Marcelle had not posted hers against her will, she might not have had this monition. To return to the Castle as a bride, martyred for the family redemption, was really only a way of returning to the Convent. It meant a life of penance for the good of others. To think of her mother sunning herself again upon the battlemented terrace, or sleeping—if only as guest—in the great panelled bedroom, brought a lump to her throat; her poor tenantry, too, should bless her name; she would glide among them like a spirit, very sad, yet with such healing in her smile and in her touch. "Sure the mistress is the swatest angel God iver sint, so she is." At home she would sit and spin in the old tapestried room, her own life as faded, and sometimes she would dream in the hall, among the antlers and beast-skins, and watch the great burning logs, so much more poetic than this peat smoke which hurt one's eyes. Ah, but then there was O'Flanagan. Well, he would not be much in the way. He liked riding over his new estate in his buckskin breeches, cracking his great loaded whip. She had met him herself once or twice, and the great shy creature had blushed furiously and ridden off down the first bridle-path. "I turn his horse's head as well as his," she had thought with a smile. Yes, she must sacrifice herself. How strange that the nuns should imagine you only renounced by giving up earthly life. Why, earthly life might be the most celestial renunciation of all. But Lieutenant Doherty, what of him? Had she the right to sacrifice him, too? But then she had never given him any claim upon her—she had been merely his little mother-confessor. If he had dared to love her—as his passionate protest against the veil seemed to suggest—it was at his own risk. Poor Doherty, how grieved he would be in far Afghanistan. He would probably rush upon the assegais and die, murmuring her name. Her eyes filled with delicious tears. She sat down and scribbled him a letter hastily, announcing her impending marriage, and posted it at once, so as to put herself beyond temptation to draw back. Then she dashed to her mother's room and sobbed out, "Dear heart, I consent to be martyred."

"What?" said Mrs. O'Keeffe, opening her eyes.

"I consent to be married," Eileen corrected hastily.

"Do you mean to Mr. O'Flanagan?" Mrs. O'Keeffe's face became red as the sun in mist. The cross heaved convulsively on her black silk bosom.

"To whom else? You haven't forgotten he wanted to marry me."

"No, but he has, I am fearing."

"What?" It was now Eileen's turn to open her eyes, and the tears dried on her lashes as she listened. Mrs. O'Keeffe explained, amid the ebb and flow of burning blood, that she had waited in vain for Mr. O'Flanagan to renew his proposal. At first she thought he was waiting for a decent interval to elapse, or for the Castle to be ready for his bride, but gradually she had become convinced by his silence and by the way he avoided her eye when they met and turned his horse down the nearest boreen, that Eileen had been right in calling him half-mounted. He had proposed when he imagined the Squire's fortunes were as of yore, but now he feared he would have to support the ruined family. Well, he needn't fear. The family wouldn't touch him with a forty-foot pole.

"If only your poor father had been alive," wound up Mrs. O'Keeffe, "the dirty upstart would never have dared to put such an insult on his orphaned daughter, that he wouldn't, and if Dan O'Leary should hear of it—which the saints forbid—it's not the jig that his foot would be teaching Mr. O' Flanagan."

The bathos of this anti-climax to martyrdom was too grotesque. Eileen burst into a peal of laughter, which was taken by her mother as a tribute to her lively vituperation. Decidedly, life was deliciously odd. Suddenly she remembered her posted letter to Doherty, and she laughed louder.

Should she send another on its heels? No, it would be rather difficult to explain. Besides, it would be so interesting to see how he replied.

V

Holly Hall—Eileen's first place—was in the English midlands, towards the North: a sombre stone house looking down on a small manufacturing town, whose very grass seemed dingied with coal-dust. "A dromedary town," Eileen dubbed it; for it consisted of a long level with two humps, standing in a bleak desert. On one of the humps she found herself perched. Below—between the humps—lay the town proper, with its savour of grime and gain. The Black Hole was Eileen's name for this quarter; and indeed you might leave your hump, bathed in sunlight, dusty but still sunlight, and as you came down the old wagon-road you would plunge deeper and deeper into the yellowish fog which the poor townspeople mistook for daylight. The streets of the Black Hole bristled with public-houses, banks, factories, and dissenting chapels. The population was given over to dogs and football, and medical men abounded. Arches, blank walls, and hoardings were flamboyant with ugly stage-beauties, melodramatic tableaux, and the advertisements of tailors. After the Irish glens and the Convent garden the Black Hole was not exhilarating.

Mr. Maper, the proprietor of Holly Hall, was a mill-owner, a big-boned, kindly man, who derived his Catholicism from an Irish mother, and had therefore been pleased to find an Irish girl among the candidates for the post of companion to his wife.

As he drove her from the station up the steep old wagon-road he explained the situation, in more than one sense. Eileen's girlish intuition helped his lame sentences over the stiles. Briefly, she was to polish the quondam mill-hand, whom he had married when he, too, was a factory operative, but who had not been able to rise with him. He was an alderman and a J.P. That made things difficult enough. But how if he became Mayor? An alderman has no necessary feminine, not even alderwoman, but Mayor makes Mayoress. And a Mayoress is not safe from the visits of royalty itself. Of course the Mayoress was not to suspect she was being refined; "made a Lady Mayoress," as Eileen put it to herself.

She entered with a light heart upon a task she soon found heavy. For the mistress of Holly Hall had no sense of imperfections. She was a tall and still good-looking person, and this added to her fatal complacency. Eileen saw that she imagined God made the woman and money the lady, and that between a female in a Paris bonnet and a female in a head-shawl there was a natural gap as between a crested cockatoo and a hedge-sparrow. Mrs. Maper indeed suffered badly from swelled self, for it had subconsciously expanded with its surroundings. The wide rooms of the Hall were her spacious skirts, bedecked with the long glitter of the glass-houses; her head reached the roof and wore the weathercock as a feather in her bonnet. All those whirring engines in the misty valley below were her demon-slaves, and the chimneys puffed up incense at her. When she drove out, her life-blood coursed pleasurably through the ramping, glossy horses.

Mrs. Maper, in short, saw herself an empress. It was simply impossible for her to realise that there were eyes which could still see the head-shawl, not the crown. Her one touch of dignity was grotesque—it consisted of extending her arm like a stiff sceptre, in moments of emphasis, and literally pointing her remarks with her forefinger. Sometimes she pointed to the ceiling, sometimes to the carpet, sometimes to the walls. This digital punctuation appeared to be not only superfluous but irrelevant, for Heaven might be invoked from the floor.

With this bejewelled lady Eileen passed her days either on the Hump, or in the Black Hole, or in the environs, and but for her sense of humour and her power of leading a second life above or below her first, her tenure of the post would have been short. The most delicate repetitions of mispronounced words, the subtlest substitution of society phrases for factory idioms, fell blunted against an impenetrable ignorance and self-sufficiency. Short of dropping the pose of companion and boldly rapping a pupil on the knuckles, there seemed to her no way of modifying her mistress. "Who can refine what Fortune has gilded?" she asked herself in humorous despair. The appearance of Mr. Maper at dinner brought little relief. It was a strange meal in the lordly dining room—three covers laid at one end of the long mahogany table, under the painted stare of somebody else's ancestors. Eileen's girlish enjoyment of the prodigal fare was spoiled by her furtive watch on the hostess's fork. Nor did the alderman contribute ease, for he was on pins lest the governess should reveal her true mission, and on needles lest his wife should reveal her true depths. Likewise he worried Eileen to drink his choicest wines. Vintages that she felt her father would have poised on his tongue in mystic clucking ecstasy stood untasted in a regiment of little glasses at her elbow.

She repaid them, however, by adroit educational remarks.

"How stupid of me again!" she said once. "I held out my hock glass for the champagne! Do tell me again which is which, dear Mrs. Maper."

"I suppose you never had a drink of champagne in your life afore you come here," said Mrs. Maper, beamingly. And she indicated the port glass.

"No, no, Lucy, don't play pranks on a stranger," her husband put in tactfully. "It's this glass, Miss O'Keeffe."

"Oh, thank you!" Eileen gushed. "And this is what? Sherry?"

"No, port," replied Mr. Maper, scarcely able to repress a wink.

"You'll have to tell me again to-morrow night," said Eileen, enjoying her own comedy powers. "My poor father tried to teach me the difference between bird's-eye and shag, but I could never remember."

"Ah, Bob's the boy for teaching you that," guffawed the mill owner. "I stick to half-crown cigars myself." His wife shot him a dignified rebuke, as though he were forgetting his station in undue familiarity.

Afterwards Eileen wondered who Bob was, but at the moment she could think of nothing but the farcical complications arising from the idea of Mrs. Maper's providing Mr. Maper with a male companion secretly to improve his manners. Of course the two companions would fall in love with each other.

After dinner things usually woke up a little, for Eileen was made to play and even sing from the scores of "Madame Angot" and other recent comic operas—a form of music that had not hitherto come her way, though it was the only form the music-racks held to feed the grand piano with. Not till the worthy couple had retired, could she permit herself her old Irish airs, or the sonatas and sacred pieces of the Convent.

VI

Accident—the key to all great inventions—supplied Eileen with a new way of educating her mistress. The cook had been impertinent, Mrs. Maper complained. "Why don't you hunt her?" Eileen replied. Mrs. Maper corrected the Irishism by saying, "Do you mean dismiss?" Eileen hastened to accuse herself of Irish imperfections, and henceforward begged to learn the correct phrases or pronunciations. Sometimes she ventured apologetically to wonder if the Irish way was not more approved of the dictionary. Then they would wander into the library in the apparently unoccupied wing, and consult dictionary after dictionary till Eileen hoped Mrs. Maper's brain had received an indelible impression.

One Sunday afternoon a friendly orthoepical difference of this nature arose even as Mrs. Maper sat in her palatial drawing room waiting for callers, and they repaired to the library, Mrs. Maper arguing the point with loud good humour. A glass door giving by corkscrew iron steps on the garden, banged hurriedly as they made their chattering entry. The rows of books—that had gone with the Hall like the family portraits—stretched silently away, but amid the smell of leather and learning, Eileen's lively nostrils detected the whiff of the weed, and sure enough on the top of a stepladder reposed a plain briar pipe beside an unclosed Greek folio.

"The scent is hot," she thought, touching the still warm bowl. "Bob seems as scared as a rabbit and as learned as an owl." Suddenly she had difficulty in repressing a laugh. What if Bob were the corresponding male companion!

"I see Mr. Robert has forgotten his pipe," she said audaciously.

Mrs. Maper was taken aback. "The—the boy is shy," she stammered.

What! Was there a son lying perdu in the house all this while? What fun! A son who did not even go to church or to his mother's receptions. But how had he managed to escape her? And why did nobody speak of him? Ah, of course, he was a cripple, or facially disfigured, morbidly dreading society, living among his books. She had read of such things. Poor young man!

After dinner she found herself examining the family album inquisitively, but beyond a big-browed and quite undistorted baby nursing a kitten, there did not seem anything remotely potential, and she smiled at herself as she thought of the difficulty of evolving bibs into briar pipes and developing Greek folios out of kittens.

From Mrs. Maper's keenness about the University Boat Race as it drew near, and from her wearing on the day itself a dark blue gown trimmed profusely with ribbons of the same hue, Eileen divined that Bob was an Oxford man. This gave the invisible deformed a new touch of interest, but long ere this Eileen had found a much larger interest—the theatre.

She had never been to the play, and the Theatre Royal of the Black Hole was the scene of her induction into this enchantment. In those days the touring company system had not developed to its present complexity, and the theatre had been closed during the first month or so of Eileen's residence in Dromedary Town. But at length, to Mrs. Maper's delight, a company arrived with a melodrama, and as part of her duties, Eileen, no less excited over the new experience (which her Confessor had permitted her), drove with her mistress behind a pair of spanking steeds to the Wednesday matinee. Mrs. Maper alleged her inability to leave her homekeeping husband as the cause of her daylight playgoing, but Eileen maliciously ascribed it to the pomp of the open carriage.

They occupied a box and Eileen was glad they did. For instead of undergoing the illusion of the drama, she found it killingly comic as soon as she understood that it was serious. It was all she could do to hide her amusement from her entranced companion, and somehow this box at the theatre reminded her of the Convent room in which she used to sit listening to the pious readings anent infant prodigies. One afternoon it came upon her that here Mrs. Maper had learned her strange pump handle gestures. Here it was that ladies worked arms up and down and pointed denunciatory forefingers, albeit the direction had more reference to the sentiment.

It was not till a comic opera came along that Eileen was able to take the theatre seriously. Then she found some of the melodies of the drawing room scores wedded to life and diverting action, sometimes even to poetic dancing; the first gleam of poetry the stage gave her. When these airs were lively, Mrs. Maper's feet beat time and Eileen lived in the fear that she would arise and prance in her box. It was an effervescence of joyous life—the factory girl recrudescent—and Eileen's hand would lie lightly on Mrs. Maper's shoulder, feeling like a lid over a kettle about to boil.

When they came home Eileen would gratify her mistress by imitations of comedians. Presently she ventured on the tragedians, without being seen through. She even raised her arm towards the ceiling or shot it towards the centre of the carpet pattern, and Mrs. Maper followed it spellbound.

But from all these monkey tricks she found relief in her real music. When she crooned the old Irish songs, the Black Hole was washed away as by the soft Irish rain, and the bogs stretched golden with furze-blossom and silver with fluffy fairy cotton, and at the doors of the straggling cabins overhung by the cloud-shadowed mountains, blue-cloaked women sat spinning, and her eyes filled with tears as though the peat smoke had got into them.

VII

In such a mood she was playing one Saturday evening in the interval before dinner, when she became aware that somebody was listening, and turning her head, she saw through the Irish mist a man's figure standing in the conservatory. The figure was vanishing when she cried out a whit huskily, "Oh, pray, don't let me drive you away."

He stood still. "If I am not interrupting your music," he murmured.

"Not at all," she said, breaking it off altogether.

As the mist cleared she had a vivid impression of a tall, fair young man against a background of palms. "Eyes burning under a white marble mantel-piece," she summed up his face. Could this uncrippled, rather good-looking person be Bob?

"Won't you come in, Mr. Robert?" she said riskily.

"I only wished to thank you," he said, sliding a step or two into the room.

"There is nothing to thank me for," she said, whirling her stool to face him. "It's my way of amusing myself." She was glad she was in her evening frock.

"Amusing yourself!" He looked aghast.

"What else? I am alone—I have nothing better in the world to do."

"Does it amuse you?" He was flushed now, even the marble mantel-piece ruddied by the flame. "I wish it amused me."

Now it was Eileen's turn to gasp. "Then why do you listen?"

"I don't listen—I bury myself as far away as I can."

"So I have understood. Then what are you thanking me for?"

"For what you are doing for—." his hesitation was barely perceptible—"my mother."

"Oh!" Eileen looked blank. "I thought you meant for my music."

His face showed vast relief. "Oh, you were talking of your music! Of course, of course, how stupid of me! That is what has drawn me from my hole, like a rat to the Pied Piper, and I do thank you most sincerely. But being drawn, what I most wished to thank the Piper for was—"

"Your mother pays the Piper for that," she broke in.

He smiled but tossed his head. "Money! what is that?"

"It is more than I deserve for mere companionship—pleasant drives and theatres."

He did not accept her delicate reticence.

"But you have altered her wonderfully!" he cried.

"Oh, I have not," she cried, doubly startled. "It's just nothing that I have done—nothing." Then she felt her modesty had put her foot in a bog-hole. Unseeingly he helped her out.

"It is most kind of you to put it like that. But I see it in every movement, every word. She imitates you unconsciously—I became curious to see so excellent a model, though I had resolved not to meet you. No, no, please, don't misunderstand."

"I don't," she said mischievously. "You have now given me three reasons for seeing me. You need give me none for not seeing me."

"But you must understand," he said, colouring again, "how painful all this has been for me—"

"Not seeing me?" she interpolated innocently.

"The—the whole thing," he stammered.

"Yes, parents are tiresome," she said sympathetically.

He came nearer the music-stool.

"Are they not? They came down every year for the Eights."

"Is that at Oxford?"

"Yes."

She was silent; her thumb flicked at a note on the keyboard behind her.

"But that's not what I mind in them most—"

She wondered at the rapidity with which his shyness was passing into effusiveness. But then was she not the "Mother-Confessor"? Had not even her favourite nuns told her things about their early lives, even when there was no moral to be pointed? "They're very good-hearted," she murmured apologetically. "I'm often companion—in charity expeditions."

"It's easy to be good-hearted when you don't know what to do with your money. This place is full of such people. But I look in vain for the diviner impulse."

Eileen wondered if he were a Dissenter. But then "the place was full of such people."

"You don't think there's enough religion?" she murmured.

"There's certainly plenty of churches and chapels. But I find myself isolated here. You see, I'm a Socialist."

Eileen crossed herself instinctively.

"You don't believe in God!" she cried in horror. For the good nuns had taught her that "les socialistes" were synonymous with "les athées."

He laughed. "Not, if by God you mean Mammon. I don't believe in Property—we up here in the sun and the others down there in the soot."

"But you are up here," said Eileen, naively.

"I can't help it. My mother would raise Cain." He smiled wistfully. "She couldn't bear to see a stranger helping father in the factory management."

"Then you are down there."

"Quite so. I work as hard as any one even if my labour isn't manual. I dress like an ordinary hand, too, though my mother doesn't know that, for I change at the office."

"But what good does that do?"

"It satisfies my conscience."

"And I suppose the men like it?"

"No, that's the strange part. They don't. And father only laughs. But one must persist. At Oxford I worked under Ruskin."

"Oh, you're an artist!"

"No, I didn't mean that part of Ruskin's work. His gospel of labour—we had a patch for digging."

"What—real spades!"

"Did you imagine we called a spoon a spade?" he said, a whit resentfully.

Eileen smiled. "No, but I can't imagine you using a common or garden spade."

"You are thinking of my hands." He looked at them, not without complacency, Eileen thought, as she herself wondered where he had got his long white fingers from. "But it is a couple of years ago," he explained. "It was hard work, I assure you."

"Did your mother know?" Eileen asked with a little whimsical look.

"Of course not. She would have been horrified."

"Well, but most people would be surprised."

"Yes. Put your muscle into an oar or a cricket bat and you are a hero; put your muscle into a spade and you are a madman."

"You think it's vice versa?" queried Eileen, ingenuously.

"Much more. At least," he stammered and coloured again, "I don't pose as a hero but simply—"

"As what?" Eileen still looked innocent.

"I simply think work is the noblest function of man," he burst forth. "Don't you?"

"I do not," answered Eileen. "Work is a curse. If the serpent had not tempted Eve to break God's commandment, we should still be basking in Paradise."

He looked at her curiously. "You believe that?"

"Isn't it in the Bible?" she answered, seriously astonished.

"Whatever the primitive Semitic allegorist may have thought, work is a blessing, not a curse."

"Then you are an atheist!" Eileen recoiled from this strange young man.

"Ah, you shrink back!" he said in tones of bitter pleasure. "I told you I lived in isolation."

Eileen's humour shot forth candidly. "You'll not be isolated when you die."

His bitterness passed into genial superiority. "You mean I'll go to hell. How can you believe anything so horrible?"

"Why is that horrible for me to believe? For you—" And she filled up the sentence with a smile.

"I don't believe you do believe it."

"There's nothing you seem to believe. I do honestly think that you can't be saved if you don't believe."

"I accept that. The question, however, is what kind of belief and what kind of saving. Do you suppose Plato is in hell?"

"I don't know. He invented Platonic love, didn't he? So that might save him." She looked at him with her great grey eyes—he couldn't tell whether she was quizzing him or not.

"Is that all you know of Plato?"

"I know he was a Greek philosopher. But I only learned Greek roots at the Convent. So Plato is Greek to me."

"He has been beautifully Englished by the Master of my College. I wish you'd read him."

"Is the translation in the library?"

"Of course—with lots of other interesting books, and such queer folios and quartos and first editions. The collector was a man of taste. Why do you never come and let me show them you?"

"You'd run away."

"No, I wouldn't," he smiled encouragingly.

"Yes, you would. And leave your pipe on Plato!"

He laughed. "Was I rude? But I didn't know you then. Come to-morrow afternoon and show you've forgiven me."

The new interest was sufficiently tempting. But her maidenliness held back. "I'll come with your mother."

Disgust lent him wit. "You're her companion—not she yours."

"True. Nor I yours."

"Then I'll come here."

"Bringing the Plato and the folios—?"

"Why not? You can't forbid me my own drawing-room."

"I can run away and leave my crochet-hook behind."

"You'll find me hooked on whenever you return."

"Well, if you're determined—by hook or by crook! But you're not going to convert me to Socialism?"

"I won't promise."

"You must. I don't mind reading Plato."

"He's worse. He isn't a Christian at all."

"I don't mind that. He's B.C. He couldn't help it. But you Socialists came after Christ."

"How do you know Socialism isn't a return to Him?"

"Is it?"

"Aha! You are getting interested.... But I hear my mother coming down to dinner. To be continued in our next. À demain, is it not?"

He held out his shapely white hand, and hastened through the conservatory into the garden.

"Going to dig?" Eileen called after him maliciously.

VIII

Eileen became interested in Robert Maper, for the old books he opened up to her were quite new and enlarging. She had imagined the Church replacing Paganism as light replaced darkness. Now she felt that it was only as gas replaced candle-light. The darkness was less Egyptian than the nuns insinuated. Plato in particular was a veritable chandelier. It occurred to her suddenly that he might be on the black list. But she was afraid to ask her Confessor for fear of hearing her doubt confirmed. To tell the good father of the semi-secret meetings in the library would have been superfluous, since there was nothing to conceal even from Mrs. Maper, though that lady did not happen to know of them. Eileen did not even use the garden door. Besides, there was never a formal appointment, not infrequently, indeed, a disappointment, when the library held nothing but books. Robert Maper merely provided that possibility of an innocent double life, without which existence would have been too savourless for Eileen. Even a single line of railway always appeared dismal to her; she liked the great junctions with their bewildering interlanglements, their possibilities of collision. And now that Lieutenant Doherty had faded away into Afghanistan and silence—he did not even acknowledge the letter announcing her approaching marriage—Robert Maper proved a useful substitute.

One day Mr. Maper senior invited her to drive down with him and go over the factory, and as Mrs. Maper was not averse from impressing her employée by the sight of the other employes, she was permitted to go. Nothing, however, would induce Mrs. Maper to adventure herself in these scenes of her early life, touching which she professed a sovereign ignorance. "Machines are so clattery," she said. "My head wouldn't stand them. I once went to that exhibition in London and I said to myself, never no more for this gal."

"And you never did go any more since you were a girl?" asked the companion, with professional pointedness.

"No, never no more," replied Mrs. Maper, serenely, "once is too often, as the gal said when the black man kissed her."

Eileen laughed dutifully at this quotation from the latest comic opera, and went off, delighted to companion the husband by way of change. He proved quite a new man, too, in his own element, bringing the most complicated machinery to the level of her understanding. Room after room they passed through, department after department full of tireless machinery, and tired men and women, who seemed slaves to the whims of fantastic iron monsters, all legs and arms and wheels. It took a morning to see everything, down to the pasting and drying and packing rooms, and as a last treat Mr. Maper took her to the engine-room, whence he said came the power that turned those myriad wheels, moved those myriad levers, in whatever department they might be and whatever their function. Eileen gazed long at the mighty engine, rapt in reverie. She could scarcely tear herself away, and when at last Mr. Maper brought her into the counting-house, she had forgotten that she must meet his son there. The white-browed clerk in corduroys did not, however, raise his eyes from his ledger, and Eileen was grateful to him for preserving the piquancy of their relation.

She did not find it so piquant, though, in the library next Sunday afternoon when he was clutching at her hand and asking her to be his wife. She awoke as from a dream to the perception of a solemn and grotesque fact.

"Oh, please!" and she tried to tear her hand away.

He clung on desperately. "Eileen—don't say you don't care at all."

"I'm not Eileen, and I particularly dislike you at this moment. Let me have my hand, please."

He dropped it like a stinging nettle. "I was hoping you'd let me keep it," he murmured.

"Why?" She was simple and pitiless. "Because we read Plato together? That was platonic enough, wasn't it?"

"You can jest about what breaks my heart?"

"I am very sorry. I like you."

His breathing changed, "like a fish thrown back into the water," Eileen thought. She hastened to add, "But it's not what a wife should feel."

"How do you know what a wife should feel?"

Eileen screwed up her forehead. "If I felt it, I should know, I suppose."

"No, you mightn't. You've liked to come here and talk to me."

"Because I like books. And you talk like a book."

"That was before I fell in love. I didn't talk like a book just now."

"When you took my hand! More like a book than ever. I've read it all—lots of times."

"Oh, Eil—Miss O'Keeffe—you are very cruel."

Eileen smiled. "I am not—I'm very kind—I threw you back into the water."

He gasped, as though out of it again. "Do you mean I am not grown enough?"

She flushed and improvised on his theme. "Not quite that. You hooked yourself, as you threatened to do. But suppose I had landed you. You know the next step—hot water. What a lot you would have got into, too!"

"You are thinking of my mother?"

"Yes, raising Cain, I think you said once. Oh, dear, swim about and be thankful." And a vision of Mrs. Maper's amazement twitched the corners of her lips and made them more enchanting.

"I'm not so cold-blooded as all that. But if you do throw me back, let it be with the promise to take me again, when I am grown. I don't say it to tempt you, but you know I shall be very rich."

"Indigestible, do you mean?"

"Oh, please let us drop that metaphor! Metaphors can never go on all fours."

"Certainly not when they have fins."

"Don't jest, Eil—Miss O'Keeffe! Let me redeem you from your sordid life."

"Why is it sordid? You said work was divine."

"You can work in a higher sphere."

"And this is the Socialist! I really thought you'd want me to turn factory lass."

"You are laughing at me."

"I am perfectly serious. I won't drag you down from Socialism, and a head-shawl wouldn't become me."

"Why, you'd look sweet in it. Dear, dear, Miss O'Keeffe—"

"Good-by."

"No, you shan't go." He barred her way. Her airiness had given him new hope.

"If you don't behave sensibly, I'll go altogether—give notice."

"Then I'll follow you to your next place."

"No followers allowed. Seriously, I'll leave if you are foolish."

"Very well," he said abruptly. "Let's go on reading Plato," and he turned to the book.

"No, no more Dialogues, in or out of Plato."

She was smiling but stern. He opened the library door and bowed as she passed out.

"Remember," he said. "I will remain foolish for ever."

"You have too long an opinion of yourself," was Eileen's parting flash.

IX

The next evening she sat in the drawing-room before dinner, softly playing an accompaniment to her thoughts. Why didn't she feel anything about Robert Maper except a mild irritation at the destruction of so truly platonic a converse? In a book, of which his proposal savoured, she would have found him quite a romantic person. In the actuality she felt as frigid as if his marble forehead was chilling her, and what she remembered most acutely was his fishlike gasping. Then, too, the contradictoriness of his social attitude, his desire to make her a rich drone, his shame at his mother, his reclusive shyness—all the weaknesses of the man—came to obscure her sense of his literary idealism, if not, indeed, to reveal it as a mere coquetry with fine ideas and coarse clothes. And then for a moment the humour of being Mrs. Maper's daughter-in-law appealed to her, and she laughed to herself in soft duet with the music.

And in the middle of the duet Mrs. Maper herself burst in, with her bodice half hooked and her hair half done.

"What's this I hear, Miss Hirish Himpudence, of your goings-on with my son?"

Eileen swung round on her stool. "I beg your pardon," she said.

"Oh, you can't get out of it by beggin' my pardon, creepin' into the library like a mouse—and it's a nice sly mouse you are, too, but there's never a mouse without its cat—"

"She'd have done better to do your hair and mind her business," said Eileen, calmly.

Mrs. Maper's forefinger shot heavenwards. "It was you as ought to have minded your business. I didn't pay you like a lady and feed you like a duchess to set your cap at your betters. But I told Mr. Maper what 'ud come of it if we let you heat with us, though I didn't dream what a sly little mouse—"

The torrent went on and on. Eileen as in a daze watched the theatric forefinger—now pointed at the floor as if to the mouse-hole, now leaping ceilingwards like the cat,—and her main feeling was professional. She was watching her pupil, storing up in her memory the mispronunciations and vulgarisms for later insinuative improvement. Only a tithe of her was aware of the impertinence. But suddenly she heard herself interrupting quietly.

"I shall not sleep under your roof another night." Mrs. Maper paused so abruptly that her forefinger fell limp. She was not sure she meant to give her companion notice, and have the trouble of training another, and she certainly did not wish to be dismissed instead of dismissing.

"Silly chit!" she said in more conciliatory tones. "And where will you sleep?"

But Eileen now felt she must obey her own voice—the voice of her outraged pride, perhaps even of Brian Boru himself. "Good-by. I'll take some things in a handbag and send for my box in the morning."

Mrs. Maper's hand pointed to the ceiling. "And is that the way you treat a lady—you're no lady, I tell you that. I demand a month's notice or I shall summons you."

At this juncture it occurred to Eileen that this might have been her mother-in-law, and a smile danced into her eyes.

"Himpudent Hirish hussy! Oh, but I'll have the lore of you. Don't forget I'm the wife of a Justice of the Peace."

"Very well; you get Justice, I want Peace." And Eileen fled to her room.

She had hardly begun packing her handbag when she heard the door locked from the outside with a savage snap and a cry of, "I'll learn you who's mistress here, my lady."

Eileen smiled. She was only on the second floor, and captivity revived all her girlish prankishness. She now began to enjoy the whole episode. That she was out of place, out of character, out of lodging even, was nothing beside the humour of this incursion into real life of the melodrama she had mocked at. Was she not the innocent heroine entrapped by the villain? Fortunately, she would not need the hero to rescue her. She went on packing. When her handbag was ready she looked about for means to escape. She opened her windows and studied the drop and the odd bits of helpful rainpipe. Descent was not so easy as she had imagined. Short of tearing the sheets into strips (and that might really bring her within the J.P.'s purview) or of picking the lock (which seemed even more burglarious, not to mention more difficult) she might really remain trapped. However, there would be time to think properly when she had packed her big box. Half an hour passed cheerfully in the folding of dresses to an underplay of planned escapes, and she had just locked the box, when Mrs. Maper's voice pierced the door panel.

"Well, are you ready to come to supper?"

The governess's instinct corrected "dinner." Mrs. Maper when excited was always tripping into this betrayal of auld lang syne, but she preserved a disdainful silence.

"Eileen, why don't you hanser?"

Still silence. The key grated in the lock.

Eileen looked round desperately. The thought of meeting Mrs. Maper again was intolerable. The mirrored door of the rifled wardrobe stood ajar, revealing an enticing emptiness. Snatching up her handbag and her hat, she crept inside and closed the door noiselessly upon herself. "The wardrobe mouse," she thought, smiling.

"Well, my lady!" Mrs. Maper dashed through the door, in her dinner-gown and diamonds, her forefinger hovering, balanced, between earth and heaven. She saw nothing but an answering figure ribboned and jewelled, that dashed at her and pointed its forefinger menacingly.

The appearance of this figure as from behind the glass shut out from her mind the idea of another figure behind it. The packed box, neat and new-labelled, the absence of the handbag and of any sign of occupancy, the open windows, the silence, all told their lying tale.

"The Hirish witch!" she screamed.

She ran from one window to the other seeking for a sign of the escaped or the escapade. She was relieved to find no batter of brains and blood spoiling the green lawn. How had the trick been done? It did not even occur to her to look under the bed, so hypnotised was she by the sense of a flown bird. Eileen almost betrayed herself by giggling, as at the real stage melodrama.

When Mrs. Maper ran downstairs to interrogate the servants—eruption into the kitchen was one of her incurable habits—Eileen slipped through the wide-flung door, down the staircase, and then, seeing the butler ahead, turned sharp off to the little-used part of the corridor and so into the library. She made straight for the iron staircase to the grounds, and came face to face with Robert Maper.

Twilight was not his hour for the library—she saw even through her perturbation that he was pacing it in fond memory. His face lighted up with amazement, as though the dead had come up through a tombstone.

"Good-by!" she said, shifting her handbag to her left hand and holding out her right. Her self-possession pleased her.

"What!" he cried. And again he had the gasp of a fish out of water.

"Yes, I came to say good-by."

"You are leaving us?"

"Yes."

"Oh, and it is I that have driven you away!"

"No, no, don't reproach yourself, please don't. Good-by."

He gasped in silence. She gave a little laugh. "Now that I offer you my hand, it is you who won't take it."

He seized it. "Oh, Eil—Miss O'Keeffe—let me keep it."

"Please! we settled that."

"It will never be settled till you are my wife."

"Listen!" said Eileen, dramatically. "In a few minutes your mother and father will be seated at dinner. Your mother will have told your father I've left the house in disgrace. Don't interrupt. Would you be prepared to walk in upon them with me on your arm and to say, 'Mother, father, Miss O'Keeffe has done me the honour of consenting to be my wife'?"

With her warm hand still in his, how could he hesitate? "Oh, Eileen, if you'd only let me!"

The imagination of the tableau was only less tempting to Eileen. It was procurable—she had only to move her little finger, or rather not to move it. But the very facility of production lessened the tableau's temptingness. The triumph was complete without the vulgar actuality.

"I can't," she said, withdrawing her hand. "But you are a good fellow. Good-by." She moved towards the garden steps. He was incredulous of the utter end. "I shall write to you," he said.

"This is a short cut," she murmured, descending. As her feet touched the grass she smiled. How they had both tried to stop her, mother and son! She hurried through the shrubbery, and by a side gate was out on the old wagon road. More slowly, but still at a good pace, she descended towards the Black Hole, now beginning to twinkle and glimmer with lights, and far less grimy and prosaic than in the crude day.

X

While packing her big box, she had decided to try to lodge that night with a programme-girl she had got to know at the Theatre Royal, and the motive that set her pace was the desire to find her before she had started for the theatre.

The girl usually hovered about Mrs. Maper's box. Once Eileen had asked her why she wasn't in evidence the week before. "Lord, miss," she said, "didn't you recognise me on the stage?"

Eileen thus discovered that the girl sometimes figured as a super, when travelling companies came with sensational pieces, relying upon local talent, hastily drilled, for the crowds. Mary became a Greek slave, or a Billingsgate fishwife, with amusing unexpectedness.

Eileen's next discovery about the girl was that she supported a paralysed mother, though the bed-ridden creature on inspection proved to be more cheerful than the visitors she depressed. Mr. Maper had sent her grapes from his hothouse only a few days before, and in taking them to the little house Eileen had noticed a "Bedroom to Let."

To her relief, when she reached the bleak street, she could see that though the blind was down, the bill was still in the window. Her spirits bubbled up again. Ere she could knock at the door, the programme-girl bounced through it, hatted and cloaked for the theatre.

"Miss O'Keeffe!" She almost staggered backward. Eileen's face worked tragically in the gloom.

"There are villains after me!" Eileen gasped. "Take this bag, it contains the family jewels. That bedroom of yours, it is still to let?"

"Yes, miss."

"I take it for to-night, perhaps for ever. The avenger is on my footsteps. The law may follow me, but I shall defy its myrmidons in my trackless eyrie."

"Oh, Miss O'Keeffe! You frighten me. I shouldn't like to have all these jewels in my house, and with my mother tied to her bed."

Eileen burst into a laugh. "Oh, miss!" she said, mimicking the programme-girl. "Didn't you recognise me on the stage?"

"Mary Murchison!" gasped the programme-girl. "Oh, Miss O'Keeffe, how wonderful! You nearly made my heart stop—"

"I am sorry, but I do want to take your bedroom. I've left Mrs. Maper, and you are not to ask any questions."

"I haven't time, I'm late already. Fortunately, I only come on in the second act."

"That's nice; put my bag in and I'll come to the theatre with you." The thought was impromptu, an evening with a bed-ridden woman was not exhilarating at such a crisis.

"You ought to be an actress yourself," the programme-girl remarked admiringly on the way.

Eileen shuddered. "No, thank you. Scream the same thing night after night—like a parrot with not even one's own words—I should die of monotony."

"Oh, it isn't at all monotonous. It's a different audience every night, and even the laughs come in different places. My parts have mostly been thinking parts—to-night I'm a prince without a word—but still it's fun."

"But how can you bear strange men staring at you?"

"One gets used to it. The first time they put me in tights I blushed all through the piece, but they had painted me so thick it wasn't visible."

"In short, you blushed unseen."

Eileen wished to go to the pit, but her new friend would not hear of her not occupying her habitual box, since she knew that the management would be glad to have it occupied if it were empty. This proved to be the case, and put the seal upon Eileen's enjoyment of the situation. To spend her evening in Mrs. Maper's box was indeed a climax.

She borrowed theatre-paper and scribbled a note to her ex-employer, giving the address for her trunk. An orange and some biscuits sufficed for her dinner.

Not till she was in her little bedroom, surrounded by pious texts, did she break down in tears.

XI

The next morning, as she sat answering advertisements, the programme-girl knocked at the door of the bedroom and announced that Mr. Maper had called.

Eileen turned red. It was too disconcerting. Would he never take "no" for an answer? "I won't see him. I can't see him," she cried.

The girl departed and returned. "Oh, Miss O'Keeffe, he begs so for only one word."

"The word is 'no.'"

"After he's been so kind as to bring your box down!"

"Oh, has he? Then the word is 'thanks.'"

"Please, miss, would you mind giving it to him yourself?"

"Who's Irish, you or I? I won't speak to him at all, I tell you."

"But I don't like to send him away like that, when he's been so kind to mother."

"When has he been kind to your mother?"

"Those grapes you brought—"

"That was old Mr. Maper."

"So is this."

"Oh!" Eileen was quite taken aback, for once. "All right, I'll go into the parlour."

He was infinitely courteous and apologetic. He had been very anxious about her. Why had she been so unkind as to leave, and without ever a good-by to him?

"Oh, hasn't your wife told you, then?"

"She has told me you were rude, and that you left without notice, and she wants me to prosecute you. I suppose you lost your temper. You found her rather difficult."

"I found her impossible," said Eileen, frigidly.

"Yes, yes, I understand." He was flushed and unhappy. "You found her impossible to live with?"

Eileen nodded; she would have added "or to make a lady of," but he looked so purple and agitated that she charitably forbore. She was wondering whether Mrs. Maper could really have been so mean as to omit her share in the quarrel, but he went on eagerly:—

"Quite so, quite so. And what do you think it has been for me?"

She murmured inarticulate sympathy.

"Ah, if you only knew! Oh, my dear Miss O'Keeffe, while you've been in the house, it's been like heaven."

"I'm glad I've given satisfaction," she said drily.

"Then what do you give by going? I assure you the day you came to the works it was like heaven there too."

"You forget the temperature," Eileen smiled. "However, it was a very nice day, and I thank you. But I can't come back after—"

"Who asks you to come back?" he broke in. "No, I should be sorry to see you again in a menial position, you with your divine gifts of beauty and song. The idea of your getting a new place," he added with a fall into prose, "makes me feel sick."

"I value your sympathy, but it is misplaced," she replied freezingly.

"Sympathy! It isn't sympathy! It's jealousy. Oh, my dear Miss O'Keeffe!" He seized her limp hand. "Eileen! Let me help you—"

As the true significance of his visit, and of the purple agitation, dawned upon her, the grim humour of the position overbore every other feeling. Her hand still in his, she began to laugh, and no biting of her lips could do more than change the laugh into an undignified snigger. Instead of profiting by his grip of her, he dropped her hand suddenly as if a hose had been turned on his passion, and this surrender of her hand reduced Eileen to a passable gravity.

"I'm very sorry, Mr. Maper. But really, life is too horribly amusing."

"I'm very sorry it's me that affords you amusement," he said stiffly.

"No, it isn't you at all, it's just the whole thing. You've been most kind all along. And I dare say you mean to be kind now. But I don't really need any help. Your wife's threats of prosecution are ridiculous, she made my longer stay impossible. I could more justly claim a month's notice from her."

"That's what I thought. I've brought you a month's salary." He fumbled in his pocket-book.

"Don't trouble. I shall not accept it."

"You shall," he said sternly. "Or I'll prosecute you."

Eileen's laugh rang out clear. This time he laughed too.

"Now, don't you call life amusing?" she said. "Here am I to take a cheque under penalty of having to pay it."

"Well, which shall it be?"

"Such a cheque is charming." And she held out her hand. He put the cheque in it and shook both warmly. They parted, the best of friends.

"Come to me for a character, of course," he said.

"Don't you come to me," replied Eileen, with a roguish smile.

XII

Eileen's next place was—as if by contrast—with a much more genteel family, and a much poorer, though it flew higher socially. It lived in a house, half in a fashionable London terrace, half in a shabby side street, and its abode was typical of its ambitions and its means. Mrs. Lee Carter drew the line clearly between herself and her governess, which was a blessing, for it meant Eileen's total exclusion from her social life, and Eileen's consequent enjoyment of her own evenings at home or abroad, as she wished. This unusual freedom compensated for the hard work of teaching children in various stages of growth and ignorance how to talk French and play the piano. Her salary was small, for Mrs. Lee Carter's ambition to live beyond her neighbours' means was only achieved by pinching whomever she could. She was not bad-hearted; she simply could not afford anything but luxuries. Eileen wondered at not being asked sometimes to perform at her parties, till she found that only celebrities ever did anything in that house.

This was a period of much mental activity in Eileen's life. The tossing ocean of London life, the theatres that played Shakespeare, the world of new books and new thought, her recent perusal of Plato and of man, all produced fermentation. But every night she knelt by her bedside and said her "Ave Maria" with a voluptuous sense of spiritual peace, and every morning she woke with a certain joy in existence and a certain surprise to find herself again existing. Her old convent-thought recurred. "We are worked from without—marionettes who can watch their own performance. And it is very amusing." Once she read of a British action in Afghanistan against border-tribes, and she wondered if Lieutenant Doherty was in the fighting. Since she had ceased to be his mother-confessor he had become very shadowy; his image now rose substantial from the newspaper lines, and she was surprised to find in herself a little palpitation at his probable perils. "One's heartstrings, too, are pulled," she thought. "I don't like it. Marionettes should move, not feel." These reflections, however, came to her more often anent her family, and the struggles of her kin for a livelihood touched her more deeply than any love. "We are like bits of the same shattered body," she thought. "In these cold English families everybody is another body." She sent most of her salary to Ireland, and her pocket-money came from singing in the choir on Sunday.

The bass chorister was a very amusing man. His voice was sepulchral but his conversation skittish. Eileen's repartees smote him to almost the only serious respect of his life, and one day he said: "Why, there's a future in you. Why don't you go on the stage?"

"What nonsense!" But the blood was secretly stirred in her veins. She saw herself walking along the Black Hole with the programme-girl, but her point of view had been modified since she had received a similar suggestion with a shudder. If she could play Rosalind to a great London audience, the staring men-folk would matter little.

"Why not?" went on the bass tempter. "A humour like yours with such a voice and such a face!"

"The stage is full of better voices and better faces."

"No, indeed. Why, there isn't a girl at the Half-and-Half—" He stopped and almost blushed.

She smiled. "Oh, I don't mind your going to such places. What is the Half-and-Half, a place where they drink beer?"

"Oh, it's just our slang name for a little music-hall that's just between the East End and the West End, with a corresponding programme."

"Our slang name?"

"Well—" he paused. "If you'll keep it very dark—but of course you will—I appear there myself."

"You! What do you do?"

"I sing patriotic songs and drinking-songs—"

"Aren't they the same thing in England?"

"Don't say that on the stage or they'll throw pewter pots. They're very patriotic."

"That's just what I said. What's your name—I suppose you change it?"

"Yes—as I hope you will yours—some day."

"I shan't take yours."

"Nobody arxed you, miss," he said. "And, besides, mine is copyright—Jolly Jack Jenkins. I make a fiver a week by it."

"A fiver!" The bass chorister suddenly took on an air of Arabian nights. At this rate she could buy back the family castle. Her struggling brothers—how they would bless their magician sister—Mick should have a London practice, Miles a partnership in an engineering firm.

"You come with me and see Fossy," continued Jolly Jack Jenkins.

Eileen declined with thanks. It took a week of Sundays to argue away her objections—religious, moral, and social. To play Rosalind to fashionable London was one thing: to appear at a variety theatre or low-class music-hall, which nobody in her world or Mrs. Lee Carter's had ever heard of, was another pair of shoes. Yet strange to say, it was the last consideration that decided her to try. Even if admitted to the boards, she could make her failure in secure obscurity. It would simply be another girlish escapade, and she was ripe for mischief after her long sobriety.

"But even your Mr. Fossy mustn't know my real name or address," she stipulated.

"Who shall I say you are?"

"Nelly O'Neill."

"Ripping. Flows from the tongue like music."

"Then it's rippling you mean."

"What a tongue! Wait till Fossy sees you."

"Will he ask me to stick it out?"

"Oh, Lord, I wish I had your repartee. But I'm thinking—Nelly O'Neill—doesn't it give you away a bit?"

"Keeps me a bit, too. I shouldn't like to lose myself altogether—gain reputation for another woman."

Fossy proved to be a gentleman named Josephs, who in a tiny triangular room near the stage of the Half-and-Half listened critically to her comic singing, shook his head and said he would let her know. Eileen left the room with leaden heart and feet.

"Wait for me a moment, please," Jolly Jack Jenkins called after her, and she hung about timidly, jostled by dirty attendants and painted performers. She was reading a warning to artistes that any improper songs or lines would lead to their instant dismissal, and regretting more than ever her incompetence for this innocent profession, when she heard the bass chorister's big breathing behind her.

"Bravo! You knocked him all of a heap."

"Rubbish! Don't try to cheer me."

"You!" Jolly Jack Jenkins opened his eyes. "You taken in by Fossy! He'll suggest your doing a trial turn next Saturday night when the public are least critical, you'll make a furore, and he'll offer you two guineas a week."

"A pleasing picture, but quite visionary. Why, he didn't even ask for an address to write to!"

"Oh, I dare say he thought care of me would find you. No, don't glower at me—I don't mean anything wrong."

"I hope you didn't let him misunderstand—"

"You asked me not to let him know too much. Fossy has to do so much with queer folk—"

"Yes, I saw he had to warn them against improper songs."

Jolly Jack Jenkins exploded in a guffaw.

"I'm sorry I came," said Eileen, in vague distress.

"Fossy isn't," he retorted. "He was clean bowled over. In that Irish fox-hunting song all the gallery will be shouting 'Tally-ho!' Where did you pick it up?"

"I didn't pick it up, I made it up for the occasion."

"By Jove! I have to pay a guinea to a bloodsucking composer when I want a song. Oh, Fossy's spotted a winner this time."

"Why is he called Fossy?"

"I don't know. Nobody knows. I found the name, I pass it on."

"Perhaps it's a corruption of Foxy."

"There! I never thought of that! You are a—!"

The jolly chorister's mouth remained open. But the prophecy that had already issued from it came true in every detail.

XIII

Despite her private stage-fright, Nelly O'Neill, the new serio-comic, made a big hit. Her innocent roguery was captivating; her virginal freshness floated over the footlights, like a spring breeze through the smoky Hall.

"Well, you are an all-round success," cried Jolly Jack Jenkins, pumping her hand off at the wings, amid a thunder of applause, encores, and whistles.

"You mean a Half-and-Half!" laughed Nelly through Eileen's tears. She had given herself to the audience, but how it had given itself in return, flashing back to her in electric waves its monstrous vitality, its apparently single life.

The Half-and-Half was one of those early Victorian halls of the people, with fixed stars and only a few meteors. The popular favourites changed their songs and their clothes at periodic intervals, but they would have lost favour if they had not remained the same throughout everything. A chairman with a hammer announced the turns, and condescendingly took champagne with anybody who paid for it. Eileen soon became an indispensable part of this smoky world. She signed an agreement at three guineas a week for three years, to perform only at the Half-and-Half. Fossy saw far. Eileen did not. She jumped for joy when she got beyond eyeshot. She felt herself jumping out of the governess-life. Second thoughts and soberer footsteps brought doubt. She had intended telling Mrs. Lee Carter as soon as the trial-performance was over, but now she hesitated and was lost. Half the charm lay in the secret adventure, the dare-devilry. Besides, as a governess she had a comfortable home and a respectable status, and she had already seen and divined enough of the world behind the footlights to shrink from being absorbed into it. What fun in the double life! She had never found a single life worth living. She would belong to two worlds—be literally Half-and-Half. Nelly O'Neill must only be born at twilight. But she felt she could not be out uniformly every evening without some explanation.

"Mrs. Lee Carter," she said, "I have to tell you of a peculiar chance of augmenting my income that has come to me."

Mrs. Lee Carter, wearing plumes and train for a court reception, paled. "You are not going to leave me!"

The naïve exclamation strengthened Eileen's hand.

"I don't quite see how to do otherwise," she said boldly.

"Oh, dear, I wish I could afford more. I know you're worth it."

Eileen thought, "If you'd only give your guests good claret instead of bad champagne!" But she said, "You are very kind—you have always been most considerate."

The plumes wagged.

"I try to please all parties."

Nelly O'Neill thought, "And to give too many." Eileen said, "Yes, you've given me my evenings to myself as it is, and considering the new work is only in the evenings, I did think of running the two, but I'm afraid—"

"If we lightened your work a little—" interrupted Mrs. Lee Carter, eagerly.

"I shouldn't so much ask that as to have perfect freedom like a young man—a latch-key even." Never had Eileen looked more demure and Puritan.

"Oh, I hope you won't be working too late—"

"The people who go there are engaged in the daytime. I'd better be frank with you; it's an extremely unfashionable place towards the East End, and I quite understand you may not like me to take it. At the same time I shall never meet anybody who knows me. In fact, it's a dancing and singing place."

"Oh!" said Mrs. Lee Carter, blankly. "I didn't know you could teach dancing, too."

"You never asked me.... Of course, if you prefer it, I could come here as a day governess and leave after tea.... You see it's a longish journey home: I'm bound to be late...."

"What's the difference? Come and go as you please.... Of course, you won't mind using the back door when there's a party ... the servants...."

For the deception Eileen at first salved her conscience Irish-wise by sending every farthing to her mother under the deceiving pretext of rich private pupils. She would not even deduct for cabs. Sometimes she could not get an omnibus, but she almost preferred to walk till she was footsore, for both riding and walking were forms of penance. The stuffy omnibus interior after the smoky Hall was nauseating, and in those days no lady thought of climbing the steep ladder to the slanting roof. But it sometimes happened that a crawling cabman coming westward would invite her to a free ride, and Eileen would accept gratefully, and, moreover, gain from conversations with her drivers new material for her songs.

This period of her life was almost as amusing as she had anticipated; her only depressions came from the children of the footlights, and the necessity of adjusting herself superficially to her environment, under pain of unpopularity. Her isolation and the privacy of her home-life already made sufficiently for that. And to be disliked even by those she disliked Eileen disliked. Her nature needed to wallow in warm admiration. She got plenty.

When, fifteen months later, she agreed to pay Fossy a hundred pounds for modifying her contract so as to enable her to appear at other Halls, she said with a smile, "You deserve it. You are the only man at the Half-and-Half who hasn't made love to me."

Fossy grinned. "If I had known that, I should have demanded a larger compensation."

Even the bass chorister had not been able to resist proposing, though his grief at being refused was short-lived, for he died soon after by a fall from one of those giant wheels that were the saurians of the modern cycle. Eileen shed many a tear over Jolly Jack Jenkins.

With the growth of her popularity before and behind the footlights came heavier calls upon her geniality, and, like a hostess who tries to pay off her debts in one social lump sum, Eileen got "a Sunday out," and Nelly gave a lunch at a riverside hotel to a motley company of popular favourites. It was expensive; for the profession, even in those days, expected champagne. It was appallingly protracted; for the party, having no work to do that evening, showed no disposition to break up, and brandies-and-sodas succeeded one another in an aroma of masculine cigars and feminine cigarettes. It was noisy and hilarious, and gradually it became rowdy. The Singing Sisters sang, but not in duet. The Lion Comique, whose loyal melodies were on every barrel-organ, argued Republicanism and flourished that day's copy of Reynolds's Newspaper, The Beauteous Bessie Bilhook—"the Queen of Serio-Comics" was scandalously autobiographic, and the old plantation songster—looking unreal with his washed face— was with difficulty dissuaded from displaying his ability to dance on the table without smashing anything. The climax was reserved for the demure one-legged gymnast, who suddenly produced a pistol and discharged it in the air. When the panic subsided, he explained to the landlord and the company that he was "paying his shot."

"That's a hint for me to discharge the bill," said Nelly, adroitly, and, thanking everybody effusively for the happiness afforded her, she hurried home to Oxbridge Terrace, to wash it all away in nursery tea. The young Lee Carters made a restful spectacle with their shining innocent faces, and she almost wished they would never grow up.

As her success grew, offers from the pantomimes and even the legitimate stage began to reach her. But now she would not make the step. At the Halls she was her own mistress, able to arrange at her own convenience with orchestras. Even Rosalind would have meant long rehearsals and a complex interference with her governess-life.

At the theatres, too, to judge by all she heard, a sordid side of the profession was accentuated. The players played for their own hands, and even the greatest did not disdain to "queer" the effects of their subordinates, whenever such effects did not heighten their own. Hamlet had been known to be jealous of the ghost, and the success of his sepulchral bass. It was in fact a world of jostling jealousies, as hidden from the public as the prompter. In the Halls she was her own company and her own playwright and her own composer. She had her elbows free.

And even here Bessie Bilhook, whose vanity was a byword in Lower Bohemia, and who had arrogantly assumed the sovereignty of the Serio-Comics, refused to appear on the same programmes unless her name was printed twice as large as Nelly O'Neill's, and was further displayed on a board outside, alone in its nine-inch glory. Again, actresses were recognised by the newspapers; the Halls had as yet no status. Their performers were not so photographed; indeed, Eileen refused to sit. She desired this obscurer form of celebrity. If her fame should ever reach Mrs. Lee Carter, the game would be nearly up. Her poor mother might even suffer the shock of it; perhaps the professional future of her brothers would be injured. Her sedate life had grown as dear as her noisy life, she loved the transition to the innocent home circle.

Yet in this very domesticity lay a danger. It provoked her to an ever broader humour on the stage. She let herself go, like a swimmer emboldened by a boat behind. Eileen O'Keeffe she felt would rescue Nelly O'Neill if licence carried her too near the falls. It was so irresistibly seductive, this swift response of the audience to the wink of suggestion. Like a vast lyre, the Hall vibrated to the faintest breath of roguishness. Almost in contemptuous mockery one was tempted to experiment....

One day, in a sudden horror of herself, she pleaded illness and hurried back to her mother for a holiday.

XIV

The straggling village looked much the same, the same pigs and turkeys rooted and strutted, the same stinging turf-smoke came from the doors and windows (save from one or two cabins unroofed by the Castle tyrant), the same weeds grew in the potato-patches, the same old men in patched brogues pulled their caubeens from their heads and their dudeens from their mouths, as she went past, half-consciously studying the humours for stage reproduction. It was hard for her to remember she wasn't "the Quality" in London, or that the Half-and-Half existed simultaneously with these beloved woods and waters. In only one particular was the village changed. Golf links had been discovered near it, a club-house had sprung up and the peasants found themselves enriched by the employment of their gossoons as caddies. The O'Keeffes were prospering equally—thanks to her subsidies—although she hadn't yet bought them back their castle. "All's for the best in the greenest of isles," she told herself, as she sat basking in family affection.

And yet the wave of melancholia refused to ebb. Indeed, it swelled and grew blacker. The remedy seemed to intensify the disease; a holiday but gave her time to possess her soul, and brood upon its stains, her childhood's scene but enabled her to measure the realities of her achievement against the visions of girlhood. Life seemed too hopeless, too absurd. To amuse the gross adult, to instruct the innocent child—what did it all mean to her own life? She was tired of doing, she wanted to be something; something for herself. She was always observing, imitating, caricaturing, but what was she? A nothing, a phantasm, an emptiness.

"Eileen avourneen," said her mother, suddenly. "I wish you were married."

Eileen opened her eyes. "Dear heart, is this another offer from the castle?" And she laughed gently.

Mrs. O'Keeffe's fingers played uneasily with her bosom's cross. "No, but I should feel happier about you. It—it settles people."

"It certainly does," Eileen laughed, and her celebrated ditty, "The Marriage Settlement," flashed upon her. "Oh, dear," and her laugh changed to a sigh. "The marriages I see around me!"

"What! Isn't Mrs. Lee Carter happy?"

Eileen flushed. "I shouldn't like to be in her shoes," she said evasively.

"Officers seem to make the best husbands," said Mrs. O'Keeffe.

"Because they are so much away?" queried Eileen, with a vague memory of her Lieutenant Doherty.

That night the melancholia was heavy as a nightmare, without the partial unconsciousness of sleep. This blackness must be "the horrors" she had heard women of her stage-world speak of. She wanted to spring out of bed, to run to her mother's room. But that would have meant hysteric confession, so she bit her lips and stuck her nails into the sheet. Perhaps suicide would be simplest. She was nothing; it would not even be blowing out a light. No, she was something, she was a retailer of gross humours, a vile sinner; it might be kindling more than a light, an eternal flame. "Child of Mary," indeed! She deserved to be strangled with her white ribbon. And she exaggerated everything with that morbid mendacity of the confessional.

Two days later she went for a walk along the springy turf of the valley. The sun shone overhead, but from her spirit the mist had not quite lifted. Suddenly a small white ball came scudding towards her feet. She looked round and saw herself amid little flags sticking in the ground. Distant voices came to her ear.

"This must be the new game that's creeping in from Scotland," she thought. "Perhaps I ought to have a song ready if ever it catches on. Ah, here comes one of the young fools—I'll watch him—"

He came, clothed as in a grey skin that showed the beautiful modelling of his limbs. His face glowed.

"Ouidà's Apollo," she thought, but in the very mockery she trembled, struck as by a lightning shaft. The blackness was sucked up into fire and light. "Am I in the way?" she said with her most bewitching smile.

He raised his hat. "I was afraid you might have been struck."

"Perhaps I was," she could not help saying.

"Oh, gracious, are you hurt?" His voice was instantly caressing.

"Do I look an object for ambulances?"

He smiled dazzlingly. "You look awfully jolly." Later Eileen remembered how she had taken this reply for a line of poetry.

A week later the Hon. Reginald Winsor, younger brother of an English Earl, was teaching Eileen golf.

It had been a week of ecstasy.

She thought of Reginald the last thing at night and the first thing in the morning and dreamed of him all night.

Now she knew what her life had lacked—to be caught up into another's personality, to lose one's petty individuality in—in what? Surely not in a larger; she couldn't be so blind as that. In what then? Ah, yes, in Nature. He was gloriously elemental. He wasn't himself. He was the masculine. Yes, that was the correlative element her being needed. The mere manliness of his pipe made its aroma in his clothes adorable. Or was it his big simplicity, in which she could bury all her torturing complexity? Oh, to nestle in it and be at rest. Yet she held him at arm's length. When they shook hands her nerves thrilled, but she was the colder outwardly for very fear of herself.

On the ninth day he proposed.

Eileen knew it would be that day. Lying in bed that morning, she found herself caught by her old impersonal whimsy. "I'm a fever, and on the ninth day of me the man comes out in a rash proposal." Ah, but this time she was in a tertian, too. What a difference from those other proposals—proper or improper. Her mind ran over half a dozen, with a touch of pity she had not felt at the time. Poor Bob Maper, poor Jolly Jack Jenkins, if it was like this they felt! But was it her fault? No man could say she had led him on—except, perhaps, the Hon. Reginald, and towards him her intentions were honourable, she told herself smiling. But the jest carried itself farther and more stingingly. Could he make an "honourable" she told herself her? Ah, God, was she worthy of him, of his simple manhood? And would he continue proposing, if she told him she was Nelly O'Neill? And what of his noble relatives? No, no, she must not run risks. She was only Eileen O'Keeffe, she had never left Ireland save for the Convent. The rest was a nightmare. How glad she was that nobody knew!

The proposal duly took place in a bunker, while Eileen was whimsically vituperating her ball. The fascination of her virginal diablerie was like a force compelling the victim to seize her in his arms after the fashion of the primitive bridegroom. However the poor Honourable refrained, said boldly, "Try it with this," and under pretence of changing her golfsticks possessed himself of her hand. For the first time his touch left her apathetic.

"Now it is coming," she thought, and suddenly froze to a spectator of the marionette show. As the Hon. Reginald went through his performance, she felt with a shudder of horror over what brink she had nearly stepped. The man was merely a magnificent animal! She, with her heart, her soul, her brain, mated to that! Like a convict chained to a log. Not worthy of him forsooth! "There's a gulf between us," she thought, "and I nearly fell down it." And the Half-and-Half rose before her, clamouring, pungent, deliciously seductive.

"Dear Mr. Winsor," she listened with no less interest to her own part in the marionette performance, "it's really too bad of you. Just as I was getting on so nicely, too!"

"Is that all you feel about—about our friendship?"

"All? Didn't you undertake to teach me golf? I haven't the faintest desire not to go on ... as soon as we have escaped from this wretched bunker. Come! Did you say the niblick?"

Reginald's manners were too good to permit him to swear, even at golf.

"One's body is like an Irish mud-cabin," Eileen reflected. "It shelters both a soul and a pig."

XV

Nelly O'Neill threw herself into her work with greater ardour than ever. But her triumphs were shadowed by worries. She was nervous lest the Hon. Reginald should turn up at one of her Halls—she had three now; she was afraid her voice was spoiling in the smoky atmosphere; sometimes the image of the Hon. Reginald came back reproachfully, sometimes tantalisingly. Oh, why was he so stupid? Or was it she who had been stupid?

Then there was the apprehension of the end of her career at the Lee Carters'. The young generation was nearly grown up. The eldest boy she even suspected of music-halls. He might stumble upon her.

Her popularity, too, was beginning to frighten her. Adventurous young gentlemen followed her in cabs—cabs were now a necessity of her triple appearance—and she never dared drive quite to her door or even the street. Bracelets she always returned, if the address was given; flowers she sent to hospitals, anonymous gifts to her family. Nobody ever saw her wearing his badge.

A sketch of her even found its way to one of Mrs. Lee Carter's journals.

"Why, she looks something like me!" Eileen said boldly.

"You flatter yourself," said Mrs. Lee Carter. "You're both Irish, that's all. But I don't see why these music-hall minxes should be pictured in respectable household papers."

"Some people say that the only real talent is now to be found in the Halls," said Eileen.

"Well, I hope it'll stay there," rejoined her mistress, tartly. Eileen recalled this conversation a few nights later, when she met Master Harold Lee Carter outside the door at midnight with a rival latch-key.

"Been to a theatre, Miss O'Keeffe?" asked her whilom pupil.

"No; have you?"

"Well, not exactly a theatre!"

"Why, what do you mean?"

"Sort of half-and-half place, you know."

By the icy chill at her heart at his innocent phrase, she knew how she dreaded discovery and clung to her social status.

"What is a half-and-half place?" she asked smiling.

"Oh, comic songs and tumblers and you can smoke."

"No? You're not really allowed to smoke in a theatre?"

"Yes, we are. They call it a music-hall—it's great fun. But don't tell the mater."

"You naughty boy!"

"I don't see it. All the chaps go."

She shook her head. "Not the nicest."

"Oh, that's tommyrot," he said disrespectfully. "Their women folk don't know—that's all."

Eileen now began to feel like a criminal round whom the toils thicken. In the most fashionable of her three Halls, she sang a little French song. And she had taught Master Harold his French.

Of course, even if Nelly were seen by Eileen's friends or acquaintances, detection was not sure. Eileen was always in such sedate gowns, never low-cut, her manners were so suppressed, her hair done so differently, and what a difference hair made! In fact, it was in her private life that she felt herself more truly the actress. On the boards her real secret self seemed to flash forth, full of verve, dash, roguery, devilry. Should she take to a wig, or to character songs in appropriate costumes? No, she would run the risk. It gave more spice to life. Every evening now was an adventure, nay three adventures, and when she snuggled herself up at midnight in her demure white bed, overlooked by the crucifix, she felt like the hunted were-wolf, safely back in human shape. And she became more audacious, letting herself go, so as to widen the chasm between Nelly and Eileen, and make anybody who should suspect her be sure he was wrong. And occasionally she paid for all this fever and gaiety by fits of the blackest melancholy.

She had gradually dropped her habit of prayer, but in one of her dark moods she found herself slipping to her knees and crying: "Oh, Holy Mother, look down on Thy distressed daughter, and deliver her from the body of this death. So many wooers and no spark of love in herself; a woman who sings love-songs with lips no man has touched, a lone-of-soul who can live neither with the respectable nor with the Bohemians, who loves you, sanctissima Maria, without being sure you exist. Oh, Holy Mother of God, advocate of sinners, pray for me. If I had only something solid to cling to—a babe to suckle with its red grotesque little face. You will say cling to the cross, but is not my whole life also a crucifixion? I am rent in twain that a thousand fools may laugh nightly. Oh, Holy Mother, make me at one with myself; it is the atonement I need. Send me the child's heart, and I will light a hundred candles to you.... Or do you now prefer electricity? Oh, Maria mavourneen, I cannot pray to you, for there is a mocking devil within me, and you will not cast her out." And she burst into hysteric tears.

XVI

As she was about to start one evening for her round, Mrs. Lee Carter's maid brought up a bombshell. Superficially it looked like a letter with foreign stamps, marked "Private" and readdressed with an English stamp from Ireland. But that one line of unerased writing, her name, threw her into heats and colds, for she remembered the long-forgotten hand of Lieutenant Doherty. She had to sit down on her bed and finish trembling before she broke the seal and set free this voice from the past.

"DEAR MOTHER-CONFESSOR,—You will be wondering why I have been silent all these years and why I write now. Well, I will tell you the truth. It wasn't that I believed you had really gone into the Convent you wrote me you were joining, it was the new and exciting life and duties that opened up before me when I got to Afghanistan, far from post-offices. Afterwards I was drafted to India and had a lot of skirmishing and tiger-shooting, and your image—forgive me!—became faint, and I excused myself for not writing by making myself believe you were buried in the Convent. ["So, after all, he never got the letter telling him I was going to marry back the Castle!" Eileen mused joyfully through her agitation.] But now that I am at last coming home in a few months, no longer a minor, but nearer a major (that's like one of your old jokes)—somehow your face seems to be the only thing I am coming back for. It's no use trying to explain it all, or even apologising. It's just like that. I've confessed, you see, though it is hopeless to get straight with my arrears, so I won't attempt it. And when I found out how I felt, of course came the horrible thought that you might be in the Convent after all, or, worse still, married and done for, so what do you think I did? I just sent this cable to your mother: 'Is Eileen free? Reply paid. Colonel Doherty.' Wasn't it clever and economical of me to think of the word 'free,' meaning such a lot—not married, not a nun, not even engaged to another fellow? Imagine my joy when I got back the monosyllable, meaning all that lot. I instantly cabled back 'Thanks, don't tell her of this.' ["So that's what mother was hinting at," thought Eileen, with a smile.] It was all I could do not to cable to you: 'Will you marry me? Reply paid.' ["What a good idea for a song!" murmured Nelly.] Put me out of my agony as soon as you can, won't you, dearest Eileen? Your face is floating before me as I write, with its black Irish eyes and its roguish dimples...."

She could read no more. She sat long on her bed, dazed by the rush of bitter-sweet memories. The Convent, her father, her early years, this dear boy ... all was washed together in tears. There was something so bizarre, unexpected and ingenuous about it all; it touched the elemental in her. If he had excused himself even, she would have tossed him off impatiently. But his frank exposure of his own self-contradictoriness appealed subtly to her. Was this the want in her life, was it for him she had been yearning, below the surface of her consciousness, even as she had remained below the surface of his? Here, indeed, was salvation—providential salvation. A hand was stretched to save her—snatch her from spiritual destruction. The dear brown manly hand that had potted tigers while she had been gesticulating on platforms—a performing lioness. Distance, imagination, early memories, united to weave a glamour round him. It was many minutes before she could read the postscript: "I think it right to say that my complexion is not yellow nor my liver destroyed. I know this is how we are represented on your stage. I have sat for a photograph, especially to send you."

The stage! Why should he just stumble upon the word, to chill her with the awful question whether she would have to tell him. She was late at her engagements, her performance was perfunctory—she was no longer with "the boys," but seated in a howdah on an elephant's back, side by side with a mighty hunter, or walking with a tall flaxen-haired lieutenant between the honeysuckled hedges of an Irish boreen. It struck her as almost miraculous—though it was probably only because her attention was now drawn to the name—that she read of Colonel Doherty in the evening paper the gasman tendered her that very evening, as she waited at the wing. It was a little biography full of deeds of derring-do. "My Bayard!" she murmured, and her eyes filled with tears.

She wrote and tore up many replies. The first commenced: "What a strange way of proposing! You begin by giving me two black eyes to prove you've forgotten me. I am so different in other people's eyes as well as in my own it would be unfair to accept you. You are in love with a shadow." The word-play about her eyes seemed to savour of the "Half-and-Half." She struck it out. But "you are in love with a shadow," remained the Leit-motif of all the letters. And if he was grasping at a shadow it would be unfair for her to grasp at the substance.

The correspondence continued by every Indian mail after his receipt of her guarded refusal; he Quixotic, devoted, no matter how she had changed. He loved the mere scent of her letter paper. Was she only a governess? Had she been a charwoman, he would have kissed her cheeks white. The boyish extravagance of his passion worked upon her, troubling her to her sincerest core. She would hide nothing from him. She wrote a full account of her stage career, morbidly exaggerating the vulgarity of her performance and the degradation of her character. She was blacker than any charwoman, she said with grim humour. The moment she dropped the letter into the box, a trembling seized on all her limbs. She spent three days of torture; her fear of losing him seeming to have heightened her love for him.

Then Mrs. Lee Carter handed her a cable.

"Sailing unexpectedly S.S. Colombo to-morrow—Doherty." She nearly fell fainting in dual joy. He was coming home, and he would cross her letter. Before it could return they would be safely married. It should be destroyed unread.

"Is anything wrong?" said her mistress.

"No, quite the contrary."

"I am glad, because I had rather unpleasant news to tell you. But you must have seen that when Kenneth goes to Winchester, there will practically be nothing for you to do."

"How lucky! For I am going to be married."

"Oh, my dear, I am so glad," gushed Mrs. Lee Carter.

Afterwards Eileen marvelled at the obvious finger of Providence unravelling her problems. She had never relished the idea of finding another place, not easily would she find one so dovetailing into her second life; she might have been tempted to burn her boats.

She prepared now to burn her ships instead. Her contracts with the Halls were now only monthly; Nelly O'Neill could easily slip out of existence. She would not say she was going to be married—that would concentrate attention on herself. Illness seemed the best excuse. For the one week after the Colombo's arrival she could send conscience money. The Saturday it was due found her still starred; she did not believe his ship would get in till late, and managers would particularly dislike being done out of her Saturday night turn. Perhaps she ought to have left the previous week, she thought. It was foolish to rush things so close. But it was not so easy to give up the habits of years, and activity allayed the fever of waiting. She had sent an ardent letter to meet the ship at Southampton, saying he was to call at the Lee Carters' in Oxbridge Terrace on Sunday afternoon, which she had to herself. Being only a poor governess, she would be unable to meet him at the station or receive him at the house on Saturday night, even if he got in so early. He must be resigned to her situation, she added jestingly. On the Saturday afternoon she received a wire full of their own hieroglyphic love-words, grumbling but obeying. How could he live till Sunday afternoon? Why hadn't she resigned her situation?

As she was starting for the Halls for the last time, in the dusk of a Spring day, a special messenger put into her hand a letter he had scribbled in the train. He was in London then. Her heart thumped with a medley of emotions as she tore open the letter:

"Oh, my darling, I shall see you at last face to face—" But she had no time to spend under the hall-light reading it. In her cab she struck a match and read another scrap. "But, oh, cruel one, not to let me come to-night!" She winced. That gave her a pause. If she had let him come—to the Half-and-Half! He would turn from her, shuddering. And was it not precisely to the Half-and-Half that honour should have invited him? The Half-and-Half arrived at the cab window ere she had finished pondering. She thrust the letter into her pocket.

XVII

Would she ever get through her three Halls? It did not seem as if she had strength for the Half-and-Half itself. She nerved herself to the task, and knew, not merely from the shrieks of delight, that she had surpassed herself. Happy and flushed she flung herself into her waiting cab.

She had the 9.45 turn at her second and most fashionable Hall—a Hall where the chairman had been replaced by programme numbers—and then would come her third and last appearance at 10.35. It was strange to think that in another hour Nelly O'Neill's career would be over. It seemed like murdering her. Yes, Eileen O'Keeffe would be her murderess. Well, why not murder what lay between one and happiness? As she waited at the wings, just before going on, while the orchestra played her opening bars, she glanced diagonally at the packed stalls, and her heart stood still. There in the second row sat Colonel Doherty, smoking a big cheroot. Instinctively she made the sign of the cross; then swayed back and was caught by the man who changed the programme-numbers.

"Is No. 9 come?" she gasped.

"I think so; aren't you well, Miss O'Neill?"

"For God's sake, give me breathing space," she said, with a last wild peep at the Colonel. Yes, there was no mistaking him after the three new portraits he had sent her. He was in cheerful conversation with a stout, sallow gentleman of the Anglo-Indian stage-type. Both were in immaculate evening-dress and wore white orchids. How fortunate she had refused to send any photograph in return, pleading ugliness but really afraid of theatrical sketches that might find their way to the officers' mess!

The band stopped, changed its tune, No. 9 appeared on the board; there was a murmur of confusion.

"No, by Heaven, I'll face the music," she said with grim humour. She almost hustled the hastening juggler out of the way. She was in a whirlwind of excitement. So he was there—well, so much the better. He had saved her from lying. He had given her an easy way of confessing. Words were so inadequate, he should see the reality: the stage to-night would be her confessional. She would extenuate nothing. She would throw herself furiously into the fun and racket; go to her broadest limits, else the confession would be inadequate. Then ... if he survived the shock ... why then, perhaps, she'd insist on going on with this double life...! He had risen in his seat. No, no, he must not go away, she could not risk the juggler boring him.

"I'm better; I mustn't be late at my next shop," she murmured apologetically as the number and the music were changed back.

"Ah, she's come—she was late," came the murmurs of the audience as it stirred in excited expectation.

She flung on roguish, feverish, diabolical, seductive in low-cut bodice pranked with flowers. It was a frenzy of impromptu extravagance, dazzling even the orchestra; each line accentuated by new gesture, the verses supplemented by new monologue; a miracle of chic and improvisation, and the house rose at it. Out of the mist before her eyes thunder seemed to come in great roars and crashes. She almost groped her way to the wing.

She was recalled. The mist cleared. She bowed direct at him, smiling defiance from her sparkling eyes. He was applauding with his hands, his stick, his lungs! Was it possible?—yes, he had not recognised her!

Now came a new revulsion. Again she felt herself saved. She sang her other songs straight at him, and exaggerated them equally, half to tempt Providence, half as a bold way of keeping Eileen still concealed. She heard his companion chuckling, "By Jove, Willie, she's mashed on you," as she threw a farewell kiss towards him. Then she hurried to her dressing-room and took out his letter. She had transferred it to the pocket of her theatrical gown, but had not as yet found time to finish it. Even before she re-perused it, another emotion had begun to possess her, a rush of resentment. So this was how he amused himself while waiting to clasp her in his arms! How would he ever live through the hours till Sunday afternoon, forsooth! She was jealous of the applause he lavished on Nelly O'Neill, incensed at his levity, at his immaculate evening-dress, at his white orchid. How dare he be so gay and debonair? Her anger rose as she read his protestations, his romantic professions. "O my darling, I shall sit up all night, thinking of you, re-reading all your dear letters, recalling our past, picturing our future. In short, as old Landor puts it:—

"'A night of memories and of sighs
I consecrate to thee.'"

She crumpled the paper in her hand. There was a knock at the door; Fossy poked his head in. He had risen in the world of Halls, even as Nelly O'Neill.

"Might I present two friends of mine? They want so much to know you."

"You know I never see anybody, and that I have to hurry off."

"Then, I was to give you this bouquet."

He handed in a costly floral mass. Amid it lay a card, "Colonel Doherty." She crumpled his letter more viciously.

"Tell them I can give them ten minutes only. Oh, Fossy, it's an amusing Show, isn't it?"

"It was a rattling good show," said Fossy, half puzzled. "Come in, boys."

Entered the Anglo-Indian twain with shining faces and shirt-fronts, cheroots politely lowered.

"Oh, smoke away, gentlemen," cried Nelly O'Neill, facing them in all the dazzle of her flesh and the crudity of her stage-paint, and her over-lustrous eyes, "don't mind me. Which of you is the Colonel?"

The stout, sallow gentleman jocosely pushed his tall flaxen-haired companion forward. "Oh, I knew the Major was out of it," he grinned.

"Not at all, Major," said Nelly. "I only wanted to know which I had to thank for these lovely flowers."

"You have yourself to thank," said the Colonel, smartly. "By Jove! You gave us a treat. London was worth coming back to."

"Ah, you've been away from London?"

"Just back this very day from India—"

"And of course the first thing after a good dinner is the good old Friv—" put in the Major.

"Thank you, Major," said Fossy. "That's handsome of you. And now I'll leave you to Miss O'Neill."

"That's handsomer still," said the Colonel. And the three men guffawed. Eileen felt sick.

The Major began to talk of the music-halls of India; the Colonel chimed in. They treated her as a comrade, told her anecdotes of the coulisses of Calcutta. The Colonel retailed a jest of the bazaars.

"I permit smoke, not smoking-room stories," she said severely. At which the twain poked each other shriekingly in the ribs. After that Eileen let the Colonel have rope enough to hang himself with, though she felt it cutting cruelly into her own flesh. It was an orgie of the eternal masculine, spiced with the aroma of costly cigars.

"I'm so sorry," she said, when she had let them have a quarter of an hour's run. "I really must fly." And she seized the bouquet, and carefully adjusted his card in the glowing mass. "Won't you come and have tea with me to-morrow? About four."

The Colonel winced. "I fear I have another appointment."

"Oh, rot! I'll bring him," said the Major. "Where do you hang out?"

"22 Oxbridge,"—her hesitation was barely perceptible—"Crescent."

The Colonel started. "Do you know it, Colonel?" She looked at him ingenuously.

"No, but how odd! My other appointment is at 22 Oxbridge Terrace."

"How funny!" laughed Eileen. "Just round the corner. Then you'll be able to kill two ladies with one cab." And she fled from the Major's cachinnation.

XVIII

She had missed her turn at the third Hall, but she did not care. She went on and gave a spiritless performance. It fell dead, but she cared less. Her head throbbed with a dozen possibilities. She was still undiscovered. As she sat resting on her couch ere resuming her work-a-day gown, her nerves stretched to snapping point, and old Irish songs crooning themselves irrelevantly in her brain, a telegram was handed her.

"He has found out," she thought, going hot and cold. She tore open the pink envelope... and burst into a shriek of laughter. The dresser rushed in, wondering. Nelly O'Neill merely held her sides, jollity embodied. "Oh, the Show, the Show!" she gasped, the tears streaking her painted cheeks.

The telegram that hung between her fingers in two sheets ran: "Reply prepaid. I don't know the ways of the stage so I send you this as a sure way of reaching you to ask when and where I may have the pleasure of calling upon your friend, Miss O'Keeffe, and renewing the study of Plato.—Robert Maper, Hotel Belgravia."

"Any answer, miss?" said the imperturbable doorkeeper.

The answer flashed irresistibly into her mind as he spoke. Oh, she would play up to Bob Maper. Doubtless he imagined her fallen to the level of her métier, though he wasn't insulting. She scribbled hastily: "Robert Maper, Hotel Belgravia. I am waiting at the Hall for you. Come and take me to supper.— EILEEN O'NEILL." She gave instructions he was to be admitted. Then she relapsed into her hysteric amusement. "Oh, the merry master of marionettes, the night my love comes from beyond the seas, you send me to supper with Robert Maper." She waited with impatience. Now that the long-dreaded discovery had come, she was consumed with curiosity as to its effect upon the discoverer. At last she remembered to wash off the rouge and the messes necessary for stage-perspective. Her winsome face came back to her in the mirror, angelic by contrast, and while she was looking wonderingly at this mystic flashing mask of hers, there was a knock, and in another instant she was looking into the eyes burning unchanged under the white marble mantel-piece.

"Ah, there you are!" she said gaily, and shook his hand as though they had met the evening before. "Where shall we go?"

He accepted the situation. "I don't know—I thought you would know."

"I don't—I never supped with a man in my life."

He flushed with complex pleasure and surprise. "Really! Oh, Eileen!"

"Hush! Call me Nelly, if you must be Christian. I suppose you think you may, now."

"I—I beg your pardon," he stammered, disconcerted.

"Don't look so gaspy—poor little thing! It shall be thrown back into the water. Will you carry my bouquet?"

"With pleasure." He grasped it eagerly, and carried it towards the stage door and a hansom.

"It wanted only that," she said. "Oh, the Show, the Show!"

"I don't understand you."

"Do I understand myself?" They got into the hansom. "Where shall we go?" she repeated.

"Places all close at twelve on Saturday night."

"Ah, do they? Your hotel also?"

"No, of course one may eat at one's own hotel. If you don't mind going there—"

"If you don't mind, rather."

"I? Who is my censor?"

"Ah, the word admits I'm discreditable. Never mind, Bob. See how Christian I am."

"No, no, I've felt it was all my doing. Indirectly I drove you to it—oh, how you have weighed on me!"

"Really, I'd quite forgotten you."

He winced and gasped. "Hotel Belgravia," he called up through the trap-door.

"Very strange you should find me," she said, as they glided through the flashing London night.

"Not in the least. I knew you blindfold, so to speak. You forget how I used to stand outside the drawing-room, listening to your singing."

"Eavesdropper!" she murmured. But he struck a tender chord—all the tender chords of her twilight playing that now rose up softly and floated around her.

"Eavesdropper if you like, who heard nothing that was not beautiful. And so I hadn't to look for you. As a matter of fact, I wasn't looking but consulting my programme to know who number eleven was, when you began to sing."

"If you had looked you wouldn't have recognised me," she said, smiling.

"Probably not. The stage get-up would have blurred my memories."

She began to like him again: the oddness of it all was appealing. "Nevertheless," she said, "it is strange you should just find me to-night, for I—"

"No, it isn't," he interrupted eagerly. "I've been every night this week."

"Ah, eavesdropping again," she said, touched.

"I wanted to be absolutely sure—and then I couldn't pluck up courage to write to you."

"But you did to-night?"

"You looked so tired—I felt I wanted to protect you."

A sob came into her throat, but she managed to say coldly, "Was I very bad?"

"To one who had seen you the other nights," he said with complimentary candour.

She laughed. "How is your mother?"

"Oh, she's very well, thank you. She lives in London now."

"Then your father has retired from—"

"He is dead,—didn't you hear?"

"No." Eileen sat in shocked silence. "I am sorry," she murmured at length. But underneath this mild shock she was conscious—as they rolled on without speaking—of a new ease that had come into her life: some immense relaxation of tension. "A hunted criminal must breathe more calmly when he is caught," she thought.

XIX

"Lucky I'm in evening dress," she said, loosening her cloak as they went through a corridor, shimmering with dresses and diamonds, to a crowded supper-room.

"But you're always in evening dress, surely."

"I might have been in tights." And she had a malicious self-wounding pleasure in watching him gasp. She hurried into a revelation of her exact position, as soon as they had secured a just-vacated little table in a window niche. She omitted only Colonel Doherty.

He listened breathlessly. "And nobody knows you are Eileen O'Keeffe, I mean Nelly O'Neill?"

She laughed. "You see you don't know which I am."

"It's incredible."

"So much the worse for your theories of credibility. The longer I live, the less the Show surprises me."

"What show?"

"Oh, it's too long to explain. Say Vanity Fair." Her thumb fell into its old habit of flicking the table. There was a silence.

"I am sorry you told me," he said slowly.

"Why?"

A waiter loomed over them.

"Supper, Sir Robert?"

She glanced quickly at her companion.

"Yes," he said. "Ma buonissima! I leave it to you. And champagne."

"Prestissimo, Sir Robert." He smirked himself off.

"Why does he call you that?" she asked.

"Oh, didn't you know my poor father was made a Baronet, after we entertained Royalty?"

"No; how strange your lives should have been going on all the time!" The pop of a cork at her elbow startled her. Then she lifted her frothing glass. "Sir—to you!"

He clinked his against it. "To the lady of my dreams."

"Still?" She sipped the wine: her eyes sparkled.

"Yes; I've still a long opinion of myself."

She put out her hand quickly and pressed his an instant.

"Thank you!" he said huskily. "That was why I said I was sorry to know that to the world you were still a governess. Of course I was glad, too."

"I don't understand. I always said you were more Irish than I."

"I was glad you had kept yourself unspotted from the stage-world."

"Good God! You call that unspotted! What are men made of?"

"You were in a bad atmosphere. Your lips caught phrases."

"Nonsense. I'm a crow, not a parrot; a thoroughly sooty bird."

"It was your whiteness that attracted—your morning freshness. You don't know what vulgarity is."

"You don't know what I am."

"I know you to your delicious finger-tips. And that's why I am sorry you told me so much. I wanted to ask Nelly O'Neill to marry me. Now she'll think I'm only asking Eileen O'Keeffe, the daughter of the Irish gentleman."

Her eyes filled with tears. "No, they both believe you capable of any folly. Besides, somebody would find out Nelly all the same." And a smile made a rainbow across her tears.

The arrival of the soup relaxed the tension of emotion. In mid-plate she suddenly put down her spoon and laughed softly.

"What is it?" he said, not without alarm at her transitions.

"Why, it would be one of those stock theatrical marriages, into which we entrap titles! Fascinated by a Serio-Comic, poor silly young man. She played her cards well, that Nelly. Ha! ha! ha! Who would dream of Plato's dialogues? And you talk of incredible!"

"I am content to be called silly." He tried to take her hand.

"Well, don't be it in public. You will rank with Lord Tippleton who married Bessie Bilhook, and made a Lady of her—the only ladyhood she's ever known."

"No, I can't rank with him," he smiled back. "I'm only a Baronet."

"It sounds the same. Lady Maper!" she murmured. "But, oh, how funny! There'd be two Lady Mapers."

"My mother would be the Dowager Lady—"

"That's funnier still."

He ate in silence. Eileen mused on the picture of the Dowager, her forefinger to heaven.

"The Royalty—how did that go off?" she said, as he carved the chicken.

"With fireworks. For the reception father built a new house and furnished it with old furniture. Royalty stopped an hour and a quarter. Oh, she was wonderful. I mean my mother. Copied your phrases—see what an impression you made."

"And what have you been doing since you came into the title?"

"Looking for you."

"Nonsense!" She dropped her fork. "But you knew I had people in Ireland."

"I never knew exactly where."

"But what put you on the track of the music-halls?"

"Nothing. I never dreamed of looking for you there. I just went." Master Harold Lee Carter's phrase flashed back to her memory, "All the chaps go."

"But what about the Black Hole—I mean the works?"

"They go on," he said. "I just get the profits."

"And how about your Socialism?"

"You taught me the fallacy of it."

"I? Well, that's the cream of the joke."

"Yes. Don't laugh at me, please. When you came into my life, or rather when you went out of it—yes, I am Irish—I saw that money and station are the mere veneer of life: the central reality is—Love."

Again her eyes filled with tears, but she remained silent.

"And I saw that I, the master, was really poorer than the majority of my serfs, with their wives and bairns."

"You are a good fellow," she murmured. "I—I meant to say," she corrected herself, "what have you done with your clothes?"

"My clothes!" he echoed vaguely, looking down at his spotless shirt-front.

"Your factory clothes! Wouldn't it be fun to wear them at supper here? Do you think they could turn you out? I don't see how, legally. Do test the question. Yes, do. Please do." And she laid her hand on his black sleeve. "I won't marry you if you don't."

"I did think you were serious to-night, Eileen," he said, disappointed.

"How could you think that, if you read the programme, as you say? 'Nelly O'Neill, Serio-Comic.' Allons, ne faites cette tête mine de hibou. Admit the world is entirely ridiculous and give me some more champagne." Her eyes glittered strangely.

A clock struck twelve.

"What, midnight!" she cried, starting up. "I must go."

"No, no;" he took her hand.

"Yes, yes; don't you know, at the stroke of midnight I change back to a governess."

"Well, the magic didn't work, for that clock's very slow. Sit down, please."

"You have spoken the omen. I remain Nelly O'Neill and drop Eileen for ever. Vogue la galère."

"Absit omen!" He shuddered.

"Why not? What do you offer me? The love of one man. But my public loves me as one man—with a much more voluminous love—I love it in return. Why should I change?"

"Shall we say merely because the public changes? I am constant."

"Yes, you are very wonderful.... And if it's to-morrow already, my fate will be settled to-day. Drink to my destiny."

"I drink to our destiny," he said, raising his glass.

"No. Only to mine. It will be decided this afternoon."

"You will give me your answer this afternoon?" he cried joyfully.

"I don't say that. It's my answer I shall know this afternoon. Yours you shall have to-morrow afternoon. You don't mind giving me one day's option of your hand?"

"One day's! When you have had—"

She interrupted impatiently. "Let bygones be bygones. You shall have a letter by Monday afternoon. But, oh, Heavens! how could we marry? You believe in nothing!"

"There's the Registrar."

She pouted: "Dry legality. No flowers, no organ, no feeling sweet and virginal in a long veil. Oh, dear! Besides, there's mother—"

"I don't object to the church ceremony."

"I'm glad. The law may end marriage. Marriage shouldn't begin with law. It ought to look beautiful at the start, at least, though one may know it's a shaky scraw."

"A shaky what?"

"Oh, it's an Irish term for a bit of black bog that looks like lovely green meadow. You step out so gaily on the glittering grass, and then squish! squash! down you go to choke in the ooze."

"Don't be so pessimistic. It would be much more sensible to think of marriage as solid meadow-land after your present scramble over a shaky what-d'ye-call it."

"True for you! I give you the stage as the shakiest of all scraws. But where is solid footing to be found? The world itself is only a vast bog that sucks in the generations."

"I am sorry I asked you to be serious," he said glumly. "You're such a quick-change artiste."

"I must quickly assume the governess or I'll lose my character," she said, rising resolutely.

He put her cloak tenderly round her.

"You know I'll take you without a character," he said lightly.

"If I had no character I might be tempted to take you," she retorted dispiritingly. "Thank you so much for my first supper."

XX

Eileen slept little. The dramatic possibilities of the interview with Colonel Doherty were too agitating and too numerous. This time the marionette-play needed writing. Who should receive him when he called? Eileen O'Keeffe or Nelly O'Neill?

Either possibility offered exquisite comedy.

Eileen—as plain as possible—with a high, black dress, drooped lids, stiffly brushed hair, even eyeglasses perhaps, with a deportment redolent of bread-and-butter and five-finger exercises, could perhaps disenchant him sufficiently to make him moderate his matrimonial ardour, even to hurry off apologetically to his serio-comic Circe round the corner. What a triumph of acting if she could drive him to her rival! Then as he went through the door—to loosen her hair, throw off her glasses and whistle him back to Nelly O'Neill!

The part was tempting; it bristled with opportunities. But it was also too trying. He might begin by taking lover's liberties, and the strain of repulsing him would be too great. Besides, she wasn't clear how to play the opening of the scene. But then there was another star part open to her.

Nelly O'Neill's rôle was much easier: it played itself. She had only to go on with the episode. And the way the episode went on would also serve to determine finally her attitude when the moment came to throw off the mask and turn to governess. The only difficult moment would be the first—to obfuscate him immediately with the notion that he had mixed up the two addresses. Even if she failed and he realised his ghastlier blunder, it would only precipitate the dramatic duel which she must face sooner or later. All these high-strung possibilities deadened the horrible pain she knew her soul held for her, as soldiers carry wounds to be felt when the charge is over. She fell asleep near morning, her battle planned, and slept late, a sleep full of strange dreams, in one of which her drunken father counted her, and couldn't decide how many she was. "It's two I am, father asthore, only two, Eileen and Nelly," she kept crying. But he counted on.

Towards four in the afternoon she posted herself at the window. It was absolutely necessary to the comedy that she should open the door to him herself. At last a cab containing him halted at the door. She flew down, just supplanting the butler.

"How good of you, Colonel!" she cried. "But where is the Major?"

It was exquisitely calculated. She had pulled the string and the marionette moved with precision. A daze, a flash, a stammer—all the embarrassment of a man who believes that in a day-dream he has given a second address first.

"Miss—Miss O'Neill," he stuttered, mechanically removing his hat.

"Nelly to my friends," she smiled fascinatingly. "Come in!" Christopher Sly was not more bewildered when he opened his eyes on the glories of his Court.

"What—what is this address?" he blurted, as she prisoned him by closing the door.

"Why?... Oh, I know. Ha! ha! ha! You've come to the Crescent instead of the Terrace."

"That confounded cabman! I'm sure I told him the Terrace."

"Don't swear. He's more accustomed to the Crescent. So many pros coming home late, and all that!"

He hesitated at the foot of the stairs. "I really think I ought to call there first...."

Now all the coquette in Nelly O'Neill rose to detain him, subtly tangled with the actress. She pouted adorably. "Oh, now you're here, can't you put her second for once?"

"I didn't say it was a her."

"A she," corrected the governess, instinctively. Nelly hastened to add, "No man leaves a woman for a man."

"This is such an old appointment," he pleaded in distress.

"I see. You want to be off with the old love before you are on with the new."

"Nothing of the kind, I assure you."

"What! Not even the new?"

"Oh, that part!" He smiled and followed her up. "You won't mind my going soon?"

"The sooner the better if you talk like that!" She threw open the door of her little sitting-room. How well the Show was going!

"A soda and whisky, Colonel? I suppose that's your idea of tea." She had the scene ready. She had got it all up like a little play, writing down the articles on a sheet of paper headed "Property List": "Cigars, cigarettes, syphons, spirits, sporting-papers," all borrowed from Master Harold Lee Carter to entertain a visitor.

But at the height of the play's prosperity, while the Colonel clinked tumblers with Nelly, came a contretemps, and all the farce darkened swiftly to drama as the gay landscape is overgloomed by a thundercloud.

It all came from Mrs. Lee Carter's benevolent fussiness, her interest in the man who had come to marry her governess. A servant knocked at the door, stuck her head in, and said, "Mrs. Lee Carter's compliments, and would you like some tea?"

"No, thank you," said Eileen, hurriedly.

But as the door closed, the Colonel's glass fell to the ground, and he rose to his feet. His bronzed face was working wildly.

"Mrs. Lee Carter!" he gasped. "You—you are Eileen!"

"Here's a mess," she said coolly, stooping to wipe up the carpet.

"Eileen! Explain!" he said piteously.

"It's you that ought to be explaining. I've all I can do to pick up the nasty little bits of glass."

"My brain reels. Who are you? What are you? For God's sake."

"Hush! Who are you? What are you?"

"I know what I was—your lover."

"Whose? Mine or Nelly's?"

"Good God, Eileen! You saw how anxious I was to get to you. That I was subtly drawn to Nelly is only a proof of how you were in my blood. But you're not really Nelly O'Neill. This is some stupid practical joke. Don't torture me longer."

"It tortures you that I should be Nelly O' Neill!" All the confessed sweetness of her position came up into clear consciousness: the lights, the laughter, the very smell of the smoke endeared by a thousand triumphs. How dared he speak of Nelly O'Neill as though she couldn't be touched with a pitchfork! Yes, and Bob Maper, too—her anger ricocheted to him—with his priggish notions of saving her from black bogs! And who was it that now stood over her like a fuddled accusing angel? She pulled out his letter and read viciously:—

"'A night of memories and of sighs
I consecrate to thee.'"

"I was dying to rush to you—you wouldn't see me. And the Major dragged me—"

"Through all that mud? All those Indian escapades?"

He groaned, "And you listened—!"

"Am I not your mother-confessor?"

He seized her by the wrists. "Don't madden me! You're not really on the Halls? You are living here as governess. It is some prank, some masquerade! Say it is!" He shook her. She tried to wrest her hands away.

"Not till you tell me the truth! You haven't been lying to me all these months?"

A sudden remembrance came to give her strength and scorn. "I have told you the truth, only my letter crossed you on the ocean. When it returns to England, you will see."

His grip relaxed, he staggered back. "Come," she said, pursuing her unforeseen advantage. "We will talk this thing over quietly. I always said you were in love with a shadow. But I find it was I who imagined a Bayard."

"And what have I done and said worse than other men?" Again Master Harold Lee Carter's complacent sentiment came to her. Men were all alike, only their women folk didn't know.

"Worse than other men!" She laughed bitterly. "I wanted you better—all the seven heavens better—saint as well as hero, with no thought but for me, and no one before me or after me. Oh, yes, it sounds a large order, but that's what we women want. Don't speak! I know what you're going to say. Skip me. Talk of yourself."

"You get what you want. The other's only make-believe. It passes like water from a duck's back. You women don't understand. The white fire of your purity cleanses us, and that is why we will have nothing less—"

"Ah, now you have skipped to me. I'm not pretending there isn't an evil spirit in me to match yours. It split away from me and became Nelly O'Neill. You asked which I was? I am both. Here, I am a respectable governess. Let me ring for Mrs. Lee Carter. She'll give you my character. The white fire and all that." She pressed the bell.

"Don't be so absurd. Give me time to collect my senses."

"All right, pick up the pieces, while I collect these." She stooped over the bits of glass.

"But for Heaven's sake don't bring that woman into it—"

The door opened. "Yes, miss?"

"Another glass, please." The servant disappeared.

"I do hope you won't break this one. In what country is it that the bridegroom breaks a glass in the marriage ceremonial? Oh, yes, I remember. Fossy told me. Among the Jews. There's a lot in the profession. Not that it's such a marrying profession. And to think I might have been a regular bride! But I've lost you, my dear boy, hero of a hundred hill-fights, I know it—and the moment you've picked your little bits of senses together, you'll know it, too. Alas, we shall never go tiger-hunting together.

"'A night of memories and of sighs
I consecrate to thee.'"

"I don't say I won't keep my promise," he said sulkily.

"Your promise! Hoity toity! Upon my word! I'm no breach-of-promise lady—Chops and tomato sauce indeed! I recognise that we could never marry. There would always be that between us!"

Her fascination gripped him in proportion as she let him go.

"I don't know that I should mind if nobody really knows," he began.

"You! It's I that would mind. And I really know. Could I marry a man who had told me smoking-room stories? No, Eileen is done with you. Good-by!"

"Good-by? No, I can't go. I can't face the emptiness. You've filled me and fooled me with love all these weeks. Good God! Do you owe me nothing?"

"I leave you something—Nelly O'Neill! Go and see her. Now you're off with the old love. You mark what a prophetess I was. Nelly'll receive you very differently. No cant of superiority. You'll be just a pair of jolly good fellows. You'll sit up drinking whisky together and yarning anecdotes. No uncomfortable pretences; no black bog posing as white fire; no driven snow business, London snow nicely trodden, in. And the tales of the world you tell me—how useful they'll come in for stage-patter! Oh, we shall be happy enough! We can still pick up the pieces!"

"Eileen! Eileen! you will drive me mad. What do you mean? You know I could never have a wife on the Halls. It would ruin me in the clubs, it would—"

"In the clubs! Ha! ha! ha! Every member of which would be delighted to have tea with me! But who's proposing to you a wife on the Halls? You said I owed you myself, and it's true, but you don't suppose I could marry a man I didn't respect? I told you we're not a marrying profession. Come, let's kiss and be friends."

He drew back as in horror. "No, no, Eileen, I respect you too much for that."

She looked at him long and curiously. "Yes, the sexes don't understand each other. Well, good-by. I almost could marry you, after all. But I'm too wise. Please go. I have a headache and it is quite possible I shall scream. Good-by, dear. I was never more than a phantom to you—a boyish memory, and a bad one at that. Don't you know you gave me a pair of black eyes? Good-by: you'll marry a dear, sweet girl in white muslin who'll never know. God bless you."

XXI

Sir Robert Maper simply could not get up on the Monday morning. The agony of suspense was too keen, and he lay with closed eyes, trying to drowse his consciousness, and exchanging it in his fitful snatches of sleep for oppressive dreams, in one of which Eileen figured as a Lorelei, combing her locks on a rock as she sang her siren song.

But she did not prolong his agony beyond mid-day.

"MY DEAR SIR ROBERT,—Both of us are dead and gone, so, alas! neither can marry you. Don't be alarmed, we are only dead to the world, and gone to the Continent. 'Get thee to a nunnery.' Hamlet knew best. If I could have married any man it would have been you. You are the only gentleman I have ever known. But I don't love you. It's a miserable pity. I wish I did. I wonder why 'love' is an active verb in all languages. It ought to have a passive form, like 'loquor' (though that passive should be reserved for parrots). Forgive the governess! I seem to have undergone 'love' for two men, but one was a fool and the other not quite a rogue, and I dare say I never really loved anybody but myself (and there the verb is very active)! I love to coquet, but the moment a man comes too close, I feel hunted. I dare say I was secretly pleased to find my hero tripping, so as to send him packing. Was ever hero in such a comic plight? Poor, unlucky hero! But this will be Greek to you—the kind you can't read. Oh, the men I could have married! It is curious, when you think of it, the men one little woman might marry and be dutifully absorbed in. I could have been a bass chorister's wife or a Baronet's wife, the wife of an Honourable dolt, and the wife of a dishonourable dramatist. J'en passe et des meilleurs. I could have lived in Calcutta or in Clerkenwell, been received in Belgravia or in Boulogne. Good Lord! the parts one woman is supposed to be fit for, while the man remains his stolid, stupid self. Talk of the variety stage! Or is it that they all want the same thing of her?

"Talking of the variety stage, there would have been the danger, too, of my thirsting for it, even with a Dowager Lady for a stepmother. The nostalgia of the boards is a disease your love might not have warded off. You are well rid of both of us.

"You said—at my first and last supper—that money and station are the mere veneer of life, the central reality is love. That is true, if by love you read the love of God, of Christ. Do you remember my going one day over the works with your poor father? Well, after I had been through rooms and rooms of whirring machinery infinitely ingenious and diversified—that made my head ache—they took me to a shed where stood in a sort of giant peace the great engine that moved it all. 'God!' was my instant thought, and somehow my headache fled. And ever since then, when I have been oppressed by the complex clatter of life, my thought has gone back to that power-room, to the great simple force behind it all. I rested in the thought as a swimmer on a placid ocean. But the ocean is cold and infinite, and of late I have longed for a more human God that loved and forgave, and so I come back to the Christ. You see Plato never satisfied me. Your explanation of the B.C. glories was sown on barren soil. I grant you a nobility in your Plato as of Greek pillars, soaring in the sunlight, but somehow I want the Gothic—I long for 'dim religious light' and windows stained with saints. Oh, to find my soul again! If I could tell you how the Convent rises before me as a vision of blessedness—after life's 'shaky scraw'—the cool cloisters, the rows of innocent beds, the delicious old garden. There are tears at my heart, as I think of it. What flowers I will bring to my favourite nun.... God grant she is still alive! What altar-cloths I will weave with my silver and gold! Yes, the wages of sin shall not be death, I will pay them to the life eternal; my dowry as the bride of Christ. I, too, shall be laid on the altar, my complex corrupt soul shall be simplified and purified, and the Holy Mother will lead me by the hand like a little child. But all this will be caviare to you. Adieu. I will pray for you.

"Eileen.

"P.S.—It is a convent that trains the young, so I shall still be a Governess."

"And perhaps still a Serio-Comic," thought the Baronet, bitterly.

Israel Zangwill – A Short Biography

Israel Zangwill was born in London on 21st January 1864, to a family of Jewish immigrants from the Russian Empire. His father, Moses, was from modern-day Latvia, and his mother, Ellen Hannah Marks Zangwill, from modern-day Poland.

Zangwill was initially educated in Plymouth and Bristol. At age 9 he was enrolled into the Jews' Free School in Spitalfields in east London. The school was for the children of Jewish immigrants and added to its teaching, of both secular and religious matters, with supplies of clothing, food, and health care.

Zangwill excelled here. He began to teach part-time at the school and eventually full time. Whilst teaching he also studied with the University of London and by 1884 had earned his BA with triple honours in philosophy, history, and the sciences.

He had already co-written a tale entitled 'The Premier and the Painter' when he resigned as a teacher owing to differences with the managers of the school. Zangwill now turned to journalism for his new career path, initiating Ariel, The London Puck, as well as working in various capacities for the London press.

His writing earned him the sobriquet "the Dickens of the Ghetto" primarily based on his much lauded novel 'Children of the Ghetto: A Study of a Peculiar People' in 1892 and its glimpse of the poverty-stricken life in London's Jewish quarter.

As a writer he was keen to reflect on his political and social outlooks. His simulation of Yiddish sentence structure in English aroused great interest. His mystery work, 'The Big Bow Mystery' (1892) was the first locked room mystery novel. Social satire flowed with 'The King of Schnorrers' (1894). A follow up to 'Children of the Ghetto' was 'Ghetto Tragedies' in 1894 and 'Dreamers of the Ghetto' in 1898 which included essays on famous Jews such as Baruch Spinoza, Heinrich Heine and Ferdinand Lassalle.

Zangwill was also involved with narrowly focused Jewish issues as an assimilationist, an early Zionist, and later a territorialist. In the early 1890s he had joined the Lovers of Zion movement in England. A few years later, in 1897, he took part in the "pilgrimage" of English Jews to Palestine. That same year he also joined Theodor Herzl (considered the father of modern political Zionism) in founding the World Zionist Organization and would take part in the first seven Zionist congresses. Zangwill was much admired as an orator and spoke movingly and eloquently on the issues he was passionate on.

In 1901 he had written that "Palestine is a country without a people; the Jews are a people without a country". On Herzl's visits to London, they worked closely together. In a debate at the Article Club in November 1901 however Zangwill was still mis-using the facts: "Palestine has but a small population of Arabs and fellahin and wandering, lawless, blackmailing Bedouin tribes." And made a direct plea to "restore the country without a people to the people without a country. For we have something to give as well as to get. We can sweep away the blackmailer—be he Pasha or Bedouin—we can make the wilderness blossom as the rose, and build up in the heart of the world a civilisation that may be a mediator and interpreter between the East and the West."

In 1902, Zangwill wrote that Palestine "remains at this moment an almost uninhabited, forsaken and ruined Turkish territory". But from this point on Zangwill began to see things differently which would, in 1905, result in his breakaway from Zionism.

Zangwill quit the established philosophy of Zionism when his plan for a homeland in Uganda was rejected and instead founded his own organisation; the Jewish Territorialist Organization. Its stated goal was to create a Jewish homeland in whatever territory in the world could be found for them. At that point in time suggestions were as varied as Canada, Australia, Mesopotamia, Argentina, Uganda and Cyrenaica.

Amongst the challenges in his life he found time to write poetry. He had translated a medieval Jewish poet in 1903 and his own volume 'Blind Children' in 1908 shows his promise in this new endeavour.

In 1908, Zangwill told a London court that he had been naive when he made his 1901 speech and had since recognised that the Arab population was twice that of the United States.

Zangwill was a supporter of both feminism and pacifism, but his greatest effect was as a writer who gained a wide audience with the idea of combining ethnicities into a single, American nation. The hero of 'The Melting Pot', proclaims: "America is God's Crucible, the great Melting-Pot where all the races of Europe are melting and reforming... Germans and Frenchmen, Irishmen and Englishmen, Jews and Russians – into the Crucible with you all! God is making the American."'

'The Melting Pot' made Zangwill's name as an admired playwright. The title itself was popularised as the phrase to use to describe American absorption of immigrants when it ran in the United States.

When the play opened in Washington D.C. on 5th October 1909, former President Theodore Roosevelt leaned over the edge of his box and shouted, "That's a great play, Mr. Zangwill, that's a great play." In a later letter in 1912 Roosevelt went further "That particular play I shall always count among the very strong and real influences upon my thought and my life."

'The Melting Pot' shone a spotlight on America's growth through the input of its new waves of immigrants. Zangwill was writing as "a Jew who no longer wanted to be a Jew. His real hope was for a world in which the entire lexicon of racial and religious difference is thrown away."

According to Ze'ev Jabotinsky, Zangwill told him in 1916 that, "If you wish to give a country to a people without a country, it is utter foolishness to allow it to be the country of two peoples. This can only cause trouble. The Jews will suffer and so will their neighbours. One of the two: a different place must be found either for the Jews or for their neighbours".

In 1917 he wrote "'Give the country without a people,' magnanimously pleaded Lord Shaftesbury, 'to the people without a country.' Alas, it was a misleading mistake. The country holds 600,000 Arabs."

With the end of World War I, and a more clearly defined idea of a Jewish settlement in Palestine, Zangwill once more returned to the Zionist effort and made efforts on behalf of the Balfour Declaration, proclaiming the right of a Jewish homeland in Palestine

In 1921 Zangwill wrote "If Lord Shaftesbury was literally inexact in describing Palestine as a country without a people, he was essentially correct, for there is no Arab people living in intimate fusion with the country, utilizing its resources and stamping it with a characteristic impress: there is at best an Arab encampment, the break-up of which would throw upon the Jews the actual manual labor of regeneration and prevent them from exploiting the fellahin, whose numbers and lower wages are moreover a considerable obstacle to the proposed immigration from Poland and other suffering centers".

Despite his advocacy on Jewish matters he would be disappointed to know that despite Israel now being established the quarrels of the Middle East continue to divide.

Israel Zangwill died on 1st August 1926 in Midhurst, West Sussex.

Israel Zangwill – A Concise Bibliography

The Bachelors' Club (1891)
The Old Maid's Club (1892)
Children of the Ghetto: A Study of a Peculiar People (1892)
Grandchildren of the Ghetto (1892)
The Big Bow Mystery (1892)
Merely Mary Ann (1893)
The King of Schnorrers (1894)
The Master (1895) (based on the life of George Wylie Hutchinson)
Without Prejudices (1896)
Dreamers of the Ghetto (1898)
Ghetto Tragedies, (1899)
"The Return to Palestine", New Liberal Review, (Dec. 1901)
Children of the Ghetto (1902)
"Providence, Palestine and the Rothschilds", The Speaker, vol. 4, no. 125 (22 February 1902)
Selected Religious Poems (1903) Translation of the Jewish Medieval Poet Solomon in Cabirol.
The Grey Wig: Stories and Novelettes (1903)
The Serio-Comic Governess (1904)
Merely Mary Ann (1904)
Ghetto Comedies, (1907)
Blind Children (1908) Poetry
The Melting Pot (1909)
Italian Fantasies (1910) Travel
Chosen Peoples, (1919)
The War For The World (1916)
The Principle of Nationalities (1917)
Chosen Peoples (1918)
Hands Off Russia: Speech by Mr. Israel Zangwill at the Albert Hall, February 8th, 1919. London: Workers' Socialist Federation, n.d. (1919)
The Voice of Jerusalem. (1921)

Filmography

Children of the Ghetto (1915, based on the play Children of the Ghetto)
The Melting Pot (1915, based on the play The Melting Pot)
Merely Mary Ann (1916, based on the play Merely Mary Ann)
The Moment Before (1916, based on the play The Moment of Death)
Mary Ann (1918, based on the play Merely Mary Ann)
Nurse Marjorie (1920, based on the play Nurse Marjorie)
Merely Mary Ann (1920, based on the play Merely Mary Ann)
The Bachelor's Club (1921, based on the novel We Moderns)
We Moderns (1925, based on the play We Moderns)
Too Much Money (1926, based on the play Too Much Money)
Perfect Crime (1928, based on the novel The Big Bow Mystery)
Merely Mary Ann (1931, based on the play Merely Mary Ann)
The Crime Doctor (1934, based on the novel The Big Bow Mystery)

The Verdict (1946, based on the novel The Big Bow Mystery)

Israel Zangwill was born in London on 21st January 1864, to a family of Jewish immigrants from the Russian Empire. His father, Moses, was from modern-day Latvia, and his mother, Ellen Hannah Marks Zangwill, from modern-day Poland.

Zangwill was initially educated in Plymouth and Bristol. At age 9 he was enrolled into the Jews' Free School in Spitalfields in east London. The school was for the children of Jewish immigrants and added to its teaching, of both secular and religious matters, with supplies of clothing, food, and health care. Zangwill excelled here. He began to teach part-time at the school and eventually full time. Whilst teaching he also studied with the University of London and by 1884 had earned his BA with triple honours in philosophy, history, and the sciences.

He had already co-written a tale entitled 'The Premier and the Painter' when he resigned as a teacher owing to differences with the managers of the school. Zangwill now turned to journalism for his new career path, initiating Ariel, The London Puck, as well as working in various capacities for the London press.

His writing earned him the sobriquet "the Dickens of the Ghetto" primarily based on his much lauded novel 'Children of the Ghetto: A Study of a Peculiar People' in 1892 and its glimpse of the poverty-stricken life in London's Jewish quarter.

As a writer he was keen to reflect on his political and social outlooks. His simulation of Yiddish sentence structure in English aroused great interest. His mystery work, 'The Big Bow Mystery' (1892) was the first locked room mystery novel. Social satire flowed with 'The King of Schnorrers' (1894). A follow up to 'Children of the Ghetto' was 'Ghetto Tragedies' in 1894 and 'Dreamers of the Ghetto' in 1898 which included essays on famous Jews such as Baruch Spinoza, Heinrich Heine and Ferdinand Lassalle.

Zangwill was also involved with narrowly focused Jewish issues as an assimilationist, an early Zionist, and later a territorialist. In the early 1890s he had joined the Lovers of Zion movement in England. A few years later, in 1897, he took part in the "pilgrimage" of English Jews to Palestine. That same year he also joined Theodor Herzl (considered the father of modern political Zionism) in founding the World Zionist Organization and would take part in the first seven Zionist congresses. Zangwill was much admired as an orator and spoke movingly and eloquently on the issues he was passionate on.

In 1901 he had written that "Palestine is a country without a people; the Jews are a people without a country". On Herzl's visits to London, they worked closely together. In a debate at the Article Club in November 1901 however Zangwill was still mis-using the facts: "Palestine has but a small population of Arabs and fellahin and wandering, lawless, blackmailing Bedouin tribes." And made a direct plea to "restore the country without a people to the people without a country. For we have something to give as well as to get. We can sweep away the blackmailer—be he Pasha or Bedouin—we can make the wilderness blossom as the rose, and build up in the heart of the world a civilisation that may be a mediator and interpreter between the East and the West."

In 1902, Zangwill wrote that Palestine "remains at this moment an almost uninhabited, forsaken and ruined Turkish territory". But from this point on Zangwill began to see things differently which would, in 1905, result in his breakaway from Zionism.

Zangwill quit the established philosophy of Zionism when his plan for a homeland in Uganda was rejected and instead founded his own organisation; the Jewish Territorialist Organization. Its stated goal was to create a Jewish homeland in whatever territory in the world could be found for them. At that point in time suggestions were as varied as Canada, Australia, Mesopotamia, Argentina, Uganda and Cyrenaica.

Amongst the challenges in his life he found time to write poetry. He had translated a medieval Jewish poet in 1903 and his own volume 'Blind Children' in 1908 shows his promise in this new endeavour.

In 1908, Zangwill told a London court that he had been naive when he made his 1901 speech and had since recognised that the Arab population was twice that of the United States.

Zangwill was a supporter of both feminism and pacifism, but his greatest effect was as a writer who gained a wide audience with the idea of combining ethnicities into a single, American nation. The hero of 'The Melting Pot', proclaims: "America is God's Crucible, the great Melting-Pot where all the races of Europe are melting and reforming... Germans and Frenchmen, Irishmen and Englishmen, Jews and Russians – into the Crucible with you all! God is making the American."'

'The Melting Pot' made Zangwill's name as an admired playwright. The title itself was popularised as the phrase to use to describe American absorption of immigrants when it ran in the United States.

When the play opened in Washington D.C. on 5th October 1909, former President Theodore Roosevelt leaned over the edge of his box and shouted, "That's a great play, Mr. Zangwill, that's a great play." In a later letter in 1912 Roosevelt went further "That particular play I shall always count among the very strong and real influences upon my thought and my life."

'The Melting Pot' shone a spotlight on America's growth through the input of its new waves of immigrants. Zangwill was writing as "a Jew who no longer wanted to be a Jew. His real hope was for a world in which the entire lexicon of racial and religious difference is thrown away."

According to Ze'ev Jabotinsky, Zangwill told him in 1916 that, "If you wish to give a country to a people without a country, it is utter foolishness to allow it to be the country of two peoples. This can only cause trouble. The Jews will suffer and so will their neighbours. One of the two: a different place must be found either for the Jews or for their neighbours".

In 1917 he wrote "'Give the country without a people,' magnanimously pleaded Lord Shaftesbury, 'to the people without a country.' Alas, it was a misleading mistake. The country holds 600,000 Arabs."

With the end of World War I, and a more clearly defined idea of a Jewish settlement in Palestine, Zangwill once more returned to the Zionist effort and made efforts on behalf of the Balfour Declaration, proclaiming the right of a Jewish homeland in Palestine

In 1921 Zangwill wrote "If Lord Shaftesbury was literally inexact in describing Palestine as a country without a people, he was essentially correct, for there is no Arab people living in intimate fusion with the country, utilizing its resources and stamping it with a characteristic impress: there is at best an Arab encampment, the break-up of which would throw upon the Jews the actual manual labor of regeneration and prevent them from exploiting the fellahin, whose numbers and lower wages are moreover a considerable obstacle to the proposed immigration from Poland and other suffering centers".

Despite his advocacy on Jewish matters he would be disappointed to know that despite Israel now being established the quarrels of the Middle East continue to divide.

Israel Zangwill died on 1st August 1926 in Midhurst, West Sussex.

Israel Zangwill – A Concise Bibliography

The Bachelors' Club (1891)
The Old Maid's Club (1892)
Children of the Ghetto: A Study of a Peculiar People (1892)
Grandchildren of the Ghetto (1892)
The Big Bow Mystery (1892)
Merely Mary Ann (1893)
The King of Schnorrers (1894)
The Master (1895) (based on the life of George Wylie Hutchinson)
Without Prejudices (1896)
Dreamers of the Ghetto (1898)
Ghetto Tragedies, (1899)
"The Return to Palestine", New Liberal Review, (Dec. 1901)
Children of the Ghetto (1902)
"Providence, Palestine and the Rothschilds", The Speaker, vol. 4, no. 125 (22 February 1902)
Selected Religious Poems (1903) Translation of the Jewish Medieval Poet Solomon in Cabirol.
The Grey Wig: Stories and Novelettes (1903)
The Serio-Comic Governess (1904)
Merely Mary Ann (1904)
Ghetto Comedies, (1907)
Blind Children (1908) Poetry
The Melting Pot (1909)
Italian Fantasies (1910) Travel
Chosen Peoples, (1919)
The War For The World (1916)
The Principle of Nationalities (1917)
Chosen Peoples (1918)
Hands Off Russia: Speech by Mr. Israel Zangwill at the Albert Hall, February 8th, 1919. London: Workers' Socialist Federation, n.d. (1919)
The Voice of Jerusalem. (1921)

Filmography

Children of the Ghetto (1915, based on the play Children of the Ghetto)
The Melting Pot (1915, based on the play The Melting Pot)
Merely Mary Ann (1916, based on the play Merely Mary Ann)

The Moment Before (1916, based on the play The Moment of Death)
Mary Ann (1918, based on the play Merely Mary Ann)
Nurse Marjorie (1920, based on the play Nurse Marjorie)
Merely Mary Ann (1920, based on the play Merely Mary Ann)
The Bachelor's Club (1921, based on the novel We Moderns)
We Moderns (1925, based on the play We Moderns)
Too Much Money (1926, based on the play Too Much Money)
Perfect Crime (1928, based on the novel The Big Bow Mystery)
Merely Mary Ann (1931, based on the play Merely Mary Ann)
The Crime Doctor (1934, based on the novel The Big Bow Mystery)
The Verdict (1946, based on the novel The Big Bow Mystery)

www.ingramcontent.com/pod-product-compliance
Lightning Source LLC
Chambersburg PA
CBHW052025020726
47501CB00004B/1243